THE HARLEQUIN & The DRANGÙE

THE HARLEQUIN & THE DRANGÙE

LIANE ZANE

ZEPHON ROMANCE

AN IMPRINT OF ZEPHON BOOKS

Digital Edition JULY 2020 ISBN: 978-1-7351318-1-8

First Print Edition ISBN: 978-1-7351318-0-1

Second Print Edition ISBN: 979-8-9850781-7-6

Cover design by Perla Enrica Giancola

SECOND EDITION

To my children

ONE

Olivia Markham had just ordered her first beer of the night when the young Canadian tourist watching the World Cup alone in the noisy lobby of the Hilton Vienna got a phone call. Olivia sat forward, alert. Perhaps it was the online predator who was grooming the girl. She waited for her subject to swipe her smartphone's screen and answer, resisting the impulse to press her Bluetooth earwig more firmly into her ear. The eavesdropping program worked and she knew it.

A brusque male voice sounded in Olivia's ear. "Melissa."

That sure didn't sound like Melissa's lovely middle-aged auntie.

Olivia slipped her own smartphone from her messenger bag and glanced around the crowded seating area before routing the incoming number through a trace program. None of the other hotel patrons, either fans of the German team or drunken conference attendees, looked her way. A quick, tight grin flitted across Olivia's face. Though she could attract more than her fair share of attention in an evening gown on stage, she had been blessed with the ability to hide in plain sight when necessary. The young woman, only seventeen if Olivia's intel could be trusted, drew male stares, however.

That was by design, unfortunately. Tall and dressed in a white silk blouse with an open network of bands across her back, the foolish Melissa wore red lipstick too mature for her age and ordered mixed drinks freely from the bar. Not illegal in Vienna where the drinking age was only sixteen, Olivia reminded herself, yet not exactly wise behavior. So far, she'd socialized only with her fellow tour members, who'd drifted to their rooms half an hour ago. But the longer she remained in the lobby by herself, the more likely she'd pick up a companion, suitable or not.

Unless the predator, who called himself Asmodeus, lured her out of the hotel first. *Asmodeus*. A demon's name.

"Hey," Melissa said, blushing and twisting into her armchair. *Definitely seventeen*, Olivia thought. "I was afraid you'd never call. I'm getting lonely." She swiveled and gave the crowd around her an appraising look. "Though I see a couple of guys here who look like they'd buy me a drink if I asked."

Olivia clinched her lips around an exasperated sigh. She couldn't understand why the teen's aunt had left her to her own devices in a foreign hotel. Oh, she'd heard the girl, her posture confident and her tone assured, explaining to the retired couples traveling on the same bus tour with her that she'd already interned with a Canadian government agency and traveled extensively for the past two years. Olivia wasn't buying it, though. Despite her smooth words and relaxed demeanor, Little Miss Ontario was not the savvy world traveler she thought she was. In many areas of life, faking it until you make it led to success with flying colors, but Olivia knew all too well the terrifying consequences when you got in over your head. She'd so wanted to shake the grandparents fawning over the teen's apparent poise and ambition. Would they be there to save her when she'd gotten herself into trouble because she'd tangled with someone who saw through her puffed-up pretense? Someone like Asmodeus.

In the past year, three young women who'd had contact with Asmodeus had later gone missing. Olivia had been following him online for six months hoping to catch him in more than innuendos and catfishing. In reality, she had nothing more than a marrow-deep hunch that Asmodeus was a predator, and it was precisely because she couldn't document and quantify the reasons that she knew he was as bad as they come. That was the only thing they had in common: the ability to hide in plain sight. His success at hiding his trail made him all the more dangerous. Worse, he knew it. Olivia had stumbled upon more than one sly joke Asmodeus had left on a comment thread for anyone who cared to notice, arrogant in his certainty that no one recognized the breadcrumbs he left to his crimes. And his chosen moniker? Its mocking conceit drove her crazy. Too bad for Asmodeus that Olivia would never grow cocky and give herself away. And she would never give up.

"You don't want to do that."

His ominous intonation sent a chill down Olivia's spine, but Melissa only laughed. "Why not?"

"I wouldn't like it." The silky cold response pooled in Olivia's stomach.

Melissa laughed again. "Jealous? Serves you right."

Olivia wanted to shake her.

"Really?" There was an unmistakable edge to this single word.

"Really," Melissa said. "You're just some disembodied Internet voice." She glanced around the lobby. "I much prefer a warm, flesh-and-blood man."

"You do *not* want to make me angry, Melissa."

The ingénue sat up and leaned over. An intent, sly expression slid over her young features. "Am I? Making you angry, Asmodeus?"

Bingo. The number came from a cellphone. Now to see if it had a GPS. Olivia's gaze slid toward Melissa. Where in the world had she learned such hard-core seduction? She was playing with Greek fire, the kind that clung to your skin and only spread when you threw water on it. Olivia pressed *send* on the text she'd already composed to Melissa's aunt. Then she sent a text to the hotel's night manager, who stood at the reception desk waiting for her alert. Catching his gaze, she nodded, and he picked up the phone to call the aunt's room. Provided this delicate dance timed itself well, she'd have enough information on Asmodeus to find him, *and* Melissa would be safely whisked away before the situation escalated out of Olivia's control.

"You are." The cold anger in Asmodeus's voice lit the banked embers of Olivia's own fury. She tamped tight controls around it; she would channel its energy to take this bastard out. "I don't like games. You've already tried my patience once."

Melissa's tinkling laughter serrated Olivia's nerves. She could only imagine how Asmodeus felt hearing it. "Games? What games? *I* asked you to call *me*. It's the least you can do to show you're serious."

"Oh, I'm serious. Deadly serious. You stopped answering my email. That's a game, Melissa."

Olivia shuddered, and studied Melissa, who didn't seem the least bit perturbed by Asmodeus's use of the word *deadly*. Then again, Melissa thought it was a game despite her words. An exciting but ultimately harmless game. She couldn't know that Asmodeus was in Vienna right now. They'd always communicated online, and Asmodeus had led the naïve girl to think he lived and worked in the States. She'd told him that she was traveling, never dreaming that he would find her. Never dreaming that she'd spent four months flirting with a psychopath who believed he owned her.

Olivia fingered the St. Michael medal hanging from a slender chain around her neck. She wouldn't have known Asmodeus was here, either, or even who his prey was if her mysterious source hadn't tipped her off earlier this evening. This was the third time in the two months since she'd arrived in Vienna that she'd gotten critical information about sexual predators in an almost preternatural manner.

Melissa sat up, anger tightening her features. "That's not a game, asshole. That's what happens when you don't give me *your* cell number. I want to talk to you, not read your cryptic messages."

Olivia looked at her smartphone screen. No GPS signal. Likely a burner phone from a big-box store. *Damn.* Now she'd have to hope the call didn't end before she could trace the cell signal back to its source. Biting her lip, she began triangulating Asmodeus's location.

"Not only have I called you, I've come for you."

Olivia's gaze flitted to Melissa. The first look of uncertainty crossed the teen's brow. Squinting, she glanced around the Hilton's lobby. "Come for me? What do you mean, 'come for me'?"

"I'm in Vienna, Melissa."

"Vienna?" The girl's unease sharpened her voice. "How did you know I'm in Vienna?"

Olivia's heart thumped. She'd known her source was accurate, but hearing it from Asmodeus made it real. She prayed he wasn't moving. Walking or driving would make it difficult to get a fix. She peeked at her smartphone again. So far so good. She'd traced Asmodeus's cell signal to a Viennese cell tower. Just a few more seconds, and she'd know down to the block where he was.

"I know many things. I know you gave your aunt a sleeping pill so you could stay out and have some fun, didn't you?"

Guilt slid across the teen's face—only to be replaced with a crafty expression. "You remembered that. You remembered that little detail from one of our chats." Her face and body relaxed as she slouched back into the easy chair with her drink dangling from one hand. Her gaze traveled around the lobby again, but this time she appeared bored. "I don't recall telling you I'm in Vienna, but then I say a lot of things to a lot of people I don't remember."

There was a short silence. Olivia squeezed her eyes shut. Stupid, stupid girl, doubting herself and providing Asmodeus with a plausible reason for his knowledge. It must be like shooting fish in a barrel for him. He didn't have to work very hard at all with this one.

"Do you recall writing that you were 'dying to meet in person'?"

Melissa sipped her drink while Asmodeus spoke. "Um-hm." She nodded and let the empty tumbler dangle again. Five meters away, a blond male, gesticulating after a German goal, paused as he caught sight of her. She smiled and wiggled in her seat in such a way that her large breasts rose and fell, and he lowered his arms. He looked back at the large, flat-screen TV showing the World Cup and then looked at Melissa again. "I'm just not sure I'm all that impatient right now. As I said, there are other guys right here." She paused. "You know what they say."

"What's that?"

"A bird in the hand or some shit like that." Melissa raised her empty tumbler in a salute to the blond male.

Olivia leaned over, placed her left elbow on her thigh, and began rubbing at the dull pain that had started to throb in her forehead. She watched the trace program on the smartphone in her right hand as it bounced from cell mast to cell mast. Any moment and she'd know how close Asmodeus was.

"Melissa," Asmodeus snarled. "Don't toy with me. I want you to meet me."

Gotcha. Olivia's pulse stuttered and then raced. Asmodeus was somewhere in the block. *Crap*. She looked up at the oblivious target.

Melissa's grip on her phone had gone slack. She seemed transfixed by the blond fan, whose athletic physique suggested that he did more than watch soccer on TV. "No, *you* meet me. I'm happy where I am." She lifted the smartphone from her cheek and swiped at its screen. Smiling, she leaned forward and set it on the coffee table in front of her and jiggled the empty tumbler at her admirer, who stood up and walked toward her.

Right. So the aunt was a no-go, but Mr. World Cup would likely keep Little Miss Ontario occupied long enough for Olivia to hunt Asmodeus down. All she had to do was send him a text from Melissa's number saying she was sorry—*jk lols* and all that—and then offer to meet him across the street in the Stadtpark in front of the Schubert statue in fifteen minutes.

That done, Olivia glanced at the couple ordering drinks before snatching up her messenger bag. Once outside the Hilton, which sat at the northeast corner of the park, she headed north toward the Weiskirchnerstrasse entrance. At this hour, few pedestrians wandered the sidewalks of Vienna's city center, and there was little traffic on the roads. The concert at the Weiner Kursalon had ended more than an hour ago, so most concertgoers had likely left, though some might linger over coffee and dessert at the Steirereck Restaurant across the lake from the Schubert Monument. Only the homeless occupied the benches after she crossed the Weinfluss River. That served her purposes well.

Once inside the 19th-century English-style park, Olivia hurried down the broad path before veering behind a large tree. In the dark, it would be difficult for any chance passerby to see her clearly as she changed. There was little enough to do to get ready. She already wore a white unitard with a tank-style top and a flowing white chiffon skirt. The layered skirt had a handkerchief hemline that split high in the middle to reveal Capri-length leggings—giving her great freedom of movement. She kept her custom-fitted, flat white-leather shoes on. Casual from a fashion standpoint, they served her well during her martial-arts training. Then she pulled out a pair of white sap gloves lined with Kevlar and weighted with powdered steel from her messenger bag. After tugging the gloves on, she slid a two-foot baton crafted from a specially tempered stainless-steel alloy into a hidden sheath in the back of the tank top. Last, she grabbed a small square of white and black cloth from the bag and tucked it into the space between her breasts. Though dressed and carrying herself like a dancer, no one who saw her would believe her entirely innocuous. She had shed her invisibility at the same time she shed her demure skirt. In her case, however, anyone who saw her would be inclined to limit her threat to that of a *femme fatale*.

She checked the smartphone's screen. Asmodeus had replied to her text with a smiley emoticon. She swiped the app to replace her content with something harmless in case someone should find her phone and dropped it into the messenger bag, which she'd leave under a convenient shrub on her way to the statue. If she got the chance, she'd come back for it. If not, no biggie. Inhaling a deep breath, Olivia consulted her watch.

Eight minutes until the rendezvous.

As she stepped into the warm night air, Olivia looked up. Stars like finely crushed diamond dust glittered against the blue-black night sky. A hush blanketed the nearly empty park, amplifying distant sounds. Somewhere along the promenade that bordered the Weinfluss River to her left, a woman laughed, a melodic trill followed by the rich baritone of a man's voice. Olivia's step hitched and slowed, and she glanced towards the spontaneous music of seduction. Only lovers strolled at this hour, arm-in-arm, heads dipped toward one another, whispering hopes and desires. Lovers, spies, and criminals.

Pressing her lips together and lifting her chin, Olivia turned away from the voices and strode down the path leading to the west side of the lake where it was darker and quieter. After she'd gone 15 meters, she swerved behind a large oak and dropped her messenger bag against its trunk. Drawing the square of cloth from her bodice, she shook it out with a flick of her wrist. Then she donned the hood she now held, one modeled on the Japanese *zentai* head covering. As with typical *zentai* hoods, hers stretched over her head, face, and neck as a thin fabric skin that obscured her features without restricting sight or breathing. She'd had it made from silk and spandex into a black-and-white harlequin mask.

Olivia stepped back on the path as her right hand pulled the baton out of its snug sheath on her back. This time when she flicked her wrist from side to side, each end of the baton extended with an ominous *snick*. Now she held a high-tech *bō* with a textured rubber grip in the middle and weighted, antenna-like ends. She couldn't help grinning. She should have chosen Darth Maul as inspiration for the design of her hood since she held the real-world equivalent of a double-bladed light saber. Or maybe she should have considered the recent comic-book anti-heroine the Black Sparrow as a role model.

However, Olivia preferred the color white. If any of them could take Black Sparrow as a role model, it would be Beta. Stasia, on the other hand, would be the comic-book heroine Miss Fury. Both those sexy, dangerous fictional ladies were drawn wearing black half-masks and cat suits. The next time she met up with her friends, Olivia would tell them about their comic alter-egos, though she could hear their pained groans in response. Her friends would, in fact, be quite surprised to learn that she even knew what a superhero was. They had the mistaken impression that she'd grown up on the Farm and spent every waking moment spying for the Company.

Olivia sprinted toward the Schubert statue, her steps soundless. When she arrived, she realized she might have been a bit premature in assuming victory over Asmodeus without a single parry or strike of her *bō*. It was a failing her *sensei* had reminded her of each time he stood over her, his own staff angled for a stabbing blow to the throat.

"It's not enough to see several steps ahead, Olivia. You must also execute each one."

In the clearing before the seated composer stood the World Cup fan, his forearm around Melissa's throat and his other around her hips. Her head lolled, her dark hair falling to obscure her face.

At least he didn't have a weapon. It would have made taking him a challenge.

Still, Olivia liked a challenge. Because, as she told her *sensei* each time she responded to what looked like an impossible situation by finding a way to block or parry him, it wasn't enough to see and execute a series of moves. She also needed to respond and take control.

Stopping five meters from the silent pair, she kept her feet apart, her left foot forward and her shoulders facing away from the threat. The *bō* she held in front of her, her hands gripping the middle third a shoulder-width apart in a combat-ready stance.

"She alive?" asked Olivia, nodding toward Melissa. She adopted the husky whisper she'd decided fit her self-imposed role.

"For now." That's when she saw the metallic gleam at Melissa's throat. "But I'm going to liberate her soul."

"Is that so?" she asked, assessing his hold on Melissa, the intensity in his gaze, the steadiness of his hands. *Keep talking, my friend.* "Maybe she'd like to keep it for a while longer."

"That's the problem." He laughed. Something in the sharp sound brought the hairs on Olivia's nape to attention. "Humans and *Elioud* alike cling to this fallen world."

"*Elioud*?" asked Olivia, easing her feet forward a few centimeters. Something about the word sounded familiar, but despite speaking six languages fluently and another dozen enough to survive, she had no idea what it meant.

He cocked his head. "Don't play coy. I've got eyes." He tightened his hold on Melissa, who moaned.

Olivia decided to change the topic. "But not a lot of sense."

"What?"

There. She'd taken him off guard, and he'd eased his hold on Melissa a bit. The light from the nearby lamppost flashed off something that looked more like an ice pick than a knife blade. Perhaps she could goad him into coming for *her.*

"You've got to get past me whether you 'liberate' her soul or not."

He smiled and relaxed more. "Not at all. I just have to wait."

That was unexpected.

"Wait?" she asked and lunged, swinging the *bō* overhand toward his head.

He threw his arm up to block the blow, keeping his other arm around Melissa's waist. The *bō* whipped against his forearm. Olivia heard the distinct snap of breaking bone.

He didn't flinch or drop the weapon. Instead, he stepped forward and jabbed it at her face.

Olivia jerked back and feinted to the other side, whirling the *bō* over his head with a whistling sound. He followed her feint, awkward as he held the unconscious teen and slashing his weapon in front of him. His thrusts met empty air as Olivia sprang to rain blows on his now-unprotected torso and back. She connected several times, the weighted disk on the *bō*'s tip cracking against his skull and spine, before dancing away from his thrashing arm. He stood swaying but didn't collapse. Melissa hung head down over his left arm, her hair and arms swinging.

"Why the hell don't you fall down?" Olivia asked, exasperated.

He grinned at her. Blood trickled down his earlobe and along the side of his neck. The harsh shadows clinging to the hollows of his face accentuated the evil gleam in his eyes. A faint sulfurous odor tickled her nose.

Olivia charged at him again, both hands gripping the middle third of the *bō* as she plied the ends against his head and the backs of his thighs. The fury of her onslaught drove him backwards, stumbling. He tripped over the low hedge circling the base of the Schubert Monument. As he flung his weapon hand up to try to maintain his balance, Olivia whacked the back of his hand. The weapon dropped and he fell, his legs tangling with Melissa's arms and legs. His free hand scrabbled behind him, but Olivia darted forward and grabbed the weapon before flinging it behind her. It certainly looked like an ice pick. Then she stomped on the back of his hand.

Hard.

Bones crunched and sinew popped. A sharp whine clawed its way out his throat.

Olivia took two quick steps back, swinging the *bō* down at the same time to rest on his Adam's apple. The grin never left him. The contrast between his expression and the animal sound emanating from his throat brought bile to her mouth and sent a jolt down her spine. Nevertheless, she kept her face impassive and her breathing even. She hadn't even broken a sweat.

"Jig's up, Asmodeus."

He threw his head back and howled a laugh. At the same time, the high-pitched wail continued to pierce the night. *Now* the cold sweat started between her shoulder blades. "I'm not Asmodeus," he said as he looked at her. "He's waiting for us to capture you."

Olivia stole a glance over her shoulder. A group of men fanned out on the path five meters behind her. She'd let herself be distracted and trapped. Another failing her *sensei* had noted time and again. None appeared armed, but she knew better. She counted quickly. Nine. That was going to be a real challenge.

"He's going to wait a long time then," she said and swiped a low roundhouse kick at the man's head, knocking him out. The eerie, pained sound cut off. Then she jumped to face the silent group, her *bō* held at the ready. Nodding, she said, "Bring it." Her hoarse voice abraded the still air.

One of the men, keeping his gaze on her, bent over and picked up the soccer fan's lost ice pick.

Then he stood up and took a step toward her.

TWO

Olivia charged, swinging the *bō* toward her opponent's head, switching to a low strike to his thigh when he lifted his hand to block. She followed the hit with a swift kick to the side of the knee, and he crumpled. By then, the other eight were rushing at her, and she didn't have time or sight to spare for him or the ice pick. Spinning, she swung the *bō* around her, connecting here with a shoulder and there with a rib. One opponent got inside her guard, so she jabbed the heel of one hand at his face, hammering his nose with a sickening crunch, then tugged hard on his shirt to bring him down in front of two of his comrades, who lost their balance and fell in a jumble on top of him.

Pivoting, she found that the other five had shifted behind her. Two pairs separated and stood back, silent. The fifth man, the largest of the whole group, stood assessing her. Olivia's heart hammered in her chest, but her hands holding the *bō* were steady. A second later the large man came at her.

Olivia aimed her blows at his head, but he didn't try to block. Instead, after she beat a staccato rhythm on his skull, he shook the assault off as if her *bō* were only a noisome fly. A wide grin split his face.

Crap.

Out of the corner of her eye, she saw the four men she'd brought down struggle upright.

Double crap.

The large man lowered his head—*he lowered his head*—and shoved toward her.

Olivia tossed her *bō* up, grabbed the back of his shirt as she stepped out of his path, and flung him toward the ground. His momentum, aided by his weight, sent him crashing. She caught the *bō* and turned, jabbing at the base of his neck as she did.

After that, the melee turned into a flurry of strikes, feints, and kicks. Olivia countered everything they brought at her, surprised at how uncoordinated and ineffectual they were. Very few of their blows had landed, and the ones that had had lacked strength. They fought like a bunch of sloppy bar drunks, telegraphing roundhouse swings and head butts. Though she hadn't yet tired, her bodysuit clung to her sweaty skin, and she'd begun to breathe heavily. She'd just sent a front kick into an opponent's lower groin, bending him over with a grunt, when she caught the sly smile another two shared.

The truth settled in a sickening pool in the pit of her stomach.

They were playing her. Playing with her, like a pack of wolves nipping at the flanks and heels of a bull moose. Any moment now, when they'd judged she'd worn herself out or grown overconfident, they'd pile on her.

Good thing she was smarter than an average bull moose. It was time to take off the kid gloves.

This time she aimed her blows to kill instead of incapacitate. Not an easy maneuver with a *bō* but not impossible—especially if the one wielding the staff committed to the kill. When she cracked a weighted tip against her attacker's head, she aimed for his temple, swerving to whip the other end across the windpipe of the attacker behind her before the first had dropped to the ground.

For a long heartbeat, no one moved. Though the park lights illuminated the area in which they fought, the thick, dark trees beyond the monument absorbed the light. To Olivia's heightened senses, the silent blackness beyond thrummed with menace. She scanned the path, but nothing moved except the eyes and heaving chests of the seven men facing her. Olivia had no idea why half of them were still standing. One attacker's nose was smashed and his features obscured by blood. Another's knee had been crushed so badly that he hopped on his good leg like a sparrow. Another carried an injured arm close to his chest. All had visible bruises and welts. The odd sulfurous scent had grown stronger and held a taint of rotting meat. She inhaled, making her eyes water. Blinking, she heard Melissa moan. The low sound broke the spell. In the next instant, three attackers ran at her, and it was all she could do to keep from going down on the ground, a place she definitely didn't want to be.

One man got under her guard and punched her exposed ribs. Crying out, Olivia held onto his extended arm and pulled him closer and down to knee him in the gut. The sharp pain in her side as she did took much of the strength out of the maneuver, but she'd unbalanced him. Shoving him into the second attacker, she slashed the *bō* across the third attacker's eyes. Screaming, he staggered back, falling over the first two on the ground. Olivia shuffled backwards, her broken rib shooting pain through her whole torso. In the earlier scuffle, she'd glimpsed the ice pick lying not far from Melissa's prone form. She might need it with these inhuman jokers.

She'd just brushed something with her toe when the remaining four attackers descended. Scooping it up without looking, she slammed the *bō* into the ground so that the extensible arms slid back into the base. As she rose, she swung the heavy metal baton into the first attacker's jaw, breaking it, before twisting to punch the ice pick at a second attacker.

It wasn't enough.

Neither injured man went down or even seemed to notice that she'd struck him. She had just enough time and presence of mind to notice their glittering, dead gazes. A heartbeat later, they'd both broken through her guard. One grabbed the wrist of the hand holding the ice pick while he punched at her face, snapping her head back. His partner chopped at her other wrist, causing her to drop the baton. The second pair drove in behind them, landing a punch and a kick at her thigh. The stench swirling around the four men gagged her, and her knees weakened as her vision splintered into brilliant shards.

Her *sensei* would not be pleased. Then again, he'd never taught her to fight off a horde of zombies.

Olivia let her body sag, dragging the attacker still holding her wrist down to the ground with her. His body tumbled, absorbing several blows from his comrades as he fell. Pinned beneath his grunting form, Olivia searched with her free hand for her dropped baton.

She wanted to crush one final skull before they killed her and Melissa.

On such a beautiful July night in the City of Music where even the motion of the stars against the heavens suggested a waltz, the *drangùe* should have been discussing opera with the vivacious woman whom he had escorted along the promenade beside the Weinfluss River after dessert at the Steirereck Restaurant. He should have been debating Mozart and Verdi, all while listening to the steady beating of her heart beneath her clear, mellifluous voice. Instead he found himself sprinting down a darkened path toward the sounds of a brutal beating.

Given the summer break in Vienna's concert season, the performance at the Weiner Kursalon had been only mediocre, but even a third-string Viennese orchestra plays heartbreakingly well, and he had not been to a concert in some time. His date had been far from mediocre. She had been lovely, smart, and knowledgeable about music and opera, yet with an enchanting innocence that made him feel protective in a way that he had not felt in a lifetime. He wondered if he had hurt her with his abrupt departure, his insistence that he would call her tomorrow. The furrows on her forehead as she stood on the sidewalk where he had left her waiting for a taxi made him think that she doubted him. Shaking his head and letting a soft expletive leave his lips, he ignored the sharp pain behind his breastbone at the thought. It was what it was. He could not change his duty or his destiny. It had indeed been a lifetime since he had learned that adamantine lesson. He was his father's son. He was a *drangùe*.

Despite knowing his duty, and despite his long years of fulfilling it, nothing had ever prepared him for the sight that met his eyes as he approached the well-lit Schubert statue on the other side of the Weinfluss. A lithe figure in white stood amongst an encircling group of battered and disheveled men, each of whom sported multiple bruises and bleeding cuts. Though the woman—he could tell little more about her thanks to the close-fitting head covering that she wore—stood motionless, the *drangùe*'s long experience fighting hand-to-hand read deadly alertness in her posture. She held a curious weapon, a long black staff with weighted ends, in a trained ready stance, and though her white tank was already dark with sweat, she looked strong and capable of fighting for as long as necessary. He stopped outside the illuminated circle to evaluate the situation. Maybe his aid wasn't needed.

A low moan came from a young woman lying near the base of the Schubert statue. The *drangùe*'s heart twisted, but before he could act, he sensed rather than saw the attack on the figure in white. As she pivoted to strike at one of the three men who lunged, another charged, his fist striking her exposed ribs. The figure in white cried out. It was not a loud cry, but its sharpness, combined with the thud of knuckle on bone, told the *drangùe* that her attacker had broken at least one of her ribs.

A white-hot fury lit him. The *drangùe* inhaled, his breath scorching his throat and nostrils. But he never lost focus. He waited a moment longer to assess the remaining four men who stood, silent and intent, watching their companions attack the figure in white. They needed to be dealt with first. The *drangùe* saw the figure in white grab the assailant who had punched her, knee him, and then shove him into a second attacker before whipping her staff across the third man's eyes. The man screamed, staggered over his two partners, and fell. The woman limped back from the other four men, only dropping her gaze for a moment as she reached for something on the ground. That was enough for them to launch themselves at her.

The figure in white rose up to meet them with something that flashed in the light in one hand and her staff, now transformed into a baton, in the other. The *drangùe* heard bone crack as she hammered the baton into an attacker's jaw. Her second hand sliced at another attacker, and the *drangùe* saw blood pour from an eye socket. Even as he cheered mentally at her incredible skill and heart, warning bells sounded in the back of his mind. They should have dropped like dead weights. Instead, they kept coming. The one-eyed man grabbed a wrist and hit her in the face while the slack-jawed villain struck the baton from her other hand. The *drangùe* saw the blows that came after that, the kick and the punch, the figure in white pulling an attacker down, the eager swings of arms and feet, but these details blurred in his awareness as he sprang from the darkness into battle.

The men proved to be little more than fleshy, jointed sacks less satisfying to hit than his punching bag. He clamped onto the nearest attacker's shoulder, pulling him close as his other hand slipped around to the man's chin and he twisted hard. Flinging the dead man aside, the *drangùe* grabbed another. This one fought, pushing his soft, flabby belly against the *drangùe* as his fists flailed. His pants and grunts filled the *drangùe*'s ears. Behind them, a third attacker rose. By now, the *drangùe*'s battle senses had awakened, and he saw the man's thermal outline and heard his racing heart a fraction of a second before the blow. Roaring, the *drangùe* spun, blocking the downward slash of the third attacker's hand with the second's back. The man screamed from the simultaneous stab and the scorching heat of the *drangùe*'s grip.

The *drangùe* locked gazes with the third man as he dropped the second to the ground. What he saw there knocked his fury back a little. The man's eyes glittered, emotionless and staring. A moment later, the *drangùe* punched the man so hard his head snapped back, and he dropped to the ground in a boneless heap. Then the *drangùe* swiveled to grab the last man off the figure in white.

He was too late.

The figure in white held her baton under the man's chin, her legs wrapped around his torso and squeezing as she tugged hard against his windpipe. It was only a matter of seconds before she had finished him. The *drangùe* bent down and shoved the body away before pressing a hot fingertip against the man's neck to make sure there was no pulse. The figure in white lay for a moment, chest heaving, her arms and legs sprawled in an attitude of utter weariness. He scanned her for any more injuries. Red welts and gathering bruises mottled her pale flesh, visible along her arms and upper back and shoulders. The right side of her outfit was ripped to reveal a thin bloody line that grazed her ribs. As he reached to pull the fabric aside to make sure that the wound was as shallow as it appeared, she flinched.

"Who are you?" Her weak voice sounded more curious than frightened. His sensitive hearing caught traces of a foreign accent in her German. *American?*

"Let me see how deep that is," he ordered, ignoring the question. The huskiness of his voice surprised him. *No huskier than usual,* he assured himself. *Exhaling hot, smoky air tends to do that.*

"It's just a scratch." She coughed and winced. "Damn bastard tried to stab me with an ice pick. If I hadn't rolled when I did, he would have, too."

The *drangùe* willed his fingers to cool to something closer to normal human temperature before stroking her upper arm. She'd looked so invincible and deadly only moments before, but now that he knelt next to her, he could see how fragile and delicate she really was. Despite having the muscular physique of a dancer or gymnast, she could not weigh more than one hundred twenty five pounds or stand taller than five six. In other words, half his weight and more than a head shorter. He felt his ire rise.

"Let me see it." This time he growled.

She went still, and he regretted his words. Gritting his teeth, he slid a fingertip along the wound. She shivered under his touch, and for a moment he forgot that he only wanted to know whether she was hurt or not. He had the urge to slip his whole hand, palm flattened, across her abdomen, to feel the banded muscle there. He resisted.

"Told you," she whispered, and he removed his finger.

He looked up then, wanting to see her eyes. That was when he got a good look at the head covering she wore. It was a black-and-white harlequin mask, but nothing like the elaborate ones he had seen in Venice for Carnival. Instead of a hard, painted shell, white fabric stretched over her entire head and most of her neck, detailing the structure of her face and neck while obscuring her features. The mask's own features had a clean, almost alien cast with large black eyes, a single quirky eyebrow, an extravagant tear on one cheek, and firmly closed lips. This, then, was a mime whose expression never changed.

"At least one of your ribs is broken." It was not a question.

She laughed this time, but the laugh choked off on a sob. "Nothing worse than I've felt before," she said when she got her breath back. "But one of them hit me pretty hard. You're all blurry. And it looks like you have glowing wings."

Shocked that she had seen more than a shimmering nimbus from his harmonic vibrations, the *drangùe* forced himself to stay calm. It would do no good whatever to burn her when he touched her. To distract himself, he gazed around the area, aware all at once that he had been so focused on the harlequin that he had let his battle senses go dormant. That was when he felt the other presence lurking in the deepest shadows behind the Schubert statue. Someone watched. Quickly he looked at the scattered bodies. One or two breathed yet, but otherwise gave no sign of impending threat. The young woman he'd seen earlier now slouched against the base of the statue, her head drooping into a hand and the other hand on her stomach. She began retching, twisted, and threw up. She was a good 10 meters away from him and closer to the watcher. The *drangùe*'s unease increased.

He lowered his voice as he leaned over the harlequin to use both hands to examine her shapely legs. "We are not alone."

She stilled again. "Where?"

He admired her presence of mind, although after watching her fight he expected nothing less. No doubt she had questions but knew that now was not the time for them. "On the other side of the statue. My gut tells me that it is not a friend."

"Who's throwing up?"

"The young woman that you were defending." He finished his examination and sat back. "Do you think that you can walk? Your legs seem uninjured."

"I'm fine. Help Melissa."

"I will, after I help you." He did not give the harlequin a chance to protest. Instead, he grabbed her hand and hauled her to her feet. To anyone else, her slight intake of breath would have been imperceptible, but he heard it. He scowled. "Wait here."

A faint aura, perhaps a remnant of the harlequin's thermal reading, remained as the *drangùe* turned. Tucking this perplexing detail away to examine later, he sprinted to the young woman, who had finished throwing up and now gazed around wide eyed. When he reached her, she looked up, her jaw slack. Bright red lipstick smeared her mouth and mascara tracked down her cheeks. It was not a becoming face. At the sight of his radiant form, her mouth fell open.

"Melissa?"

She flinched. "How-how did you know my name?" In her rough voice, it was hard to distinguish the accent of her English. She swallowed and looked away. "What are you going to do to me?"

He answered in English. "I am going to help you and your friend get medical care."

Confusion flitted over her features. "Friend? What friend?"

The *drangùe* looked back at the harlequin, who stood upright and graceful in a relaxed stance, both arms loose at her sides. But she held the baton again in her left hand. That and the alert tilt of her head as she appeared to scan the trees beyond him and Melissa told him that, broken rib or not, she had recovered enough to defy anyone to attack her. He smiled to himself. Then he remembered Melissa's question.

"A Good Samaritan," he said, his low voice pitched to reach the harlequin's ears only. She swiveled her head to aim the painted eyes at him. Although her expression was hidden, he read her surprise at the intimacy of his voice in the subtle movement of her head. It occurred to him that it would be an intriguing challenge to decipher her responses without the usual facial cues.

"Same as you," she murmured. He wondered if she knew that he could hear her.

At her words, something like a premonition coursed through the *drangùe*. Frowning, he kept his gaze on the harlequin as he spoke to Melissa, who stood blinking in the light from the nearby lamppost, which was much amplified by his presence.

"You have had a great shock," he said, pitching his voice to a soothing timbre, "and this is not a safe place. Let me escort you out of the park and take you to the hospital."

As he knew it would, his tone lulled her into a calmer, compliant state. Blinking several times, she stood and leaned toward him. He wrapped an arm around her waist while scanning the darkness beyond the statue. The air around them had grown oppressive to his senses, like pressure building before a storm. He urged the young woman to walk. Together they headed up the path toward the Weiskirchnerstrasse entrance to the park where he'd already arranged for his driver to meet them.

The harlequin waited until Melissa and he had passed and then fell in behind them, walking backwards to watch their exit. Her heat radiated along the sensitive line of his spine while the strong beating of her heart thundered in his ears. It took only a moment for him to realize that their hearts beat in unison, though he could not know whether that was a coincidence or through a fortuitous alignment, but as soon as he noticed, his own heart rate sped up. Hers followed suit. Her breath hitched, and she stumbled a little. As she caught herself, he felt her piercing gaze through her face covering. He forced himself to focus on Melissa, who'd started to sob. Pulling her closer, he raised his temperature slightly as he began to hum. She relaxed into his warmth, so much that he feared that he'd need to carry her. The harlequin gave an exasperated sigh.

"You are not sympathetic to Melissa's plight?" He made no effort to turn back to the harlequin. Rather he again pitched his voice to reach her ears.

She snorted and turned to flank the wilting young woman. They had made it to the park entrance without being followed. The *drangùe* saw with surprise that she now carried a messenger bag. *How had she gotten that without him noticing?*

"Who are you?" asked the harlequin in a husky whisper. This time when she asked he knew that she wouldn't be ignored. "Your accent. I can't place it. It's not German, that's for sure."

He sighed and moved his hand to Melissa's upper arm, putting some distance between them. It was necessary to wean her from his support by the time they made it to his waiting car and driver.

"A Good Samaritan." He paused. "Same as you." He wished then that he could see her expression as he echoed her earlier murmured words. Was she smiling or frowning? He himself frowned and increased his harmonics as well as the length of his stride.

"Why can't I see you?" she asked. "I thought it was because I'd gotten hit, but nothing else is hazy. Just you. In fact, if anything, I'd say you just got *hazier*."

Melissa stopped walking. "You said you're taking me to the hospital." From the rising petulance in her voice, he gathered that she was recovering from her earlier shock. She looked at the harlequin, her eyes narrowing as she took in the painted face and torn white suit for the first time. "Who the hell are you?"

The *drangùe*'s patience stretched thin. If he were honest, it was something more than annoyance that he felt right now. He ignored the young woman and answered the harlequin. "One of the mysteries of the universe, I am afraid." He waved toward the street where a black Mercedes waited at the curb. "Now here is my driver." He turned to the patiently waiting man. "These women need to be driven to St. Elizabeth's. You have the direction?"

The driver, who had gotten out of the car as they approached, inclined his head and opened the rear door. "Please, ladies," he said as he gestured for them to slide into the seat.

The harlequin was having none of it. She grabbed Melissa, who squealed, at the same moment as her weighted staff appeared in her other hand with a *snick*. The *drangùe* was impressed. Not only had he not anticipated such an act, but she'd executed both moves gracefully even though she was injured.

"Yes?" he asked, low and soft, no hint of smoky heat in his voice. From the corner of his eye, he saw the surprise on his driver's face. No doubt that loyal, opinionated servant would express his astonishment at great length later when they were alone.

"We're not getting into that car. I still can't see you." Strong emotion strained her low voice. "Whatever technology you're using to obscure your features leads me to conclude that you're not the Good Samaritan you'd have me believe. In fact, now that I think about it, it was *too* convenient for you to show up when you did, am I right, Asmodeus?"

The *drangùe* jerked and gave an involuntary hiss. His driver took a step toward them, his hand out, but the *drangùe* hardly registered the shocked concern on his driver's face.

The harlequin's spine straightened a fraction. "You know that name." It wasn't a question.

Before he could answer or ask his own questions, Melissa, long ignored, acted. She elbowed the harlequin in her broken rib and twisted free as the harlequin doubled over with a sharp gasp. The *drangùe* reacted without thinking, leaping to the injured woman's side as Melissa darted down the sidewalk only to be stopped by his driver. The harlequin dropped her staff, swayed, and then crumpled. He caught her before she hit the pavement. The heat and pain radiating from her hurt side shot through him like a thunderbolt, and his heartbeat sped up. Grimacing, the *drangùe* compelled his heart to calm, feeling her breath stutter and then match his. She wriggled weakly.

"Shh," he urged, drawing her closer to his chest and wrapping his arms around her shoulders.

Crooning wordlessly, he stroked a warm palm along her injured side, willing the broken bone to knit. An urge to remove her mask and see her face took him, and he pulled back slightly. He had grabbed the edge of the covering and begun to slide it up her graceful neck, his gaze drawn to the erratic pulse at its base, when a *polizei* car pulled in behind the Mercedes, its lights flashing. Two officers jumped from the car, calling out to them to remain where they were.

Melissa started screaming and struggling, breaking free from his driver's grasp as one of the officers came up, her hand on her holster. At the same moment, the harlequin, who had sagged against him, surged forward, knocking him off balance as she drove the base of one palm under his chin. He released her in response. By the time he had recovered, she had turned away, snatched up her staff and the messenger bag, and begun sprinting in the river's direction. The second *polizei* officer, who had reached the spot where the *drangùe* stood, raised his pistol and shouted at her to stop. She kept running. As the officer squeezed the trigger, the *drangùe* knocked his wrist up and away.

The harlequin ran through the intersection across from the Hilton Vienna, dodging cars. She never looked back. They lost sight of her on the dark sidewalk beyond the hotel.

Exasperated, the *drangùe* turned to the second *polizei* officer, who reached to restrain him. He stilled the harmonics and the light emanating from him while slipping into the easy smile he had perfected over the years to diffuse tension.

All the *polizei* officers would see and remember was a tall, dark-haired man in evening wear that was a little disarrayed from brawling. It would take only a few moments of special charm to send them on their way to St. Elizabeth's with the young woman.

"Officer," he said in German, infusing the words with warmth and connection. The man stilled and stood blinking. "I am so glad that you have arrived at the most opportune moment possible. This young lady"—he waved toward Melissa, who now stood gesticulating and chattering while the female *polizei* officer and his driver listened, "was beset upon in the park by a gang of thugs when I happened upon them. I am afraid that she needs medical attention."

"Was that one of thugs you were detaining?" the man asked, lifting his chin in the direction that the harlequin had disappeared. "Why did you ruin my shot?"

The *drangùe* kept his gaze trained on the other man. "Who?" he asked, his feigned innocence underscored by his will. "Do you not think that you should call for reinforcements and investigate? They cornered her near the Schubert statue."

After that, everything proceeded as the *drangùe* knew it would. An ambulance arrived and the female officer escorted Melissa to St. Elizabeth's. Three more *polizei* cars screeched to a halt at the curb, their lights flashing, and the officers emerged, running to the park entrance while the first male officer continued to take statements from the *drangùe* and his driver. Although his driver lacked his boss's special abilities, he had the right temperament and experience to confirm that only the *drangùe* and the traumatized Melissa had emerged from the Stadtpark. Later, the *drangùe* would visit her in the hospital to ensure that she suffered no long-lasting damage from the incident and to ask his own questions about the men and the harlequin. Unfortunately, he would not be able to investigate the crime scene until after the Vienna *polizei* had already processed it, but they did not have the same ability to analyze it as he did. Likely there would be something they had overlooked that would tell him more. If, as he suspected, the attackers were no ordinary human gang, the *drangùe* expected to find plenty of evidence that the *polizei* had neither the ability to find nor the power to handle.

After all, the harlequin had mentioned Asmodeus.

Asmodeus stood on the outskirts of the police investigation at the Stadtpark among a knot of officials. Although he had no official capacity here, he had delighted in using one of his avatars to insert himself into the situation. Of course, he could always compel people to share what they knew with him, but he much preferred the more subtle and satisfying manipulation of humanity. He chortled to himself, startling the nearest *polizei* officer, who looked up from where he knelt by a body on the ground. An uneasy and subconscious recognition of Asmodeus's true nature crossed the officer's face, to be wiped clean as his own gullibility explained away what his gut knew. Asmodeus continued to smirk, knowing full well that it would torment the man's waking moments for weeks and his dreams for much longer. Yet the man would blame the carnage around them for recalling Asmodeus's unblinking stare and the unaccountable mirth that didn't reach his eyes.

Of course, who would blame any of the *polizei* for losing sleep over what they had discovered when they arrived in this stately and quiet park in the heart of Vienna? Apparently, the attackers had been a group of drug-addled soccer fans who'd continued to beat each other to a literal pulp after their intended victim and her heroic rescuer had escaped. Even the hardened *polizei* detective with twenty years' experience had seen nothing like it. While three of the nine men still lived, their conditions had been listed as critical and they weren't expected to last through the night. None of them had any official identification on them. Early results from the national fingerprint database came up empty, and the fingerprints had been sent on to their counterparts at Interpol. None of the battered faces lent themselves to immediate identification, though the forensics experts remained hopeful that once they'd been cleaned prior to autopsy that identifying features or marks would emerge. A forensic anthropologist would be brought in to reconstruct the faces if necessary. And there was always the chance that dental records would provide at least one or two identifications.

Beneath the meticulous data collection ran a current of disgust and fear so strong that Asmodeus could taste its sweetness on his tongue. That alone merited his presence here even if he learned nothing useful from these worthless investigators. As far as he could tell, they had no idea that the "heroic" passerby had withheld information about a certain figure in white wearing a head covering painted with a harlequin's face. Then again, the hero was no ordinary man, was he? Asmodeus chortled again. He'd simply been looking for a little diversion when he realized that someone was tracking him online. Watching a woman dressed like a ridiculous fantasy superhero come to save the bait that he'd dangled had sent Asmodeus into orgiastic flights of anticipation. When she'd proved to be a tougher target than he could have anticipated, he'd been so transported by the blood and brutality that he'd felt a release such as he hadn't in decades. It seems that he had drawn a Wild *Elioud* to his trail, and the spiritual power discharged from her death would feed him for some time.

Even so, he'd felt sharp regret as the fight had drawn to a close, a fight she had been destined to lose no matter how preternaturally talented with a stick she had turned out to be. However, the regret had lasted only a moment as his minions overwhelmed her, bringing her to the ground like a wounded deer. He'd tasted her fear along with the metallic scent of blood. At that moment, ecstasy awaited him.

That moment was stolen from him.

The *drangùe*, a powerful *Elioud* by the sheer white brilliance of his harmonics, had burst from the darkness with the power of a speeding comet. All at once, the sure victory had transformed into defeat. The *drangùe* dispatched three of the attackers, leaving the harlequin to subdue the fourth and final. Asmodeus, long used to disciplining the howling emotions that buffeted him, stifled his initial rage and anguish to move closer to observe their interaction. He'd given his presence away, though that unfortunate slip had yielded valuable information. He had baited his harlequin, and she had in turn unwittingly baited one of his greatest enemies. As a result, Asmodeus had drunk in the sight of the *Elioud* kneeling by the injured woman, the *drangùe*'s protective urge and desire rolling from him in shockwaves. In doing so, the *drangùe* had just revealed a major vulnerability. It was almost too delicious to bear.

The question for Asmodeus now was how best to pursue the hero by using the harlequin.

THREE

Only a single shot chased Olivia as she fled, her side aching though no longer excruciating. She dared not look back to see whether anyone followed. Once she was sure that she'd outrun any ability to distinguish her features in the dark, she tugged the *zentai* hood from her head as she ran and stuffed it into her messenger bag. Her baton followed. Inside the bag she'd stuffed a lightweight hooded tunic. This she pulled out and slipped on. The loose gray fabric fell to her mid-thigh, hiding the messenger bag and obscuring her own form. At this point she'd almost reached the Wien Mitte Mall and the closest U-bahn station. Darting a glance toward the security camera aimed at the mall entrance, she used both hands to raise the tunic's hood over her head as she approached, experienced enough to be confident that no one examining the video later would be able to identify her.

Good fortune stayed with her as she entered. A group of rowdy World Cup fans jostled and chattered as they headed toward the metro. Olivia picked up her pace and fell into step with those in back. She palmed one of the fan's U-bahn cards while he joked with his friends, who then teased him when he couldn't find it. She slipped it into his back pocket as they made their way to the train. When the group got on the metro, she got on with them. It didn't matter that they were getting on the green line, which meant that she'd have to transfer a couple more times to get on the orange line. She wouldn't have taken the train straight to the Westbahnhof station, the one closest to her flat in the sixth district, anyway.

Despite being surrounded by a dozen or so tall, muscular men, Olivia kept her head angled so that the train's security camera wouldn't capture her features. Absently she found her St. Michael medal. Rubbing it with her thumb, she debated whether to get off at the station where she kept more clothes in a public locker for just such an eventuality or bide her time among the soccer fans when someone jostled her from behind. She took a step forward, pivoting at the same time to see who it had been. A young woman about the same height and build as Olivia stood gazing at her, her large, luminous eyes innocent and yet knowing.

"This is yours, yes?" she asked in heavily accented English while holding out a backpack.

Olivia didn't reply immediately. Instead she studied the bag. *What was this woman up to?*

"Yes, yes, it is yours. I saw you drop it at the Wien Mitte station." The young woman passed her the backpack, her fingers touching Olivia's briefly. Something sparked between them, not quite static electricity but similar. Olivia's fingers closed reflexively over the straps, and then the young woman had turned away to speak to someone on the other side of her, Olivia and the backpack forgotten. For a moment, a very visible and very luminous nimbus limned the young woman's form. Olivia blinked hard and deliberately. Then she started to reach for the other woman. Before she could get her attention, the train pulled into the next station, and then all of the soccer fans moved in a boisterous jumble out the doors and onto the platform. She let them trail away and up the escalator, joking and laughing, but couldn't find the young woman among them. A shiver ran down her spine.

As the last person exiting stepped past her, Olivia came back to herself. Moving swiftly, she avoided the security cameras on the platform and found a dark corner to investigate the contents of the backpack. Inside, she found a red hooded sweatshirt with the words VIENNA, AUSTRIA embroidered on the front. There was also a soft knit cap, a pair of jeans in her size, and high-top sneakers, also in her size. Shaking her head, Olivia pulled the jeans out first, slipped off her shoes, and then tugged the jeans over her leggings. The rest of the items she donned quickly before pushing the tunic, her shoes, the *zentai* hood, and her baton into the backpack. Her transformation took less than a minute, allowing her to jump on the escalator before the last exiting passenger had reached the top. The messenger bag and smartphone she dumped in a trashcan before boarding the next train on the brown line.

After that, it was another hour before she'd transferred stations another time, arrived at her final stop, and then walked twenty minutes to her flat. It was 2 a.m.

Olivia had let herself in without turning the lights on when she felt a dark presence in the main room. Something whistled toward her.

She had the baton extended into its *bō* form before her opponent's chain whip caught her. The heavy steel dart on the ancient battle weapon wrapped around her *bō* instead of piercing her torso, and she jerked. The dark figure on the other end lurched forward. Olivia grabbed the figure's wrist, twisting the *bō* into an upright position at the same time, and then pulled her attacker into her. Her rib was still sore, though it didn't hurt as much as it had. She growled.

"Beta." She let go of the other woman's wrist and shoved.

Beta staggered back, dragging her chain whip. In seconds she had pulled its sections up into a compact mass in her left hand. "Liv."

Olivia sighed and turned a table lamp on. She slid the backpack down and dropped it on the sofa next to her. "Want something to drink? *I* need something."

Beta shrugged and slouched against the wall next to the sofa. "Nice red sweatshirt," she said in Czech.

"It is indeed," Olivia said as she walked into the kitchen area. She got a glass of water and drank it down. It felt as though she hadn't had anything to drink in hours, which was true. Crushing fatigue had started to set in along with the bruises she knew mottled her upper back and torso. A stinging cut over her right eye and tenderness along her jaw promised to test her makeup skills in the morning. "Thanks for the practice defending against a sneak attack."

"You reacted slowly." Beta came over and pulled out a chair at the small dining table. "If I'd really intended to hurt you, I would have succeeded."

Olivia looked at her friend. As usual, Beta wore a black-leather biker jacket and black-leather riding jeans. The chain whip had disappeared into an inner pocket. Olivia pulled the stranger's sweatshirt over her head and tossed it onto the sofa with the backpack. Then she turned to the cabinet over the refrigerator and pulled out a bottle of Tuzemák, a Czech spirit distilled from sugar beets and flavored to taste like rum. She glanced back at Beta as she reached for shot glasses. Carrying everything to the table, she set the glasses down and poured two shots. She tossed hers back as Beta watched and then poured another.

"How many?" asked Beta, her low voice almost a whisper.

"Nine." Olivia looked at her friend, who watched her closely, her coal-dark eyes unfathomable. "But you'd think it was three times that many given how hard it was to put them down."

Beta scowled and knocked her own shot back. She slammed the shot glass down and motioned for Olivia to hit her again. It was the most violent reaction that Olivia had ever seen her have. She suspected that beneath Beta's ultra-cool exterior there was a core of molten passion, one that her friend released only as a flick of her deadly chain whip. She thought again of the bright star plummeting toward her, the small silver flag at its base rustling. Only the most talented and focused martial artist mastered the chain whip. With its sections, it was more challenging to control than a whip made from a seamless leather strip. Olivia's *sensei* said the martial artist either bent the chain whip to her will or the chain whip broke the martial artist.

She grinned as she poured her friend's second shot. Beta's seven-section chain whip functioned as her third arm.

"Asmodeus?" asked Beta.

Olivia sighed and sank into a chair, pouring herself a third shot. She should really get an ice pack and some ibuprofen, maybe a med kit for the cut over her eyebrow.

"No." She straightened. "But he didn't get the girl, either."

Saluting Beta with her shot, she tossed the Tuzemák back. The alcohol had started to work, leaving a pleasantly warm trail down her throat to pool in her stomach. She felt her shoulders relax and her thoughts grow fuzzy. Calm washed over her. She was alive and home.

Beta got up and went to the cupboards. She pulled out a medical kit and ran some water into a small plastic bowl. Grabbing a tea towel, she carried the kit and bowl to the table and sat next to Olivia. Silently she began washing the cut over Olivia's eye using a syringe before drying her forehead with the towel.

"How bad?" asked Olivia, closing her eyes.

She wanted to slouch, to sleep right there, but Beta's gentle swipes stung. And her friend had some news yet to share.

Beta said nothing, simply drew a tight breath between her front teeth. After a moment, Olivia heard her tug on nitrile gloves and snip the applicator on the skin glue.

"That's not supposed to go on the face," Olivia said with her eyes still closed.

"Then you should not move."

Holding the edges of the cut closed with one hand, Beta began applying the glue over it. She layered more glue over the first coat and then applied a third, and final, coat. In less than three minutes, the glue would set. Now the warmth from the activated polymer competed with that of the alcohol in Olivia's veins. She found her thoughts drifting to the mysterious stranger who had intervened at precisely the right moment to save her life, and that of Melissa.

"The scar will be minimal," Beta said as she stripped off her gloves.

"Did our online friend send a message about me?" Olivia asked.

Beta nodded. "Stasia will be here before first light."

Olivia opened her eyes and stretched, though by now she felt drained as the adrenaline receded. Drained, exhausted, and chilled. Beta got up, returned the items to the kitchen, and filled the tea kettle. While it heated, she went to Olivia's bedroom and returned with a robe, a blanket, fuzzy socks, and slippers. Without speaking, she hauled Olivia to her feet and draped the robe over her shoulders before leading her to the sofa. Olivia plopped onto the cushions, grateful for their firmness. Beta tucked the blanket around her before kneeling and removing her shoes. She tugged the socks onto Olivia's freezing feet followed by the slippers.

Olivia dozed while Beta left to make the tea and a tray of food. Then she let Beta feed her as though she were a small child, her head drooping and her eyes closed. The sweet, hot tea and honey-slathered toast satiated something hollow inside her, and she managed to swallow the last bite as Beta eased her onto her side on the sofa. As she slept, she dreamt of the fight in the Stadtpark. In the way of dreams, her attackers floated around her as blurry menaces, amorphous blobs that dissipated whenever she tapped them with her *bō*. Only their brilliant eyes and gaping maws came in focus, and every one held an icepick. They swarmed her, stabbing and stabbing, but never finding the right spot to liberate her soul.

The pain took her breath away, but then he was there, tall and surrounded by a brilliant nimbus that scattered the icepick-wielding ghouls. She sighed as he drew her into his arms again, already anticipating his warm healing touch and tender crooning. In fact, in her dream, she understood his words on some primal level, deep inside her gut. What he said as he caressed her face, running a finger over her cut, left her with a bittersweet yearning that stayed long after she awoke. She looked up as the ache pierced her, expecting to see only hazy features, but she saw him. Though she couldn't bring his face into focus later, she knew that he was astoundingly beautiful and terrible at the same time. He could destroy her with one flick of his mighty hand, yet he would not, now or ever.

When she awoke, early daylight pulled the shadows from her flat in long strokes, revealing furniture, books, and picture frames as well as the two women sitting at her dining table, their heads bowed close as they talked in low voices. She'd only gotten five hours of sleep, yet she felt deeply refreshed. Stretching, she sat up.

"Stasia."

Beta and Stasia glanced at her together. Purple shadows darkened Stasia's eyes and her caramel-colored hair needed a brush. Even so, she was stunningly beautiful with large, almond-shaped eyes, high cheekbones, and a wide, dramatic mouth.

"Sì, *cara?*"

Olivia got up and went to Stasia, bending to hug her. Stasia smelled like anise and vanilla, simultaneously exotic and comforting.

"What's wrong? Why are you and Beta both here?" She looked at Beta, hoping her apology showed. "Don't get me wrong. I wish you could be here every time I take on a horde of zombies."

Beta and Stasia exchanged a weighted glance.

"What?" Olivia asked. "Don't tell me you've both fought zombies too."

"*Zombi*?" Stasia laughed without humor. "Indeed, that is a good word for them, *cara*. But they are more accurately called pawns because they do the bidding of someone very powerful."

Olivia went to put the kettle on. "That could describe any number of people. But most people possess an instinct for survival. Or lack the will to go on if they're badly injured. I had to use lethal force on these guys. And even then, some of them kept getting up. Hence the comparison to zombies."

She turned to rummage through the refrigerator for breakfast. She felt ravenous, which always happened after a strenuous fight.

"Dead gaze? Slack jaw? The scent of rotting eggs and meat?" Beta asked in an emotionless voice.

Stasia's voice, on the other hand, crackled with strong emotion. "A sharp, pointed weapon and talk of liberating your soul?"

Olivia whirled, breakfast forgotten. "What?"

She stared at her two friends and sisters in arms. She had recruited Beta two years before and Stasia a few months later, both during missions for the CIA. Though she knew as much as the Company did about these women, there was much that she still didn't understand. What she did know was that they all shared a passion for preventing sexual predation in all forms. They'd also both had her back when it counted, multiple times. Beyond those two things, nothing else mattered.

"We have encountered them too, Liv."

Stasia got up and went to the refrigerator, gesturing for Olivia to sit. Beta kicked a chair out from the table and nodded to it. Olivia sat. Stasia pulled out eggs, milk, cheese, and mushrooms.

Olivia looked at Beta. "Details."

Beta's enigmatic eyes returned her gaze. "At first, it was just three or four at a time in the tourist areas. Drugs, I thought. Something designer that increases adrenaline and deadens the pain response. But then I found the first body."

Stasia looked over her shoulder as she cracked an egg. "Tell her."

Olivia reached out and placed her hand over Beta's. "Was she tortured?" She heard the catch in her own voice and felt a painful squeeze in her chest.

"*He* had been stabbed at the base of the spine with something very long and pointed."

Olivia's breath caught. "Like an icepick?"

"Yes."

Stasia had started slicing mushrooms. "Among the refugees there are stories of packs of men roaming camps who attack the most vulnerable. Women, children, the old. Like wild dogs, they must be shot to prevent them from repeating their attacks. Two weeks ago, I traveled to Macedonia where I have contacts. At my request, two of these pawns were tranquilized so that I could interrogate them."

Olivia waited while Stasia poured beaten egg and milk into a pan, layering cheese and mushroom. The kettle whistled, so she got up and poured hot water into a clean mug and added some to the other two mugs on the dining table. She sat down again. Although she felt refreshed from sleeping, her body ached all over. She needed a shower and fresh clothes, too. She looked across the table at Beta, who sipped near-boiling liquid from her steaming mug. Beta's dark gaze met hers. The Czech lifted an eyebrow and sipped again.

Stasia set a plate in front of her. "Eat." She turned back to the stove. "The interrogation was like questioning a stubborn eight year old. Two stubborn eight year olds. Not very useful, but it did provide some clues."

She glanced over her shoulder and saw that Olivia wasn't eating. Waving her hand at Olivia's plate, she slid a spatula under Beta's omelet and flipped it. Olivia frowned and took a few bites to appease Stasia only to find that her appetite had returned. As a result, she forked in large, cheesy chunks and burned her tongue in the process, bringing water to her eyes. Across from her, Beta's own eyes turned up, but the hint of a smile didn't reach her lips. Olivia ignored her.

"What clues?" she asked around a mouthful of egg.

Stasia lifted the pan and slid an omelet onto a plate, which she set down in front of Beta. Then she poured the egg mixture into the pan one final time and turned sideways to look at them, her hand holding the spatula on her hip.

"First, these people call themselves *bogomili* after a heretical medieval sect. Their leader has instructed them to 'liberate' souls by puncturing their victims in the back."

"Ah. Yes, that does sound familiar." Olivia pushed the empty plate away from her and drew her mug of tea closer. Her thoughts had cleared and now she felt able to focus on what Stasia and Beta had to tell her. "I almost got liberated, in fact." She rubbed at the long, thin tear in the side of her suit. The memory of warm male fingers brought goosebumps. "Good thing I rolled first."

Stasia sat down with her own omelet, which she sprinkled with a fine coating of black pepper. "I managed to get the two *bogomili* to tell me more about their beliefs, though I also spent some time researching the original heresy."

Olivia sipped her tea, aware that Beta had seen her reaction after she'd touched her side. She pretended not to see the curiosity in the other woman's expression. Some details of the fight didn't need to be shared.

Stasia continued. "The original *bogomili* were followers of a Bulgarian priest named Bogomil, who founded a sect in the 10th century based on dualism."

"That's a basic Gnostic belief," Olivia said, "the idea that there are two equal and opposing forces for good and evil in the universe. Good is spirit and light. Evil is matter and darkness. It's been around forever. Mani taught it in the Persian Empire during the third century, for example. In keeping with Gnostic beliefs, I suppose Bogomil thought that Satan created the world?"

Stasia nodded. "Yes. As you can imagine, Bogomil's idea that God and Satan are equals did not sit well with the Catholic Church, which also teaches that God created the universe and it is good. The Pope sent emissaries to try to correct Bogomil's doctrinal errors, but eventually the Church had to defeat the *bogomili*, who had spread throughout the East and West. Some say Bogomil's ideas made it as far as England."

"You're telling me that someone has resurrected Bogomil's name after all these centuries?"

"They are *zombi* beliefs," Beta said. "Why not a *zombi* name?"

"Let me guess the reason they're 'liberating' souls." Olivia twirled her now-empty mug between two hands. "If Satan created matter, then the human body is by default evil. Everything in this world is. Killing the body frees the soul to rejoin God in the spiritual realm."

"A kindness really," Beta said as she raised her mug.

"What about the behavior? The smell? Are they drugged?"

Stasia shrugged. "It seems likely, though the tests I ordered were inconclusive. Also, their behavior did not change over time. As for the smell...." Stasia stood and started collecting their plates. "They are mortifying while still alive."

"Wait...what?" asked Olivia, uncertain she'd understood properly. "Do you mean they are decaying?"

"From the inside out," Stasia said, a note of disgust shivering her voice. "So I guess you could call them *zombis* after all. Beta, show her the weapon."

Beta reached into an inside jacket pocket and pulled out a wicked-looking object that resembled an icepick. However, Olivia could see in the light of day that it had a carved wooden handle that would look out of place in a hardware store. Beta tossed it up and caught it by the narrow tip before offering it to Olivia. Olivia hefted its weight in her palm before studying the handle's carving. A fantastic hybrid of lion's head and serpent's tail, the handle would have been at home among artifacts from ancient Mesopotamia that she'd seen in the British Museum. The sun's rays surrounded the lion's head while a crescent moon and star flanked either side of its body.

"Does it have a name?"

"The *bogomili* call it a *subulam*, or awl. The carving is of *Chnoubis*, an ancient Egyptian Gnostic icon."

"The lion's head and sun on top represents the spiritual world. The serpent's tail represents the created world down below." Olivia studied the carving, her lips pressed together. She couldn't be sure, but it was possible that this was the same weapon that she'd mistaken for an icepick last night.

"Altogether it represents the demiurge," Stasia said.

"In other words, Satan." Olivia stood and stretched. "Okay, this is getting ridiculous. I'm chasing a predator named Asmodeus, which is a demon's name. As if that's not bad enough, now you're telling me he's got a fan club of psychotic killers who poke their victims in the back as a way to speed them to Heaven."

"Yes." Stasia looked at Beta before looking back at Olivia. "There have been strange stories of defenders appearing during some of these attacks. Some say they are giants. Others describe them as beings shrouded in blinding light. They are beautiful beyond belief. Or they strike terror in the witnesses. Some hear music while others get blinding headaches. Many whisper that they are angels."

Olivia laughed. "Then the witnesses and victims are the ones taking drugs. Or being drugged. Did you test them too? The young woman last night certainly was."

"Why is this funny, *cara*? You came home battered and bruised." Stasia's eyes flashed and her hands flew to underscore her angry words. "What have you not told us?"

Olivia's humor vanished. Sighing, she sat down again. "Asmodeus knew I was coming. He sent the *bogomili* to ambush me." She paused and searched their faces. "I couldn't handle them all alone. I would have died last night if this guy hadn't shown up and pulled them off me. A *very large* guy whose features I couldn't make out because I thought my vision was blurry from getting hit."

Beta, who had never left her seat at the table, shifted closer. "Asmodeus?"

"I don't know." Olivia looked at both these women, wondering for the first time since she'd recruited them how much they trusted her. "I let him escort me and the young woman I'd been following out of the Stadtpark, but when he tried to get us into a car with a driver, it occurred to me that his goons may have gone too far. Maybe he'd stepped in to rescue us only because he wanted to take us somewhere more private for his fun and games."

"You told me last night that Asmodeus did not get the young woman." *Was that a slightly accusatory note in Beta's voice?*

"He didn't, but not because I stopped him." Recalling the final moments with the stranger, Olivia rubbed her side. "The *polizei* showed up, so I took the opportunity to run."

"That cut in your side had already started to heal by the time I saw you," Beta said, watching her. "Your bruises are almost gone." Her dark eyes glinted as she leaned even closer. "The cut over your eye," she nodded with her chin, "has already healed enough that the skin glue has peeled off. I see only a faint pink line. You are a fast healer, Liv, but not that fast."

Olivia gasped and fingered the skin above her right eyebrow.

"*Cara*," Stasia said, pacing into Olivia's small living area, pivoting, and pacing back. "This is too big for you alone. It is obviously more than a serial predator tracking victims online."

"I agree," Olivia said, dropping her hands to her knees and sitting straighter. "Since you're here, I assume you two will help?"

Both women nodded.

"Well, then, this is how we're going to handle it. Beta, go back to the Stadtpark. The ambush happened near the Schubert statue. My rescuer came down the path from the direction of the promenade, but he claimed that someone was watching us. Look for proof that he wasn't lying when you examine the scene. Stasia, find out what the *polizei* know and check on the victim. The closest hospital is St. Elizabeth's, so start there. Maybe she remembers something we can use. Recover the weapon if you can. I'll go over everything again to see if there's something I missed." She paused before adding, "And I'll request a meet with my source."

"Is that wise?" Stasia asked.

Beta scowled.

Olivia sighed. "In light of how things went south last night, I think it's time to put a face and a name to this person."

"I prefer to remain your faceless, nameless partner," Beta said.

Stasia's brows furrowed. "I suspect that your asset already knows more than he or she has shared. Still, I agree with Beta. It is too soon to reveal more than necessary."

Olivia nodded. "Fair enough." She smiled. "What happens on the Dark Web should stay on the Dark Web."

Stasia looked skeptical while Beta's expression remained carefully neutral.

"You will be careful, *sì*?"

"Of course, *cara*," Olivia said as she stood. She leaned over and hugged Stasia. "Thank you for coming." She smiled over her shoulder at Beta, who would not appreciate a hug. "Let's meet back here at eight tonight."

Beta and Stasia nodded and had made it halfway to the door when Olivia remembered something.

"Wait!"

Both women turned back, wary surprise on their features.

"Do either of you know the term *Elioud*? The guy holding the victim last night said something about 'humans and *Elioud* alike clinging to this fallen world,' and he seemed to allude to me being in the latter category. Any idea what it means?"

Stasia shook her head. Beta frowned. Her right hand crept up inside her jacket, although Olivia didn't know whether she was reaching for her chain whip or the disturbing *subulam*.

Olivia herself felt the urge to clasp her St. Michael medal, which was strangely warm against her upper chest. Rubbing it, she said, "All this talk of demons and angels and liberating souls...." She heard the nervous thread that ran through her voice and squared her shoulders. She wasn't about to become superstitious at this stage.

Stasia crossed herself surreptitiously while Beta just crossed her arms over her chest and continued to scowl.

Olivia held their gazes with her own. "As far as Asmodeus and his noxious crew are concerned, my definition of *Elioud* is one who defends the innocent from monsters. And will never, ever give up."

Stasia grinned. Beta relaxed into a loose fighting stance and rolled her shoulders back.

It would be some time before Olivia realized how eerily accurate her definition of *Elioud* had been. Or how exactly it applied to her.

FOUR

"Not enough cleavage, Ms. Markham. And ditch the blond. Our target favors brunettes."

Olivia couldn't stop her spine from stiffening at the brusque voice behind her. She'd been reading through her daily briefing at her desk when the new station chief accosted her. A slight frisson of unease coursed through her. The man had been in Vienna for only a week, yet she never heard him approach. Apparently Joseph Fagan deserved his legendary reputation in the field. Too bad he couldn't turn it off now that he ran field officers from the safety of an office in the Landstrasse. Schooling her features into alert professionalism, she swiveled in her chair and forced herself to hold his cold gaze. Every single time she did, an involuntary thought came: *I hope I never stand across from his muzzle.*

"Who's the target?"

"Mihàil Kastrioti, Albanian." Fagan stood, unblinking. "Did you forget something, Ms. Markham?"

Damn. The man demanded deference. Nevertheless, she'd only give it to him reluctantly.

"No, *sir*, I don't think so." She smiled, forcing it to sound sweet. "Please continue."

Fagan blinked once. Olivia understood in a flash of insight that he'd been surprised. She tucked that away. Anything she could do to throw him off his game, however little, bore further analysis.

"Kastrioti comes from one of the oldest clans in Albania. Since the Communists left in the early 90s, the Kastrioti clan has sought to increase its wealth via emerging industries related to the petroleum sector."

"Oil is one of Albania's few natural resources," Olivia said, playing the role of eager intern to the hilt.

"Indeed." The dryness of Fagan's tone suffocated further chirpy observation. "Though in the current market not bringing in the profits that it did even two years ago. A fifty percent decline in the price of oil has to have hurt even Kastrioti's wealth, which is rumored to be vast."

Olivia popped up a hand to eye level. Fagan's answering glower warmed her heart. "The Kastrioti clan has a long history in Albania. Is he related to Gjergj Kastrioti, the national hero from the Middle Ages?"

"Yes, Ms. Markham. He's a direct descendant, though there are few records extant to confirm that claim. In fact, Kastrioti may have inherited his illustrious ancestor's *nom de guerre*."

"The Dragon of Albania?" Olivia heard the surprise in her voice. "We think the Dragon runs one of the dominant mafia families in the Balkans, the Krasniqi clan."

Fagan studied her. "On the surface, Mihàil Kastrioti appears to be nothing more than a very successful businessman with refined tastes and playboy habits. Unfortunately, he also happens to associate with some questionable people and turn up where bad things happen. Interpol has been watching him, but so far they have yet to link him definitively with the Krasniqis. Here"—he tossed a manila folder on her desk—"here's some research on Kastrioti that hasn't been digitized. Familiarize yourself with it. He's in Vienna meeting with various plastics companies. I'd like you to use your position at ABA-Invest in Austria to get closer to him."

"Hence the need to show my cleavage?" Now it was Olivia's turn to study Fagan. What would he do if she refused to follow his lead? Well, she'd always been given leeway to handle field assignments as she saw fit, and she had no intention of wearing a wig and dressing slutty because Snake-Eyes Fagan said so. She smiled. *Snake-Eyes. That's a good one. I think I'll keep it.*

She realized that Fagan was watching her so she sat up and tried to look more alert.

"You're not good at taking orders, are you, Ms. Markham?" Something in his tone niggled. Olivia realized that he hadn't blinked since she'd surprised him. *Maybe Mr. Roboto is a better name. Nah. He's cold and inhuman in a predatory way, not like an android.*

"I have no trouble doing what needs to be done," she said, enunciating each word very carefully. "My personnel file confirms that." She waited a beat. "*Sir.*"

"No one has a perfect record, Ms. Markham. Not even you. I advise you to consider that when choosing to disregard my orders."

He waited a long moment, long enough for sweat to prickle along Olivia's spine and palms. She felt her lips tighten as she stared back at him.

Blink, you bastard!

Fagan blinked.

It was a victory of coincidence, but the tension dissipated. Relief flooded Olivia. She'd take what she could get.

She opened the folder and scanned the top document showing Mihàil Kastrioti's itinerary while in Vienna. "Kastrioti has an appointment with Frau Reiter about getting seed money to incubate new business in Austria. She likes me. She'll be happy to include me in her meeting with him."

"Just make sure Kastrioti is equally enthusiastic about spending time with *you.*"

Fagan stood there for a moment longer, but his demeanor had stopped bothering Olivia. She couldn't swear that the next time she saw him she'd be calm and unrattled, but she'd handle the next time as it came.

"Yes, sir." She played this one straight. No need to yank his chain too often. Also, it wouldn't do to rely on bravado if he did spook her again. He was too smart not to notice and take advantage of it.

After Fagan left, she read through the paperwork he'd dropped off. There wasn't much, but what there was held the kind of insight that only someone intimately familiar with a target could provide. She suspected that Fagan had scoured his personal case files and called in favors to create a profile of Kastrioti that contained the name of his favorite wine, his favorite dish, where he vacationed, and the name of his tailor among a myriad other minute and telling details. Although Kastrioti was unmarried—he'd made it onto a tabloid list as one of Europe's most eligible bachelors—he had a reputation for enjoying the company of beautiful brunettes. After she'd absorbed the information, Olivia looked at the enclosed surveillance photos at last.

The man in the photos was quite possibly the most beautiful man she'd ever seen. And the most dangerous-looking one. He had dark hair long enough to comb back with sideburns to the bottom of his ears. There was a photo of him clean shaven and wearing a tailored suit, his hair smooth. Another photo showed him in jeans and layered long-sleeve Henley shirts, his hair becomingly mussed and several days' beard covering his strong jaw. But the photo that held her attention caught him at the gym, his chest bare under an open hoodie. He had massive shoulders and well-defined abs, something that she appreciated but could overlook. She'd seen her share of fine male specimens at Langley and in the field, especially the black-ops specialists she'd teamed with. It would take more than hours in a gym to make an impression on her.

No, what sent a pang to her breast and sped her breathing was the look on his unguarded face. The brilliant blue eyes under straight brows radiated a resigned sadness, suggesting an old hurt. In a suit, Mihàil Kastrioti was suave, aloof, imperious even. The man in the gym photo was naked and vulnerable in more ways than one. Olivia should have felt satisfaction that her target had obvious chinks in his defenses, but instead, she found herself sorry for him. It was hard to imagine that he was the Dragon that the CIA and Interpol hunted.

"What happened to you?" she whispered, touching a fingertip to his face and stroking it over his strong shoulders.

Nevertheless, she would do whatever needed to be done to learn his secrets. Because if he had anything to do with the sex trafficking that the Krasniqis controlled, she was going to take him down.

At the precise moment of Olivia's fierce vow, her target experienced a painful surge of energy that caused him to drop his guard so that his opponent's left hook caught his chin. Mihàil Kastrioti dropped like a bag of bricks to the mat of his private gymnasium. Before Mihàil could recover, his opponent had dropped onto him from above, grabbed his wrists, and rolled, twisting so that he was perpendicular to Mihàil's head. In moments, his opponent controlled one of Mihàil's arms with his legs, and Mihàil's other arm with one of his. He struck Mihàil's head with his elbow, keeping him stunned, and wrapped this arm around his neck in the crucifixion chokehold.

Mihàil pounded on the mat signaling his submission.

His opponent tightened his hold. Despite his pain, Mihàil felt the rumbling in the other man's chest and heard his strained laughter. He pounded harder and growled through his clenched teeth. Just when he thought his instincts would take over before he blacked out, his opponent released the hold and collapsed onto the mat next to him.

"Cut it a bit close, didn't I?" András asked, grinning around his mouth guard.

Mihàil only snorted and shoved away before rising to stand. He fingered his tender, swelling jaw and frowned. Then he waved at András to engage again, put his hands up, and began to circle. András grunted and began bouncing on his toes, feinting first left and then right. Mihàil jabbed with his right three times in succession, forcing András off balance as he blocked. Seeing the opening this created, Mihàil punched with his left, snapping András's head back. The trouble was that András was taller and heavier. He simply popped upright and grinned again.

"Your date that bad?" he asked as he danced back and forth so quickly that Mihàil barely got his left arm up in time to block his punch.

"You could say that." Mihàil kept his gaze pinned on his opponent. "Or maybe I am bored with fighting you."

"No, that's not it." András shook his head. "She was stunning. But you never take them seriously, do you?"

"Do *you*?" Mihàil asked.

He felt more than saw the attack that came from behind and to the side. *Miró*. He'd returned from the errand that Mihàil had sent him on. Ducking,

Mihàil drove a shoulder into his new opponent and lifted. From the opposite side, András darted in to his unprotected flank. Mihàil pivoted, carrying Miró with him until he slammed into András. Both of his opponents crashed to the mat. Mihàil jumped on Miró's exposed back, pinning him on top of András in a sweaty man sandwich. He yanked Miró's head back and wrapped an arm around his neck while punching at András, who began bucking in an effort to dislodge them. Miró bucked with him, which was more than enough to break Mihàil's hold. As soon as that happened, Miró fell sideways as András surged up. Mihàil rolled away and sprang to his feet before either could recover their own feet and trap him.

"Do they know anything?" he asked Miró while keeping his arms up and his gaze focused on András.

"As usual, not much."

"Any evidence?"

András rushed him before the question had left his mouth. Mihàil blocked the first blow and caught the other man by the shoulders before delivering a head strike. He backed away as András staggered backwards.

"They found this." Miró threw an object that flashed in the gym's bright overhead lighting. It stuck in the wall next to the floor-to-ceiling mirror on the far side.

Both Mihàil and András swiveled to look at it.

"Damn," András said.

Mihàil spit out his mouth guard and signaled that he was done with their workout. He scowled. "That complicates our mission here."

"So do the witnesses."

Mihàil, who'd lifted a water bottle to his mouth, sent a sharp look at Miró instead. "Witnesses?"

Miró nodded. "Plural. The girl taken to St. Elizabeth's and a ghostly woman identified on CCTV running toward the Wien Mitte station. I can handle the one in the hospital, but the identity of the other one has eluded the local *polizei*. She appears to have some training in evading surveillance." He handed Mihàil a grainy image captured from the CCTV video. It showed a blurry figure in white in an otherwise dark setting.

"Fascinating," Mihàil said almost to himself, studying the image.

András shrugged. "No matter. I can track her."

"That will be much more challenging now that she has moved to the top of their suspect list."

"What?" Mihàil's surprise took everyone off guard, including himself. Then he laughed. "Humans are so predictable. As long as they are looking for her, they will not see us. However, the only one who knows that we are in Vienna will also be looking for her for obvious reasons."

"Do you really think he can use her to find you?" András asked. His normally laughing eyes had narrowed in worry. "We cannot let that happen, Mihàil."

"That is easy." Mihàil paused and looked at each of his men. "We find her first."

"He clearly did not plan for what happened," Miró said. "He lost control of the situation or there would not have been any witnesses. Perhaps we can use his sloppiness to our advantage. Now that we know he is in Vienna too, she will lead us to him."

Mihàil frowned. "She is an unknown quantity, *Elioud* or not. My guess is that she does not know what she is yet. And we do not know how large his operation here is. We will have to handle this very carefully or we will be the ones who lose control. If that happens, everything we fight for is in danger. I want you both on reconnaissance as well as your normal duties. We need to know more about our surroundings."

He pulled off his gloves and began peeling the underlying boxing tape from his hands. "In the meantime, I have a meeting scheduled tomorrow with the Director of Eastern Europe at ABA-Invest in Austria. I will not let this new situation take my focus from our mission."

"Is that wise?" András asked. He leaned against the full-length mirror, his arms crossed. "The ABA is very high profile. He may not need the harlequin to find you if you are too visible. Maybe you should delay until we have handled him."

Mihàil shook his head. "No, we go forward as planned." He stepped up to the wall and pulled the *subulam* out, hefting it in his hand. "I have every intention of being ready for him."

Later that afternoon, Olivia sat outside the Café Mozart enjoying an espresso and a slice of *sachertorte*, the famous cake that Franz Sacher created in 1832 for an Austrian prince. It was a beautiful, mild day and tour guides led large groups of tourists along the sidewalk toward the Vienna State Opera House, the St. Stephen's Cathedral, and the historic shopping district of Kärntner Strasse. For a moment, she indulged in innocent fantasy, pretending that it was 1840, and she was a princess who'd slipped away for a secret assignation. She'd just taken a tiny bite of the dense chocolate and apricot jam covering the cake when a woman stopped at the table. Without haste, Olivia sipped her espresso, letting the hot coffee melt the rich cake flavors on her tongue before swallowing.

When she looked up at last, Olivia saw that the newcomer had ice-blond hair cut in a messy pixie style, a white-linen blouse with cap sleeves and cinched with a wide black-leather belt, a white pencil skirt, and white stiletto pumps. She wore dark sunglasses and carried an impractical white-leather clutch with a gold letter *Z* dangling from the clasp.

Olivia gestured at a chair. "Please. Sit."

The woman smiled. Her red lipstick stood out against her pale skin. She slid into the chair across from Olivia, laid her clutch on the table, and raised an elegant, long-fingered hand toward a suddenly frantic waiter. Olivia noticed that the woman's lacquered nails were the same vibrant shade of red as her lipstick. Strangely, the waiter didn't come to their table, hurrying inside instead.

Her visitor aimed her dark lenses at Olivia. When she spoke, she pronounced her words with a cultured English accent. "Ms. Markham, I presume?"

Olivia nodded, watching the mysterious woman. The brilliant sun haloed the stranger's hair, causing her features to disappear in a white haze. Olivia picked up her espresso and sipped as she blinked to clear her vision. *Why didn't I think to sit on that side of the table so that she was the one blinded?*

"And you are?" she asked, speaking in English as well. "I'd like to know who to thank for helping me these past few months."

Her words hung in the air as the waiter returned and set an espresso in front of the woman. When he set a small plate with a slice of cake in front of her, it rattled against the espresso cup.

She placed a gentle hand on the waiter's forearm. Calm washed down him so clearly that Olivia found herself spooked. "Thank you, Eduard."

The waiter beamed and bowed before turning on his heel and leaving. The woman waited to speak until he was out of earshot.

"You may call me Zophie." She forked up a sliver of cake to eat, running a delicate pink tongue over her lips. "Oh, this is simply divine!"

Olivia's own desire for cake had vanished. Patting her lips with her napkin, she set it on the table next to her cake plate. "You're not exactly what I expected."

"Oh, I never am," the other woman assured her. She gave her a sly glance. "But you're never what anyone expects, either. Am I right?"

Olivia squirmed. Annoyed, she said, "Asmodeus knew I was coming. Why is that? Did you set me up?"

"Hardly," Zophie said, taking another bite. "I'm in the business of thwarting Asmodeus and his kind, not aiding them. Besides, he's perfectly capable of discovering when someone is watching him. He doesn't need my help."

This news alarmed Olivia, who'd been certain that she'd covered her online tracks. A thought occurred to her. "You might have helped him inadvertently. After all, if he can trace my involvement, then why not yours?"

Zophie laughed and waved a languid hand. "He's perfectly aware that I'm watching him, but he can't do anything about it. It's all part of the terms that he lives under."

"What terms? If you know what he's doing, why don't you stop him?' Olivia's frustration grew.

Zophie's lips pursed and she shook her head slowly. "I'm bound by the same terms not to intervene."

She must have sensed Olivia's confusion because she took Olivia's hand between both of hers. A powerful shock ran up Olivia's arms and to her chest, causing her heart to palpitate. Her hand felt cold between Zophie's warm ones.

"Do you remember how powerless you were to help your cousin? You tried to tell your aunt and uncle. You tried to tell your parents. You tried to convince Emily, pleading and pleading with her not to meet Jin that last time. You tried to stop her, but she had her own free will, and so he beat her to death in that garage and dumped her body in a stream two weeks after high-school graduation. She never made it to college with you."

Olivia couldn't breathe. She stared at this stranger holding her hand. A cloud moved over the sun and the sound of the noisy tourists faded until she sat in a tiny vacuum, pinned to her chair.

"If you want to stop Asmodeus, it's up to you to listen and believe. And then act on what I tell you. So far, you have trusted me. You must continue to trust me. I will always help you if I can."

"How do you know about Emily?" Olivia whispered through stiff lips. She began to tremble as hot and cold waves washed through her.

The stranger tilted her head. "Ah, Ms. Markham. Are you ready to listen to that answer?"

At that moment, Eduard returned with another espresso, which he placed in front of Olivia. Zophie nodded and smiled at him, and he left whistling.

"Drink that. It will help."

Olivia wanted to protest but instead followed the stranger's admonition as if in a trance. The hot, bitter liquid helped, however, and the violent shaking subsided.

"There. See? I always tell you the truth, hard as it is for someone in your line of work to believe." She slid her fork under the final morsel of cake. "Michael says that I enjoy my assignments too much, but he's too serious to eat cake."

The medal on the chain around Olivia's neck suddenly felt warm and heavy. She grasped it between her thumb and forefinger, a sudden intuition filling her with more terror.

"Why, yes, dear," Zophie said, licking her fork. "He did assign me to look out for you. That's why I made sure to bring a friend with me to the park last night. I believe you met him?"

"That wasn't Asmodeus?"

Zophie's laughter pealed. The sun emerged and the day brightened. She raised a dainty finger to her eye behind the dark lenses, appearing to wipe away a tear.

"Oh, what a fabulous joke, Ms. Markham! Ah, I needed that." She picked up her cup and drank the last of the espresso. "Please don't make the mistake of sharing it with him when you meet because he won't find it as funny as I do. No, he was born to destroy predators such as Asmodeus. Someday you two will make an incomparable team. The one greater than the sum, if you know what I mean."

Olivia squirmed again. *What is it about this woman that sets me off?* "I choose my own partners."

Zophie patted her hand. "Of course you do, dear. I suppose you might be silly enough not to choose him. I hope not. You're going to need all the help you can get against those nasty creatures, the *bogomili*. Remember them?"

The breath hissed between Olivia's teeth.

"Oh, and be sure to ask him about the *Irim* and the *Elioud*. He can explain it all so much better than I can. I never do tell anything straight on, I'm afraid. It's a grievous fault, one of many. Michael constantly chastises me for it."

Zophie uncrossed her long legs and stood. Olivia felt a stab of envy at the fluid grace of her movements.

"I've so enjoyed our talk. Sadly, it's time for me to go. We should always meet for espresso and cake. It's quite heavenly."

She paused and pulled her sunglasses from her face. The sight of her eyes sent a shock of recognition through Olivia. This woman had given her the red sweatshirt and backpack last night at the U-bahn station. "Please give my regards to Beta and Stasia. I so look forward to meeting them."

Olivia's mouth dropped open. Before she could respond, Zophie slid the sunglasses back onto her face, picked up her clutch, and strolled away. In moments, the crowd of tourists had swallowed her up.

FIVE

W hen Mihàil arrived at the ABA-Invest in Austria offices next to the Vienna State Opera House, an assistant apologized for the Director of the Eastern European division, Frau Reiter, who had been called into an emergency meeting. She ushered him into a conference room with the promise that someone would come along in a few moments to make sure that he was comfortable. Mihàil nodded and took the opportunity to stretch his legs under the conference table and close his eyes. He'd had a busy evening, no less for the fact that he and András had attempted to follow the trail of the mysterious harlequin. Over the years he'd learned to grab rest whenever and wherever he could. The cushioned leather chairs in the ABA conference room offered more comfort than most places he'd napped.

Their night may have been long, but it was far from fruitless. After viewing more CCTV footage, Mihàil had been very impressed at how thoroughly the harlequin had disappeared among the World Cup fans surging through the Wien Mitte station after the German win. Then he'd noticed the young soccer fan searching through his pants and jacket pockets while his friends appeared to enjoy his predicament. Though he couldn't be sure, his instincts told him that she'd gotten onto the green line with the fan and his friends. They'd identified the number of the train car from the CCTV footage, and then András had gotten on the same one. András, an exceptional tracker and not one to admit defeat, had managed to discern a faint trace of the Wild *Elioud* on that car.

It was a start at finding her. He wondered how much his enemy already knew about her route.

Now it was up to Miró to get the CCTV footage from inside the car during the relevant time period. If all went well, they'd find another clue to her next stop. It required patience and painstaking effort on top of their natural talents, but Mihàil trusted that the right outcome would be reached. He could only hope that they'd reach it in time.

All at once his head fell sideways, and he jerked upright.

Someone cleared a throat from the doorway.

Confused embarrassment filled Mihàil. He never fell asleep so soundly anywhere outside of his homes, and even then only the Albanian one afforded enough security to let him let go so completely that he didn't hear someone approach as he slept. However, he had the disconcerting feeling that he'd been observed for some time while he napped. Swiveling in the chair, he came face to face with a woman.

In those first few moments, her beauty floored him, though he couldn't have said why. He spent a lot of time in the company of beautiful women as part of his cover, so he should have been immune to silky, shoulder-length blond hair, large blue-gray eyes, full lips, and flawless fair skin. But apparently he wasn't.

"Herr Kastrioti?" she asked. She had an unusual voice, slightly husky with more polished notes threading through it. Her accent, though so slight humans probably couldn't detect it, was American.

What were the chances? Then again, he knew how often coincidence actually affected his life, that is to say, not very. She certainly had the height, build, and posture to be his mysterious harlequin.

Coming to his feet, he said, "Yes. Sorry. I must have dozed off."

"That's quite understandable. Late nights with too much to drink and too many women." Before his startled mind could formulate a response, she nodded toward his chair. "Please, sit. Frau Reiter has asked me to bring you refreshments while you wait. She's terribly sorry. She's aware that your time is valuable, but it can't be helped."

At her words, Mihàil realized that she held a full tray. Ignoring her protests, he grasped the tray and set it on the conference table. A quick survey of its contents showed a teapot, two cups, spoons, milk, sugar, lemon, and a plate of pastries.

"I can bring coffee if you prefer," she said. There was a strange note in her voice. *Worry?*

"No, no. This will be fine. I love tea."

Mihàil moved to pour at the same time that she did. His elbow banged against her forehead with a shockingly dull sound. He stepped back.

"Are you all right?" he asked, his hand outstretched to catch her as she stepped away at the same time.

What the hell? His customary charm had fled with his nap. For the first time in longer years than he cared to remember, he felt out of sorts as though he'd gotten up on the wrong side of the bed as the Americans liked to say. He'd thrown a lot of elbow strikes that had knocked out more than a few opponents, which was exactly why he feared that he'd given her a concussion. Shock swiftly gave way to pain on her features. That was even more swiftly replaced with what appeared to be a practiced calm.

She laughed and it sounded genuine. "I'm sorry, Herr Kastrioti." She rubbed at the spot. "That was entirely my fault. I'm fine."

He squinted. Her rubbing had drawn his attention to a fresh hairline scar above her right eye. *Interesting.*

"Please, call me Mihàil. And you are?"

She blushed, a lovely shade of red that started at her breastbone and made its way up her neck and face like watercolor on wet paper. He found it fascinating. He hadn't seen a woman blush in half a century. Almost all modern women were too cynical and experienced to blush, at least those he met throughout Western Europe. He would have guessed that was also true of American women, though this one seemed quite young, perhaps only a few years out of university. The blush drew his gaze to the rapid tattoo of her pulse in her neck, which gave away the roiling emotions under her carefully controlled demeanor.

"Olivia. Olivia Markham." She cleared her throat. "You may call me Olivia."

Mihàil, acting on impulse, took her hand and bowed over it in the old style, which he missed. Olivia Markham likely had never had a man bow over her hand judging by the way her blush deepened to an almost painful crimson. Mihàil decided to push his effect and brushed his lips over her knuckles. He heard her soft intake of breath, which should have left him satisfied save that he himself grew a little breathless at such an intimate touch.

"Olivia. What a charming name," he said, his voice a little gruffer than he'd intended. *How original. So witty, Mihàil.* He let her hand go and smiled, hoping she hadn't heard the gruffness.

She smiled and turned back to the tea tray. As she poured, she said, "Frau Reiter has also commissioned me to begin discussing your business development ideas. I'm familiar with how ABA operates as well as how Frau Reiter thinks, so you will find the transition to working with her seamless, I assure you."

Mihàil accepted a cup of tea from her hand and sat back down. Olivia offered him sugar and lemon, which he declined, and milk, which he did accept. He selected two pastries at random from the plate she proffered him, but then deposited them without another thought onto the small plate that she set in front of him.

"I have already read through the materials you supplied on your existing holdings and financials."

Olivia sat down at his right and sipped her tea before looking at him. The shade of her eyes had turned a haunting green-gray with a darker green around the iris. He'd never seen eyes so changeable in hue before and found himself staring at her. Catching himself, he tried to recover with a deliberate stare. Let her think it was all a part of his aggressive business persona.

"Well, then, you already have a clear idea about the realm of possibilities for Kastrioti Venture Partners in Austria. Obviously, we need to find something that leverages our oil that is less tied to the vagaries of the price of a barrel."

"Obviously." She studied him over the rim of her cup. "But I think you already have at least one solution in mind. You've purchased existing industrial real estate in Budapest as well as Tirana and Zagreb."

He smiled. She hadn't been intimidated.

"I see you told the truth, Olivia. You read through *all* of my financials, including the fine print. Not only that, but you've identified precisely the relevant information for my trip to Vienna and my visit to ABA today."

She seemed pleased at his words, sitting up a little straighter and pouring more tea for both of them. As she did so, her hair slipped from behind her ear and curtained her profile. Mihàil wanted to lean forward and tuck it behind her ear. Instead, he picked up a dry-looking pastry and took a bite.

"I think I can guess why you purchased the sites that you did," she said, handing him his refilled cup.

"And that is?"

"Rivers, trains, and production facilities that can be converted with minimal costs to produce detergents and other household cleaning products."

"Household cleaning products? Why not polymers?"

"First, Budapest already has a trained workforce, one that's out of work, by the way, since Henkel transferred all of its production here. Second, you've already funded a small pilot plant at the Technical University of Vienna based on what they call cyber-physical systems for 'industry 4.0.' That means you're planning to be at the forefront of the next industrial revolution."

Olivia saw admiration sweep over Mihàil Kastrioti's face after her analysis and couldn't believe how pleased she felt as a result. It had taken all of her training and discipline to this point to stay focused, despite having maneuvered to lead the meeting without Frau Reiter in the first place. It didn't help that she was tired after two late nights. The previous night, Beta and Stasia had come to her flat, each with intel that raised more questions than it answered.

Beta's survey of the Stadtpark site had been interrupted by the arrival of a tall, brown-haired man who was neither *polizei* nor other law enforcement. Wearing a t-shirt, faded jeans, and combat boots, he looked more like an Eastern European gang member. Beta put him at six-six and about 250 pounds, so taller and heavier than Olivia's memory of her rescuer. She also estimated that this giant had plenty of hand-to-hand training given the way he carried himself. Nothing she couldn't handle, she assured Olivia and Stasia, but she'd prefer not to engage him unless necessary. When the stranger had arrived, she'd been on the other side of the Schubert statue where it was easy enough to climb a tree to watch him kneel to study the flattened grass. The normally unflappable Beta was trying to interpret his actions when the stranger rose and turned to look at her hiding spot. He'd stood there for a long moment stripping her cover with his gaze until a gaggle of visiting Chinese orchestra students had pulled up short in front of the police barricades, staring at the stranger in mute stupefaction. He'd done something really bizarre then, in Beta's estimation. He'd grinned, kissed his first two fingers, and flicked them in her direction before turning and sauntering away. Though Beta found evidence that someone had been on the other side of the Schubert statue, she could tell nothing about this individual except that he wore a man's dress shoe, size 15.

Stasia hadn't been as fortunate to arrive before her interloper, however. She'd gotten to St. Elizabeth's only to be told that Melissa no longer remembered anything from the time she left the Hilton to the time she arrived at the hospital. Combined with the fact that the duty nurse had commented on the exceptionally dreamy visitor that Melissa had had earlier in the morning, this convinced Stasia that someone had scared Melissa into not talking. From the woman's overwrought description, this stranger apparently was also over six feet tall, well built *and* well dressed, but his hair was black with a frosting of gray at the temples. The *subulam* recovered at the scene had also disappeared from *polizei* evidence.

And now Olivia sat across the table from a third hulking man recently in town from the Balkans. *Coincidence?* Her experience and intuition told her that was unlikely.

Fortunately, her own Company boss had gifted her with a free work pass to gain Mihàil Kastrioti's trust.

That formidable subject leaned closer to her now. A warm, spicy scent wafted into her nose. Her body relaxed in turn. An image of him sleeping in that same chair teased her. He'd looked so angelic that she'd been tempted to smooth the dark hair off his forehead and place a kiss there.

"Exactly."

For a moment, she felt lost. *Exactly what?* And then she remembered.

"But Herr Kastrioti, the industrial revolution must start here in Austria. ABA incubates Austrian startups."

"Austrian startups funded by large, international conglomerates. I am happy to incorporate my new business in Vienna where I can work with the best R&D laboratories and engineers in the world. However, when my plants and products are thoroughly designed and tested, full-scale production will be at those three sites that you named."

She frowned. "Where you can decrease your operating costs while depriving good Austrians jobs that should have been theirs."

"While bringing advanced technologies to countries left behind by industrial revolutions one through three." The heat in his deep voice flared in his gaze as well, and Olivia imagined she saw wisps of smoke curling around his face. "Albania, my home, is one of the poorest countries in the world, Frau Markham. We were just coming out of the communist dark ages and expanding our man-ufacturing capabilities when the worldwide economy soured. Now the price of oil has hit rock bottom. People are hungry. And when people are hungry, they do stupid, bad things."

Though he never raised his voice, its intensity along with the brilliance of his gaze skewered her to her chair. She hadn't missed his use of her last name either. Olivia shivered. For a moment, she panicked. She did *not* want to be on the other side of anything, not even a negotiation, from this intimidating man. She almost believed his passion was real until she remembered that he could be the Dragon of Albania, a ruthless, brutal oppressor of Albanians and other vulnerable people, especially women and children. At that thought, she recalled her years of training as a martial artist followed by her training at The Farm. Liquid steel flowed down her spine and raised her chin. She didn't have to let her intimidation control her. *He* wouldn't control her.

She shifted in her seat and reached for the folder of documents that she'd brought into the conference room earlier while he slept. "If you mean what you imply, then you should have no issues with various workplace standards and codes that Austrian law stipulates for factories operated in Austria, including a workers' compensation fund and paid maternity leave. That will be included as part of our agreement when I help you to incorporate your new enterprise here." She brought her gaze to his, letting him see her determination.

For a long, magnetic moment their gazes held. Something like fear fluttered in her stomach and tickled her chest, but she felt hot, not cold.

He broke the silence.

"I would not have it any other way, Frau Markham. In fact, I invite you to tour my Tirana site and speak with the employees there. I have already issued invitations to several potential business partners to travel later this week on a fact-finding mission before committing to working with Kastrioti Industries. It would be a simple measure to include you."

Olivia blinked, considering. To give her time to think, she opened the folder and pretended to scan the various boilerplate documents there. She'd already learned that Kastrioti had filed flight plans for his private jet and had started to identify the passengers and purpose. He'd saved her the trouble *and* offered her the perfect opportunity to observe him and his operations more closely, perhaps even to find the missing link between him and the Krasniqis.

She looked at him, surprised to see him watching her closely. Shutting the folder, she smiled and saw his eyes enlarge. They really were the most amazing blue against his tanned, scruffy cheeks. For an instant, she wished that they'd met under other circumstances, that she could have met him without all the second-guessing about his nature and business. Almost as soon as she'd thought it, however, she dismissed the idea as ludicrous. After Emily, she would always second-guess a man's nature, Company assignment or not.

"That sounds like an ideal proposition," she said. She stood and handed him her business card. "If you would be so good as to forward me the travel details, I will clear the trip with Frau Reiter."

Stasia arrived at the Hilton Vienna wearing dark sunglasses, slim black slacks, and her favorite black leather boots with the high, chunky heels. In her over-sized leather bag with the large, round handles, she'd tucked her *surujin* next to her smart phone, a thumb drive, and a set of lock-picking tools. Beyond that, she'd brought lip gloss and a wallet with a little cash and clean ID and credit card. Anything else she needed for this little mission she'd pick up or improvise. She strode to the hotel bar, noting the admiring glance of several males in the lobby without acknowledging them, and chose a table near the bar entrance. All she needed was one to follow her.

"A *negroni*, please," she said when the server arrived for her drink order.

"How unusual." The florid American who'd approached her table would do. He wore a suit with the top button of his button-down undone and a nametag on his left lapel. "I prefer a martini." He looked at the server. "Put them on my tab."

Stasia smiled as though she was delighted by this news. She made a show of reading the name from his tag, bending close so that her hair brushed his shoulder as she looked down. "How very Bond of you, Dr. Kilcourt."

He grinned and nodded, raising the empty glass in his hand. "Is that an Italian accent I hear?"

She dipped her chin. "And you must be here for the American medical conference."

"I am. I am indeed." He sidled up to her table, setting his glass on it.

She smiled at him again. This shouldn't take long.

He leaned closer to her. "So tell me, has anyone ever told you that you look like a young Sophia Loren?"

Only about a million times, you ass. His breath assailed her.

Keeping her gaze on his, Stasia tilted her head and said, "Do you really think so?"

He tried to focus his bleary gaze on her as he raised a hand to touch her hair, which hung down in soft waves to her shoulders. She'd worn a silk scarf tied around her hair to encourage the comparison.

"My God, you even have her dimpled chin. And that eye liner." He bent his face into her hair, drawing in a loud breath. "Meow."

As he inclined toward her, Stasia felt in his right jacket pocket for his room key. *Damn! Not there.*

Pulling back, she said in a low voice, "Watch it, Mr. Bond. Cats have claws."

A fine spray of liquor-scented saliva misted the air as he laughed at her coy words. Stasia contained her disgust and blinked, refusing to wipe her face with her scarf. She'd shower as soon as she got back to Olivia's flat. The server arrived with their drinks, Dr. Kilcourt's martini a pale, transparent olive green and her *negroni* a vibrant shade of red-orange. She pulled the burnt-orange twist from the cocktail using a delicate fingernail and nipped at its end, smiling at him sideways as she chewed the bitter peel. Dr. Kilcourt stared at her mouth as she did so. When she offered him the twist, he bent over and bit from it, his large, wet lips engulfing her fingers before pulling back and leaving a trail of slime. He kept his gaze on hers or she would have grimaced and wiped her fingers on her slacks. Instead, she slipped her right hand into his left jacket pocket and palmed his room key.

Time to give him the brush off. She stuck Dr. Kilcourt's room key into the waistband of her slacks.

"I bet you taste as piquant as your drink," he said in a stage whisper.

Stasia smiled and lifted the *negroni* in a toast before skillfully spilling it on her companion. Exclaiming in mock distress, she began scrabbling for napkins with such dramatic flair that the server hurried over to help. Next ensued a comedy of errors in which Stasia timed her moves to create the utmost distraction and mess, drawing in another server and several patrons from the conference. As confusion reigned, she snatched her bag and headed to the front desk where she complained to the attendant that her keycard no longer worked. The attendant obligingly reset it to the same room that Melissa and her aunt had booked. Having tracked the aunt's location using her cellphone's GPS, she knew that the woman was at the hospital. Now was the time to search their room and laptops.

From his vantage in the hotel lobby, Miró watched the Italian woman as she smiled at the Hilton employee, who checked her proffered ID before rewriting the room code on the drunken American's keycard. He'd enjoyed the little show that she'd put on moments before as she batted her eyes while picking the man's pocket.

She was good. *Damn good.*

No one else had noticed the fine narrowing of her eyes or the hard look that flitted over her face as her suitor sucked on her graceful fingers. Miró's determination to stay in the background wavered at that, but he trusted his instincts and let her handle it. He wasn't as compelling as Mihàil or as bold as András, but he could definitely handle the likes of the American doctor and not make a scene. In fact, when the good doctor managed to extricate himself as the Italian woman strode toward the elevators, Miró stepped in. No one noticed anything unusual about Miró's improvised friendly back slap in which he delivered a harmonic jab before easing the unconscious man down onto a cushy loveseat. He'd even kept his back to the lobby security camera during the intervention.

Because he was good too. *Damn good.*

Having already copied the Canadians' user files from two laptops and scoured their room, Miró left the hotel. It wouldn't pay for the Italian to see him, no matter how much he would like to discover whether he could put a genuine smile on her lovely face.

Six

I f it weren't for the good fortune at finding his enemy in Vienna, Asmodeus might have regretted coming to the City of Music. Being here for more than a few hours certainly tried his temper and ate at his being. At least it was summer. That meant a lower quality of music. He relished each missed note and mangled intonation, hanging onto their rare discord as a lifeline. So it was that he took more care than usual to move among the Viennese, moving from pockets of cacophony to islands of noise to avoid the classical strains of Mozart and Strauss that permeated the city air. Sometimes, however, when he could stomach it no more, he deliberately strolled past a street musician—usually a violinist or a cellist—and even though he suffered a splitting headache afterwards, he relished the twanging pop as every single string on the instrument snapped.

This afternoon he'd been forced to travel to the third district, and just being here made his teeth ache. He found the back table in the darkest corner of the café and waited for his contact to arrive. When his acolyte entered, Asmodeus studied him. The man fancied himself above the law and smarter than his colleagues at the intelligence agency. He had no conscience, no moral compass save whatever benefited him, but he was just as likely to target others to relieve boredom as he was to gain some advantage. It was all about control and game play. As humans went, he was a pitiless predator among the milling sheep. Unlike the *bogomili*, he wasn't a mindless lunatic foaming at the mouth and eager to savage vulnerable victims. He saw clearly that there was a spiritual war between two powers, and he'd chosen one side over the other for the adrenaline rush it gave him. He also thought it was the winning side.

In that he was not wrong.

His acolyte sat down across from Asmodeus and dropped a packet on the table in front of him.

Asmodeus left it there, narrowing his eyes at his acolyte's direct gaze. For now, he let the man look upon him as though they were equals. There would come a time, however, when he would relish chastising this human for his insolence.

"You have set someone on Kastrioti?" he asked at last when his acolyte had the grace to squirm a little.

His acolyte tapped the envelope. "Her picture is inside. She's quite a clever young thing, though probably too clever for her own good."

Asmodeus tilted his head. "Do I detect a note of covetousness for the woman in question?" He laughed. "And she only sees a middle-aged balding man with a paunch and glasses?"

His acolyte stiffened.

Asmodeus dismissed the man's reaction with a wave, looking away to pull a thick stack of paper from the envelope. In this digital day and age, the old-school route of paper and in-person meetings remained harder to hack and track, though he found the online world filled with exciting prospects. The delectable Melissa had been only one of a multitude of ripe, malleable targets. It was almost as if the Father of Lies himself had invented the Internet and its oh-so-intuitive graphic interface, the World Wide Web. Naïve humans promoted the decentralized information highway as a great democratic equalizer and means for freedom of expression. Savvier humans wanted to traverse it without the prying eyes of governmental overlords, forgetting the everyday dangers of social engineering. Predators like his acolyte and demons like Asmodeus exploited the irrational trust people placed in their relationship with technology.

As he considered the photo of the female intelligence officer, Asmodeus asked, "What have you discovered about the Wild *Elioud*?"

It was always the Wild *Elioud* who were the most unpredictable players in this age-old spiritual war, though not many managed to channel their innate power into being a disciplined, independent warrior for a righteous cause. It would have been better if she'd let her weak human nature guide her, so that Asmodeus or any of a multitude of demons could take her under their wings so to speak and turn her. In recent years, they'd grown quite successful at finding and recruiting these hybrid descendants of angels who were unaware of their bloodlines.

"She's trained for one thing. She knew to avoid security cameras and blend with a crowd. Probably had a go-bag stashed at one of the stops. I've had analysts scanning hours of video, but so far nothing."

"Hmm." Asmodeus continued to stare at the field officer's face. Something about the eyes...eyes were indeed windows to the soul, but photos didn't steal them. They hid them. *Just like a harlequin mask.*

This photo was just a headshot, but the shape of the neck and the shoulders were consistent with the vigilante do-gooder who'd broken up his little abduction and taken out his hit team with the help of the *drangùe*.

"Tell me more about this field officer." He flipped the photo over. "Olivia Markham."

His acolyte's gaze sharpened. He'd scented Asmodeus's deeper interest. *One of the reasons he's so useful. For the time being.*

"She joined the Company even before graduating from college. Almost from the start, she was flagged for exceptional skills. She speaks six languages fluently and can learn enough of another language to succeed in new missions. She's also highly skilled at hand-to-hand combat. Her instructors at the Farm ranked her first in her class across the board. Her current NOC is as a master's student in the International Development program at the University of Vienna. As part of her studies, she's been working an internship at ABA-Invest Austria."

"Ah. I see now how you were able to draw Kastrioti out. His weakness. Even after all this time, he cares too much about the people of Albania."

"What are the chances she's our Wild *Elioud*?"

Asmodeus looked at his acolyte. "I'd say exceptional. That is the word you used to describe Markham, is it not?"

His acolyte began to grin, a wide, shit-eating grin that would have made weaker mortals uneasy at best. "So perhaps our search for her isn't stalled after all? I'd say we had some divine intervention if I didn't know better."

Asmodeus chuckled at this, pleased that his acolyte showed no fear at the sound. Psychopaths never did fear what their more empathetic human brethren did. It was both a blessing and a curse. A blessing when dominating those same weak brethren. A curse when not understanding their own vulnerability before someone as powerful and malign as Asmodeus.

"Oh, I'm sure that my own personal guardian angel had a hand in moving this engagement along, but she's forbidden from anything beyond watching and warning them."

His acolyte leaned forward, eager. "Kastrioti has invited Markham to accompany him on a fact-finding mission to Albania in four days. We can use that to our advantage, isolate him."

Asmodeus shook his head. "I said that his *love for* Albanians is his weakness. Albania itself makes him stronger. There he has resources and people to draw on that make him practically invulnerable. No, our best strategy is to isolate him while he is in Vienna. He now knows I am here but not where. Neither of us knows much about the other's position, but we both know about *her*."

He pointed to Markham's photo. His acolyte looked thoughtful.

"She's the key. Kastrioti will be cautious about revealing who he is while he's in Vienna, so that gives us an advantage."

"Why?"

"Because we will not be cautious in exploiting her to get to *him*. She believes that he's running the Albanian mafia, does she not?"

His acolyte's grin returned in full force. "She believes he's the Dragon of Albania."

Asmodeus smiled at last.

Miró's cell buzzed on the table next to him. "Yes?"

"It's Karl." Karl was the local *polizei* officer that Miró had recruited to keep an eye on the sole surviving *bogomili* at St. Elizabeth's. "He's conscious. The hospital staff is with him now, but I'm going to have to call this in as soon as the doctor gives me the all clear. I'd estimate another thirty minutes before that happens. Someone will be dispatched promptly to talk to him."

"Understood. Thank you."

Miró stared at the image of the Italian woman on his computer screen. *Anastasia Fiore*. Her employer was the *Agenzia Informazioni e Sicurezza Esterna*. *She is a spy.*

He logged off his laptop and snapped it shut. Snatching up his cellphone, he gathered his belongings into a messenger bag and headed for the entrance of the Austrian National Library. He hit Mihàil's number with his thumb as he exited the building at a brisk clip. Mihàil answered on the second ring.

"Two things. First, I am headed to St. Elizabeth's to interrogate the surviving *bogomili*. I will send András a text to meet me there, but I think he may still be somewhere in the ninth district tracking the harlequin. I have a limited window of opportunity, so I may be alone on this."

"Unlikely that Asmodeus is desperate enough to risk another *bogomili* on an attack inside a hospital with crucifixes on every floor," Mihàil said. "But stay sharp. He will not leave this one alive for long. Follow the usual precautions as you exit the building. No need to endanger any humans."

"Copy that."

"I am not far from St. Elizabeth's, so if things get chaotic, let me know."

"Copy that too."

"What is the second thing?"

"I was in the Hilton lobby when an Italian woman came in matching the description that Karl gave me, so I waited. I have to admit, I am impressed. She managed to gain access to the victim's hotel room in less than fifteen minutes, though her method was a little flamboyant for my tastes."

"Did you arrive before she did?"

"Of course. I also got her photo. Mihàil, she works for the Italian foreign intelligence."

"Interesting."

"Yes, yes it is." Miró paused as he looked both ways before crossing the street. To anyone else who may have noticed him leaving the library, his step off the curb took him into thin air. It wasn't that he disappeared, exactly. It was more that he shifted his harmonic vibrations to a different wavelength so that he blended with his surroundings. And then he picked up his speed. He'd arrive at St. Elizabeth's in five minutes instead of the twenty-five that humans needed for the same distance.

"She is *Elioud,*" he said. "It all adds up. She is your harlequin."

Silence answered him. He waited, aware that Mihàil considered his assessment. He'd cut across the Stadtpark and made it to the Hilton before Mihàil spoke.

"No, not mine, I think."

"I did not mean it like that."

"Neither did I. Listen. Andràs glimpsed a dark-haired woman at the Stadtpark watching him. He said that he had been studying the ground where the harlequin had lain when he sensed her thermal signature behind him. He did not think it matched the harlequin's, remember?"

Miró had reached St. Elizabeth's while Mihàil reminded him about Andràs's report. He hurried across the lobby, avoiding the elevator to take the stairs instead, sprinting up them three at a time.

"There are two Wild *Elioud* in play?" he asked before whistling. "That has not happened in a very long time."

"I agree. And we have no way of knowing yet which one is the harlequin. Or whether the other is Dark or Grey. With Asmodeus around, we have to wonder." Mihàil paused. "Fortunately, I think I have identified the second *Elioud.*"

Miró halted at the top of the second-floor landing. "You have?"

"Yes. And I am going to take her to the opera."

Miró smiled. "That is one way to find out whether she has chosen a side or not. You will not want to forget your earplugs in case she starts screeching like torn sheet metal."

Mihàil sounded deadly confident. "That will not be a problem. I am taking her somewhere that the ambient sounds will enable me to drown out whatever discordant gibberish comes out of her throat if that happens."

The intern who delivered office mail stopped at Olivia's desk just before five and handed her a heavy, cream-colored linen envelope the size of a greeting card. Frowning, she flipped it over to see a red-foil seal on the flap. A stylized two-headed black eagle, the national symbol of Albania, told her who had sent it. Her frown deepened. Someone in Kastrioti's organization had emailed an itinerary for the trip to Tirana, which she'd duly forwarded via secure email to Fagan. She hadn't expected to hear from Kastrioti again until she arrived at the runway and his private jet.

Breaking the foil seal, she slid the heavyweight linen panel card from the envelope. Bold, black letters in a very fine hand scrawled across its face.

"Please do me the honor of joining me this evening. I find that business is not always best conducted in a boardroom but rather in a more relaxed setting. Not every question can be answered with charts and factory tours."

Kastrioti had signed his first name. *Mihàil*.

She fingered her St. Michael medal, which was warm where it lay between her breasts, and read the message two more times. Her heartbeat picked up.

Before she could decide how to answer his invitation, she heard a voice in the hallway outside her cubicle. When she looked up, she saw a man in a suit carrying an armload of long-stemmed red roses cushioned with baby's breath. He stopped in front of her desk.

"Frau Olivia Markham?"

Something about the delivery man seemed familiar, but the flowers had disarmed her usual vigilance to such an extent that she ignored what she would normally have followed up. Instead, she stood as a few colleagues peered over their partitions or gathered around the delivery man.

"These are for me?"

"Yes." He held the roses out.

Frau Reiter had come out of her office farther down the hallway and now watched the exchange.

"Well, take them, Olivia!" she said and stepped forward to look for a card.

Finding it, she studied the red-foil seal before reading the message. She looked up at Olivia, who had accepted the roses and cradled them against her chest. Surprisingly heavy, their heady perfume filled her nose.

"It simply says, 'Tonight. 7:30.'" She motioned toward the bundle with her chin. "If those roses are any indication of what you should wear, Olivia, I say it should be little and black and come with a pair of high heels."

"With diamond drop earrings," a female colleague said.

"No, a strand of pearls and your hair up," another said.

"Perhaps you can post a photo on your Facebook page," a male colleague said. The woman next to him scowled at him.

Olivia's thoughts whirled. She felt off balance in a way that she'd never felt before.

"I haven't even decided whether I'm going," she said to the group around her.

"Of course you're going," Frau Reiter said. "Unless of course you think you're being pressured...." She let her words trail off and gazed at Olivia.

Olivia dipped her nose closer and inhaled. She looked up and smiled at her boss. "No one pressures me, Frau Reiter." She looked back at the delivery man. "Are you waiting for a message?"

He inclined his head. "Should you accept Herr Kastrioti's invitation, I am to drive you."

Olivia blinked several times before raising her wrist to look at her watch and then at Frau Reiter, who nodded at her silent question.

"Well, then, I guess we'd better leave if I'm to have time to change into that little black dress with heels."

"As you wish, Frau Markham," the man said, inclining his head again. "Please be so good as to wait here while I bring the car from the garage. I will call the front desk to alert you when I am at the front door."

"That's not necessary," she said, coming around the desk to join him.

He'd started to turn away but turned back at her words. His next words were surprisingly gentle but firm.

"It *is* necessary, Frau Markham."

Olivia said nothing as he walked away, wondering instead where she'd seen him before. And what she'd gotten herself into. After he disappeared, several of her female colleagues returned to admire her bouquet, so Olivia took the opportunity to hand it off while she sent a text message to Beta and Stasia with the news that she was spending the evening with Kastrioti. Beta didn't respond, but Stasia sent a brusque text filled with demands for details, which she chose to ignore. She didn't intend to get into a text debate over the wisdom of going out with the suspected Dragon of Albania without backup. Then she sent a text to her CIA handler about the impromptu meet.

She'd just wrapped her arms around her roses when the receptionist rang her desk phone. When she came out of the ABA offices, she saw Kastrioti's driver standing next to a Mercedes sedan with tinted windows. He opened the rear door for her as she approached. She handed him the roses and got into the car, telling him the street address for her flat. As they drove, she studied the back of the driver's head. She didn't allow the nagging sense that she'd seen him before derail her, but it made it impossible to relax and enjoy the luxury of being driven home.

It's not a date, Olivia.

An hour and a half later, she came out of her building's front door to find the driver waiting next to the Mercedes, his hands crossed in front of him. He was too well trained to say anything when she approached, but she saw the flicker in his gaze and was gratified. If he'd remained entirely unmoved at seeing her in her little black dress and Christian Louboutin heels, it might have taken a little air out of her sails. After all, the man had likely held the door for a dozen models and high society women in designer clothing and shoes. Although she rather doubted that any of those women had carried a Kahr CM9 9mm handgun in her clutch or worn a knife sheath on her thigh.

When he opened the rear door, she saw that Mihàil Kastrioti waited in the back seat. Her heart pinged. Getting in a car with a potential predator was extremely risky even for a highly trained operative.

"Thank you," she murmured to the driver as she got in.

He nodded and shut the door after her.

"Good evening, Herr Kastrioti," she said, settling into the seat. She clutched her bag against her lap, the slight weight of the Kahr nevertheless comforting.

"Please, Mihàil."

"Good evening, Mihàil." His name came out of her a little too quickly. She heard the way her voice caressed its breathy syllables and blushed. She refused to drop her gaze, however.

"Good evening, Olivia. You look even more beautiful than you did this morning." Appreciation colored his deep voice, sending a warm shiver through her.

The back seat of the Mercedes, spacious during her drive to her flat, had contracted in Mihàil's presence. Olivia found herself breathing a little more shallowly to conserve what air remained around his large frame. Her shoulder brushed against his, and she wished that she'd brought a wrap. Even though he wore a suit jacket, she wanted another layer of fabric between her skin and his.

"Are you cold, Olivia? You are covered in gooseflesh." Mihàil leaned forward. "Pjetër, please adjust the air conditioning. It is too cold for Frau Markham."

Olivia started and forced herself to smile at Mihàil, which was challenging given the piercing blue of his eyes. He looked capable of reading her thoughts. "No, no. I'm fine." *I'll be plenty warm once I've sat next to you for a few minutes. You're a human heater.*

She felt funny, actually. A flush washed over her. She shifted a fraction toward the outside of the seat. Maybe she was coming down with something. Her knife sheath pinched, which had the effect of slowing her racing pulse and clearing her thoughts. She needed to get it together. Maybe she could use her obvious attraction to him to her advantage.

Breathing out to steady herself, she shifted to face him more directly.

"Thank you for the beautiful roses." She infused her voice with her gratitude, aware that real emotion served to distract a target more effectively than any manipulation. "I've never smelled anything so heavenly."

He watched her closely as she spoke, his head and body tilted to give her his full attention. At her confession, he smiled. It wasn't a large smile, just a slight tilt of the outside corners of his lips, but happiness radiated from his eyes. She couldn't look away from his gaze and felt something cold and hard start to melt inside her chest.

"I am pleased that you like them. They were grown on my property here in Austria, but the cultivar comes from my estate in Albania. My mother loves roses and bred this one from several other species native to the Balkans, though hers are not as long stemmed. That has been my own refinement."

Olivia glanced over to see Pjetër's eyes in the rearview mirror. Something told her that Mihàil had not given all the other models and beautiful society women bouquets of his mother's favorite rose.

"I'm flattered that you've shared them with me," she murmured, looking down to hide her thoughts.

A charged silence settled between them. Olivia brought her gaze up and made an effort to peer through the tinted window, which obscured the city around them. In doing so, she realized that they were headed north rather than east. When she turned to ask Mihàil where they were going, she caught him watching her. The intensity in his gaze reminded her of his impassioned speech that morning about helping the Albanians with his new business. All trace of his earlier good humor had vanished. Uneasiness wended through her gut. No matter how quickly she could remove her weapon, he would be on her before she could fire a round. And as massive as his chest was, she wasn't sure that it would do anything other than enrage him. She needed to keep her wits about her.

Calm down, Olivia. He doesn't have any idea about who you work for or why you're here. He's not planning an abduction or anything sinister like that.

She stiffened her spine and resisted the urge to touch her tongue to her dry lips. Instead, she held his gaze and asked, "Where are you taking me? I'd expected to head into the Old Town." She gestured toward herself. "Hence the dress."

"And shoes. Never forget the shoes." He smiled again. "I have never seen Louboutin worn so well. You should have no trouble navigating the crowd."

"Crowd?" Olivia asked, puzzled. It didn't sound as though he intended any harm. If he did, they wouldn't be going someplace with a lot of witnesses.

"At the Vienna Music Film Festival. It should be more crowded than usual. This is the first year that productions from the Metropolitan Opera in New York are being screened. Tonight highlights from Verdi's *Rigoletto* will be shown on the big screen in the City Hall Square."

Olivia didn't know what she'd expected of tonight's outing, but it certainly wasn't an opera about a young woman who sacrifices her life for her womanizing lover. The news hit her as hard as a surprise punch to the back of the head. It sounded too much like what had happened to Emily.

SEVEN

Mihàil watched as the color drained from Olivia's face when he told her about their destination. The only *Elioud* who couldn't stand music, the language of the angels, were those who rejected divine grace. If Olivia Markham hated music, she wouldn't risk her life to protect humanity, the vocation of any *Elioud* seeking redemption. The only question now was whether she was a Grey *Elioud*, that is, ambivalent about having angel blood, or a Dark *Elioud*, a descendent who had chosen the side of the Evil One. Grey *Elioud* could be turned to fight for good, but Dark *Elioud* must be shackled to wait for final judgment.

He looked out his window as he steeled himself for what he must do.

Beside him, Olivia's faint nimbus limned her form. It was as unique as a fingerprint, though her angel ancestry was so distant that it would never radiate very strongly. He glanced back toward her. She'd looked down as he'd mentioned *Rigoletto,* hiding her beautiful, luminous eyes. In the few seconds that her gaze appeared focused on her hands clutching her bag, he drank in the sight of her. Above average in height and slender, she nevertheless appeared both strong and graceful with the lean muscles of a dancer.

Or martial artist.

He ignored the thought.

She'd gathered her silky blond hair into a sleek chignon and wore a pair of delicate crystal-drop earrings. The only other jewelry she wore was a fine silver chain with a tiny medallion. She also favored very natural-looking makeup with only a hint of mascara and eyeliner and pale lip gloss. He picked up a complex scent with hints of rose, freesia, and ginger from her perfume, which she'd applied so sparingly that it became more of a sensuous tease than a cloying miasma. She kept her nails short and painted a pale pink. The only dramatic flair she'd indulged were the red-soled heels by French designer Louboutin that must have taken a serious dent out of her salary as an intern. The little black dress she wore with such allure had definitely come off the rack somewhere.

Caught up in her beauty, Mihàil missed the sense of Olivia's next words.

"Pardon?" he asked, pulling his focus back together from surveying her appearance.

"I asked why you invited me tonight, Herr Kastrioti."

"Mihàil." He watched the flutter in her throat as he insisted once again that she use his first name. It sounded like music when she did.

She did not.

Instead, she looked at him, her gaze direct and unblinking.

"Why did you invite me tonight?"

He thought about his words, watching her as she watched him. "Because I believe that you see me as a wealthy playboy more interested in spending time with beautiful women than in investing in my country." There was a quick flicker in her eyes that confirmed that his guess was at least partly right. "I also sense that you do not trust me for some reason, something more than the caution one would have while negotiating a business deal."

Again the confirming flicker followed by a nervous circle on her clutch with the tip of her thumb.

She swallowed. "So you think to charm me into losing my reservations about you?"

He held her gaze as much because he couldn't look away from their ever-changing blue-green-gray as because he sensed that she needed to see the truth in his eyes. "Honestly? Because I wanted to get to know you better." *That is the truth.* "I have learned that it pays to know who I am up against in all my dealings." He let a warning note slip into his voice. "I do not handle surprises very well."

She blinked several times. Her thumb had stilled its circuit on the black leather of her bag.

"Since you're being so honest, I should tell you that I'm a graduate student in international development. You're the first major client that I've taken the lead on."

Mihàil settled back against his car seat. They were almost at the city square, unfortunately. He'd really like to continue this conversation without the noise of the hundreds assembled there—and his duty to aid anyone in distress. He caught Pjetër's gaze in the rearview mirror. His driver dipped his head almost imperceptibly. He'd gotten the message and would drive around the square to the north side, giving them a few more minutes alone.

"I am aware that you're an intern, yes," he said, looking back at Olivia, who seemed startled at his words. "Why the surprise? ABA researched my background as well. But that means that Frau Reiter thinks very highly of you—or perhaps not so highly of me?" He smiled a little to show that he had no hard feelings about that possibility.

She laughed. "Oh, she's highly suspicious of handsome men, but she's willing to overlook that defect for a strong development deal." She pursed her lips a little and looked at him sideways. "She thought I could negotiate one better than she could given your—ah—playboy tendencies."

Mihàil ignored the implication that he'd allow himself to be so distracted by Olivia that he'd agree to less favorable terms. He had something more pressing to discover. "Is that why you do not trust me? Because you think I am handsome?"

He heard her soft intake of breath and felt his own pulse pick up. She looked toward the car window, but the surrounding buildings blocked much of the light from the setting sun. There wasn't much to see through the tinted windows of the Mercedes.

When she looked back, she let him see the truth in her eyes. "You know quite well that I'd have to be inhuman not to find you incredibly attractive."

It was just a figure of speech, but Mihàil couldn't help wondering. Was it an unconscious slip? Does she know that she's something not quite human? At the same time, something shifted inside his chest at her words. He knew that human women found him physically attractive—along with his wealth, of course—but most of them had little interest in anything beyond the superficial. It tended to work out well from the standpoint of providing him a persona that no one took very seriously, least of all the women that he escorted around the major cities of Europe. Olivia on the other hand had shown more curiosity and concern about his plans than most authorities and investors. As a result, in the space of only a few hours, her opinion of him already mattered.

At that moment Pjetër pulled over and shifted the car into park. He gave Mihàil an apologetic look.

"It appears that we have arrived." Mihàil opened his door, sending Pjetër a mental warning to stay put. His driver scowled.

He came around the car and opened Olivia's door. She stuck a high-heeled foot out onto the pavement, her dress riding up a little to show her upper thigh. Mihàil looked away and clenched his fingers on the frame of the car window. A tendril of perfume wafted toward him as she stood. All at once electricity filled the air around them like the moments before a lightning strike. Inhaling through his nostrils, Mihàil slipped a hand onto the small of her back, which was firm and warm under his palm. As he touched her nimbus, harmonic sparks flared into the early evening sky and his breath heated. He tasted smoke and felt the temperature of his palms and fingertips rise.

Olivia glanced over her shoulder, startled. Mihàil focused on lowering his body temperature and swallowing the smoky air in his lungs. And pretending that nothing out of the ordinary had happened.

Urging her forward with slight pressure on her back, Mihàil kept his eyes straight ahead on the milling crowd of people that spilled into Felderstrasse Street from Rathausplatz, the Vienna City Square. As the largest cultural and culinary event in Europe, Vienna's annual music festival was immensely popular. Thousands of people came daily during the eight weeks the free event ran, and tonight's broadcast of *Rigoletto* especially appealed to the musically savvy Viennese, some of whom had already seen it performed live in New York, himself included.

Mihàil looked down at Olivia, who scanned the massive crowd with an impressive alertness for a graduate student.

"Shall we find some food?" he asked, nodding to the kiosks on the far side closest to the Burgtheater. "Or wine first? The caterers offer specialty drinks if you'd prefer a cocktail or something non-alcoholic."

Mihàil, who'd been looking ahead, felt Olivia stiffen. Glancing where her gaze had fastened, he glimpsed a man striding along the left side of the central paved area toward them. Although the man had done nothing overt to draw attention to himself—in fact, he was dressed as a casual visitor—both his gait and his posture were at odds with the chatting, smiling festivalgoers who strolled and stood in groups holding plastic tumblers filled with cocktails and wine. The man disappeared among a cluster of people, but his infrared signature had already imprinted on Mihàil's memory.

Hundreds of chairs had been arranged in concert seating before the Vienna City Hall, an immense neo-Gothic structure with an ornate façade and five towers. Bleachers curved around the backside of the main paved area. Although the broadcast of *Rigoletto* on the gigantic screen wouldn't begin until nine-thirty, many of the seats had already been filled. As they headed toward the food and dining area, Mihàil considered the wooded area behind the barricades that corralled the festival from the rest of the square. Charmingly lit, smaller paved pathways drew visitors from the festival to stroll through a park-like setting, wine in hand and music in the air. They offered a romantic interlude for those so inclined. And tonight he felt inclined.

"Can we walk by all of them and see what they're offering?" Olivia asked as they drew near to the food kiosks. "Do we have time?"

"Before the opera?"

"Yes." Again that flicker of unease in her gaze.

"It will not start until twilight, so more than enough time to decide what to try." Mihàil kept his face forward. "I am sorry if I chose poorly. Opera is not for everyone."

She glanced up at him, surprise evident on her face as they approached the first vendor. "What?"

Mihàil stopped. "American?" He gestured toward the cart. "You are American, are you not?"

Now Olivia looked a little shocked. "That's not in my profile. How do you know that?"

Mihàil tilted his head. What had spooked her so much? "Simple. I can hear your accent. It is very slight, I assure you. I just have excellent hearing."

The throng of people visiting the two-dozen international food vendors engulfed them before she spoke again.

"No, I'd rather eat something else. Something less European. Something spicy." She gave him a sideways glance that he couldn't read. But his gut told him that her preference wasn't entirely based on her own whim.

"That is not in my profile," he said, steering her through the crowd, which parted at his stern glance. When she glanced at him, a question in her eyes, he clarified. "I like spicy food."

"Just a good guess," she said. The sideways glance again. "I like spicy food, too."

He was forced to step closer to avoid a tall man walking in the opposite direction. "Well then, I believe our best bet is either Indian or Mexican. Neither is very hot here, I am afraid."

She swerved into him as her path forward narrowed, and he reacted by putting his arm around her waist to steady her. He expected her to stiffen, but for a moment she melted against him and his temperature spiked before he could stop it. She felt so good in this truncated embrace that his imagination leapt to holding her in both arms for longer—a lot longer. He felt her slight tremble, saw the flutter of her pulse at her throat, and heard her swallow. Instead of pulling away, she eased into a longer stride, opening a bit of distance between them. She did it so gracefully, smiling up at him as she did that he didn't feel the sting of her rejection.

"How about both?"

"Both it is."

They walked through the crowd until they'd found both kiosks and asked people waiting what was being served. Then Mihàil escorted Olivia to an open table in the covered eating area before returning for food. As he stood in line at the Mexican cart while holding a tray of Indian food, he noticed a man watching him farther down near the wine bar. The watcher turned away as soon as Mihàil's gaze swept over him, but he hadn't moved fast enough. For a normal human subject, perhaps, but not for a *drangùe* whose instincts had been honed over centuries. Mihàil's battle senses came fully awake.

When he returned to Olivia, she sat upright and alert with her bag on the table next to her. Setting the trays down on its glossy wooden surface, he sat next to her, aware that they were entirely exposed.

"Sangria?" He held a plastic tumbler out. "I decided against the mango lassi."

She accepted the tumbler with a distracted smile, toying with the simple silver chain around her neck. He tried not to notice that it dipped between her breasts.

"Something wrong?"

"Yes." She took a deep breath and looked at him, her hand dropping from the chain to wave at the air around them. Claude Debussy's *Préludes* played in the background. "Debussy. I'm not a fan."

Mihàil studied her. "Not even *Clair de Lune?*"

She shrugged and looked sheepish. "Not really."

Mihàil tasted metallic disappointment on his tongue. "Do you like any music?"

"Really?" Her incredulous tone reminded him that she was a graduate student—and much, much younger than he was. He suddenly knew what she was going to say before she did. "Just because I don't like wandering piano playing that's essentially musical wallpaper you think I don't like music? Is that actually music we're listening to? It's bordering on being atonal."

She sipped from the sangria, but her shoulders had hunched. Mihàil scanned the area around them, wondering where the two watchers were.

"*Rigoletto?*" he asked, pretending to be absorbed in his food.

"It's not the music. I love opera actually." She started to finger the chain at her neck again. He felt her gaze on him and looked up. "It just reminds me of someone I lost."

Mihàil recognized the stark pain in her eyes and heard the slight catch in her voice. He'd reached across to press a hand on her forearm when there was an enraged shout behind them. Olivia spun on her seat.

Terrified people scattered from a man swinging a bladed weapon about him in the middle of the aisle between the kiosks. At his feet lay another man, convulsing, his hands clutching his throat. Blood spread in a widening pool beneath him. The weapon caught a blond woman on the back. She sprawled. The attacker whirled and leaped. Two more victims fell to the pavement. In moments the music film festival dissolved into a kaleidoscope of running, shoving people, overturned tables and chairs, and screams.

Mihàil launched himself at the attacker.

The man whirled in time to see Mihàil land in a crouch near him. His eyes glistened in the lights from the awning over the tables. He brandished the weapon, a machete, while gripping a boy who looked about twelve around the upper shoulders. He laughed, spittle flying.

From the concert area came more shrieking and suddenly maddened people rushed back toward them. The attacker in front of Mihàil laughed again. People parted around them, but the machete lashed out. Once. Twice. Someone screamed. Fell. The attacker struck out with his foot. Another yelp that died on a whimper as the attacker kicked again. Mihàil never took his eyes from the man. He saw the paramilitary gear, the black boots and tactical vest. He saw the earpiece. This killer, this dreg of humanity, was not alone. Without turning his head, Mihàil sensed the infrared signatures of three men with controlled movements before City Hall. One walked down each side while the third stood in the center beneath the screen.

Farther down the square toward the Burgtheater came more yelling and some gunfire. Frantic people surged back toward City Hall. The narrow paved lane between the food vendors had become a frothing, seething mass of witless, defenseless people.

They are herding them into this area.

Mihàil flashed a call for Miró and András as he lunged for the attacker's hand. He scarcely felt the icy slice of the machete's blade on his forearm as he slammed his other forearm under the man's chin, snapping his head back.

Olivia, petrified, watched as Mihàil blocked a machete blow before plowing into the attacker. Mihàil followed him down. The boy the attacker had held ran to a woman under a table, who pulled him down to hide with her. The scent of hot blood, urine, and feces from the wounded assaulted the air. A woman brushed past her. Recognizing Zophie's short white-blond hair, Olivia snapped out of her trance. Before she could form a coherent thought, Zophie shot a glance beyond her.

Olivia twisted.

The tall bearded man reaching for her missed. Grabbing his upper arm, Olivia leveraged his momentum to throw him to the pavement where he rotated to his back. She was on him instantly.

Crazed people broke from them with all the instinctive madness of a herd of wild animals from an attacking predator. Open pavement widened around them.

Straddling his chest and upper arms with her thighs, she punched his head over and over. As she did, he bucked and thrashed, dislodging her before she could subdue him. Then he shoved her away and reached for his assault rifle where it had landed when she'd pulled him to the ground. Rolling, she sprang to her feet. This one seemed less out of control than his partner. She was sure they were partners given the similarity of dress and the matching earpiece.

She wanted that earpiece.

He nailed her with his gaze and grinned.

Shaking her head, she pointed to his assault rifle. On instinct she addressed him in the dialect spoken in Syria, Levantine Arabic. "Too close, *akhi*. You will miss me."

Shock washed over his face.

Olivia smiled. As she did, she slid her dress up her thigh and pulled the knife from its sheath.

He sneered and raised his assault rifle.

Tossing the knife up, she caught it with hardly a glance.

His eyes widened.

She threw.

The knife pierced his left eye, and he fell backwards, the assault rifle clattering to the pavement. Olivia hurried over and pulled the knife out, wiping it on his pants before slipping it back into her sheath. Bending over, she pulled the earpiece from the dead man's ear and searched inside his vest for the associated two-way radio. Grabbing the Syrian's assault rifle, she detached the magazine, which she threw under the nearby tables. There was probably a round already chambered, but she didn't have time to disable the trigger. Instead, she tossed the weapon over the counter at the closest food vendor. Behind her, she heard a burst of automatic rifle fire. It was closer than it had been the previous time.

Almost immediately, the mass of humanity that had given her and the shooter a wide berth filled in the clearing, some of the desperate individuals running over the shooter's lifeless body. She stood up and looked for Mihàil in the last place she'd seen him. They knocked into her and nearly toppled her on her five-inch heels. For a moment she wondered whether she'd be able to make it out of this stampeding herd of humanity alive. She could always take off her Louboutin heels and prod people away with them.

And then Mihàil was there.

Before she could react, he'd leaned over and slid his arms under her thighs and back. He felt uncomfortably hot, but she had no time to wonder why. Straightening, he turned and started to carry her between two food vendors and toward the shelter of the trees beyond. She tugged on the lapel of his jacket to make him look down at her. He tilted his ear close as she strained to make herself heard over the cacophony.

"My clutch. There's a weapon."

He frowned and pivoted, not an easy thing to do in the increasingly tight quarters. Rough male voices sounded from both ends of the rectangular dining area. Then more gunfire ripped through the night air. She saw dark-haired men with tactical vests and assault rifles guarding the entrance from the central part of the square. Looking back over Mihàil's massive shoulder, she saw a lone man with an assault rifle at the narrower Universitätsring entrance. Clearly the attackers wanted to contain them within this natural barricade of tables, chairs, umbrella stands, and awnings, not to mention the food vendors lined up next to each other. It was going to be tough to escape to the nearby grassy and tree-filled sections of the square.

Wading through the hysterical people packed around them, Mihàil returned to the table where only five minutes before they'd been tensely discussing styles of music.

"There!" Miraculously, her clutch lay undisturbed.

Mihàil grabbed it, thrust it at her, and pushed his way through the crowd to the Mexican food vendor. On the other side of the counter at least a dozen people crouched, shivering, some weeping quietly, one man talking on his cellphone, and two teen girls texting. One woman, who looked Mexican, had managed to wedge herself under the counter half inside a cabinet. Most looked at Mihàil and Olivia with stricken faces, but one or two refused to raise their eyes. Mihàil placed a finger on his lips. That's when Olivia saw the bloody sleeve.

"You're wounded!" she whispered, her heart choking her.

He bent to set her on her feet. The man on the cellphone scooted out of the way without being asked.

Mihàil's blue gaze threatened to scorch the air around them. A hint of smoke tinged the air.

"You know how to use the weapon." It wasn't a question. "Do you think you can take out the shooter over there?" He gestured with his chin toward the Universitätsring entrance. "Whatever they are going to do will start any moment."

Nodding, she slipped the earpiece and two-way radio into her clutch, which she slung around her neck and across her torso. Then she bent to remove the Louboutin heels before pulling the Kahr from her clutch. Turning to the one woman wearing an apron and gloves, she said, "Can you turn the lights out here?"

The woman nodded.

"Do it and then tell the people on either side of you. Tell them to pass it on." She realized that surprise showed on Mihàil's face and shrugged. "No night-vision goggles."

She turned to go.

"Wait!" Mihàil placed a burning palm on her forearm. "Stay there. I will text you info as it becomes available."

"Copy that." She turned again to go.

"Olivia?" Mihàil's tense voice stopped her.

"Yes?" She turned back to look at him, the Kahr at her side.

He pulled her close against his chest, his gaze drilling into her. "Be safe."

And then he kissed her so hard she felt it all the way into her bare heels on the paved stone of the square.

EIGHT

Mihàil eased her down to the ground, gave her one last burning look, and then sidled along the front of the kiosks toward City Hall and the armed men that she'd glimpsed earlier. She wasn't sure what he planned to do. The festival's security was dead or they wouldn't be in this situation. Given the shooter's tactics—herding hundreds of civilians into a confined space at dusk—they were organized and deliberate. Who knew if the *polizei* would arrive before the shooters killed everyone? Whatever Mihàil managed to do to distract or disable any of them would save lives until the authorities got here. His aggressive takedown of the machete man proved he was more than willing and able to act. She just hoped that his judgment kept him from getting himself killed.

As Olivia watched Mihàil crouch to hurry along the front of the kiosks toward City Hall, the lights on the kiosk next to her snapped off. Shaking her head to clear it, she began picking her way along the kiosks towards the smaller entrance across from the Burgtheater. More kiosks darkened as she stepped. She heard sobbing and angry male voices over the confused babble. The pleasant evening had turned hot, and the scent of sweat and fear mingled with Persian and Japanese food and spilled beer and lemonade. Someone shoved into her, but she pivoted and let him lurch into the space behind her. She'd only gone the length of one kiosk before she heard distant sirens.

After that, she had to force her way between bodies, praying the whole time that her movement didn't cause too great a ripple through the crowd to draw the shooter's notice. Several times she had to show her weapon or press it into someone's side to get someone to open enough space for her to squeeze through.

She gritted her teeth. If only she could climb to the awning over the kiosks and vault between them. But no. She had to take the hard way. She paused, panting and damp, and pulled out the two-way radio and wrapped the earpiece around her ear. She heard more Levantine Arabic in a very harsh, deep voice asking for reports from the two dead guys in the center. She pictured a wiry black beard and dead eyes and breath scented with *bharat* spice mix, heavy on the clove and cardamom.

"They're dead, *ikhwa*," she said in her most cheerful, confident voice. "I can't say how machete man died, but the *akhi* with the assault rifle took a knife to his left eye."

She waved her Kahr at a man blocking her forward progress. When he didn't budge, she whacked him with the barrel. It was more of a tap, really. Whimpering, he laid a hand alongside his face and turned enough for her to get past.

"Who is this?" Now the deep voice sounded cold. A furious cold. Olivia pictured Mihàil laying hands on him. How cold would he be then?

"Ever see that American movie *Die Hard*, *akhi*?" Silence greeted her. "No? Well, I'm Bruce Willis. Yippie-ki-yay."

Olivia had eyes on the shooter at the Universitätsring entrance now. Even in the dark, he was easy to see through the trembling shoulders wedged around her because he stood alone a good 10 meters from the crowd on a platform. He paced, his assault rifle held ready to mow down those in front of him.

She heard a woman screaming through the radio. It cut off abruptly. *Shit*.

"Yippie-ki-yay, *ukhti*." The cold voice was clearly unimpressed with her, *his sister*, and whatever nonsense she was speaking.

Olivia ducked behind the last kiosk, grabbing the mouth of the startled woman beneath her to keep her from screaming out. Placing a finger on her own lips to signal the terrified people huddling there, she crawled over them to the counter, the Kahr held high.

Olivia kept her voice confident, shoving aside the knowledge that the evil bastard had killed a woman in response to her goading. Best to keep jabbing at him. "Too bad you didn't see it, *akhi*. Bruce Willis takes out all the terrorists by himself, a few at a time."

Hiking her dress up, she eased herself onto the counter. The shooter pressed his free hand to his ear. Cold Voice shouted orders for him to fire at the crowd. It was now or never.

He raised the barrel of his assault rifle at the same moment that Olivia sighted down the barrel of her Kahr. Inhaling and holding, she squeezed the trigger. The man dropped to the platform, his rifle jerking up and spraying bullets into the night sky.

The crowd screamed and shoved, many of those on the inside unable to see anything.

Olivia jumped down into the square and ran toward the shooter's body. Snatching up the assault rifle, she turned back to the square. She swung the rifle up and shot out the nearest lights on posts among the tables of the dining area.

"Go, go, go!" she yelled, waving her arm at the front people who wavered and then fled, streaming across Universitätsring toward the Burgtheater. "Quickly! Keep your head down and don't stop!"

Cold Voice barked questions over the two-way radio, but Olivia ignored them and prayed he wouldn't send anyone to investigate. If they were fortunate, the *polizei* would be here by the time the terrorists realized that she'd taken their rear guard out. She wanted to leave with the fleeing crowd, but Mihàil had told her to stay and wait for information. Pulling her cellphone out, she checked. No texts.

Squinting toward the concert area, Olivia searched for the telltale presence of terrorists. There were at least three in front of City Hall. Her gut told her that at this level of planning and execution there had to be more on the perimeter. If it were up to her, there'd also be a sniper somewhere on the loggia of City Hall. Which meant that even if the terrorists hadn't thought of it, she should go there with the captured assault rifle. Unlike the average terrorist who blindly sprayed bullets, she'd learned the Marine adage "one shot, one kill" at Langley.

And her cover was rapidly dispersing through the exit to the street.

Making her decision based on real-time facts on the ground, Olivia jumped onto the grass beside the platform where large trees provided cover for her to advance toward City Hall. She'd only gone a few meters when she heard Cold

Voice ordering his group to engage the *polizei* approaching from the four sides of the Rathausplatz. Gunfire peppered the woods ahead of her where she saw men in tactical gear running among the trees. Keeping close to the barriers erected behind the bleachers along the sides of the square, she sprinted toward the front. When she got closer, she saw the bodies of two security officers on the pavement just outside the barricade. *The same ones guarding the entrance earlier.*

The challenge would come when she reached the end of the cover—and smack in the middle of the current fusillade. She needed the *polizei* to fall back. And a distraction from the other side of the plaza.

She'd barely had the thought when her cellphone buzzed.

Mihàil's text read, "Go now."

Up ahead, *polizei* began retreating across the street, taking cover inside the portico of the building on the corner. Cold Voice shouted for terrorists to converge on the side of the square away from her position. Peering from behind the barriers, she saw the terrorist ahead turn away from her. As soon as he did, she shifted the assault rifle to her back where it hung by its strap and ran forward through the temporary barricade, up the short flight of stairs, and into the portico at the front of the Rathaus where she leaned against a column to catch her breath.

Feeling every cut and scrape on her bare soles, Olivia looked around the column to the square. Confused shouting erupted over the two-way radio, and the closest terrorist ran away. She didn't hesitate. Darting down the length of the portico, she wrenched the door open and ran into the building. More security officers lay crumpled inside, their blood pooling on the stone of the first floor. Ignoring them, Olivia headed for one of the two parallel Grand Staircases leading up to the Festival Hall and the balcony overlooking the square. The red carpet cushioned her sore feet, but she was breathless and drenched by the time she made the hall. And she didn't know if there was a sniper or where he was.

Festival Hall, almost as long as an American football field and half as wide, was dark. It wasn't empty, however. Dozens of tables and chairs had been set up for a gala banquet. Olivia paused inside the pointed-arch doorway and scanned the space for movement. Then she made herself re-scan the hall before committing to crossing it. Good recon was like carpentry, her trainer at Langley had said.

"Measure twice, cut once. Look twice, don't get dead."

Seeing and hearing nothing, Olivia crept through the room holding the assault rifle against her body to minimize any sound from its movement. When she stepped out onto the loggia, for a heartbeat she wished that she was here for another reason. Though it too was dark, the view out across the Rathausplatz toward the Burgtheater was breathtaking. Or would have been if there hadn't been pandemonium down below. Olivia eased onto the balcony projecting from the end tower on the west side of the loggia, the one closest to the side of the square where the terrorist leader had directed his members.

"Focus, Olivia," she said while rubbing her St. Michael medal between her forefinger and thumb. *Where is Mihàil?*

She lifted the assault rifle, positioned it snugly against her shoulder, and adjusted the scope as she searched the square for Mihàil. Her heart skipped a beat when she found him standing shoulder to shoulder with a muscled giant wearing a t-shirt, jeans, and combat boots, a group of festival goers huddled behind them and a terrorist aiming an assault rifle at them. Two other terrorists lay on the square between them, their clothes smoking.

Olivia didn't have time to puzzle the reason for that out. She just inhaled and prepared to shoot the terrorist still standing. As she did, she saw movement out of the corner of her eye.

After kissing Olivia, Mihàil had made his way through the jammed Rathausplatz, his blood boiling. Literally. Hot smoke spurted from his nostrils. His fingers, clenching and unclenching, radiated. He'd felt the pavement heat beneath his shoes. There would be scorched footprints for investigators to puzzle over later. Terrified people had shifted away from him, but none cried out. On some level, they knew what he was and no one wanted to draw his attention. A few surreptitious elderly hands had crossed chests as he passed.

That was ten minutes and many charred terrorists ago.

András and Miró had arrived soon after he'd taken the machete-wielding terrorist down. They'd hunted the terrorists on the perimeter, leaving those in the square for Mihàil, who'd also led many of the festival attendees to safety after Olivia had taken out the shooter at the Burgtheater entrance. He'd seen her run through the security barrier only moments before, an assault rifle swinging from her back. Tendrils of hair had escaped the smooth coil on the back of her head, and her sweaty arms glistened when she passed through the light on the square, but the determined look on her face and her headlong dash transformed her into an avenging angel. Emotion swirled through him as he watched. Pride and something else.

Now András stood next to him, his own heat blasting the air and a ferocious scowl transforming his features. The big Hungarian had taken a few bullets and blood stained his t-shirt and jeans, but the bullets had melted after piercing his flesh, which ejected the offending material as it healed itself. Bullet fragments spattered across his clothes.

The terrorist facing them had cold, but rational, eyes, unlike the others. Unlike them, he aimed his assault rifle instead of squeezing the trigger and waving his arm around while hoping to hit something.

"The woman is dead," he called out in accented German.

Mihàil's heart turned over, hard, but he kept his face expressionless.

"I doubt that," he said and stepped forward.

Even for Mihàil, what happened next happened fast.

The assault rifle recoiled against the terrorist as he shot. Andràs growled and dove forward, his arms outstretched. Mihàil spun away from the bullet's trajectory, his hand snatching it from the air as it whistled past his shoulder. At the same instant, the terrorist collapsed, swinging his assault rifle up as his dying grip clenched the trigger and sent a staccato of shots into the night sky. Half a heartbeat later, Andràs tackled the lifeless sack before it hit the pavement.

Mihàil crushed the bullet in his fist and flung the smoking chunks away as he sprinted toward the Rathaus. He spared only a glance at the blackened hole in the terrorist's forehead as he passed. Later, he would grieve for the lives lost tonight, innocent and terrorist alike. All life was precious to *Elohim*, and death robbed these souls of the grace that living gave them, the chance to regret the wrongs they'd done, ask for forgiveness, and try to make amends. Right now, however, he could only think of Olivia and the terrorist's last words. What if a terrorist had been lurking inside, ready to act while she focused on the drama below? Had she left herself vulnerable in an effort to save him? Mihàil sensed her above him on the balcony, yet he couldn't discern anything beyond her presence. He didn't know whether she was injured or dying.

He wrenched the Rathaus door open and ran inside. The stone and marble interior insulated against the outside din. András would adjust his harmonics and slip away once he'd done what he could to calm and guide the traumatized crowd outside. He, however, had to find Olivia. Flinging himself at the closest Grand Staircase, Mihàil leapt three steps at a time until he reached the floor with the Festival Hall. Across the dark hall and through the balcony doors, the infrared outline of bodies, two upright and one prone, flared brilliant vermillion.

Olivia.

Mihàil didn't need his vestigial wings to fly to Olivia, who stood next to Miró. Both turned to look at him as he stepped onto the balcony, Olivia's gaze unfocused, Miró's grim. At their feet lay the smoldering remains of a man, his infrared signature vivid red, not from life but as a result of spontaneous internal combustion. In other words, his internal temperature had risen so quickly that he'd incinerated, leaving only dense, human-shaped ashes with a visible blue-white core. Sweat slicked Olivia's skin in the heated air, yet gooseflesh covered her arms while massive shivers rolled through her.

Without a word, Mihàil picked Olivia up and carried her away from the terrible scene. She didn't resist. She didn't say or do anything, in fact. Despite the circumstances, Mihàil felt the rightness of her weight in his arms and against his chest. When he glanced down, he couldn't see where his nimbus ended and hers began. It gave him the strangest feeling, leaving him slightly disoriented. He was also almost certain that Olivia and his harlequin were one and the same. Though she'd used a nine millimeter and assault rifle instead of a *bō* and martial arts, Olivia's grace, dexterity, speed, and quick thinking in a volatile and deadly situation equaled those of the masked harlequin.

Miró matched his pace as they descended the stairs.

"András will meet us at your car. Pjetër has found a quiet side street a few blocks away. We just need to get out of here without being seen." He looked down at Olivia and back up again. "She is in shock. Think you can adjust her harmonics for her?"

Mihàil wondered if Miró saw the same merging of their nimbuses or if he simply asked the most logical question.

"Long enough to leave the building," he answered and lifted Olivia higher. She'd stopped shivering and relaxed against his chest, but she made no move to hold onto him and gave no sign that she knew where she was or who was holding her.

As they reached the first floor of the Rathaus, Miró tapped Mihàil's shoulder. "There's something you should know about the dead guy on the balcony."

Something in his voice caused Mihàil's battle senses to go on alert. Halting, he squinted, his mouth setting in a grim line. "What did he do to her?"

Miró shook his head. "Nothing. I got to him first. Mihàil, he wasn't a terrorist. He was an operative, likely CIA."

Mihàil's mouth twisted. The two men he'd seen in the square before the attack. They'd moved like CIA. And Olivia had noticed. Why? More importantly, their presence couldn't be a coincidence.

Focusing again on Miró, he said, "That's not all."

Miró, whose own face looked grim, shook his head again. "András and I came across some operatives clearly in a position to take out terrorists, but they hadn't. They didn't try to stop us though."

"Odd." Mihàil looked down at Olivia. "Perhaps our Wild *Elioud* has gotten on the wrong side of the CIA." Very wrong if the CIA would allow terrorists to draw her out to kill her.

On the floor below, the entrance doors opened to admit an officer in tactical gear. More followed.

Without another word, Mihàil and Miró shifted their harmonics until they became invisible to human sight. Mihàil's shift caused sympathetic vibrations to ripple through Olivia's nimbus. It flared and brightened as a candle flame flares and brightens in a gust. He hummed to encourage her harmonics to shift farther. It was no easy task. As a Wild *Elioud*, she wasn't easily manipulated. Her shock was a minor blessing in that sense. She'd be more open to his guiding her. His potent blood and their earlier connection took care of the rest.

"Olivia," he said, removing the dampening on his voice that kept him from overwhelming humans when he spoke. "You need to trust me."

Olivia startled and looked up at him. She clasped his lapel and held his gaze. In the warm fluorescent light, her blue-gray eyes blazed with sudden recognition. And trust.

"Thank you," he whispered as her harmonics shifted along with his.

Now it was only a matter of getting out of here.

Plunging down the final set of stairs, they passed by the officers unseen and out into the square. Overhead, helicopters hovered, beaming spotlights at the tumultuous scene. While police herded civilians into groups, soldiers holding weapons scurried to secure the perimeters of the square. Emergency medical personnel set up aid stations near the bleachers to evaluate people for transport to local hospitals. Flashes from police photographers' cameras popped everywhere. Next to the large screen stood a knot of men in dark suits listening to a tall, gray-haired man who seemed to be issuing commands. Sirens blared blocks away in all directions. A cacophony of shouts, loud voices, boots on pavement, radio chatter, helicopter blades, truck engines, and slamming car doors competed with the smell of blood, sweat, spilled food, exhaust, and charred flesh.

In this chaos they walked north unimpeded, turning the corner onto Felderstrasse and continuing west past the Rathaus. Mihàil's influence on Olivia's harmonics lost strength as they wended their way through the throngs of personnel, official vehicles, and media trucks. She returned to the lower and slower human spectrum halfway up the block. He and Miró shifted their own harmonic vibrations back to match. Although she'd responded to his earlier plea, Olivia now buried her face against his chest. She needed to be someplace warm and safe when she came out of her shock. Someplace where he could explain what had happened on the balcony. And begin to tell her more about who and what she was.

They'd reached the intersection with Rathausstrasse when the *polizei* detained them at a blockade.

"No one beyond this barrier, sir," a young officer said. Five other armed officers stood in a semi-circle around the waist-high barricade spanning the street.

Miró, glancing at Mihàil, stepped forward. A couple of inches shorter than Mihàil and less broad with graying hair at his temples, Miró projected a quiet seriousness that commanded respect.

"Please, we need to take this woman to Vienna General Hospital." He gestured north to the hospital, a five-minute drive, and infused his voice with undeniable charm. "My friend's car and driver are at the end of this block."

Confusion flitted across the officer's face. Clearly, she was so well trained that even Miró's *Elioud* charm couldn't completely block out her strong desire to follow orders.

"There are paramedics to assist you," she said, lifting her hand to rub her temple. It wasn't surprising. Resisting an *Elioud*'s charm caused humans to have severe headaches. "No one is to leave until statements can be taken."

"Perhaps I can be of service," said a man wearing a gray suit behind the officer. He stepped closer to the barrier. His German held a trace of an American accent.

Mihàil's battle senses emitted a high-pitched warning at the newcomer's approach. Next to him, Miró stiffened. Below average in height and balding, the middle-aged man didn't present any obvious threat save for his cold stare. It was a predatory stare.

The man in the gray suit turned to the officer. "We'll take responsibility for them. You may go back to your duties."

Beneath the officer's carefully blank expression, Mihàil read her dislike of the newcomer. She said nothing, however, simply nodded and turned back to her colleagues at the barricade.

The man in the gray suit gestured, his gaze on a point behind them. Mihàil heard steps and swiveled, stunned to see four armed figures. They wore full facemasks and gloves and held weapons pointed at him and Miró. Whatever material had been used on their clothing, it hid their thermal signatures. A moment of doubt entered his head. Asmodeus couldn't disguise his nature behind an unfamiliar avatar, and yet Mihàil's gut told him that it was no coincidence that his and Miró's battle senses had been foiled. He wondered what other nasty surprises might be in store for them.

"We'll accompany you, gentlemen," said the man in the gray suit. "We want to ensure that you don't disappear."

Mihàil kept his gaze on the man in the gray suit while he sent a mental call for Andràs. At his side, Miró waited for his signal.

"You're not planning on being difficult, are you?" asked the man in the gray suit. He nodded and one of the men prodded them with the tip of his weapon.

"Not at all," Mihàil said, taking a few steps. They needed to clear the blockade and put distance between themselves and the officers stationed there.

They'd gone halfway down the block when a sharp whistling sliced the air, followed by a grunt and a thud. Nearly at the same moment, a whooshing brought another thud. Mihàil and Miró spun around to see two shooters on the ground. The second two men shot at two figures on the perimeter of their small group, pivoting to follow the figures as they ran. Mihàil wrapped his arms around Olivia, but silver flashed and a dark wind whipped. One shooter screamed as something bright snaked around his wrist and yanked. The last shooter dropped when something smashed into his head. Miró looked over at Mihàil, his eyes uncharacteristically wide.

On either side of them stood two black-hooded women, one holding a silvery segmented whip, whose end she swung in a rapid blur at her side, and the other whirling a chain with a weighted end over her head.

The woman with the chain stepped forward into the light from a streetlight.

"*We* are planning to be difficult," she said.

NINE

The man in the gray suit studied them. As he did, Mihàil's sensitive hearing picked up a burst of audio from his hidden earwig. Mihàil didn't need to hear the words to know that more operatives would be on their way. He glanced toward the barricade. As he'd suspected, the hooded women had already disabled the *polizei* there. He smiled. Whatever else they were, these Wild *Elioud* were very talented.

"We thank you for your escort, but it is no longer needed," he said.

András materialized behind the man in the gray suit. He loomed over the much shorter man, who nevertheless remained unaware of his presence.

An instant later, a government-issue 9mm SIG Sauer appeared in the man in the gray suit's hand. He fired at the woman with the segmented whip. One shot was all he managed. As the woman launched herself in an acrobatic flip away from the bullet's trajectory, András reached over his shoulder and grabbed the SIG Sauer out of his hand. The man pivoted on his heel, his mouth gaping so awkwardly that Mihàil wondered if he'd ever been taken by surprise before. Andràs grinned, its lopsidedness making him look boyish. But he destroyed that impression by squeezing the pistol in his massive, heated paw. The SIG Sauer glowed dull red and warped out of shape. Andràs threw the resulting lump onto the pavement.

Mihàil nodded, and Andràs gave the man a lazy tap on the jaw. He crumpled like tissue paper to the ground.

Mihàil looked at the hooded woman who'd spoken. She stood in the same spot under the streetlight, but now her weighted chain hung loose in her hand, still but ready. That's when Mihàil saw that it was a *surujin,* a traditional Okinawan weapon.

"You realize that she is going with me?" he asked, pitching his voice so that it sounded as though he spoke into her ear. She flinched, though it was so slight no human would have caught it.

Then she stepped up, the *surujin* rising into a vicious whirl above her head. She released its latent fury at Miró, who'd been easing himself closer. A heartbeat later the woman with the segmented whip sprang off the roof of a car, her whip lashing out at Andràs. The agility of their coordinated attack impressed Mihàil, who almost wished that they would succeed. Unfortunately for them, Mihàil's crew had some extraordinary abilities that martial arts and weapons had little effect against.

The segmented whip wrapped around Andràs's upper torso, capturing both of his arms. The attacker pulled, which tightened the segments. She was strong enough to make Andràs stumble a step toward her before he planted his feet. The *surujin* wrapped around Miró's lower legs. When he stumbled, he fell to his knees. Mihàil winced. There would definitely be bruises later. Fast healing but painful regardless. Miró's face tilted up. Though his intense stare spelled trouble for any opponent, Mihàil knew his friend well enough to read the keen admiration there.

A pause like an indrawn breath silenced the street. Blocks away the noise and chaos of the square echoed as if from another world.

Then Andràs growled. Instead of shrugging the segments of the whip apart as Mihàil expected, Andràs hummed. His humming rose in pitch until it matched the natural harmonics of the steel, which vibrated in response. He continued manipulating his pitch until he'd elongated the bonds between the individual steel molecules. At the same time, he increased his own harmonics so that he vibrated on a different wave pattern until there opened up a space between the steel molecules that was large enough for him to walk through. The now-empty whip hovered in an Andràs-shaped lasso before returning to its normal harmonics and collapsing onto the pavement.

Andràs smirked and gestured toward Miró, who smiled at his captor and gave a slight bow. The women stood still, although the tension in their frames suggested they prepared to act at any moment.

Miró swung his arms and knees at the same time, coming for a moment to his feet. A moment later, the *surujin* links blazed before Miró broke through them. The *surujin* weights dropped to the pavement in a puddle of molten steel. He shrugged, looking sheepish.

The Wild *Elioud* attacked while his men stood preening. The taller woman who'd carried the chain whip darted around Andràs, who swung to grab her, but she'd already snatched up her chain whip and run into the middle of the street, pivoting and whirling it. The smaller one whose *surujin* had been destroyed ran straight at Miró before jumping and wrapping her legs around his torso. She began striking him fiercely with both fists. When Miró reached to pull her off, she swung nimbly to his back and wrapped an arm around his neck and began to choke him.

"Enough!" Mihàil boomed and took a step forward. He feared that Andràs and Miró would forget themselves under such a sustained assault. His harmonics enlarged his voice, sending out powerful waves that reset the combatants' own harmonics.

All of the combatants ceased moving and looked toward him. Mihàil had no idea what expression the women wore, but his men's demeanor had lost all playfulness.

Before he could speak again, Olivia placed her hand on his forearm. Her wide, lucid gaze shone with fear. "Don't hurt them. Please."

Mihàil's heart twisted as he looked at her, and he pulled her closer instinctively. She quaked, but she didn't look away.

"Never," he said, withstanding her scrutiny. After a moment, he felt her relax. He looked at the other women. "Will you join us?"

The shorter woman hopped off Miró's back and stepped away from him. "Is that a request?"

"Yes."

She glanced over her shoulder at the taller woman, who'd already snatched her chain whip up and tucked its folded length into her jacket pocket. The other Wild *Elioud* nodded.

Mihàil didn't wait for them to respond. "Then we have a truce." He looked at Miró. "Please escort our guests to my place. I will bring Olivia with me."

The shorter woman started to say something, but Olivia spoke instead.

"Please, I think I can stand."

Mihàil set her on her feet reluctantly, although he kept a hand on her upper arm as she stood near him. A shiver raced through her, but her voice was firm when she spoke.

"Go. The faster we leave here the faster we get some answers." At that moment, a two-way radio on one of the downed *polizei* barked questions. Olivia peered over her shoulder toward Felderstrasse where an ambulance crept past the intersection, a paramedic staring and beginning to point at them. "And we can't stay here any longer."

Mihàil didn't need to see the expression on the hooded women's faces to read their acquiescence. They moved together and stood until András and Miró fell into step on either side of them. Then they followed Mihàil's team without looking back. Mihàil slipped his hand into Olivia's and began walking toward Rathausstrasse where Pjetër stood, hands crossed at his waist, next to Mihàil's Mercedes. Though his loyal retainer's face showed no emotion, Mihàil read the tension in his shoulders. No doubt the man would give him the cold shoulder for a few days over endangering Olivia and involving what he deemed the loutish Andràs in protecting her.

Mihàil opened a door for Olivia and helped her into the backseat. She slipped in, managing to look graceful despite her dirty bare feet and the long, blond tendrils of hair falling from her formerly smooth chignon. He saw her hands go to her clutch, but she didn't look at him. Was she considering using the Kahr 9mm hidden there? For her sanity, he hoped not. It would be a lot of blood and gore for nothing.

He was about to go around to the other side of the car when she slid across the seat for him. So he got in and pulled the door shut. Without asking, he pulled her into his side and sent a silent message to Pjetër to turn the heater in the back up. She sat upright and stiff at first, trembling and covered in gooseflesh. He felt the exact moment when she stopped shivering because it coincided with her relaxing against him. He said nothing, letting his own temperature rise a few degrees. Her delicate scent and the weight of her head on his shoulder opened something up inside his chest. If he could stay here in this corner of his car holding her, he would forget everything else, including his duty.

"He burned to ashes in front of me." Although she murmured the words, Mihàil heard her. "I just stood there and watched as he turned into a living ember."

Mihàil closed his eyes and prayed for the right words. He sighed. "I know."

She twisted to look at him. Her gaze still held a trace of shock, but he could see that she was already absorbing and accepting his answer.

"Your friend did it."

"Yes."

"You can do it too."

"Yes."

Her next question surprised him.

"Why?"

Why? Not 'how'? "He was going to kill you."

She looked away. Her hands began to play with the clutch in her lap. "He didn't look like a terrorist."

"What did he look like?"

Olivia shrugged. "An American?" She didn't sound convincing.

Mihàil said nothing. When she didn't go on, he said, "Miró—my friend who saved you—believes that he was CIA."

She startled and then stilled.

"You knew that—just as you recognized those operatives when we first arrived."

Mihàil felt her breath hitch and heard her heartbeat speed up. He pressed on.

"Miró and Andràs, my large friend, saw other CIA officers during the attack, officers who did nothing to intervene." He took her chin and lifted it until her gaze met his. For a moment, all he could see was the dark smoky gray rimming her irises and the lighter blue-gray filling them. Her warm breath fluttered across his cheek, drawing his gaze down to her mouth. He tilted his own head closer, fascinated as her pupils dilated in response. It seemed that he wouldn't need his *Elioud* charm to get answers. "Why is the CIA after you?"

Olivia's eyes had fluttered almost shut when Mihàil spoke, his low voice thrumming through her. Though his question caught her off guard, a part of her heard the slightly breathless quality of his speech. She opened her eyes again, feeling the pulse race in her veins, and wondered how much of her reaction was fear for her cover and how much was desire. His mesmerizing gaze held no trace of the haunted sadness that she'd seen in the gym photo. It was blue fire, its laser intensity trained on her. He smelled musky hot with the faintest tinge of smoke, just enough to make her want to laugh at the clichéd words that came to mind: *Lord, is he smokin' hot.*

Swallowing, she focused on his question. He'd obviously seen her with her Kahr and an assault rifle. How did she spin these facts to a man who could incinerate her? At that thought, she found shock threatening to overwhelm her again. She shied away from the surreal subject, but she had no good answer. Then Stasia's words came back to her: *Many whisper that they are angels.* She shut that thought down and turned to find Mihàil watching her closely. Divinely handsome, yes, but definitely human. Or she couldn't trust her own senses anymore.

Fortunately, she didn't have to answer because he asked another question.

"I take it they have yet to interrogate you about your activities then?" he asked.

Olivia didn't know what he had in mind, but her training kicked in. Better to let him tell her what was going on and follow his lead. It would buy her the time to weave a story without revealing her or her mission. She dragged her gaze away and began toying with the clasp on her clutch.

"Activities?" she asked, keeping her voice soft and unsure. "I don't know what you mean."

"Do you not?" Though his voice was low, it was far from soft. He seemed to grow warmer beside her, and the scent of smoke grew more obvious. "Not every woman carries a 9mm in her evening bag."

Olivia swallowed again, hard. Despite his obvious attraction to her and care for her safety, she was reminded that she knew very little about Mihàil's motives or plans. Nothing that had happened so far had excluded him from being the Dragon of Albania. In fact, his extraordinary capacity for violence suited an Albanian crime lord. Never mind the very real ability to reduce people to ashes suiting an Albanian dragon.

She cleared her throat and looked at him again, raising her chin slightly. "Not every European playboy knows what a 9mm looks like."

Mihàil burst out laughing and ran his hand through his hair. The smoky scent faded and his temperature cooled. "Indeed. But I think you know by now that I am not your typical European playboy." His deprecating smile took her breath away. "Though perhaps my next move is in keeping with my reputation, eh?"

His warm fingers dropped to her exposed knee beneath the edge of her dress, sending a tremor through Olivia. He bent and nuzzled the side of her neck while his fingers played with the cloth before moving it aside to stroke the soft skin of her inner thigh just above her knee. Olivia shuddered and let a tiny moan escape her. She longed for him to press his lips against the pulse beating like a terrified swallow at the base of her throat.

Instead, his hand pushed her dress up her leg, exposing the knife in its sheath.

"And you are the only beautiful woman that I have had the pleasure to escort who has worn one of these," he said against her ear. When he sat back, Olivia had to stifle a groan at the keen sense of loss.

She covered her response with an irritated huff as she pulled her dress back down. Then she moved into the far corner of the backseat. "Well, it appears we both have some explaining to do," she said, her tone haughty as she gestured between them. "As you're not such a gentleman, I won't insist that you go first."

Mihàil gave her a slightly mocking smile, tilting his head and holding his hand out, palm up. "I am indeed a gentleman because I could very easily persuade you to tell me far more than you would be comfortable sharing." There was an edge to his words that convinced her that he meant what he said.

She didn't like being intimidated, so Olivia just sat staring coldly back at him, determined to say nothing. After several long, tense moments, it became clear that Mihàil intended to wait until she did. Olivia gathered her will, firming her mouth and dipping her chin a fraction as she did. If he meant to force her, well, then he'd have to do more than glare at her. And she'd be damned if she'd make it easy. Unexpectedly, she recalled a similar scenario with Fagan in their last meeting. Fury at the memory of him standing by that barricade, weapon in hand, rose like bitter bile in her throat. As she'd approached the Rathaus, she'd heard a familiar voice on the two-way radio that she'd pilfered from the dead terrorist say that she was being handled, and when the operative had appeared on the balcony, she'd known who sent him. She'd seen the other operatives, who had not been there at her request and didn't step in to stop the slaughter. She didn't know what the hell Fagan was playing at, but he'd used her and innocent civilians to get at Mihàil.

She bent forward, her hands fisting.

Mihàil blinked. He looked startled. His surprise gave way to thoughtfulness as he leaned back into his corner, all tension gone from his posture. "Forgive me. You have had a shock. My questions can wait until we reach my home, and I can see to your comfort first. I and my friends have much to share with you and your friends as well."

Olivia frowned. Something had just happened between them, but she didn't know what. She sat upright and studied Mihàil, but he gave her a bland look. After a moment, Olivia turned and looked toward the window, which had become a mirror in the darkened night. She had no idea in which direction they were headed, but she had no reason to distrust his earlier promise not to hurt her friends.

As for her, she was beginning to suspect that Mihàil's real danger had nothing to do with pain or violence.

Miró glanced at the rearview mirror of the Porsche Cayenne Turbo S that he'd rented earlier that afternoon. Apparently, there were three Wild *Elioud*, one of whom was an Italian spy named Anastasia Fiore. Even had she never spoken, he would have known which of the two hooded women she was by the way that she moved. She sat diagonally across from the driver's seat, her head turned in his direction. Though he couldn't discern her gaze through the spandex covering her face, Miró felt its force on the back of his head. She knew that he watched her and that he was aware of her stare. He wondered how much of her anger stemmed from his destruction of her *surujin* and how much was deflected fear for Olivia Markham, who was clearly the leader of their little band. What had seemed to be a rare meeting of Wild *Elioud* was turning out to be something far more astonishing—a united squad of expert martial artists.

Next to him in the front passenger seat sat the tall Wild *Elioud* who had yet to speak. She kept her head facing forward, radiating alertness. Miró suspected that she trained all of her attention on their route. His intuition told him that she too was a spy. Something also told him that it would take more than the ordinary *Elioud* charm to disorient her memory. He glanced in the rearview mirror again. If the strength of her animosity was anything to go by, Ms. Fiore would put up a fierce fight as well.

András broke the tense silence as only András could. "About damn time you drove me in style," he said, shifting his large frame to survey the interior of the luxury SUV. "I could definitely get used to this."

Miró chose not to answer.

András shrugged and leaned into the corner of the backseat, crossing his arms. Miró saw the subtle shift in Ms. Fiore's posture as his friend's shoulder brushed against hers. He hoped she didn't have a weapon hidden somewhere in her form-fitting suit. It certainly seemed unlikely, but Miró's gaze lingered on her curves anyway.

András nodded at her. "Way to take on Mr. Ice there. Those bruises look good on him."

Ms. Fiore's posture didn't relax, but she swiveled her head toward András, who took that as an invitation to continue talking.

"He's a small bastard, but he's slippery as hell. I usually only land one out of every three punches unless I manage to pin him down."

"That does not happen often," Miró said.

"Small?" Ms. Fiore asked. She sounded incredulous.

The woman in front snorted. Ms. Fiore's head came forward before returning to aim at András.

"I know, I know. It is hard to believe how effective someone that size can be against me."

Ms. Fiore, who'd leaned forward as András blathered on, struck while his words lingered on the air. Twisting slightly, she jabbed at András's jaw with the heel of her right hand, snapping his head sideways. Before he'd righted himself, she'd grabbed him by the throat and straddled his lap, a sharp blade pricking the tender skin above his Adam's apple. Miró laughed. The hooded woman next to him turned her head in his direction.

"Perhaps your friend lacks my skill," Ms. Fiore said before leaning back.

András coughed and rubbed at the bead of blood welling on his throat. Shaking his head, he wiped his fingers on his jeans. "Point taken," he said and coughed again. He grinned at Miró before looking back at her. "I like your style."

Ms. Fiore huffed and relaxed into the corner of the backseat. Miró watched as she studied the blade of her unusual knife, which appeared to have a dagger-like tip and a handle that resembled brass knuckles. He recognized it as a rare British fighting knife from World War II called a BC-41. That was an interesting and telling detail about his little Italian spy. Plus, he couldn't help wondering where she'd had it hidden on her.

"Schönbrunn Palace on the left," said the woman in the front. "We are in Hietzing."

"Of course," Ms. Fiore said. "The imperial district with its gardens and villas."

Something in Ms. Fiore's tone made Miró wonder what exactly she knew about Mihàil. He'd make it a point to find out. It was vital to protect their base of operations in Vienna, which was currently listed as for sale by a luxury Vienna realtor when it was in reality owned by a shell company of Mihàil's. Mihàil had just had a large underground garage installed under the garden and plans had been drawn up for a rooftop addition, so it would be too bad to have to abandon it.

András's gaze met his in the rearview mirror. Miró nodded.

In the next instant, Andràs and Miró emitted blinding white light and a harmonic sound storm that enveloped the interior of the luxury SUV in angelic white noise. Only an angel or the most powerful *Elioud* could withstand its disorienting effects. Both women slumped in their seats, their heads in their hands for the rest of the short drive. Neither would have any sense of time passing or in which direction they'd headed. It was such a powerful angelic weapon that Miró regretted the need to use it. Both women would be dizzy and vulnerable, something he hated. Beyond that, he and Andràs would have a splitting headache, a hollow stomach, and crushing fatigue for a day—not ideal in a hostile environment with Asmodeus and his *bogomili* grunts popping up and spiking people.

At the gated entrance to Mihàil's imperial mansion, Miró stopped to enter the code, at the same time adjusting his harmonics and nimbus until he again appeared as a normal human. András waited until the garage door slid shut behind them before doing so himself. As Miró pulled into a spot closest to the stairs, Ms. Fiore moaned. The tall silent woman sat upright and stiff. Miró shut the SUV's engine off and turned in his seat.

"Forgive us. Herr Kastrioti prefers to keep the exact location of his residence a mystery." He paused before adding in apology, his own voice strained a little, "For that reason, certain measures have been taken to prevent identification of the building even from the inside."

"What are you?" Ms. Fiore whispered. He could feel her piercing gaze on him through her hood. In that moment, Miró couldn't prevaricate.

"*Elioud*. Descendants of angels and humans."

Andràs, serious for once, added, "Just like you two."

Asmodeus watched as the Porsche Cayenne SUV disappeared inside the gated entrance. He'd been expecting that his acolyte's little stunt with the terrorists would fail to trap the *drangùe*, but his acolyte had to learn some humility, so he hadn't interfered. Plus, the fiasco had afforded him the opportunity to observe the *drangùe* and his team undetected. And what he'd seen had been more than worth the aggravation. Two more Wild *Elioud* had appeared to disrupt the *drangùe*'s extraction, something so unheard of that he found himself astonished for the first time in eons. To be sure, Asmodeus rather regretted giving his acolyte so much leeway. The man's ham-handedness would make his future efforts at deception more complicated. Still, he relished a challenge, and the possibility of turning a trio of Wild *Elioud* into a trio of Dark *Elioud* who would follow his direction sent him into a demonic euphoria.

Even better, he'd seen the angelic white noise, which had radiated through the dark night like a beacon. Not only hadn't he been affected, it had led him to the *drangùe*'s hidden lair. Though he couldn't penetrate its defenses, it was more than enough to know where his enemy hid himself, especially now that his two underlings had the "angelic flu."

Asmodeus knew just what to do to exploit that fortuitous opportunity.

TEN

Olivia wasn't surprised when Mihàil's driver pulled up to a security gate at the end of their drive, although the well-lit underground garage took her aback somewhat. There were spots for a dozen cars, yet she could have sworn that they'd entered a residential driveway. Pjetër parked next to a single white Porsche Cayenne near an entrance to stairs. Olivia opened her door and jumped out to wait, her arms crossed at the waist. Her bare soles protested at the cold, rough concrete, but she relished their sensitivity and the alertness it brought.

Mihàil came around the rear of the Mercedes, a scowl darkening his handsome face. He said nothing, but when Pjetër got out of the driver's seat, he had a pair of men's socks, which he held out to her. Olivia had the oddest sensation that Mihàil could communicate telepathically with the taciturn man. She decided to pay attention to see whether she noticed other instances that supported that outlandish theory.

Why not? she asked herself. *What's telepathy when you can roast someone alive?*

Snatching the socks, she bent to pull them on when she caught sight of blood on the snowy white material on Mihàil's forearm. She stifled a sharp cry, but he dropped to one knee and wrapped his warm hand around her calf before leaning over to examine her foot.

"Not me," she said in a soft voice. She plucked at his shirt. "You."

He glanced at his arm and dismissed it. "I am fine." He stood and took her hand. "Let us go inside. The others are waiting."

She sunk her weight into her heels, though she was certain that he could drag her up the stairs whether she cooperated or not. "No. Let me see it."

Shrugging, he held his arm out. Olivia plucked at the torn sleeve, which was stiff with dried blood. Given the amount of blood and the length of the cut, she expected to see a bone-exposing gash. Instead, a thin, pink scar ran through the rusty brown on his skin. She ran a fingertip along the line in disbelief, and then, without thinking, raised her finger to the almost-invisible line over her eyebrow.

"Yes," he said close to her ear. "I heal quickly."

While she tried to take his words in, he slipped his hand around hers and pulled her up the stairs. His bulk blocked most of her view, but Olivia felt that something else affected her senses as he led her into the interior of his home. They walked through a number of rooms and long corridors, too many to suit a typical Viennese home, but she hadn't expected a European playboy to live modestly. The ceilings were high and the walls a pristine white, while the décor ran toward the modern with uncomfortable-looking steel frames and firm cushions in solid colors. Frankly, it looked like something in a high-end architectural magazine, impersonal and cold. It didn't suit him at all.

Mihàil strode up wide marble stairs with an ornate railing before leading her down a hall to a bedroom. Inside there was a king-size bed with a snowy duvet and plump pillows. The dresser and nightstand were black and silver. A large framed photograph of a single red rose dominated the wall above the bed while large floor-to-ceiling windows promised a light-filled room during the day. Several lamps around the room glowed warmly, softening the hard lines and planes of the furnishings.

Mihàil gestured toward some clothing laid out on the bed. "No doubt you would prefer to change out of your evening wear into something more comfortable." He waved toward a door in the far corner of the bedroom. "If you would like to freshen up, there are towels and toiletries in the bathroom. I would like to gather everyone in forty-five minutes, provided you are not too exhausted."

Olivia had stepped toward the bed to examine the long-sleeved shirt and loose trousers there. Both were plain black and made from a soft, stretchy fabric. While the material and color were understated, the weight, cut, and stitching proved to be extremely high quality. All at once Olivia couldn't wait to strip the form-fitting dress from her sweaty, tired body. She gathered the shirt to her chest

and turned to Mihàil, wondering as she did whether the clothing had belonged to the last supermodel that he'd dated. A sharp pang pierced her at
the thought.

"Thank you. I'd love a hot shower before we meet. How will I find you?"

"No need. Simply press this button on the intercom to call Pjetër, who will
escort you."

She nodded and shut the door after him. Somehow the room seemed to
expand and echo with the loss of his presence. Glancing around, she sighed
and headed toward the bathroom. After she flicked on the light switch,
she caught sight of her appearance in the ceiling-to-counter mirror on the
opposite wall. What a fright! Her blond hair had slipped from the chignon in
wide, tangled strands, and her mascara and eye liner had smeared so that she
looked like a drunken college co-ed after a night of clubbing. As she stepped
into the room, something flashed on her breast. Taking her St. Michael medal
between her thumb and forefinger, she rubbed it. The embossed edges of the
engraving consoled her.

Straightening her shoulders, she reached to pull out the pins holding up the
remaining hair strands that stuck out from the back of her head like a rooster's
tail. In moments she was undressed and under an incredibly hot shower that
eased her sore muscles with its vigorous spray. In the steamy heat, the rose
scent of the luxurious shower gel relaxed her even further. As the delicate
freesia of the shampoo mingled with the rose, she couldn't help noticing the
similarity to her favorite perfume. She wondered if that was a coincidence. No
matter. It felt delightful to suds her long hair and massage her tense scalp.

Again the thought of Fagan's actions sent her into an angry paroxysm. A
field officer was dead because of him. And she still didn't understand what he'd
hoped to accomplish. She'd barely started to interact with Mihàil, let alone get
close enough to link him to the Krasniqi mafia. She'd bet dollars to donuts that
Fagan's arrogance had led him to act when the terrorist attack intersected with
her efforts at cultivating Mihàil. A risky proposition even when all field officers
are read in on a pop-up op. A nigh-impossible scenario when the lead officer
hasn't been. Well, the man might not be used to having his field officers question

his leadership, but as soon as she got back for a debriefing that was in fact what she was going to do.

Half an hour later, Olivia stood in front of the mirror dressed in fresh clothes. Mihàil must have a type because they fit her like a dream, not too loose and not too tight. A pair of soft shoes, somewhere between a slipper and a slide, had been left at the foot of the bed. Now all that remained for the recovery of her previously neat appearance was for her to comb and braid her hair. As she wove the damp strands, her gaze strayed to the knife sheath on the counter. She could wear it around her thigh, but it would be less easily accessed under the loose pants than it had been under her cocktail dress.

Snapping the hairband she'd found in a vanity drawer around the end of her braid, Olivia snatched the sheath up and wrapped it instead around her lower leg, adjusting it until it was snug. She was surprised, frankly, that Mihàil hadn't confiscated it. She wondered if Beta and Stasia had been allowed to keep their weapons as well. Patting the braid to make sure that no loose hairs strayed outside its confines, Olivia went to the intercom.

Moments after she'd pressed the button, Pjetër knocked on her door. He nodded and led her toward a different staircase than the one that Mihàil had led her up. As any seasoned operative knows, situational awareness included careful observation, so Olivia began building a mental map of her unfamiliar surroundings. Try as she might, however, the white walls and dark wood floors blurred into confusing anonymity. Shaking her head to clear it, she thought she heard the faint tinkling of glass chimes. A mirage of prismatic color wavered at the periphery of her vision, but when she turned her head, all she saw was sterile white.

Bemused, she almost ran into Pjetër when he stopped outside the doorway to a large room. An impressionistic painting of gold-and-green framed with a heavy ornate frame dominated the far wall. It was the only thing with any color. White molded chairs with steel frames surrounded the long glass table in the center of the room. At the far end, Stasia sat, her chair tilted away from the table and one leg crossed over the other. The top foot swung in angry anxiety. Beta, on the other hand, leaned one shoulder into the corner behind Stasia, her arms folded. Hers was the stillness of vigilance. Both of her friends still wore their *zentai* hoods, which meant that Mihàil and his friends hadn't forced them to reveal their identities.

Next to the painting slouched a giant of a man in t-shirt, jeans, and combat boots, his arms crossed across his massive chest. Given his size and clothing, he could be none other than Beta's finger-kissing interloper at the Stadtpark. His mop of brown hair and boyish dimples looked nothing like the Eastern European gang member that Beta had described. He smiled and gave a little salute as she stepped into the room.

Seated nearest to her was a man in a dark suit with black hair graying at the temples. Next to the slouching giant, this man seemed nondescript until he looked at her. The cold fire in his intelligent blue eyes gave the lie to any ordinariness.

And at the head of the table sat Mihàil, darkly magnetic, his hands folded in his lap as he leaned back in his chair. He'd also showered and changed, though he'd left dark stubble on his cheeks and chin. Instead of the familiar suit, he now wore a blue-gray Henley shirt whose top two buttons were undone and the sleeves shoved up above his elbows. Despite the situation and her usual self-control, she noticed how well the knit material conformed to his broad shoulders and muscular chest and arms. She felt her heartbeat grow painfully erratic.

He looked at her, his gaze distant and reserved. Nodding at a chair next to him, he said, "If you will take a seat, we will talk while Pjetër brings food."

Olivia ignored his nod and strode to the chair next to Stasia. Seating herself, she tried to think about how to signal Beta about their weapons. Thinking clearly turned out to be more difficult than usual, however. Her fingers found her St. Michael medal of their own volition.

Mihàil's gaze remained enigmatic.

Olivia cleared her throat but said nothing.

For several moments, no one else said anything either. Tension rose until Mihàil said softly, "Enough."

The atmosphere in the room lightened so noticeably that Olivia was certain the lights had also brightened.

Mihàil sighed and pinched the bridge of his nose. Then he looked up again, directing his gaze at Olivia. "Olivia, there is no good way to lead you to this. Perhaps the best place to start is to ask you about that pendant you wear."

Olivia's thumb and forefinger ceased rubbing the sterling silver disc. She could see no reason why it mattered, one way or the other, so she answered, "It's a St. Michael medal."

"Do you believe?"

"It's complicated."

He sighed again. "So is what I am about to tell you. What do you know about St. Michael?"

She shook her head. "Not much. I wasn't raised in any church."

The slouching giant stood up, alert now. The man in the dark suit leaned toward her, his brilliant eyes flaring brighter. Both of her friends had stilled. She could feel their concentrated focus on her. They'd never asked about the medal before, and she'd never told them anything.

Mihàil tilted his head. "Then why do you wear it?"

Olivia shrugged. "I don't know exactly. I had a friend who had one. He was Catholic." She stopped. The reason she'd started wearing this medal touched a deeply buried nerve. Swallowing, she went on, "I–I was attracted to it on some level. I just felt as though I had to have one, so I got it."

"Was that all?" he asked, his voice soft and knowing.

"Like what?" she asked, bewildered.

"It has been blessed," he said gently. "You had it blessed."

"How did you know that?" she asked, her confusion growing.

"We can see the blessing." Mihàil nodded to include his friends.

"You can?" she asked. She let her skepticism color her voice. "How?"

"The same way we can raise body temperature until combustion."

Olivia flinched. Of course, she'd known he'd say that.

Mihàil leaned forward now, placing his forearms on the table in front of him. "You did not choose that medal. You were meant to have that medal because St. Michael has chosen you."

Olivia frowned. "You talk as though he's real, not some dead saint who lived hundreds, maybe thousands, of years ago."

"He *is* alive," Mihàil said. She heard the conviction in his voice. "The truth is that St. Michael is no saint. He is an archangel, meaning he holds the highest angelic rank. In his case, he is also the first among equals. There are other archangels, but St. Michael leads the angelic army against Satan and his demons. He is also the Chief Justice of the Supreme Council of the Heavenly Court. He is the patron of soldiers, police officers, and doctors. Believers call on him when facing lethal enemies, like the ones you faced in your harlequin hood."

Olivia sat up at that. Blinking rapidly, she tried to think how she could have given herself away. Next to her, Stasia shifted in her seat. *Of course!* He'd guessed given Beta and Stasia's hoods.

"That would mean you were at the Stadtpark," she hissed. "Are you Asmodeus? One of St. Michael's 'lethal enemies'?"

Pandemonium broke out at her question. The giant shouted and took a step toward the table, his hands clenching into two meaty fists. The man in the suit stood, his blue eyes flashing. Then Beta leaped onto the giant, her chain whip wrapped around his throat while Stasia sprang from her chair, vaulted onto the table in a single bound, and dove for the man in the suit, a knife in her hand. He managed to step aside, but her blade sliced along the back of his upper arm, drawing a hoarse shout from him. Clearly her friends still had their weapons.

Mihàil hadn't moved from his seat, although his eyes narrowed and his fingers dug into the surface of the table. She thought she smelled smoke in the room, whose temperature seemed to have risen twenty degrees. Coughing, she felt tears spring to her eyes. Reverberation shook the air and then a thunderous clap sent Beta and Stasia tumbling while the two men they'd attacked fell back, the giant choking and tugging at the chain whip still wrapped around his neck and the man in the suit holding his arm pressed to his chest, his face pale and the fire gone from his gaze.

Mihàil closed his eyes. Silence reigned in the room for several moments. Olivia dragged in heavy breaths, her heart and mind racing. What the hell had just happened there?

At last he looked at the man in the suit. "This too shall pass." Then he looked at Olivia, and there was such stark pain in his gaze that she flinched. "You asked me that once before. No, I am most definitely not Asmodeus."

Olivia's ears rang, and she felt dizzy.

"You're mortal enemies," she whispered, her gaze locked with his.

She'd thought he was human.

She'd wanted him to be human, needed him to be flawed, perhaps even bad, so that she could take him down, take him out, rid the world of another predator, and save innocents along the way. All while protecting her heart.

She hadn't wanted to believe he was an angel.

Mihàil.

She didn't want to say it aloud because it sounded so stupid, so absolutely ridiculous. But it came out anyway.

"Michael. You're the Archangel Michael." Her voice shook.

"No." He shook his head. "I am exactly who you think I am: Mihàil Kastrioti, son of Gjergj Kastrioti, the Dragon of Albania."

"Gjergj Kastrioti?" she asked, confused. "The one who died in 1468?" At his steady gaze, she went on, "But that's impossible. That would make you more than 500 years old."

"Five hundred seventy to be precise."

Olivia put her fingers up to her temples. A sharp pain had started behind her right eye and a tic jerked her left lid. "How can that be?"

"He's a *drangùe*," the giant said. "A dragon man."

"What exactly is a *drangùe*?" Olivia asked.

It was Beta who answered.

"The son of a dragon and a woman." When everyone turned to look at her, she shrugged. "Many Slavic heroes are said to have been sired by a *zmaj*, a dragon. That is why they were so strong and wise."

"That sounds like a legend." Olivia turned to Mihàil. "By all accounts, Gjergj Kastrioti was a man, not a dragon. And he died at 63. Of malaria."

"Yes." Mihàil nodded. "He had always been so hale, so robust, but at the end, he was frail. Even so, he was not just 'a man.' He had the blood of the *Irim* in him."

Olivia sat up at that. "The blood of the *Irim*? Are you a friend of Zophie's?"

A pointed look passed between Mihàil and his two friends.

Mihàil turned his gaze back on Olivia. "You have met Zophie?"

Olivia heaved an exasperated sigh. She still had no idea what was going on. "Yes." She leaned toward him. "She told me she'd sent a friend to help me at the Stadtpark. I take it that's you?"

"In a manner of speaking. What else did she say?"

"That I should ask you to explain the *Irim* and the *Elioud*. What are they and what do they have to do with you?"

"The *Irim* were the angels assigned to watch over humanity before the Flood. Unfortunately, they fell in love with their wards and came to live on Earth, marrying them. Their children were the *Nephilim*, a race of giants. Some also shared forbidden knowledge. As a result, the Lord Most High sent the Flood to destroy the *Nephilim*, but by then the *Nephilim* had intermarried with humanity, and their descendants became the *Elioud*."

Olivia shook her head. His words rang with truth, but she still couldn't accept them. Before she could formulate a thought, however, Stasia took a step forward and addressed Mihàil.

"According to your friend there," she jerked her head toward the one that she'd cut, "they are *Elioud*."

Mihàil inclined his head. "They are. As am I."

"He said that Beta and I are *Elioud*, too."

"You are." He turned to Olivia. "And so are you, Olivia."

In the silence following his words, Pjetër entered the room carrying a large tray. Behind him came a young man pushing a large cart. By unspoken consent, they waited while Mihàil's staff set food and drinks on the table. Although Olivia had believed herself too tense to eat, a familiar scent caused her stomach to growl. Startled, she threw a glance at Mihàil, whose face wore an expression that she couldn't read.

"New England clam chowder?" she asked him. Its existence in a suburb of Vienna in the home of a wealthy Albanian being surveilled by the CIA was too much. She sat back, stunned and defeated.

Mihàil stood, came to her side, and brought a china tureen closer before ladling some of the rich, creamy soup into the bowl in front of her. "It is your favorite, is it not, Olivia?"

She looked at him, feeling like a lost little girl. "How did you know? Can you read minds too?"

He laughed. "No. Zophie told me. She said that it would make you feel better to eat something you love while hearing such fabulous tales. That and I am to give you *sachertorte* for dessert because chocolate cures many blows to the psyche."

Olivia grasped her pendant before she realized what she was doing and dropped her hand into her lap. "How did she know that clam chowder is my favorite?"

"Zophiel is one of Michael's emissaries," he said and stood back. "She knows everything about you and your friends." He gestured toward Beta and Stasia, who stood looking down at their place settings where hot food steamed. "Please, ladies, remove your hoods. You've taken a large blow to your psyche as well. The dizziness and headache will pass with time. Eating will speed up your healing."

At his words, Olivia narrowed her eyes. That's when she noticed Stasia's white knuckles on the back of the chair in front of her, her feet spread wide as though on the rolling deck of a ship. Beta, always so tall and proud, had an unusual stiffness in her neck. Had something happened to them on their way here? Then her stomach growled again into the tense air. All at once, the giant threw his head back and laughed, and Olivia joined him. Deliberately picking her spoon up, she dipped it into her bowl and took a bite.

"Stasia, Beta, please sit down," she said after swallowing. "We might as well eat. I doubt that Mihàil plans to poison us." She looked at each of them in turn. "Plus, I'm pretty sure those are your favorite foods in front of you."

Stasia gave an exasperated sound and threw herself into a chair, simultaneously pulling her hood off. She glared around the room, her gaze lingering on the man whose arm she'd slashed, before she began eating with quick, dainty bites. Beta, on the other hand, stood a moment longer, her chain whip dangling from her hand. Slowly, she raised her free hand and tugged her hood over her glossy black curls. Then she laid the chain whip on the table, arranging it so that its links lay flat and the handle faced out, her dark, fathomless gaze focused on the room the whole time. She remained standing and began eating with her left hand. Olivia knew that she'd strike in an instant if she felt threatened.

Mihàil sat. He nodded and the other two men sat as well. "Where are my manners? I have forgotten to introduce my friends. That large Hungarian oaf is Andràs." Andràs grinned and then, wincing, rubbed at the bruises ringing his neck. "And next to me is Miró from Split in Croatia." Miró acknowledged them with an impassive nod, though his eyes narrowed slightly when he looked at Stasia. She held his gaze until he looked away.

Mihàil raised his wineglass. "Now that the introductions are made, we should celebrate the largest gathering of *Elioud* in three centuries."

"What does that mean?" Olivia asked.

She glanced at her friends. Beta had set down her fork and fixed her gaze on them. Stasia sat upright, one hand clutching the stem of her wineglass, the other in her lap. Olivia turned to look at Mihàil, whose eyes glittered.

"That depends on you. Asmodeus certainly knows about you, Olivia. It is only a matter of time before he finds Beta and Stasia, if he has not already. He will come after all of you. You should not face him without our help."

"Is he some kind of bad *Elioud*?"

"Worse," Mihàil said, his gaze grim. "He is a Dark *Irim*."

Miró spoke for the first time. "Asmodeus is a fallen angel who blames humanity for his sins."

ELEVEN

Early the next morning Stasia attacked the sandbag in Mihàil Kastri-oti's private gymnasium with ferocity. She'd awakened to the gray of predawn, her mind in turmoil and her hands itching to pound something hard. She'd have given anything for a chance to punch that smug, digni-fied-looking Miró who'd barely flinched when she'd sliced his arm open the night before. Instead, she'd thrown the heavy duvet back and gotten up, stalking to the bathroom to throw cold water on her face. When she'd returned to the room, she'd pulled out all the drawers in the dresser and opened the closet to find a variety of clothing in her size, ranging from sports bras and panties to high-end athletic wear. A bit nonplussed at the quantity, she'd dressed in a black tank and leggings before cracking her door and easing outside into the hallway intending to find Olivia and Beta, who'd been escorted to rooms on the floor below hers.

Stasia had only gotten as far as the landing on the next floor when a silent man appeared in the hallway. She recognized him as Kastrioti's driver and the man directing the delivery of their meal the night before. She wondered if he was the one who'd purchased her clothes. He seemed the most likely choice, though perhaps there were other staff members on call for purchasing women's underwear. Kastrioti was a wealthy playboy, after all. Unbidden, Miró's face filled her mind's eye. She growled. He'd damned well better not be the one responsible for what she wore right now.

"Where are Olivia and Beta?" she asked in Albanian.

The man, whose age could have been anywhere from twenty-five to sixty-five based on his piercing gaze and unlined skin, answered in Italian. "They are still sleeping, *signorina*. The master suggests that you use this time to work out in his gymnasium. He says that his punching bag will help you clear your thoughts."

Stasia blew out a loud, gusty breath as she pushed her hair back from her face, but it didn't help. Nodding, she said, "Show me the way."

That's how she found herself in the cavernous gymnasium, sweaty and determined as she practiced combinations, her taped fists flying and knuckles snapping against the worn leather. She'd prefer to swing her *surujin*, but that oaf had destroyed it.

"You should keep your guard higher," a low voice behind her advised in Italian. "You drop it when you uppercut."

Snarling, Stasia whirled as she launched a swift roundhouse kick at Miró's head. He caught it, though not quite in time. The side of her foot contacted his injured upper arm with a satisfying *thunk*. He winced but said nothing. She smiled.

"Not yet healed?" she asked, letting acid sharpen her tone. "What? Does your angel blood not heal you quickly?"

He kept her foot in his hand. "Normally, yes. However, last night's battle and the drive home have depressed my immunity a bit." He rubbed a thumb along her arch. "We call it the 'angelic flu.'"

Shivers ran up the back of her arms. Stasia ignored them. "You can let go of my foot now." She slipped her fingers into the grip of her fighting knife hidden in its sheath at her waist.

"First tell me what you know about Mihàil's Vienna residence."

"What makes you think I know anything?" She kept her gaze on his face, waiting for an opening.

"Something you said in the car on the way here. That and the fact that you work for Italian foreign intelligence. You are a spy, Anastasia Fiore."

Shock rippled through Stasia, but she pushed it aside as she pulled her knife free and slashed at his hand holding her foot. Instead of recoiling Miró caught her wrist with his free hand and tugged. Already on one foot, the move took her off balance, and she fell into his muscular chest, hard. Breathless, she looked up into Miró's icy-blue eyes and stopped struggling. Her view of the room contracted to the circumference of those penetrating irises.

"You really should stop trying to hurt me."

"Or what?"

He said nothing but dropped his gaze for an instant to her mouth. Prickles danced along the skin of Stasia's lower back and her stomach clenched.

"Or perhaps I will have to melt this too." He held her dagger up on his forefinger.

Porca vacca! How did he get that? Stasia lunged for the knife, but Miró swung it higher.

"Ah-ah. Tell me what you know about Mihàil's Vienna address."

Stasia growled and shoved back from him. He let her go. She backed out of reach and crossed her arms.

"Only that it is in Hietzing within a couple of kilometers of the palace and that a real-estate company holds the title."

Miró studied her a moment and then held her fighting knife out. She darted forward and snatched it, backing a step into a ready stance with the knife poised to defend against an attack. He didn't move. She drank in the details of his appearance, looking for a weakness. He wasn't as tall as Mihàil or András, but he towered over her nonetheless. This morning he wore a black t-shirt that hugged his broad shoulders and chiseled pectoral muscles so well that his abdominals promised exquisite definition. Stubble darkened his cheeks and jaw. The skin below his arctic eyes held a slightly purple tinge. He looked tired.

Stasia slid her fighting knife back into its sheath where its weight comforted her. Before she could walk away, Miró was right next to her, invading her space, seemingly without moving. Everything about him was unyielding and hot. So hot she could have sworn steam rose between them. Steam and sparks.

With a surprisingly light touch, he brushed her hair back. His fingers stroked her ear as they tucked the strand behind it. Stasia thought drunkenly that she should have grabbed a hairband to hold her hair out of her face. "Thank you."

Stasia blinked several times. "For what?" she finally managed to ask.

"For telling me the truth." He bent closer. His warm breath smelled sweet and rich like chocolate. "And for trusting me."

She swallowed, cleared her throat, and swallowed again before speaking. "*Prego.*"

Their gazes remained locked for a long moment until Stasia knew that he would kiss her. Inside her chest frantic butterflies fluttered against her ribcage, and her eyelids dipped as she raised her chin. Then Miró stepped back. Her eyes snapped open in time to see his gaze shutter.

He nodded. "I will let you return to your combinations, *signorina.*"

And then he'd gone. The temperature in the room plummeted.

Stasia shivered, shook herself, and then ducked her head and raised her fists. She stalked to the sandbag to pummel it until her heartrate and breathing had nothing to do with that infuriating man.

Olivia woke all at once in an unfamiliar, dim room, aware that she wasn't alone. Her training kept her from moving or even changing her breathing until she'd ascertained her situation. She became aware of the exceptional comfort of the mattress cushioning her. The heavy duvet, so white that it almost glowed in the faint light, cocooned her in smooth, soft cotton. The scent of fresh flowers hung on the air. She could pick out their shape on the nightstand and wondered if the dark blooms were Mihàil's roses. The faceted crystal vase had been waiting for her when she'd returned to the room last night. She'd fallen asleep dreaming of him, the *drangùe*. The dragon man.

A shadowy figure sat in a chair in the far corner. Although she couldn't make out her friend's features, her eyesight had improved enough for Olivia to recognize Beta's angular shoulders and alert posture.

"Did you sleep?" Her voice sounded rusty.

"A little." Beta stood and pulled the blinds back from the window, letting in the dawn.

The room faced the southwest. From the color of the sky, Olivia guessed that it was after 6 a.m. *Damn*. She was tired. Yawning, she sat up and stretched.

Beta turned. "They will be looking for you."

"I know."

"How much did you see?"

"Enough. Fagan sent me texts demanding that I report in as soon as I'm able. The longer I take the more questions I'll have to answer."

"How are you going to handle his suspicions of Kastrioti?"

Olivia's quiet laugh held no humor. "Suspicions?" She ran her hand through her tangled hair. "I have some of my own questions for Fagan."

Beta leaned forward. "Such as?"

"Why he sent an operative to kill me."

Beta hissed. "What?"

Olivia nodded. "There was an operative on the balcony overlooking the Rathausplatz when I got there. He was going to kill me, but Miró incinerated him."

Beta shook her head. The room had lightened enough for Olivia to see her friend's confusion. "Incinerated?"

"Grabbed and held onto him until flames erupted from every inch of skin. He was ashes in a matter of moments." Olivia flung the duvet back and stood. She needed to get dressed. "There were other operatives on the square before the attack. Fagan knew it was coming and didn't warn me."

Beta ran a hand down her face. She looked visibly shaken. Olivia saw her struggle to regain her usual unreadable demeanor. After a minute, she said, "You are a throwaway."

"Looks that way." Olivia pulled slacks and a short-sleeved silk blouse from the closet. If she showed up at the substation this morning, she'd have to spin a story about waking to find herself at Vienna General without any memory of how she got there. She'd go in hot and aggressive to keep it believable. "Fagan's a slippery prick. I'll admit I saw the other operatives in the square and took out the terrorist, but I'll conveniently leave out seeing the operative spontaneously combust. Let's see if he mentions the body-shaped pile of ashes on the balcony."

Turning, she added, "Mihàil saw the CIA officers in the square. He read me well enough to know that I recognized them too."

Shadows again obscured Beta's features as the window brightened behind her. "Does Kastrioti suspect you?"

Olivia shook her head. "He seems to think the CIA has targeted me."

"Will you burn your cover with him?"

"That seems premature. He might be an angel hybrid, but by his own admission, these *Irim* and *Elioud* aren't all goodness and light. He only told us that he and Asmodeus are mortal enemies. Maybe they're rivals for criminal enterprise in Eastern Europe. Fagan's aggressive but careful. He must know more than he told me if he's willing to exploit a terrorist attack on civilians and kill one of his best officers to get to Mihàil. No, as far as the dragon man is concerned, my secret identity is the harlequin from the Stadtpark."

Olivia rummaged through a drawer for trouser socks before turning to the array of shoes on a rack in the closet. Crying out, she reached down for one that snagged her gaze. She'd forgotten about leaving her Louboutin heels on a table at the Rathausplatz until just now. These were a different pair by that designer, lower-heeled and less dangerously sexy, but seeing the familiar red sole made tears prick her eyes.

"Is something wrong?"

Blinking hard, Olivia shook her head and bent to slip the shoes on. Straightening, she turned. "Come with me. I have a feeling I'll need help getting out of here."

Beta narrowed her eyes but didn't comment. Instead, she placed a firm hand on Olivia's forearm. "Liv, something happened last night." She paused, looking pained. "I do not know how we got here."

Olivia searched her friend's face. "Does this have something to do with the 'large blow to the psyche' that Mihàil mentioned?"

Beta nodded. Her dark eyes had a grave expression. "I made the mistake of telling Stasia that I saw Schönbrunn Palace and that we had entered Hietzing. She said 'of course' in a way that made it clear that she was not surprised. In the next moment, this blinding white noise enveloped me. When it stopped, we were in the underground garage, and I had a terrible headache. My neck still hurts. I think that it was the same for her."

Olivia put her hand on top of Beta's. "Don't beat yourself up."

Beta scowled. "It *will not* happen again." Her gaze challenged Olivia to argue with her. "Also, that cool one—Miró—said that 'certain measures' were in place to keep us from identifying this residence."

"Ah. That explains it."

"What?"

"I had trouble getting my bearings last night. Every time I tried to look at the walls or count stairs or doors, everything blurred together. My peripheral vision wavered, and I heard chimes." She laughed. "I thought I was just in shock."

Beta shook her head. "My head hurt so much last night that it took all of my concentration to put one foot in front of the other. What are you going to do if it happens again?"

Something that Beta said struck Olivia. She remembered that she'd twice made very intimidating men blink by refusing to back down. In fact, she'd always been very successful when imposing her will to master new situations and skills. Given Mihàil's supernatural powers, perhaps her own angel blood had something to do with that. Last night Mihàil had said that he planned to teach them more about their angelic nature and help them discover and use the gifts that they each had. Maybe angelic powers were like any other natural abilities: one could use them without even being aware that she did. The thought made her smile.

Beta frowned. "Why are you smiling?"

"I'm simply going to put my mind to finding the front door, and then I'm going to walk right out of it."

Forty-five minutes later, Mihàil knocked on Olivia's bedroom door. It was still early, and he'd hoped that she'd sleep longer after last night's events and revelations, but he'd made a mental sweep of her room a few minutes ago and found it cold and empty. As he knocked, he tested the bathroom on the far side of the bedroom for her infrared signature. The room was warm with human-sized heat concentrated in the shower, so he shrugged and turned toward the stairs. He'd instruct Pjetër to bring her to the breakfast room when she'd finished dressing.

He'd poured a second cup of coffee from the carafe on the sideboard when something niggled at the back of his mind. Something about the infrared signature in the shower...its size and shape and even the particular color of the heat resonance...it wasn't Olivia's. Too tall, too thin, and the white-hot core itself was razor-thin and buffered in a much cooler concentric band of purple-red. Beta had been in Olivia's shower. Why?

Quickly he scanned the mansion room by room and floor by floor. In the gymnasium he read the fuzzy infrared signature of a short sweaty woman whose heat evaporated from her outer edges. It was Stasia, whom he'd had Pjetër escort there an hour earlier. From the location and collapsed form of the signature, she sat on a low bench near the weights, bent over. Strangely, her white-hot core radiated at both chest and groin level. He shook his head. He didn't want to speculate about why she found her workout sexually stimulating. He'd lived long enough to know that the female body operated by its own rules. It was none of his business, even if he couldn't help recognizing it. Shoving the revelation aside, he promptly forgot it.

Next he found András in the TV room on the sectional sofa. Likely he was flipping moodily through the satellite stations as he tried to recover from his angelic flu. Although he was a large man or perhaps because of it, he suffered the most even though he had almost as much angelic blood as Mihàil, who was three-quarters *Irim*. Then again, it didn't help that Andràs acted as though he were impervious to bullets and knives, always taking more than his share during battle. He would be recuperating for most of the day. Miró, who conserved his angelic energy by nature, was in the situation room. Though he'd drained his reserves, Miró's mind remained clear enough to focus on his usual cerebral tasks. By his placement and posture, he sat at one of the desks where he could review the camera feeds periodically while working at his laptop gathering intelligence for their operations. In the kitchen, Mihàil found the larger and less dense infrared signature of the housekeeper and cook, who suffered from asthma and diabetes. Though her whole signature was warm red, she had no white-hot core and her hands and feet were an unhealthy blue. Pjetër's familiar signature appeared in Mihàil's study along with that of the young Viennese man that Pjetër had hired to help. Nowhere did Mihàil find Olivia's signature, not even in the pantry. She was gone.

Mihàil's temperature dropped as he realized what that meant. Olivia had left the protective sanctuary of his house, and he had no idea how long she'd been gone. The thought of her alone, without even her friends, chilled him to the core. She had no idea what Asmodeus was or what he could do. It had taken Mihàil only two days to confirm her identity as the harlequin. Asmodeus couldn't be far behind. In fact, it would be just like Asmodeus to instigate a terrorist attack as his latest salvo against Mihàil, who was bound as a *drangùe* to intercede to save human lives. If Asmodeus had seen Olivia in action at the festival, he'd have no doubt who she was. Or that she was with Mihàil.

Mihàil didn't have any time to waste.

Pjetër. He waited a moment before mentally commanding Stasia and Beta to come to the breakfast room. Though he typically relied on his *Elioud* charm to motivate others, in extreme circumstances such as these his will was unopposable by anyone short of a full-blooded *Irim*.

Five minutes later, his retainer appeared in the doorway. "Yes, my lord?"

"Olivia has left the residence, and I have no idea when. Take the car and head toward her flat. I doubt that she has gone there, but you can let yourself in and have a look around for clues."

Pjetër inclined his head. As he turned to leave, Stasia staggered into the room with her hands at her temples. She looked angry—and terrified. Mihàil regretted her terror, but he had no choice. He helped her to sit before kneeling and looking into her eyes.

"When did she leave?" He kept his voice low, but power reverberated in the room.

Confusion contorted Stasia's features. "What? Who are you talking about?"

"Olivia. She is gone. When did she leave?"

Stasia rubbed at her temples. "She is gone?"

"You have not spoken to her this morning?"

"No." The pain of his summons had obviously diminished because she straightened. As she did, her eyes flashed. She gestured with her taped hands at her clothes. "I was in your gym punching my frustration into your sandbag as you well know. Ask that *cretino*, Miró. He was there about twenty minutes ago."

"You have been in the gymnasium the whole time?"

"She does not know when Olivia left. I do."

Mihàil swiveled on his haunches. Beta stood just inside the doorway holding her chain whip and looking as cool as her infrared signature suggested that she was. Heat still radiated from her neck muscles, but she'd drawn most of its energy into her razor-thin core. Although she was relaxed, Mihàil wasn't fooled. She could transfer that energy instantly into action. Of the three Wild *Elioud*, she was by far the most dangerous. And that was saying something.

"When was that?" he said, clenching his back teeth against his mounting frustration and worry.

"You are unaware?" He couldn't read her expression, but he suspected that she found his lack of knowledge amusing. She'd also tuck it away for the future no doubt.

"This is not a game, Beta. If Asmodeus finds her before I do, she will not be able to withstand him."

"If Olivia does not want to be found, he will not find her."

Mihàil stood. He resisted projecting power to appear more intimidating. Now was not the time to harden Beta's resolve against him. "I have no doubt that Olivia can hide from humans. She can even, with training, elude most *Elioud*. She cannot hide from an *Irim*. Asmodeus can see her angelic essence. He knew what she was that night in the Stadtpark. If I had not intervened, he would have killed her or worse. Need I remind you that he and I are mortal enemies? He could have caused the terrorist attack to get at me. If so he will have seen her with me."

"Does he know that you live here?" Stasia's sharp tone drew Mihàil's gaze.

"Almost certainly. When we disoriented you with angelic white noise, it would have attracted his notice." Miró had entered the room without the women noticing. They both started and looked at him. He carried a short carved staff in a belted sheath. "That was the risk we took in using it." He handed the staff to Mihàil, who slipped it over his head so that the sheath hung on his back.

Stasia and Beta shared a glance.

The whites of Stasia's eyes grew more prominent. "Will Asmodeus come here?"

"No." It was Beta, who took a step toward Mihàil. "He cannot penetrate your defenses, can he?"

"No. As long as you stay inside my home, you are safe." Mihàil raked his hand through his hair. "How long, Beta? Where did Olivia go?"

Beta eyed him a moment longer, her left hand stroking the heavy dart at the end of her chain whip, which she still held with a relaxed wrist. Then she seemed to decide something.

"She left almost half an hour ago. Where she was headed, I am unsure. The Landstrasse district, I think." She shared a look with Stasia that Mihàil couldn't decipher.

"Not her flat?" he asked to be sure, forcing himself to take the time to get as much information as he could even though panic rose inside him at Beta's words. *Half an hour*. St. Michael, let him not be too late. "Or the University of Vienna? The offices for ABA-Invest Austria?"

Beta shook her head.

"We do not know all of Olivia's connections," Stasia said as she darted a glance at Miró. "When we formed our trio, we promised to respect each other's privacy."

Mihàil nodded. She was holding something back, but he didn't have time to press for more. He turned to Miró. "Let me know if you hear or see anything."

Miró nodded, but his gaze shone with concern and guilt. Understanding passed between them. Miró blamed himself for not being in the situation room when she left. And Asmodeus would use Olivia as bait to try and trap Mihàil.

As both *Elioud* warriors turned to leave, Stasia grabbed Miró by the arm. "Wait! Where are you going? We have to find Olivia!"

Mihàil left the breakfast room without a backward glance. Miró would remain in the situation room and update him as necessary as well as keep Beta and Stasia under watch. He heard his lieutenant answer as he raced downstairs to the mansion's front entrance.

"We must remain here, I am afraid, Ms. Fiore," he said, anguish coloring his quiet voice. "He will find her. Alive or not."

TWELVE

T en minutes later, Mihàil approached the southwest corner of Landstrasse, Vienna's third district, on foot. He'd run the entire way in half
the time that he could have driven it. Shortly after, Miró's voice sounded in
his ear via an invisible earwig, something they'd adopted for fighting among
humans when out of range mentally. Sometimes Mihàil marveled at the human
ingenuity that mimicked the gifts of angels—without illicit help from fallen
Irim. All too often, however, that ingenuity served evil purposes.

"*Polizei* have been dispatched to the main Belvedere Gardens near the Upper
Palace. A witness reported seeing a woman there fighting off a gang of men,
including shooting one. None of the men has fled or paid any attention to other
people except to knock one would-be rescuer unconscious."

"*Bogomili*," Mihàil swore.

He hated *bogomili* and all humans of their type. After the Flood, Asmodeus
and other Dark *Irim* had been left to wander the world to tempt susceptible humans. The most receptive became minions, willingly giving up their immortal
souls to become brain-dead puppets. The latest group belonging to Asmodeus
called themselves *bogomili*, killers who enabled the Dark *Irim* to circumvent
the prohibition against taking human life. In controlling humans, Asmodeus
gained greater agency in the world. But there was a steep cost. Every minion
sapped Asmodeus's angelic strength. And every minion made him vulnerable:
each one could be used against him. That's why *bogomili* fought to the death.
Asmodeus couldn't afford to let them live under someone else's control.

His lips pulled back in a humorless grin. As the Dark *Irim* had unknowingly
done with the surviving *bogomili* at St. Elizabeth's. Thanks to Miró's quick

intervention, the creature's harmonic signature had been masked. Asmodeus would have to focus on him to realize that he still lived.

Calling on his eidetic memory, Mihàil reviewed a mental map of Vienna. The Belvedere, a Baroque complex set in a park on the southwest corner of the Landstrasse, featured beautiful gardens designed after those in Versailles. The three large terraces of the main garden linked the Upper and Lower Belvedere palaces. Graveled walks through symmetrical beds with fountains, sculptures, clipped hedges, and small waterfalls offered a view of Vienna's Old Town to the north. That's when Mihàil realized that the recent attacks clustered around a distinct geographic area.

That was very interesting. It suggested that Asmodeus had an acolyte.

Only the most devoted humans became acolytes. They retained an ability to think, plan, and promote their chosen mentors while blending in with the rest of humanity, though perhaps a bit more selfish, a bit more grasping, and a bit more brutal. They were powerful, though unpredictable, agents for Dark *Irim* who didn't weaken the angelic strength of their mentors. *Elioud*, with the blood of the *Irim* running through their veins, made the most powerful acolytes of all. That was why Wild *Elioud*, lost descendants of the *Irim* who didn't know that they had angelic blood, like Olivia, Beta, and Stasia, were both vulnerable and prized.

Acolytes cost even more than minions, however. Asmodeus would be psychically and physically bound to his acolyte, effectively hobbling his movement. He couldn't go beyond a tight radius without suffering from angelic flu. Should his acolyte die before he could sever the bond, Asmodeus would be tied to the mortal remains until they disintegrated. If he should be imprisoned or otherwise prevented from tormenting humanity, his chosen vocation on Earth, then his spirit would be ripped apart.

Asmodeus had overextended himself in his greed and arrogance. Again.

Miró realized it at the same time. Whistling, he said, "He found a new acolyte."

"I concur." Mihàil slowed as he neared the entrance just west of the Upper Palace. "I have arrived at the Belvedere. For the moment, I want you to work on identifying the acolyte."

Before he dispatched Asmodeus's acolyte, he'd make sure that the Dark *Irim* hadn't had time to sever his bond first. Then it would only be a matter of time before he could track down the weakened angel and capture him.

"Copy that."

Though it was still early, tourists and joggers clogged the paved area on the northern side of the palace. Most stood silent as they looked out over the nearest terrace. Mihàil slowed to a normal human pace and moved around them.

Two *bogomili* and a man sprawled on the near terrace, whose white gravel paths were spattered with blood. One *bogomili* pulled his useless legs behind him as he headed toward the middle terrace. Movement there caught Mihàil's attention. Moments later figures emerged from stairs hidden at the right side of the upper terrace.

Olivia sprinted, barefoot, toward the third terrace at the head of a pack of *bogomili*.

Mihàil shot after them, his temper rising at the sight of her torn blouse and slacks. By the color gradients of her frayed infrared signature, whose core had cooled to a warm orange, she'd already expended her energy reserves.

He caught up with her before she reached the stairs to the lowest terrace.

Olivia.

She glanced over her shoulder, a startled look on her face.

Mihàil pulled the staff from its sheath on his back and lobbed it to her.

She snatched it gracefully as it arced down, pivoting to meet the closest *bogomili* with a swing that sent him flying over the edge of the terrace.

Mihàil flashed a grin, but her gaze had honed in on the approaching *bogomili* as she planted her feet in a fighting stance, the staff in her right hand and a red-soled pump in the other. Sweat slicked her bruised face and long strands of blond hair haloed her head in the early morning sun. Her chest rose and fell as she sucked in air, yet fierce determination shone from her eyes. Mihàil's heart stuttered and then beat hard. She was excruciatingly beautiful.

He brought his attention to bear on Asmodeus's minions, who'd halted in a semi-circle around them. Bruised faces and dangling limbs did little to dim the evil light in their feral eyes. More than one held a *subulam*.

Wailing sirens approached from the south. It would all be over before the *polizei* could arrive.

Mihàil closed his eyes and deepened his breathing. Fiery breath filled his lungs and heat shimmered from the pads of his fingers and his palms. Opening his eyes, he glanced at Olivia, whose breathing had calmed. Her infrared signature had also smoothed out. White-hot energy flickered and caught in her chest. She looked over her shoulder at him and heat blurred the air between them.

Hidden sword, he flashed.

Her eyes widened and then she'd dropped her shoe to unscrew the sheath from the blade.

An instant later, *bogomili* swarmed over them.

The next few minutes blurred as flesh sizzled and combusted at his touch interspersed with screams and cracks and fleshy thunks. Through it all, Mihàil sensed Olivia's whirling and slashing infrared signature, her heartbeat loud in his ear. She let out a hoarse cry as a *subulam* sliced across her upper back, and he flinched, darting a glance at her only to feel the bitter cold point of another *subulam* as it plunged into the fleshy part of his neck between his spine and his shoulder before exiting below his clavicle. Roaring in rage and agony, Mihàil grabbed his attacker's chin with one hand and his shoulder with the other before twisting sharply and dropping the smoking body.

Then he fell to his knees as pain blurred his vision. His harsh breathing filled his ears, but his battle senses told him that no *bogomili* moved around him.

Blinking rapidly, Mihàil staggered upright, clawing at the *subulam* handle. Olivia stood in front of him among half a dozen bodies, her shoulders rising and falling. Her arms shook and dark sweat stained the valley of her spine. Blood dripped from the tip of the sword in her right hand.

A tall male wearing an expensive dark suit and sunglasses stood in front of Olivia, an arm around the waist of a young woman with long, straight hair who kept her gaze on the ground. Something in her posture and facial structure looked familiar.

"Ms. Markham." The man's voice held an indeterminate, cultured accent. He gestured toward the *bogomili* on the ground. "An impressive display."

"Who are you?"

"A friend." He smiled, showing dazzling teeth in the early morning sun. "I admire your devotion and your grit in defending the vulnerable such as this young woman." He tilted his head toward the woman next to him, gripping her chin with his free hand and appearing to study her. The woman gazed up at him with wide eyes but said nothing.

A warning tingle shot up Mihàil's neck.

Olivia stepped forward. "Yes?" she said in a soft voice. Mihàil heard the threat threading through it.

So did the suited man. He turned back to them, the corners of his mouth turning down. "There's no need to be so hostile, I assure you, Ms. Markham. I rescued this pretty one from these—" here he gestured at the fallen *bogomili* and made a disdainful sound. "Does she remind you of someone? A friend perhaps?"

At his words, the young woman looked back at them. Olivia's sharp intake of breath made the hairs stand up on the back of Mihàil's neck. All at once he knew who the tall man was.

Stumbling forward, he croaked, "Olivia, no!" Pain lanced around the *subulam*. Retching, he hunched over with his hands on his thighs. His ears began to ring and his vision to waver. For a moment he could do nothing but pant and claw at the handle of the cursed weapon poisoning him.

Olivia drew closer to the couple. "Emily?" Even in his sickened state, Mihàil could hear the confused hope in her voice.

"Yes, Ms. Markham, she resembles your dear Emily, doesn't she? She even has the same disfiguring bruises on her lovely neck. You can save this innocent, my dear."

Giving a cry, Olivia dropped the sword with a clang and took two steps closer. She reached out to touch the young woman as if to make sure that she was real.

As soon as she touched the other woman's forearm, the tall man placed a palm over her heart. The white-hot energy that had welled at Mihàil's arrival surged under the tall man's palm and her heartbeat lurched. Mihàil felt a corresponding drain in his own internal energy and his vision darkened.

"No!" he roared, staggering.

The tall man's head snapped up. Grinning through his vessel, Asmodeus flashed a message to Mihàil. *Already attached, dear boy? I would not have thought it possible in such a short time, though I must admit that she is indeed a rare find. How delightful! I could not have asked for a better end to our long rivalry.*

Mihàil ignored the Dark *Irim* and blocked out pain and weakness to focus. *Olivia.*

Her shoulders twitched, but she didn't turn around.

Olivia. Sunglasses.

For a moment Mihàil thought that she was far too entranced to respond. A terrifying cold seeped from the *subulam* into his chest. And then Olivia raised a shaking hand to knock the sunglasses from the tall man's face.

Brilliant angelic light blazed from his eyes. His corresponding smile was equally brilliant as he looked down at Olivia. "Ms. Markham," he crooned. "We were about to become the best of friends, but I daresay you need some more motivation now, don't you?"

A thin keening broke from the young woman's throat, and Olivia began struggling against the tall man's hand. Pain jabbed into Mihàil's chest, forcing a grunt from him. Dark streaks threatened to erase his view of Olivia's wide eyes. Raising a leaden arm, he managed to touch the *subulam* handle. He focused inward, shepherding his waning strength to shift his harmonics to match those of the Dark *Irim* weapon. He couldn't remove the tightly wedged *subulam*, and he no longer had the internal heat to melt it, but he could disrupt its power on a molecular level. Perhaps it would be enough.

"Here, stop that!" The tall man called in a sharp voice. The keening cut off abruptly and faint scuffling sounded in the periphery of Mihàil's hearing.

Mihàil ignored everything. The *subulam* began to vibrate in sync with his harmonics. Excruciating pain reverberated in his chest as it did. He blacked out.

From the corner of her eye, Olivia saw Mihàil slump to the ground. Icy cold radiated through her, but she'd felt it waver after Mihàil grabbed at the *subulam* lodged in his chest. The tall man took his blazing gaze from her to look over at Mihàil. Olivia reacted. Stiffening her fingers, she poked them into his eyes. He let out a scream, and then his eyes hissed and popped. Shocked, Olivia staggered back as steam rose from the tall man's eye sockets. Clear jelly dribbled down onto his cheeks. Shrieking, he clapped his hands to his face. The young woman fell to the ground, gibbering and writhing. All at once, the shrieking cut off and the tall man's body collapsed in upon itself like a deflated balloon and then flames erupted all along the flattened form.

Olivia looked down at her fingers. Though they appeared normal, heat shimmered from their tips.

She didn't have time to consider anything else. Her hearing, which had always been exceptional, now exceeded believable and told her that *polizei* streamed from cars and tactical vehicles on the far side of the Upper Palace. She'd rather not have to explain what had happened here. She wasn't really sure she could. And CIA officers avoided local authorities at all costs.

Pivoting, she snatched up the sword and ran to Mihàil. She had no time to find the baton sheath. She dropped to her knees next to the large Albanian, whose pallor shook her to the core. Scrabbling at the handle of the *subulam,* she tugged. It resisted and then pulled free, the metal elongating like taffy. Horrified, Olivia shoved the handle into the pocket of her slacks. Half of the blade remained inside Mihàil.

Shaking his shoulders, she commanded through a tight throat, "Kastrioti, get up!" He moaned and his eyelids fluttered. Beneath her hands, his skin felt unnaturally cold, sending terror through her. He'd radiated such commanding heat before.

"Mihàil," he whispered.

Olivia let out an exasperated sigh through gritted teeth. "Get up, Dragon Man."

His gaze held pained humor, but his lips were tinged purple. "Yes, my lady."

Rolling onto his side, he placed his palm on the terrace and, groaning, shoved himself to a seated position. Across the upper terrace, *polizei* began running around the end of the palace and into the bystanders clustered there.

Olivia threw a glance at them and then gripped Mihàil's cold hand.

Stand.

She pulled as he pushed, and then he was on his feet, and they were lumbering toward the stairs to the lower terrace and its quadruple hedge mazes. The ornamental gardens wouldn't hide them for long, especially from the helicopter that approached. But Olivia hoped that she'd lead them out of the maze into the tree cover to the west before they could be spotted from the air.

A rough shout came from the *polizei* on the upper terrace and pounding feet followed. Olivia ran, acutely aware of Mihàil's heartbeat and breathing and his lowered temperature. She wanted him warmer, damn it! Where their palms met, heat began to spread, and joy filled her like sunshine. His hand warmed and his heart steadied. Then they entered the maze and Olivia raced to the center before running toward the western corner and the exit. The helicopter was two minutes out. It would be close.

Her free hand strayed to her St. Michael medal. *Please.*

Then they'd reached the opening in the hedge. Darting a glance back, Olivia saw running figures carrying assault weapons about to enter the middle terrace. There was no way that they'd make it across the gravel pathway without being seen. Suddenly one of the officers in the front pulled up, and shouting, gestured to the east away from where Olivia and Mihàil stood. Olivia stood still, her breath held. Some of the officers broke away and jogged across the grass. The rest followed the lead officer to the stairs.

Olivia waited. If they continued along the outside path, she'd lead Mihàil back inside the maze and behind the officers. If they headed toward the other side of the terrace or into the maze, she'd make a break for the small building to the west.

At the bottom of the stairs, the lead officer stopped and directed the *polizei* behind her away from the outside path.

Now, Dragon Man.

Olivia pulled Mihàil out of the maze and across the gravel pathway. Something made her look back up the path to the stairs. Zophie, clad in black tactical gear, boots, and a wide-brimmed cap, stood with her hands on her hips, grinning. She gestured with her chin toward the building.

Stunned, Olivia nodded and kept running. Mihàil pounded an arm's length from her, his head down. She had no time to consider his appearance, but panic tickled her stomach at his ashen features and leaden movements. And then they'd made it to the building. Hugging its front side, they ran away from the helicopter now hovering over the gardens. Thirty more seconds and the helicopter would overtake them, making their escape even more challenging. She refused to consider the possibility that they wouldn't make it.

As if reading her thoughts, Mihàil panted out, "We should separate."

Save your breath, she thought grimly, not looking at him. She grabbed his hand again and yanked him after her. They made it under the nearest tree just as the helicopter swung over the building behind them.

Her cell rang. She pulled it from her pocket. "Markham."

"You sound out of breath." It was Fagan.

"Fairly sure you know why."

"You mean because half of Vienna's law enforcement is converging on the Belvedere, which is where your GPS coordinates put you right now?"

Mihàil tugged on her hand. *Who is it?*

She looked over her shoulder and shook her head. No time to talk about this now.

"What's going on?" Fagan asked.

"It's a little complicated."

"Is Kastrioti there? Witnesses identified a man fitting his description."

Damn. "Yes."

"A team will be there in five minutes."

"No!" Olivia stopped on the far side of a tree to catch her breath. Mihàil, who'd leaned against the trunk when they halted, looked at her sharply.

She turned away from him, certain his hearing was sharp enough to catch everything she said anyway.

"What haven't you told me?" she hissed.

"Operatives have died."

"You mean like I would have last night?"

"Try the Austrian federal police officer he just took out at the Belvedere."

Olivia darted a glance at Mihàil, whose gaze was unfocused as he appeared to listen to something. Did he have a hidden earwig? Straining, she thought she could detect a faint sound. She turned back and eased a few steps away.

"Try again. I took him out." She left off the added information that the *Bundespolizei* officer hadn't been entirely human when she'd done so. Recalling the supernatural light that had streamed through his eyes, she shivered.

Fagan's harsh laugh crackled over the cell. "The only way this ends well for you is if you come in now. Otherwise you're an accomplice as far as the Austrian authorities are concerned. It won't be long before they identify you."

"Just as I thought," she said in a low, fierce voice. "You'd discard me to get him. Good luck with that, asshole." She ended the call and then lobbed the phone back toward the building where it hit the side with a sharp crack. She turned to Mihàil. "Let's go."

Mihàil's eyes narrowed, but he said nothing just fell into a jog next to her. Fifty meters through the trees up ahead appeared a major street, the Prinz Eugen-Strasse. They needed to get beyond it and inside as soon as possible. If only she hadn't had to ditch her cell. Behind them, shouts sounded as *polizei* officers picked up their trail. The helicopter beat the air coming toward them.

Crap. They were running out of options.

White van.

What?

Ahead. Someone Stasia knows.

Olivia saw a white van swerve to the curb as they emerged from the trees. The side door slid open and a man wearing a black leather jacket waved them over. "Hurry! Hurry!" His accent was definitely Italian.

Running, she climbed in with Mihàil on her heels. The man at the door slid it shut just as the driver took off with a screech. Mihàil fell into Olivia as the driver did a sharp U-turn and then took a right down a street lined with tall buildings. The sound of the helicopter faded. They had gotten into the van without being spotted from the air. The next few minutes would be critical in determining whether they'd lost all of their pursuers, but Olivia's intuition told her that they'd gotten away.

"Hey, Dragon Man, I can't breathe," Olivia complained, shoving at his massive chest. He didn't respond. Blood slicked her palm.

The man with the leather coat wrenched Mihàil over onto the floor of the van next to Olivia. Bending over, he pressed an ear to the silent Albanian's chest. He sat back, a grave expression on his face.

"Neither can he, *signorina*," he said.

Thirteen

O livia sat up, her heart pounding, and leaned over to listen to Mihàil's chest. Faint crackles came to her sensitive hearing as he struggled to breathe. Sitting upright, she scanned his features. His pallid skin had a purple tinge. Clearly he wasn't getting enough oxygen. She touched his upper chest near the puncture wound with a gentle fingertip.

"His lung's collapsed." She turned to Stasia's contact. "He needs a chest tube."

The man nodded and began searching in a storage bin behind him. As he pulled out medical supplies, he said, "We cannot risk going to a hospital."

Olivia narrowed her eyes. "You have training?"

He shrugged. "Enough to save him." He slipped on a stethoscope and bent to place its chest piece against Mihàil's chest. "What weapon was used?"

She pulled the *subulam* handle from her pocket. "This. The rest is still in his chest."

The asset focused on it, whistling softly.

"You recognize it?" Olivia asked, surprised.

He nodded. "I have never seen one broken off inside someone though. Please elevate his head."

Olivia scooted behind Mihàil, sliding her hands under his head and shoulders before cradling them in her lap. Without waiting for direction, she pulled his right arm toward her before tugging his shirt up to expose his ribcage. Muscle rippled under her fingers. The man was massive and solid. She'd never be able to move him on her own.

The asset pushed the medical supplies near her hand before rummaging for gloves. He snapped a pair of nitrile gloves over his wrists and held out a hand. "The antiseptic wipes."

Olivia grabbed a packet of wipes and tore them open. She held the paper wrapper apart so that the asset could grab the gauze to sterilize the incision site. The next few minutes passed in a tense silence except for the asset's terse requests for anesthetic, scalpel, and a number twenty-four French tube. Olivia found and opened each package, handing them over without touching the exposed implement.

As the asset readied the scalpel to cut a one-inch incision between two of Mihàil's lower ribs, Olivia grabbed his forearm. He looked at her.

"Be very careful," she said. She held his gaze. Something passed between them, some strong current that she didn't have the time to dissect. But she knew when it hit him. His eyes widened, a small bead of sweat popping out between his brows. He nodded.

After a moment, the asset set the scalpel against Mihàil's skin. Olivia looked at the wounded *Elioud* in her lap. Something sharp stabbed her breast in the same place that the *subulam* had punctured his. She smoothed the hair from his forehead. When he groaned as the scalpel sliced into his flesh, she stroked his cheek. He was so beautiful it made her throat close and her chest ache. Gratitude and relief had swamped her on the Belvedere terrace when she'd heard his voice in her thoughts. Turning her head and seeing him at her shoulder had revitalized her flagging steps and made her believe her situation wasn't hopeless. It no longer mattered whether he was an Albanian mafia lord or simply a wealthy European playboy. Or even some human-angel hybrid with unearthly powers. He'd come for her and fought side-by-side with her.

The asset sat back on his heels and ran a hand over his face. "I have drained his chest, but the rest of the blade has to be removed and the bleeding stopped or his lung will stay collapsed. He also needs IV fluids and antibiotics, which I do not have here."

"Where are you taking us?"

"A safe house, but you cannot stay long. This is strictly off-book as a favor to Stasia." He stripped his gloves and dumped them in a plastic bag. Cleaning up the rest of the trash, he continued, "The Americans have alerted us to a rogue field officer with Kastrioti. They want help bringing you in. Dead or alive."

Bitterness flooded Olivia's mouth. This was all Fagan's doing. There were still people at the Company she could trust, but they weren't here. He was. So until she could clear her name, she was out in the cold. She looked down at Mihàil. He needed protection, too.

The van lurched into a dim underground garage and screeched to a halt.

"This is where we part ways, *signorina*," said the asset, gripping the trash bag and the storage bin. "We took evasive driving measures, but it is only a matter of time before they find this van." He slid open the van's door. A black Mercedes SUV with tinted windows waited next to them. "Others will take you to the safe house."

Two men wearing dark clothing and sunglasses got out of the Mercedes SUV and came to help Olivia with Mihàil, who remained unconscious. Straining with his weight, they lifted him into the rear seat of the SUV after Olivia, who again supported Mihàil's head in her lap. The last view she had of the white van, the two assets were stripping a white coating from it to reveal tan paint and a logo. Moments later, the Mercedes SUV left the garage. One of the new pair tossed her a cellphone.

"Call Stasia."

Olivia dialed her friend. "Staz?" Her voice broke.

"Olivia, thank God." Stasia's Italian accent had thickened in worry. "Miró tracked Mihàil's cell signal, but it's good to hear your voice, *cara*."

"Likewise." Olivia took a steadying breath. The cut along her upper back where a *bogomili* had attacked her had started to burn. She wondered if she needed stitches. "Staz, Mihàil needs medical attention. Can you get someone to your safe house?"

"How bad is he?"

"He's got a piece of a *subulam* in his chest and internal bleeding. His lung's collapsed."

"*Dio santo!* Wait." Stasia spoke to someone in the background. "We must move with care, *cara*. Beta and I will check with our contacts. It must be someone who will not attract attention to us, *capito*?"

"Absolutely." Olivia cupped Mihàil's cheek and rubbed her thumb over his bottom lip. She had an intense urge to kiss him. Tamping it down, she cleared her throat and said, "We need an extraction plan. In twenty-four hours, Vienna will be shut down tight."

"*Sì*. We will arrange it and follow you separately."

Olivia watched Mihàil's chest rise and fall in shallow breaths. He'd dressed in a black t-shirt and dark slacks this morning, making him a little less intimidating, though only a little. They'd had to bend his legs to get him inside the back seat, and his broad shoulders brushed the back of the passenger seat in front of them. Despite him being unconscious and gravely wounded, his familiar scent soothed her. Closing her eyes, she tried to identify components of his cologne. Cedar, clove, and musk. And something smoky...the faintest whiff of charcoal.

The Mercedes SUV pulled into the garage for a residential building fifteen minutes later. Olivia had no idea which district they were in, but she hoped that it was far from Vienna's Old Town. The CIA substation wasn't far from that. She also suspected that the *bogomili* and Asmodeus had a base of operations near the tourist area. The image of the tall man filled her mind's eye, and she shivered. Something told her that she hadn't actually met Asmodeus. It seemed highly implausible that she would take out a Dark *Irim* on her own without knowing what she was doing. While the *bogomili* were clearly crazy and following Asmodeus's orders, that tall man had been like someone possessed. Fallen angels were demons, and demons possessed people, didn't they? She rubbed her St. Michael medal while her other hand squeezed Mihàil's shoulder. Between the heavenly Michael and the very real one next to her, she felt safer.

The assets jumped out of the Mercedes SUV. One came around to Olivia's door. She lowered the window. "Stasia sent a text. An ambulance has been dispatched to a ghost accident two blocks away. We're going to intercept it and grab IV fluids, blood, antibiotics, and morphine."

Olivia nodded. "What about a surgeon?"

"She promises to have a doctor here in half an hour, an hour maximum."

Olivia nodded again. "Grab a gurney while you're plundering the ambulance. We're going to need it to move this hulk."

Miró's battle senses had heightened to a painful pitch as he and Ms. Fiore approached the Hilton Vienna. In fact, he was so tightly wound, the hair on his head hurt his scalp. The unhealed cut on his upper arm throbbed, adding to his dark mood. It didn't help that his head already ached so hard that his eyeballs hurt, and he needed to sleep for a full day. But Mihàil needed a surgeon. And the medical conference was their best bet for getting him one without attracting attention from the authorities. Or from Asmodeus, though the Dark *Irim* was likely in an angelic coma.

Miró shook his head. Angels were beings of spirit and air. Humans were spirit trapped in flesh. Only one spirit could reside in corporal matter. *Elioud* had come from the forbidden mingling of angelic spirit with human spirit, essentially creating super humans with angelic traits. The stronger the angelic spirit, the more angelic 'blood' the *Elioud* was said to have. *Drangùe* were the strongest *Elioud* because they'd been conceived directly by *Irim*. Angelic possession, on the other hand, subsumed the human host against divine law. The Dark *Irim* would have hated every second inside his human vessel. It would have burned and sapped his strength, but when Olivia broke his hold, the rebound on Asmodeus would have been severe. Eyes were indeed windows to the soul, and Olivia had reached right into the Dark *Irim*'s. Even without training, she'd done as much damage to Asmodeus as any *Elioud* ever had.

No wonder Mihàil was so smitten with her, though he didn't know it yet.

Miró hoped Asmodeus hadn't recognized it either, but his instincts told him that the Dark *Irim* knew exactly what he was doing when he used Olivia as bait to trap Mihàil. And it had nearly worked. In all the long years that he'd known Mihàil and fought at his side, the *drangùe* had never been wounded so gravely. True, Mihàil had nearly died protecting the woman he'd loved, a human named Luljeta, but that was more than a century before he'd rescued Miró from his degrading and soul-crushing life as a *köçek*, a boy trained as a cross-dressing dancer and sex slave.

Miró would do whatever was necessary to find a surgeon to remove the Dark *Irim* weapon from his friend's chest.

The diminutive Italian spy strolled at his side without looking at him, her shoulders back and her chin raised. She'd donned a plunging black jersey dress and tied a carmine silk scarf around her graceful neck. Silver jewelry and stiletto heels added to her allure. It was a dramatic look for mid-morning, and heads turned in the large lobby as she made her way. That suited Miró, who slipped into a chair facing away from the counter and pretended to be absorbed in his cellphone. The young man she approached struggled to ask how he could help her. Miró, irritated, snorted to himself. If the young ass would just raise his gaze to her face and focus on her eyes, he might be able to marshal his thoughts and ask a respectful question.

"I have an emergency and need to find my friend Dr. Kilcourt," Ms. Fiore said. The innocence in her tone grated Miró's nerves. He knew full well that she was more deadly than sweet. "I would send him a text message, but I know he turns his cell off during these meetings. Can you tell me where to find the panel session on video-assisted thoracic surgery?"

Five minutes later, Miró followed Ms. Fiore up the stairs to the mezzanine level and the Klimt Ballroom where they both entered via separate doors. He stood next to his door, hands crossed, while she scanned the room for the obnoxious doctor from her previous visit to the hotel. After a minute, she crossed over to the left side of the ballroom and made her way down the center aisle before stopping to bend toward a man sitting on the outside row. Miró narrowed his eyes. Dr. Kilcourt sat next to the thin man with glasses and thinning hair whose face was practically smothered by Ms. Fiore's breasts.

Ms. Fiore spoke to Dr. Kilcourt before standing and walking back toward Miró, her hips swaying in exaggeration. Dr. Kilcourt followed her. Miró clenched his jaw and scowled. As she came toward him, she smiled.

"Is that smoke I smell?" she asked Dr. Kilcourt as he joined her at the door. "It is rather hot and stuffy in here, *sei d'accordo?*"

"My room is much more pleasant," he said, oblivious to Miró, who stood silent at his shoulder.

Ms. Fiore's eyes laughed at Miró, but she spoke to Dr. Kilcourt. "That sounds lovely." She slipped an arm inside his and leaned closer. She lowered her voice. "Are you really the chief of surgery at Beth Israel?"

Dr. Kilcourt leaned toward her, lowering his voice as well. "Yes, I am. I specialize in cardiothoracic surgery. And in my professional opinion, you have a very fine chest."

Miró slapped Dr. Kilcourt's back, disrupting his nervous system with a burst of harmonics for the second time in two days. He ignored his partner's smirk. The pudgy surgeon collapsed just as two men approached the door to the ballroom from the hall.

"Too many mimosas at the breakfast reception," Ms. Fiore said, swinging toward the men and stepping half in front of Miró. He saw her shoulders draw back and heard the brightness in her voice. The men's gazes swung away and fixated on her. "Could you help us get him to the elevator so that we can take him to his room?" She flashed a room key. "We do not want his boss to see him like this."

The men nodded and stepped forward. Miró stepped back and allowed Ms. Fiore to direct them with heavily accented Italian and little flutters of her hands as they each put an arm under Dr. Kilcourt's shoulders and dragged him to the elevator. There Ms. Fiore assured her concerned helpers that she could manage to navigate the short distance to her colleague's room without help and pressed the close-door button before they realized that she'd dismissed them. Miró, amused, watched the elevator slide shut on their startled and confused faces. He much preferred to blend into the periphery, but Anastasia Fiore dazzled to disarm. Properly trained, she'd be a formidable *Elioud* warrior.

Fifteen minutes later, they'd maneuvered the groggy doctor through the lobby of the Hilton and into the waiting SUV, which Miró had paid the valet to hold for them. They'd pulled a hooded Vienna sweatshirt over Dr. Kilcourt while Ms. Fiore had pulled the scarf up and over her head and donned a pair of sunglasses. Miró simply adjusted his harmonics. Security video of them would be frustratingly blurry and incomplete for anyone viewing it later, though if all went well, by then Dr. Kilcourt would be back in his hotel room convinced that he'd demonstrated his surgical prowess to a very beautiful, very grateful woman.

Mihàil's awareness came back to him through his most basic sense, that of infrared light. He allowed thermal waves to wash over him for several long moments before he exerted his will to interpret them. A familiar infrared signature with a pure-white core banded in hot orange came into focus next to him. All at once, his other senses flared to life and inundated him with sounds and smells. He breathed easily, allowing himself the time to catalogue and understand this sensory information before opening his eyes. There was no threat in his environment, just lingering vibrations that suggested previous urgent activity.

Olivia's scent rode heated currents to him. Her even breathing told him that she slept, though by the shape of her infrared signature she sat near his bed.

That made him frown.

Why was he lying in bed while she slept in a chair?

That's when the annoying pain of an IV needle taped to the back of his left hand and the cool air caressing his bare shoulders led him to the deep throbbing in his chest. And he remembered the fight at the Belvedere and the frantic dash to escape. Opening his eyes, Mihàil saw by the strength of the light illuminating the gap between blinds and window behind Olivia that it was late. Questions about how long he'd been out and where they were raced through his thoughts. Where were his lieutenants?

Miró. András. He flashed their names, but his effort was pathetic. If they weren't in the next room over, they'd never hear him as weak as his angelic strength was.

The door to the room opened and Miró stepped in. When he saw that Mihàil was awake, relief transformed his features. Though he remained grave, his shoulders relaxed.

How do you feel?

Never better. Thank you for asking. My head is a throbbing boulder and my chest feels like someone pried it open and ripped out a few vital parts. You did not operate, did you?

Miró smiled and shook his head. *No. We kidnapped a human surgeon in Vienna for a medical conference. No one's the wiser.*

Mihàil nodded and shoved himself upright. Miró frowned but didn't say anything even when Mihàil winced. Olivia stirred in her chair, and they both looked at her.

Tell me what you know.

Austrian authorities are looking for you both. All the usual means of egress are guarded or surveilled. According to Ms. Fiore, foreign intelligence agencies have also been alerted to be on the lookout for you.

What am I supposed to have done?

Murdered a Bundespolizei *officer. They have an eyewitness.*

Mihàil recalled the tall man who'd served as Asmodeus's vessel. The Dark *Irim* found some of their most receptive humans among law enforcement officials and the military. Asmodeus in particular preferred covert operatives. Their secret lives in service to flawed masters made them ideal vessels and acolytes.

Focus on the Bundespolizei. *There may be a connection to the acolyte.*

Miró nodded. *As soon as the Austrian authorities claimed that you had murdered a* Bundespolizei *officer, I started evaluating all the intel we had on that branch of intelligence service. Ms. Fiore has also helped with her connections with Italian agencies.*

That brought something to mind for Mihàil. *I owe her my thanks for the hasty rescue.*

For the surgeon as well.

Mihàil's eyebrows rose. *Indeed.* He touched the bandage on his chest. *I am afraid this will take some time to recover from.*

We are taking that into account in planning your escape. Ms. Fiore is working on false identities for you and Ms. Markham. She suggested one of those ubiquitous Danube River cruises. You will be in Budapest in three days.

"You can talk out loud now. I'm awake." Olivia stretched her arms above her head and stood. When they looked at her in surprise, she asked, "What? How often do two people stare at each other so meaningfully? Besides, he"—she dipped her chin at Mihàil—"has spoken to me telepathically several times. I just assumed that you all could do it."

She came closer to Mihàil and leaned over him to examine the bandage on his shoulder. Her long hair brushed the skin on his chest, sending sudden images of her over him in much more intimate circumstances. He gulped and shifted his thighs under the concealing sheet.

"I'm sorry," she said, her worried gaze lifting to his. "I didn't mean to hurt you."

"You did not," he said, his voice coming out gruffer than he'd intended. He cleared his throat. "Are *you* all right?"

She stood back and shrugged. "I'm fine. Just the usual bruises and cuts."

"She had to get twenty-five stitches for the laceration on her upper back," Miró said. "It will leave a scar."

Mihàil scowled.

Olivia shot his lieutenant a hard look and spoke before he could say anything. "I'm no stranger to stitches."

"Indeed, I would say that you have had more than your fair share of them," Mihàil said, noting the faint pink that suffused Olivia's cheekbones at his words. "It occurs to me, Ms. Markham, that you have been at two *bogomili* attacks and a terrorist attack in as many days. Miró, what does that suggest to you?"

Mihàil kept his gaze on Olivia, who'd gone still at his use of her last name.

Miró's discomfort radiated from him. He was a truthseeker. That meant that he was extra sensitive to the subtle interplay between harmonics, breath, and infrared signatures when interacting with people. He didn't need to question them directly, just observe their reactions to any given verbal prompt. *I cannot read her well. She is either naturally evasive or she's been trained. Or both.*

Answer the question. Aloud.

"It suggests that Ms. Markham is working with Asmodeus as his acolyte."

She looked startled. And something else. Hurt? "You think I'm helping him? That I'm some sort of follower of that evil being?"

Mihàil ignored the distress that he heard in her voice. He spoke lightly but sharpened his gaze on her. "That is one interpretation. You would not be the first *Elioud* to ally with a Dark *Irim*. It is a powerful partnership."

All at once, anger burned away the confusion in her blue-gray eyes. "Really? If I was his acolyte, why would I attack him? That was him, wasn't it? The tall guy who put his hand on me"—here she placed a hand over her heart—"and it felt like he was draining my life away? And now I'm wanted as your accomplice."

"Who did you speak to on the phone while we were escaping?"

Olivia turned and dropped into the chair. "I'm not at liberty to say."

Mihàil said nothing, just intensified his gaze on her. It was a tactic designed to make ordinary humans squirm, sweat, and eventually start spewing relevant and irrelevant information. Instead, she sat up taller, squared her shoulders, and held his gaze with a directness that impressed the hell out of him. It also infuriated him.

In response, he leaned forward, letting his temper soothe the cold ache in his chest. The air around them heated, and, as weak as he was, Mihàil still managed to project power.

"Then I am afraid that until you trust me with the truth that I will have to treat you as a Grey *Elioud*, one who has not chosen a side in our angelic war."

The whites of her eyes grew. "What does that mean?"

"It means that you are coming with me when I leave Vienna." He looked at Miró, whose expression gave nothing away. "Have Ms. Fiore create identities for newlyweds. I mean to keep Ms. Markham close."

Beta stood looking out the window toward the Belvedere, which was too far away to see even if it hadn't also been dark outside. She'd stood here since

Stasia had left with the quiet *Elioud*, the one whose cold eyes seemed to take in everything, most especially Stasia. She held her folded chain whip in her right hand and palmed its heavy steel dart. The smooth metal had scratched and pitted over the years, but it was solid and warm against her skin. She'd spent the afternoon in the gym dancing with her chain whip, swirling, leaping, and striking over and over. The control and discipline required channeled her fear, worry, and rage so that her thoughts stayed clear. The emotions were still there, bitterly compressed inside her, but they didn't own her.

A slight change in air pressure behind her sent her whirling, the dart flashing out. Despite her speed, András stood untouched an arm's length away from where she'd targeted, casually eating strudel. He'd been eating all day from what she could tell. The man was a bottomless maw. Licking his fingers, he wiped them on his jeans and looked toward the dart, which lay on the floor next to him. He toed the dart and then glanced at her.

"You should be careful with that thing. It could cause a nasty bruise." He bent over and yanked it.

Beta had been unprepared for his maneuver. She stumbled forward a step before recovering. Glowering, she jerked the chain whip, but András didn't let go. Instead, he tugged it, causing her to take another step forward despite having planted her feet.

"We can keep doing this until I pull you on your ass," he suggested, giving her a lopsided grin. A dimple mocked her from his cheek.

Beta reacted by launching herself at him, catching up the slack from the chain whip, and twisting it around his ankles as she threw herself into a rolling dive. András hit the floor with a *thud* as she sprang to her feet and circled around him, cinching the chain whip as she stepped back.

"No," she said, standing over him.

He looked dumbstruck, his wavy brown hair sliding over his forehead. *Sladký* Lord, the man was a *beast*. His shoulders were as wide as a doorway, and he was almost as tall. For a moment, fear gripped her. If he got angry, she'd do well to drop her chain whip and run for it. She ignored her fear and kept her face impassive and her breathing even.

Then he smiled a wide, beautiful smile with large white teeth. Light danced over his deep-blue eyes. "You taught me a lesson. I should know better than to challenge you with your chain whip. Truce?" He dropped the dart and held out his hand.

Beta waited. She didn't want to seem eager to trust him. He watched her, his gaze sincere. At last she took the proffered hand, which engulfed hers. Heat from his palm and fingers made her realize just how cold her own were. Goosebumps flared along the backs of her arms, but she tamped down the shiver that accompanied them, bracing her feet and hauling on his hand. She wouldn't have budged him if he hadn't flattened his other hand on the floor and levered himself to his feet. Without a word, she began peeling her whip from his lower legs. Warmth radiated from him, exuding a complex scent of smoky balsam with a lingering hint of black currant and magnolia. He smelled like a bright summer day bursting with green growing life.

"You don't talk much, do you?" he asked while she folded her chain whip and tucked it into an inner pocket of her jacket.

She saw a tiny flake of crust at the corner of his mouth, right where she remembered a dimple. She wondered what the big oaf would do if she stood on tiptoe and licked it off.

"You talk enough for both of us," she said instead.

At that, he threw his head back and laughed. It was so infectious that Beta almost chuckled. Almost.

He punched her on the shoulder and she stumbled. Wiping the corner of his eyes with his thumb, he inhaled and then grinned at her. "Your mother served only axe soup. Too bad she forgot to ask for potatoes and beef." He reached out and wrapped a massive paw around her bicep, shaking his head. "I thought so. Axe handle."

"Is there some reason you came looking for me?" she asked, ignoring his jibe about her slender build. She pulled her arm from his grip. "Or are you just lonely?"

András sobered. "Mihàil is awake. We need to get to the safe house to plan an escape for him and Ms. Markham."

She cocked her head to the side. Her instincts told her that it was a request rather than an order.

"I think not," she said, watching his open expression. "This Dark *Irim* is licking his wounds. His forces are in disarray. It will be easy for me to slip out of Vienna unnoticed. Olivia knows how to contact me once she has reached a safe destination."

Clouds descended over his gaze, chilling the air. "She who travels alone invites along dogs with fleas."

"I always travel alone," she said. "Fleas do not like how I taste. Too much axe handle, not enough beef and potatoes."

He leaned forward, his gaze suddenly blazing. "Mihàil nearly died today because of Ms. Markham. Now he must leave Vienna without finishing his business for his people."

Beta refused to give any ground. "And Olivia is wanted as his accomplice. She, too, must leave Vienna with unfinished business. I suspect that Kastrioti will not let her leave on her own, will he?"

András scowled. "She may be a Grey *Elioud*, only looking out for her own interests. He must protect himself."

"And he may be a mafia lord seeking to eliminate his rival," she said, tilting her shoulders toward the threat rather than away. As tall as András was, she had to be careful not to let him look down at her. "Perhaps Olivia has been caught between a fallen angel and a greedy man with angel blood."

The clouds darkened to a thunderhead. Lightning sparked in his gaze. A sharp smoky scent swirled around them. "*Lófasz!*" he swore. "Mihàil is a *drangùe*."

She took a step back and raised her chin. "So you keep saying." She refrained from slipping her hand inside her jacket. No need to poke the hornet's nest, at least not when she stood so close. *How could I have thought that his eyes were warm and open?* "We are at an impasse. Neither of us has reason to trust the other. One of us must trust first." She left it unsaid that it would not be *her*. Instead, she fixed him with an unblinking stare.

Something flared in András's gaze, which quickly shuttered again. After a long moment, he stepped aside. Gesturing toward the open doorway, he said, "I extend trust so that you may trust. But word to the wise: broken trust cuts twice as deep."

FOURTEEN

O livia grabbed a stack of blouses and shoved them into the suitcase on the bed in front of her. It wasn't the first time that she'd had to pack to leave in a hurry, but usually she had more input. And a go-bag filled with false identities, money, a backup weapon, and her *bō*. It was the last that she missed the most.

This time, Mihàil's man Friday, Pjetër, had arrived with a suitcase already neatly packed with a selection of her own clothing and toiletries taken from her flat. To sell their cover story, he'd also brought along a second suitcase filled with new items that a bride might pack for her honeymoon as well as a set of wedding rings. She'd peered at the lingerie before zipping the case shut again, but as soon as she saw the rings, something painful had lodged in her chest. Both bands were plain white gold, but the engagement ring had a stunning square-cut solitaire diamond. If she had to guess, it was three carats, large enough to be dangerous if she got into hand-to-hand combat. She wondered if that included an impassioned fight with her new husband.

Instead of trying on the engagement ring and wedding band, Olivia had chosen to sort through the clothing, focusing on refolding everything even though Pjetër had done a better job. He'd chosen capris and shorts, a couple of skirts, a silk wrap, and two lightweight cardigans along with the blouses that she'd repacked. At last, she turned to the second suitcase, rubbing a thumb over the engraved leather nametag. *Caterina D'Angelo*, newly married to *Alessandro*. She'd always assumed that her first marriage would be a sham for a mission, but she'd never expected it to feel so wrong.

"Your evening clothes, Caterina," Stasia said behind her. Olivia turned to see Stasia holding a hanging bag. "I gave Pjetër some suggestions for what you'd like to wear to the formal dinners on the cruise." She hesitated. "There are enough gowns, both evening and cocktail, should you extend your trip."

"Because we have no idea how long *Alessandro* and I will be together." Olivia glanced toward the doorway. She couldn't see Miró, but she knew that he was just outside, listening with his supersensitive *Elioud* hearing.

Stasia stepped closer and put her hand on Olivia's forearm. She lowered her voice. "*Cara*, this is a good plan. You need to get out of Vienna, and a river cruise is ideal. Traveling as a newly married couple will draw little attention and give you two a reason to stay out of sight."

Olivia sighed. "I know, but I'm certain that I could have made it out of Vienna alone. I've gotten out of some sticky situations before."

Stasia threw a glance over her shoulder. "Nevertheless, not naked." She waggled the hanging bag at the double meaning to her words. A *naked* field operative was one who had no cover or backup. "This is better, you will see."

She laid the hanging bag on the bed and then turned back to Olivia. "Well, where are they? *Dai*, what kind of bride doesn't show off the very breathtaking diamond that her beloved has bestowed on her?" She gave Olivia a very pointed look.

Olivia rolled her eyes and picked up the small black-velvet box sitting on the dresser behind her. *Pocket litter* was the trade term for items in a field operative's pocket that lent authenticity to a cover. She laughed as she caught sight of the engagement ring. *Pocket litter* indeed. This qualified as a Big Lie. Anyone seeing this ring would never doubt that Caterina and Alessandro were married. She slipped the wedding band on and then the diamond solitaire.

Rings shouldn't feel so weighty on a finger.

Stasia peered around her shoulder at her hand. Olivia heard her slight intake of breath. When she gazed into the mirror across from them, she caught a glimpse of something in the other woman's eyes. It flashed so quickly that she couldn't be sure, but it looked a lot like yearning. Clearing her throat, she turned around.

"What about you and Beta?" she asked. "I've already asked too much from both of you."

"You are joking, no?" Stasia's look of disbelief would have been comical if it hadn't been such a serious topic. "*Coraggio!* My handler has assigned me to dig into the Belvedere incident. He believes that the Austrians are seeking to cover up another terrorist attack. I am tasked with discovering what really happened. It should take me a few days to do a thorough job, including interviewing the surviving *bogomili* from the Stadtpark."

Olivia hadn't realized that one of the men had lived. She raised her voice slightly. "Perhaps Miró can give you some help. The Dragon Man wants proof that I'm not working with Asmodeus. His lieutenant can get it for him. That is, if you can get anything coherent out of a *bogomili.* "

A faint pink tinted Stasia's cheeks. *Interesting.* "I suspect that our new friends have talents that we do not. I will ask him to accompany me."

"Good. I'll contact you when we reach Budapest. And Beta?"

Stasia's gaze darted toward their unseen listener and back. "She left Vienna last night shortly after Mihàil awoke. She told the giant that you know how to reach her."

Olivia nodded slowly, letting Stasia see the understanding in her eyes. Beta preferred to work alone. "I do."

Stasia flung her arms around Olivia, kissing her once on each cheek before stepping back, her eyes bright. "*Buon viaggio, cara.* Until we meet again, take care of yourself."

"Thank you for everything, Staz. I owe you more than I can ever repay." Miró appeared in the doorway. Olivia was grateful that he'd allowed them the appearance of privacy. Nevertheless, she fixed him with a hard stare. "Take good care of her, *Elioud*, or I'm coming for you as soon as I'm out of this mess."

Miró inclined his head. "My duty demands nothing less, *Signora D'Angelo.*"

Olivia watched them walk out, Stasia in front and Miró shadowing her. Something told her that he had more than duty on his mind. Stasia could take care of herself, but it relieved Olivia to know that the quiet, intense *Elioud* had her friend's back.

Anyone observing the young couple strolling in the Mexicoplatz the next morning would have suspected that they were in love by the joy radiating from their expressions. That and their obvious affection as they held hands and once or twice indulged in heartfelt, though brief, kissing. Beautiful and well dressed, they were a striking match of blond and brunette, her willowy form pleasingly contrasted by his broad and muscular one. Some might have wondered if they were celebrities or models on a photo shoot, but if so, their demeanor was incomparably relaxed. By all indications, they had eyes only for themselves.

They entered the Church of St. Francis of Assisi, which dominated the square with its three red-tiled towers, and spent an hour inside. Though it was four metro stops from the center of Vienna, the Mexico Church as it is known, had its fair share of tourists from the nearby ships docked at the Reichsbrücke Dock. The couple joined a tour group already in progress, pulling small radios from her oversize bag before wedging earbuds into their ears. Some of the group noticed the newcomers, wondering why they hadn't caught a glimpse of them on their cruise only to shrug and accept that the couple might have spent most of their time inside their cabin. The couple smiled at the other tour members as they walked through, lingering at the chapel dedicated to the Empress Sisi. The man seemed particularly taken with his partner, draping her bare shoulders with a gorgeous silk shawl as they entered and carrying her heavy bag. His gaze followed her as she eagerly explored the interior of the church.

Afterwards, the couple boarded the shuttle with the rest of the group where they chatted with some gray-haired Australian tourists. They introduced themselves as Alessandro and Caterina D'Angelo, newlyweds on their honeymoon. As they disembarked at Stephansplatz, one of the Australian women caught sight of the young woman's engagement ring and exclaimed over its astonishing size and brilliance. Naturally, this caused many of the female tourists—wives, mothers, and grandmothers—to clamor for a look and to extend their well wishes to the fortunate couple. The tour guide, anxious to stick to his schedule, chided the stragglers to catch up lest they sacrifice the group's entry time into St. Stephan's Cathedral, the mother church of Vienna and one of its most recognizable symbols. Reluctantly, these women put aside their happy curiosity, but when it came time to find a place for lunch, they invited their newfound Italian friends to join them. By the time the group had finished touring Old Town and taken a bus to Schönbrunn Palace, the newlyweds had charmed them with the romance of their first meeting. None of their starry-eyed companions had any idea that a major manhunt was underway for a man and a woman who resembled the couple to an uncanny degree.

Later that afternoon, the tour group returned to the Reichsbrücke Dock and their ship. Caterina and Alessandro promised their new friends to make an appearance at dinner before heading to their suite to freshen up. Alessandro, wanting nothing but the best for his bride, had booked one of the two largest suites on the stern of the top deck. As Olivia opened the door, the full, rich scent of roses assailed her nose. Breathing in reflexively, she only glanced at the bathroom with its large walk-in shower and neutral tile on her left because directly ahead of her was a sideboard with the largest bouquet of cut roses that she'd ever seen. Flicking a glance over her shoulder, she saw Mihàil standing just inside their cabin door, a slight smile on his voluptuous mouth—a mouth that she couldn't help but want to kiss again, this time for real.

"Your mother's roses?" she asked softly, walking closer to the sideboard to drop her nose toward the fragrant blooms. "Why bother? The cabin steward isn't essential to our cover story."

Mihàil moved closer but stopped in the doorway to the inner room. To her left, Olivia saw a sitting area with a sofa, coffee table, and end tables. Beyond sheer curtains covered a sliding door to their private terrace. Over her left shoulder, she glimpsed the foot of a large bed. Everything in the suite was decorated in shades of taupe, tan, cream, and dark brown. Next to the bouquet stood a stainless-steel ice bucket, bottled water, two glasses, a coffee maker, and a bottle of sparkling wine with a card reading *Congratulations.* Two crystal flutes flanked the wine.

He shrugged, watching her. "The little things matter, *Cat.*" His Italian accent was perfect, but it was his rich baritone speaking the false nickname that sent shivers up her spine. He stepped around her and reached for the wine bottle. "If you keep faith in the little things, it translates into the big things. This is true whether it concerns a false identity or a true romance." He handed her a flute filled with sparkling wine. "To our romance."

Olivia had the odd feeling that Mihàil had just qualified their romance as "true." Confused, she tilted the flute to her mouth. Was it just an allusion to her not telling him the full truth? Or could he be referring to the obvious attraction they felt for each other? She was wise enough to know that there could never be a true romance between them as long as she was a covert operative. That life was built on faithlessness. Hadn't Fagan proven that to her? As for Mihàil himself, it mattered less and less to her whether he was the Dragon of Albania because he was the son of Gjergj Kastrioti or because he was the head of an Albanian mafia family. Either way, they were both out in the cold, running for their lives.

Maybe they'd have to adopt their new identities permanently. They could be newlyweds Cat and Aleso by day, harlequin and *drangùe* by night. Unless otherwise occupied.

She choked on her sparkling wine as the thought hit her and darted a glance at Mihàil.

He placed a hand on her shoulder, concern tightening his gaze. "Did you swallow wrong?"

Shaking her head, Olivia wiped her mouth and set the flute down. Turning back, she realized that Mihàil was quite close. At least he blocked her view of the bedroom. She wouldn't have to act nonchalant about its existence just yet. "We should get changed for dinner."

Mihàil drained his flute and set it next to hers. His eyes darkened to a deep blue and his hand slid down to knead the flesh of her upper arm. His fingers were pleasantly warm and firm. "Do you wish to shower?"

Olivia's breath caught in her chest. Her heart compressed against her ribcage. Tension crackled the air. She swallowed around a suddenly dry throat. "No. You go ahead."

He tilted his head to the side. "Hm. I had not thought of that."

"What?" she asked, unable to look away from him and intensely aware of his hand on her bare skin. It was as if she'd never been touched by another person before.

"That it would be hard to keep you in my sight if I am in the shower." His thumb began to rub gentle circles. The air around them heated. His scent, by now familiar, filled her nose with its heady fragrance of cedar, clove, and musk. A sharp smoky note added a thrilling edge to it.

Olivia felt lightheaded. She thought she was melting. She leaned toward Mihàil's hard chest, her eyes closing. This could be real. This *was* real. Hadn't he just chided her about faithfully living their false identities or something like that?

Suddenly Mihàil swore in a language that Olivia didn't know and stepped away, leaving her bereft and cold. Her eyes flew open. His own gaze had shuttered. He turned and stalked into the bedroom.

"I *will* take a shower before we head to dinner." He appeared in the doorway with a small shaving kit and a hanging bag over his shoulder. "The bedroom is all yours."

He brushed past her on the way to the bathroom. Olivia grabbed his arm as he did.

"Wait! Aren't you worried that I'll try to make a break for it?"

"And go where?" he asked. "Do you think I left the ship unwatched?" He gave her a hard, appraising look. "Though I suppose you are more than capable of swimming the Danube. Never worry. I will know if you dive over the side and recover you if I need to." He went into the bathroom, sliding the pocket door shut with a bang.

What the hell? Olivia stood there stunned until she heard the shower turn on. How would he know if she jumped into the Danube? Besides incinerate enemies and communicate telepathically, what else could *Elioud* warriors do? Look through walls like Superman with his x-ray vision?

Scowling, Olivia stepped toward the double closet across from the bathroom door. She slid the door open to see the evening gowns and cocktail dresses that Stasia had brought to the safe house. She ran her fingers over them. There were two black dresses, one long with a skirt that flared at the ankles and a sleeveless, knee-length one with a V-neck. The remaining dresses ranged in length and cool pastels, from white and peach to lavender and lilac. Materials varied from the seductively clingy jersey of the black gown to the silky drape of satin, the stiff formality of taffeta and the flowing translucence of chiffon. Fingering the material of each, Olivia darted another glance toward the bathroom. Should she garb herself in something sensual or sedate?

She ended up settling on both.

Her initial instinct was to play it safe, so she pulled out a Midi dress with long sleeves and bateau neck and held it before her as she turned toward the mirror on their stateroom door. Densely sewn peach sequins formed Art Deco patterns on a lighter peach background. The fully lined dress was both demure and elegant. But when Olivia looked at the back, she saw a plunging V-neck and a dramatic slit. She would have to go without a bra. That was decidedly not demure and likely not safe.

Hurrying to the bedroom, she slid the door shut only to be confronted by a king-sized bed. It dominated the room. Shoving that to the back of her thoughts, she shed her blouse, bra, and capris before shimmying into the body-hugging dress. It fit her snugly yet had enough stretch to let her move easily.

She darted back to the entryway to look at herself in the mirror. The dress hit below the knee, its glittering geometric patterns accentuating her waist and hips, its neckline kissing her collarbones. Studying her reflection, she decided that she'd need no jewelry other than some drop earrings. And her hair would have to be up. She held it off her neck with one hand before turning to the side.

"Your scar is nearly invisible," Mihàil said from the doorway to the bathroom, startling her.

Olivia sucked in a breath and looked over her shoulder, her heart tapping at her ribs. Mihàil leaned against the door, a towel around his waist and his hair damp. She swallowed. He had the chest and arms of a Greek warrior, his abdominal muscles defined and glistening, his pectoral muscles prominent, his shoulders broad, and his biceps bulging. Yet a thin purple line bisected his right breast where the surgeon had removed the broken *subulam*. He might have angel blood in him, but he wasn't invincible. In fact, there were dark shadows under his eyes. She'd almost forgotten how gravely wounded he'd been. How much had today's activities cost him?

"How's your incision?" she asked, nodding toward his chest.

He shrugged, but his gaze devoured her. "It is fine. I am hardly aware of these absorbable staples. Medicine has come a long way since my first battle."

Something occurred to her. "I suppose you've always been able to cauterize your own wounds."

"Yes, but without the concurrent tissue damage."

"Is that why the surgeon had to reopen your wound? Did you mean to seal it?"

He shook his head. "Normally, I would have heated the metal until it was molten and then ejected it as I sealed the wound closed. But Asmodeus consecrates *subula,* so it was poisonous to my system. I couldn't overcome it."

So Superman had Kryptonite.

She tilted her head. "You weakened it, though."

"Yes, by harmonics rather than thermodynamics. All angelic beings have the power to manipulate harmonics. It can be a very powerful tool once you know what you're doing."

"Harmonics? Doesn't that have to do with music?"

"Music is the language of the angels and the fundamental force underlying all of creation. Everything has a harmonic signature, though the level of harmony with the celestial varies. Dark angelic beings are discordant. Music hurts them on a spiritual level."

"Is that why you asked me to go to the music festival? To test my reaction to music?"

"Yes."

"Did I pass? I hated the Debussy."

He studied her. His own expression was hard to read. "And didn't care for *Rigoletto,* if I recall."

"No." She held her breath, waiting for his answer.

"You said it reminded you of someone you lost."

"Yes," she whispered, looking down.

"Emily."

Her lips felt frozen. "My cousin."

Mihàil stepped toward her. Olivia longed for him to pull her against the smooth skin of his chest and wrap her in his heat. Instead, he tilted her chin up. The look in his eyes caught her off guard. There was compassion, yes, but pain, too. The same pain that she'd seen haunting his expression in the surveillance photos that Fagan gave her what felt like a million years ago. The same pain, it came to her in an epiphany, in her own eyes right now.

"Why did you leave the safety of my Vienna home?" he asked.

"What?" Olivia's thoughts had gone fuzzy as soon as Mihàil had come within touching range. He filled her awareness, narrowing her vision to take in only him. Her heartrate sped up.

"Why did you leave my protection?" A strong emotion thickened his voice. "You would have died at the Belvedere or been taken by Asmodeus if I had not gotten there in time."

"I can't tell you," she said, shaking her head. "I wish I could, but I can't. Please trust me." She put her hand on his forearm, willing him to believe her.

He sighed and stepped away. "You are an enigma, Olivia Markham, and more than meets the eye. You are smart, beautiful, and well trained for someone who claims to be a graduate student. But your grief has made your harmonic signature unstable. That is why Asmodeus used it against you at the Belvedere. He will try again. If he can, he will use your grief to make you his acolyte."

He paused and a veil descended over his gaze. "The last time Asmodeus had an *Elioud* acolyte, thousands died."

Olivia and Mihàil sat that evening at an oval table along the starboard side of the restaurant on the ship's middle deck. The cruise offered open seating, so Mihàil maneuvered them into the seats closest to the window. Outside the Vienna skyline glowed in the early evening, and for a few moments Olivia entertained hopes that they would have the table to themselves. However, that was unlikely given the view, and they were joined by four other guests, a middle-aged British couple and two German men. The British woman sat next to Olivia, followed by her husband on the aisle side of the table. After politely shaking hands and introducing themselves, the two German men filled the remaining seats. Next to Mihàil's muscular form, the tall blond German appeared almost slender though he was athletic looking. His shorter, dark-haired friend wore wire-framed glasses. He reminded Olivia of an architect or software engineer.

As the waiter poured their wine, Amelia, a gray-haired schoolteacher with sad blue eyes, asked Olivia whether this was her first river cruise. After that, Amelia took on the role of hostess, asking questions, offering observations, filling in empty spaces in the conversation. Olivia noticed that Mihàil spoke little, letting her speak for them, reaching across the table and taking her hand in his. She didn't mind; although they'd worked out their cover story together before leaving the safe house, it would make it simple to keep their story straight if she narrated it.

Nevertheless, Olivia wondered at Mihàil's subdued manner given his charm and flirtatious behavior earlier in the day. She rather missed it. It was as though heavy clouds had covered the sun, and all that was left was a dark intensity that loomed large in her awareness—like the pull of vertigo when standing too close to a precipice. As she raised her wineglass to her lips, she glanced toward him and caught her breath at the soft halo of sunlight that limned his dark head. Blinking, she tried to clear her vision. The diffuse glow remained. When he caught her gaze on him, the halo flared and sparked. Olivia choked.

"Are you all right, my dear?" Amelia asked, concern furrowing her brow.

"Yes, thank you," Olivia murmured, remembering to sweeten her words with an Italian accent. "I am a bit dazzled by the view." She nodded toward the Vienna skyline slowly sliding by. Their ship would cruise the Danube along the Vienna shoreline before returning to dock. Early the next morning, it would sail southeast toward Bratislava in Slovakia.

Amelia nodded and handed her empty salad plate to the waiter who had come to gather them up. "It's quite lovely, but I prefer the view of Budapest by night. The Hapsburgs knew what they were about when they built a parliament building if you ask me."

"I am so looking forward to seeing it in person. Aleso has already been."

Amelia turned to him. "We're going to stay in Budapest for a few days once we dock. Jack has promised to take me to Széchenyi Bath. You should come. They say the Bath is very romantic at night."

"Plus the hot springs are good for what ails you, mate," Jack said, pointing with his chin toward Mihàil. "That and some deep-tissue massage should help that stiff shoulder of yours."

"Join us," Amelia said, reaching for a basket of dinner rolls. "We can look out for each other. Tourists are quite easily taken advantage of at popular spots like the Bath."

Mihàil's fingers tightened around hers, but he nodded and smiled at Amelia and Jack. Olivia recognized tension around his eyes that hadn't been there before. Was it pain? Or annoyance? "I have spent many relaxing hours at the Bath on previous visits to Budapest, so I purchased tickets in advance. I am not sure of our schedule."

Jack let out a snort. "Woman, they're on their *honeymoon*. Whatever possessed you to think that they'd like to spend their *romantic* visit at the Bath with you and me?" He shook his head and grabbed a roll.

Amelia bristled and turned to Jack. "What? I was just being helpful." She and Jack proceeded to bicker, taking their attention from Olivia and Mihàil.

Olivia leaned closer and asked, "Are you all right? Would you like to return to our suite?"

Mihàil had let her hand go so that she could eat. He picked it up again, toying with the diamond engagement ring with his right thumb. She was acutely aware of the strength in his warm fingers, the comfort and feeling of safety that his touch conveyed. He looked up at her, but she couldn't read the expression in his blue eyes. Even so, she wanted to brush the hair from his forehead and smooth the faint lines there.

"I am more tired than I would like," he said, "but I can make it through dinner. I will have to rely on you, however, to keep up our cover. I am afraid I am also not as alert as I should be."

Olivia studied him. "Is there something that seems off to you?" she asked in a low voice.

He held her gaze before leaning over to give her a brief kiss. As he pulled back, he murmured, "Perhaps I am wrong, but the two Germans next to me have odd infrared signatures."

Olivia blinked at that. *Infrared signatures?* Was reading infrared signatures something *Elioud* could do? Or just a *drangùe?* She picked up her water glass and sipped it, glancing over the rim at the two men. They had seemed quite alert when Amelia and Jack discussed the Széchenyi Bath. Could they be more than simple tourists?

After they'd all had after-dinner espresso and torte, Olivia forestalled any lingering conversation by announcing that she was tired from walking in the heat of the afternoon at Schönbrunn Palace. She thanked their dinner companions and said that she hoped that they'd see them while they toured Bratislava the next day. Jack stood while she was speaking. Amelia smiled and wished them both well before she too stood. Both German men pushed back from the table and stood. Though they appeared reluctant to leave, they had little reason to remain and shook Mihàil's hand before wishing Olivia a goodnight.

She slipped her hand into Mihàil's, and they headed toward their suite. Again, Olivia was struck by how right it felt to have Mihàil's fingers intertwined with hers, how comforting and intimate at the same time. His palm pressed against hers like a kiss. All at once she envisioned him over her, both hands capturing hers as his gaze captured her gaze. She had a premonition then about what it would feel like between them as he moved in her, his weight holding her within the cage of his arms, her legs holding him within their hammock. When he bent to kiss her, the circuit would be completed and sparks would fly, lips to lips, palms to palms, and groin to groin. As she imagined this scenario, their joined hands grew warm.

Without warning, energy sparked. Their hands flew apart.

Sucking in a sharp breath, Olivia stopped. They were outside the door to their suite. She looked at Mihàil in confusion only to see a thunderous expression on his face. A slight smoky scent hung on the heated air.

"Excuse me," he mumbled. "I really need some air. And I can better survey the infrared signatures of all the people on board from the deck. The bedroom is all yours. I will sleep on the sofa in the sitting room when I return."

Before she could say anything, Mihàil turned away and went outside, leaving her shivering from the sudden loss of his heat.

Fifteen

M ihàil stood near the ship's railing in the deepening twilight, acutely aware of the beautiful woman traveling as his wife in the suite next door. Her infrared signature was as familiar to him as his own now.

Their cruise ship sat wedged between two other cruise ships at the busy dock. Below him on the Handelskai, the promenade abutting the Danube that gave access to the ships, tourists streamed from shuttle buses after an evening in the city center. Some tourists had chosen to visit the closer Mexicoplatz or Lasallestrasse with its cafes and U-bahn stop that was only five minutes' walk west of the square. As they returned, they mixed with those from the buses, their combined infrared signatures blending and blurring into a vivid kaleidoscope.

Even so, Mihàil sensed András sitting on a bench under the trees planted along the center of Handelskai. He wasn't surprised to find his lieutenant there. Although they hadn't spoken after the attack at the Belvedere, Mihàil knew that András blamed himself for his general's injury. Before he made his way to Budapest on his own, András would keep watch to ensure that Mihàil escaped Vienna undetected.

Mihàil stared at his lieutenant. *She will not escape.*

It's the bogomili *I'm worried about. You're as weak as a kitten. One or two you could handle, but they come in groups of tens.*

There are no bogomili *within kilometers.*

And no backup either if they do show up. You're drained. I can see your signature.

Even without the sound of his voice, Mihàil heard András's concern. What the big Hungarian left unsaid was that he could see the discordant thread in

Mihàil's harmonics, the cold current that ran through his internal heat. The one that had been there ever since his wife had died. It weakened his *Elioud* strength like Achilles' heel.

There was no point in denying it. *That is why I need you in Vienna. Follow the plan. Miró needs to fly out in three days.*

András didn't respond for a moment. Mihàil could see his lieutenant's head move as he watched the teeming throng on the promenade.

Do you ever think about whether it's all worth it? That they're *worth it?*

The question surprised Mihàil. András had never questioned their vocation before. An image of Olivia filled his mind's eye.

I know *they are,* he flashed.

András nodded and stood. He left without looking back.

Mihàil watched the big Hungarian go, modifying his harmonics until they integrated with the jumbled chords surrounding him. It would have been more than Mihàil could have done to find the *Elioud* in the crowd when he was healthy, but tonight his senses couldn't track Andràs beyond his sightline. Andràs disappeared, leaving Mihàil with the uneasy feeling that he'd just learned how ordinary humans felt when angelic beings visited them. It wasn't very comforting.

He looked toward the Church of St. Francis Assisi, its red roofline and towers smudged against the darker blue sky. None of the infrared signatures that he'd registered after he'd come up to the deck held any threat or abnormality, though there were more than a few of them that had no bright white or electric blue and were mostly cooler orange. That was to be expected with the retired and elderly passengers. The surrounding infrared signatures, though interspersed with younger and hotter elements, held no threat or serious abnormality. The percentage of questionable infrared signatures didn't alarm him. If anything, it was lower than an average block in any large city.

As he scanned the Handelskai for the questionable individuals, he saw the two men who'd sat next to them at dinner.

Frowning, he studied their infrared signatures.

They weren't *bogomili,* whose inner core lacked any heat at all and whose signatures barely reached warm in the outer layers. But there was a colorless granule in their core that shifted within a deeper red-dark orange, as though their infrared signatures were flames. He'd seen infrared signatures like theirs many times over the centuries, though at first they had been rare. They belonged to people who had no empathy or only broken empathy. Psychopaths and sociopaths and other individuals with personality disorders had abnormal infrared signatures.

They would bear watching.

More than Olivia, a small voice whispered inside.

She doesn't trust me, he shot back.

Why should she trust him?

More importantly, why didn't he trust her? Not only had she denied being an ally of Asmodeus, she'd had every opportunity to finish him off on the escape from the Belvedere. Instead, she'd saved his pathetic life. She'd slept in the chair next to his bedside after his surgery, waiting for him to wake up. The worry in her eyes had been real. Too real.

You don't trust yourself.

That was the crux of the matter.

Mihàil let out a great frustrated breath and paced the deck.

It had been a glorious day. Once they'd arrived at the Mexicoplatz in their cover as newlyweds, he'd all but forgotten that it was an act. As he'd told Olivia earlier, the little things did matter, and he'd focused on making their cover as believable as possible.

Because he'd wanted to believe it.

He closed his eyes and called up the image of her face, the changeable blue-gray irises. Every time he'd kissed her today, she'd caught her breath, her heart raced, and then she'd relaxed into it. It could have been fear affecting her, but he'd tasted sincerity on her firm, warm lips, seen the way her eyelids fluttered shut, felt her lean against him. She'd fit inside his arms and against his chest in a way that could only be described as good. *Right.* When he'd kept her under vigilant guard, it wasn't out of fear that she'd run away. It was because he couldn't keep his gaze off her. She drew him as a lodestone draws true metal.

Just as he knew that she was drawn to him.

As they'd walked up the stairs to their deck, their hands entwined, he'd suddenly seen her thoughts as vividly as if they'd been his own thoughts. Sweet Heaven, he'd thought that they were *his* thoughts. He hadn't realized that they were sharing the same fantasy until their linked hands grew warm. Their harmonics had synced without him noticing, and their nimbuses had melded at their joined hands.

But it was more than that. His viewpoint had been hers. He'd seen their lovemaking through *her* eyes, experienced their connection through *her* senses.

Triumph and desire had arced through him with the force of an electrical charge—knocking their joined hands apart. Whatever expression had been on his face had shocked Olivia, but relief had flooded him when his brain had cleared. Never in his long life had he ever felt such an intense attraction. He wondered if they'd survive a physical coupling or be burned to a crisp.

Mihàil groaned and sat in a deck chair, dropping his forehead into his hand. His chest ached where the *subulam* had punctured it. Rubbing at the incision with heated fingertips, he let his thoughts drift. He pictured Olivia's breasts, their plump weight fitting perfectly against his palms, their rosy-brown nipples the size and texture of large raspberries. He hardened against his too-tight slacks, his skin heating until sweat dotted his upper lip. The ache in his groin made him forget his chest wound. And made his head throb.

He laughed. It sounded hoarse and strained even to his ears.

"What's so funny?" Olivia said across the deck from him.

Mihàil stood. His heart knocked against his ribcage. How had she reached this deck without him being aware of it? He couldn't remember the last time anyone, human or *Elioud,* had taken him off guard. Should Asmodeus ever find out....

She sighed. "It's hot up here. And smoky, Dragon Man. You didn't tell me you created your own lair wherever you go."

Mihàil cleared his throat. "I am sorry." He cleared his throat again. "I am not as in-control as I would like."

She crossed over to the deck chair next to him and sat down on it sideways. She still wore the body-hugging dress. Its sequins caught the faint light from the moon and glittered as she moved. When she turned back to face him, the diamond engagement ring flashed. The scent of roses and freesia wafted toward him.

"Ah. Your emotions come out as heat and smoke." At his nod, she said, "Perhaps it would help clear the air if we talk about the obvious attraction we have for each other."

Mihàil clenched his jaw. "As you wish."

Several moments passed. He didn't know what she wanted him to say, so he waited.

Finally she spoke. "I suppose it makes you angry to want a woman you think is in league with your greatest enemy, especially after you nearly died from a *bogomili* attack."

"No!" he said. It came out sounding harsher than he'd intended. For the first time ever, his *Elioud* charm failed to engage. He was going to have to work just to sound civil. Running a hand through his hair, he forced calm into his voice. "No."

"You sound angry to me."

He released his jaw and clenched it again. It didn't help. "I do not think that you are a Grey *Elioud*. I never did."

"No?" The soft question sounded rhetorical. "But you don't deny being angry?"

"I do not deny wanting you," he said.

The statement hung heavy in the heated air. He hadn't intended to project power, but somehow the immensity of his desire had infused his words. Even in the dim light he could see the shiver that ran through her. He gripped the deck chair with both hands. He didn't want to *compel* her to respond. But he sure as hell did want her to respond. He wanted nothing more than for her to climb into his lap, intent shining in her lovely eyes. He wanted her to straddle him, to bend over and grab his jaw with both hands as she kissed him, her body pressed against his. He wanted it so badly he could feel the sequins of her dress pressing against his silk shirt, taste the sweetness of her tongue and lips.

She sucked in an audible breath. "Why does that make you angry? Don't you want to want me?"

Mihàil flinched at her question. He couldn't stand to hurt her again, but he had to be blunt. It would hurt both of them less in the long run.

"No."

"Let me see if I understand. You don't think I'm an ally of Asmodeus. You want me, but you don't want to want me. Did I summarize that correctly?"

Mihàil scowled. Apparently Olivia knew how to be blunt too. "Yes."

"Why am I here then?"

"So that I can protect you."

"Really, Dragon Man? Protect me from whom? There are no *bogomili* on board, of that I'm sure. And Miró told me that Asmodeus is in some sort of angelic coma." She sounded exasperated. "Well, let me be clear. We're done with our true romance." She tugged at her hand as she spoke. "Tomorrow when we reach Bratislava, your bride will unexpectedly leave you."

At this she tossed something. It hit his chest with a cold *thud*. Mihàil scrabbled at the object as it rolled, catching it before it fell to the deck. Then she stood up and walked away. He heard her descend the stairs. Mihàil raised his fist and opened it. He already knew what he would find there. It was the engagement ring. Despite knowing that nothing had ended between them because nothing had been real, he felt hollow.

The next morning, Mihàil sat alone on the open terrace at the end of the ship, his breakfast untasted and his coffee cooling as he stared out over the Danube. It was another brilliant day, and he wished Olivia sat there sharing it with him.

She remained in the suite asleep, her long blond hair dangling in a braid over the side of the bed. He'd checked on her earlier, tempted to damn the consequences, strip his clothes, and slide into bed next to her. Instead he'd returned to the sofa where he'd lain awake the rest of the night, thinking about her.

"A chocolate croissant! How delightful!" Zophie sat in the seat across from him before plucking the pastry from his plate and biting delicately into it. "Oh," she breathed after chewing, "it's like manna."

Mihàil turned to look at her. "Would you like an espresso?" he asked.

"Cappuccino, please." His guardian angel took another bite of the pastry with her eyes closed, chewing with obvious pleasure. She was dressed as a casual tourist with a floral blouse and knee-length white walking shorts.

Mihàil raised his hand to signal the waitress and ordered a cappuccino and a fresh espresso for himself.

Zophie finished the croissant and then took a strawberry from his plate. She peered at it and then sniffed the luscious red berry before nibbling it. Then, giving a sigh, she popped the whole thing into her mouth.

Mihàil waited while Zophie tried more items, sipping his hot espresso as he did. The diminutive angel had a pixie haircut and a heart-shaped face, her brilliant eyes angelic blue. Just having her here at his table soothed the ache in his chest and eased tension between his shoulders that he hadn't realized was there. No matter what, Zophie was on his side.

"She's quite lovely, Mihàil," she said at last, picking up her cappuccino and sipping it. "Oh, such a treat even if Marco had nothing to do with creating it."

Mihàil said nothing. He'd known the Capuchin friar Marco d'Aviano. If that holy man hadn't invented the popular coffee drink named after his religious order, he would nevertheless approve of it.

"She's stronger than you give her credit for," Zophie said, looking at him directly.

"I'm a *drangùe*. My mother is a full-blooded *Irim*. And still Asmodeus found me a willing ally."

Zophie put her hand on his. His harmonics tuned into hers and for a brief moment he experienced harmony with the celestial. It was almost unbearably exquisite. "My dear, that was a long time ago. Michael himself knows how sincere your penance has been." She tilted her head. "Oh, silly man! Don't be obtuse! Olivia doesn't weaken you."

"Asmodeus already tested that idea," Mihàil said, rubbing his chest.

Zophie leaned over the table, placing her hand over his wound. Warmth burrowed into him, erasing the lingering ache. She sat back with a dramatic sigh followed by a giggle. "I know, right? I bet he thinks long and hard about touching your girl again. Shame about the vessel, but we're using Olivia's technique as a training video for new guardian angels. She's got great instincts."

Mihàil blinked. Zophie always took him by surprise. "She is not 'my girl.'"

"Your mother likes her," Zophie said with a sly smile. "She's created a new rose cultivar called The Harlequin. It's a long-stemmed white with a very heady fragrance that has hints of ginger and freesia. She's already sent it to the gardener at your estate outside Shkodër."

When Mihàil sat stunned at this news, Zophie leaned across the table again. He would have sworn that she'd grown a foot in an instant. "Don't. Let. Her. Go. Dragon. Man." She poked him in the chest at every word. "You don't want to disappoint your mother, do you?"

Olivia woke feeling wrung out and sore at heart. She'd lain awake half the night, angry and hurt and listening for Mihàil, hoping that he'd change his mind and come to her. And that had made her angrier and jabbed her heart harder, but no matter how she struggled to let the hurt, anger, and hope go, they'd played tag with each other for hours until she'd finally drifted into an uneasy sleep filled with dark, smoky dreams. Now in the clear morning light she no longer felt angry or hurt, just tired. Her *sensei* had long warned her to master her emotions or they would master her. He wanted her to be more like Beta and less like Stasia.

No, that wasn't right. Stasia *expressed* her emotions easily, but she didn't hold onto them. She might have a passionate heart, but she had a cold eye.

The scent of roses lingered in the cabin. It had been their fragrance that had finally soothed Olivia enough to sleep. She shoved away the blanket and sat up. She needed to stretch and practice her forms. Those would help her find her equilibrium and boost her mood. If she'd had her *bō*, she could have practiced on their private veranda, but there was nothing to do about that right now.

Rummaging through the drawers in the storage area, she found some leggings and a tank top. Bras, panties, and socks filled the top drawers. On the bottom of the closet she found a pair of what looked like dancer's shoes. When she stooped to pick them up, she realized that her *bō* rested behind them.

Whooping in delight, she grabbed it up and set it on the dresser. Then she stripped out of her camisole and pajama capris, dressing quickly. She had no idea where Mihàil had gone, but it wasn't a large ship. He could return any moment. She'd rather spend as little time in his company as necessary. After dressing, she considered what to bring when disembarking in Bratislava before noon. Stasia had made sure that she had a backpack. Checking it, Olivia found her *zentai* hood in the front pocket as well as a 9mm Kahr, some euros and a prepaid Visa, a Czech passport, and a burner phone. Thank God for her friends! They'd made it much easier for her to ditch Mihàil.

Olivia shoved some clothing into the backpack. As she did, gold glinted on her left hand. She stopped and stared at the wedding band. She twisted it, thinking, and then held her hand away from herself. The ring looked natural. And, as pocket litter went, fairly useful. A wedding band would help ward off the attentions of annoying but harmless men looking for a love connection. It might also delay anyone looking for her as a single woman, especially if she found accommodations for her and her absent husband.

Satisfied that she had a reason to keep wearing the wedding band, Olivia finished packing by tossing some toiletries into her improvised go-bag. Last, she slipped her collapsed *bō* into the partly zipped bag so that she could remove it quickly and left the suite. She carried it in one hand as she jogged up the stairs to the sun deck and the walking track there. A handful of gray-haired tourists walked in the morning sunshine, chatting. One elderly woman sat wrapped in a blanket at a table reading a book. Olivia ignored everyone and stretched out among the tables and chairs, letting the smell of the river and the warmth from the sun ease her tight muscles and clear her mind.

After she'd loosened up a bit, she closed her eyes and began practicing her forms. She imagined that she was standing in front of her *sensei*, his arms behind his back and a frown on his face. She released her shoulders and flowed from one sequence to the next, breathing as she extended her arms or widened her stance. The familiar movements relaxed her. After twenty minutes, sweat slicked her skin and soaked her tank top; she could feel the burn in her abdomen and loose strands of hair clung to her forehead.

"Water?" asked a voice in her ear.

Olivia startled and opened her eyes. Mihàil stood next to her, holding out a frosted bottle. His unshaven cheeks and the dark smudges under his eyes confirmed that he hadn't rested well either.

She hissed and spun away, settling into a ready stance, her hands fisted at her side. She didn't look at the deck chair to the left of Mihàil where she'd dropped her backpack. If she could get close enough, she'd grab her *bō*. Even though she could fight without it, she felt naked.

"Here." Mihàil tossed the bottle toward her.

Olivia stopped it in mid-air with a foot before kicking it back at him. He stepped aside easily.

"This really isn't the best place to spar," he said, but he'd widened his own stance and faced her.

"Then leave."

He said nothing in response, just narrowed his eyes. For a moment, reality rushed in at her. She took in his height and massive shoulders, arms, and chest. He was a good six inches taller than her and almost 100 pounds heavier. And he was a trained fighter. She wasn't some foolish young woman raised on Lara Croft and Hollywood movies with women her size busting male heads and kicking serious ass. She couldn't hope to best him in a sparring match, and he'd only make her feel worse when he shut her down with gentlemanly care. Hurt and anger flared again at that thought. Why couldn't he just be a total jerk so that her feelings for him would evaporate?

He might be trained, but he was weakened from his injury. And she *was* a damn good martial artist who'd sparred with some of the best at the Company. Her *sensei* had drilled her on how to take down a big man. The keys were surprise, aggression, and exploiting weak points. If Mihàil had any of these, that is.

Lifting her chin, she shifted her weight. She saw when he recognized the subtle movement.

"Olivia," he said, his gaze never leaving her, "I am sorry. I never meant to hurt you."

"Well, you did," she said, feinting to the right.

When he followed, his arms moving into a block, she flung her right leg into a low sweeping kick. It connected with his thigh. As he flinched reflexively, she jumped and clapped her hands over his ears. His arms rushed up a beat later to shove her own arms out and away before his flat hand connected with her mid-chest. She stumbled backwards, just missing the small herb garden growing in a raised container behind her. Mihàil had held back, but she rubbed at her breastbone anyway and regained her balance. Her St. Michael's pendant, exposed to the morning sun, burned the thin skin above her breasts.

Mihàil closed his eyes and shook his head a couple of times. His sensitive hearing must really be ringing. She grinned. He opened his eyes. Something flared in his gaze at her triumph.

"I know. Please forgive me." His plea caught her off guard, but she covered it by shifting to the left. If she could unbalance him again, perhaps she could reach her *bō*. That would go a long way to equalizing them.

He leaned almost imperceptibly to his right. "I've wanted you since the moment I set eyes on you."

"If we're being honest now," she said, "I guess I should admit I've wanted you since I saw you sleeping in that chair at the ABA offices." As she said the last words, she rushed at him. She feinted a front kick before pivoting right so close to his body that his scent followed her.

His hand shot out and grasped her left arm, which slipped from his fingers as she pivoted again behind him. *Sweat and speed*, she thought, *will do it every time*. She ran for the deckchair with her backpack. Snatching it up, she yanked the collapsed *bō* out, flinging the backpack from her as she turned toward Mihàil and extended the *bō* at the same time.

Mihàil never took his gaze from her face. "But I cannot act on it."

"Can't or won't?" she asked, surprised that the hurt flared to life again, stronger than ever. She lunged at him, swinging the *bō* around her head before striking.

He blocked it without looking, his right forearm taking the hit. It appeared that he hardly noticed the blow even though it had to hurt like hell. She got the feeling that he'd been playing with her up until now, letting her think that she'd succeeded in outmaneuvering him, that she'd managed to teach him some lessons. Confused, she backpedaled, settling into the familiar ready stance just beyond the reach of her *bō*.

"Both." Mihàil tilted his head. "Are you going to let me speak or are you going to keep attacking me?"

"I'm just getting started," she said and launched herself at him. For the next thirty seconds, she danced around him, aiming blows with both ends of the *bō*, ducking to strike at the back of his thighs only to pop up and charge at his head. He blocked the head shots with little effort, turning as she attacked, but he made no effort to block the shots to his legs. After the thirty furious seconds, Olivia danced back and settled into her ready stance, her chest heaving but her breathing silent.

Mihàil remained where he was, focused on her. His gaze shone. Her confusion grew. He looked proud *and* predatory. As though she'd acted exactly as he wanted.

"There is a lot that you do not understand, Wild *Elioud*," he said. His voice was soft, yet it filled the air around them. Olivia realized that the gray-haired tourists had left at some point after she'd pulled the *bō* out. They were all alone.

"Why don't you explain it to me?" she asked, her mind busy considering angles of attack and methods for getting him flat on his back on the deck.

"Stop that," he commanded. Though he hadn't raised his voice, there was an unmistakable—and inescapable—command to it.

She shivered and gripped her *bō* tighter with her sweaty palms, tensing to move. She tried to ease to the right, but she found that she couldn't. Her eyes widened, but her training kept her from betraying her shock further.

"I am a *drangùe*. That means that I am the son of an angel—a fiery serpent, a *dragon*—and a human. My father, the Dragon of Albania, was himself the son of an angel and a human mother."

Olivia's throat tightened and her mouth went dry. "That means you're almost a full-blooded angel," she managed to whisper. How had she forgotten that he was more than just a man? For some reason, she began to shake.

Mihàil's eyes narrowed. "Relax." His rich baritone filled her hearing and soothed her spine. She stopped shaking. "Yes, I am almost a full angel, an *Irim*. But I am not. I am an *Elioud*."

He came toward her, deliberately and slowly lifting his hands to grasp her *bō*. He pulled it from her unresisting hold and lowered it to the deck next to his foot without taking his gaze from hers. Then he took her hands and began to massage her stiff fingers. His warm ones engulfed her smaller hands.

"I am both man and angel. I cannot make love to you without accepting the consequences."

"Consequences?" she asked. Her mind had gone blank with him so near. The warm scent of him, of male musk, cedar, clove, and a hint of charcoal, disoriented her.

"Yes. Consequences." He leaned forward a little, his massive arms and chest surrounding her. She shivered. "Lovemaking is not a casual physical act, Olivia."

She swallowed. His blue eyes had darkened as he spoke of making love to her. Electricity gathered in her groin and tingled in every nerve tip. Her nipples hardened painfully. She grew wet and full. Her skin overheated. Even her comfortable leggings and tank top felt too tight. Somewhere in her rational mind, it alarmed her that Mihàil could move her from anger to desire so quickly.

Licking her dry lips, she whispered, "I've never done anything casually, Dragon Man."

He bent his head and kissed her, softly at first and then when she relaxed against him, he took her lips more aggressively with his, running his tongue over them until hers parted. Then he nipped the corner of her mouth and pulled back enough to look at her again.

"I know that." Now his gaze turned sober, desire tamped down if not gone. "Lovemaking is meant to bind two souls into one. I cannot make love to you without making you mine. Do you understand?"

He waited for her to answer. Olivia didn't really understand, but she knew that he was quite serious. She wobbled a nod, a slight frown between her eyes. He stepped away from her then, leaving her bereft of his warmth and support. The breeze from the river cooled her flushed, sweaty skin. Gooseflesh sprung up on her arms.

"I cannot make you mine, Olivia, without greater consequences." Now his face looked bleak. "I am a *drangùe*. I forgot that once, and many people died as a result."

Olivia didn't think. She acted on instinct. Stepping toward Mihàil, she took his hands and looked up into his face. He didn't resist her. She cupped his jaw with her hand and rose onto her toes to kiss him. He didn't kiss her back, but he also didn't pull away. She rubbed her thumb over his chin, the coarse stubble prickling her. He leaned his cheek into her hand and closed his eyes.

"That's a heavy burden that you bear," she said softly.

He opened his eyes, and the pain in them took Olivia's breath away. When he spoke, his voice cracked. "I had a wife. Her name was Luljeta, which means 'flower of life.' Luljeta was not an *Elioud*, and I married her against my father's wishes. She was killed by the minions of a Dark *Irim*."

All at once, Olivia understood what Mihàil had been warning her about the night before.

"You became Asmodeus's acolyte," she said, horrified wonder in her voice.

She dropped her hand from his face. Hurt flared in his gaze, but he stepped away from her.

"Yes. I became his acolyte as my father, the Dragon of Albania, lay dying of malaria while my mother watched over him. Asmodeus had minions in the

Ottoman Empire, so I joined the court of the sultan, eventually rising to lead a cavalry regiment for Suleiman the Magnificent."

He fell silent and looked toward the Danube through narrowed eyes. A muscle worked in his jaw. After a moment, he began speaking again.

"I did not want to take my rightful place as my father's heir. As a *drangùe*. I made the mistake of trying to live as just a man. I was selfish and self-centered. Then I compounded my mistake by joining with Asmodeus. What hubris!" he laughed. It was a bitter sound. "It was my own fault that Luljeta was targeted by the Dark *Irim*, but instead of admitting it, I wallowed in my grief until Asmodeus worked his charms on me. He told me everything I wanted to hear so that he could use me. Now my guilt torments me, another victory for him."

He turned back to Olivia.

"This war with the Dark *Irim* has eternal consequences. After the *Irim* disobeyed and married humans, the Archangel Michael sentenced them to penance in order to redeem themselves and rejoin the *Angeli Fidelis*, the ones who never rebelled. The Dark *Irim* rejected Michael's penance. They remain here on Earth as an angelic scourge for humanity's faults."

"The *Elioud*," Olivia said, thinking aloud. "St. Michael made them angelic protectors against the Dark *Irim*."

Mihàil nodded. "The Archangel Michael commands our forces, such as they are, against Dark *Irim* and Lucifer's demons. We defend the innocent with our lives."

Olivia felt a tingle of *déjà vu* run down her spine. Her St. Michael medal grew warm, drawing her fingers. As she rubbed it, she remembered that she'd told Beta and Stasia that *her* definition of *Elioud* had been 'one who defends the innocent from monsters. And will never, ever give up.'

She shivered. What if the monsters were fallen angels that never, ever gave up?

"And a *drangùe* is not just an ordinary *Elioud*, is he?" she asked softly.

"A *drangùe* is Archangel Michael's general. That is why I cannot make you mine." His expression grew severe and his gaze distant. "It may already be too late."

"Why?"

Mihàil looked at Olivia, and the anguish in his gaze punched her in the gut.

"Because Asmodeus recognized that I care about you at the Belvedere. He will stop at nothing to use you to get at me."

Sixteen

Their cruise ship reached Bratislava late morning. Olivia watched as the massive rectangular Bratislava Castle with its white walls and red roof sitting on a rocky, forested outcropping grew larger. Below it sat the Old Town whose matching red-roofed buildings could be glimpsed beyond the large, modern buildings that bordered the Danube. Though tiny and landlocked among the Little Carpathians, a short, low mountain range, Slovakia ranked high in terms of development and standard of living, two facts that Olivia knew from her cover as an intern at ABA-Invest Austria. She had, in fact, traveled to a conference in Bratislava this past spring and fallen in love with the charming capital. For an instant, she considered disembarking and finding a place to hole up on her own.

But the urge passed just as swiftly. Though she knew that it made more sense in terms of her invisibility to the CIA, hiding from her employer was the least of her worries. As long as she and Mihàil continued to play newlyweds, they would attract no attention from the other tourists. The fact that they'd sailed out of Vienna last night without any *polizei* or *Bundespolizei* officers swarming the ship meant that efforts to track them had been focused elsewhere, though Olivia suspected that Miró and Andràs had been very busy flitting around Vienna, here whispering a false lead, there feeding sightings of Mihàil with their angelic abilities.

No, she had only two concerns about evading detection.

The first was whether Stasia had left any trace of any of them in Vienna during their hasty plans for departure. As far as Olivia knew, the CIA had no intel tying her to Stasia beyond the mission that she'd led in Venice, and that would not lead

Fagan or anyone else to suspect that Stasia had joined her in a crusade against sexual predators using their agencies' connections.

The second was harder to quantify and definitely much more terrifying.

Mihàil had assured her that the *bogomili* were too brainless to come after them alone. But the clock was ticking on when Asmodeus would come out of his angelic coma. Mihàil wasn't sure how long that would be because it had been eons since any Dark *Irim's* angelic fire had rebounded on him. Olivia's gratitude at the respite was immense, yet incomplete. Once Asmodeus woke up, he could find her harmonic signature instantly now that he'd had his hands on her. That is, unless she'd learned how to camouflage it by then.

Or she'd found safety with Mihàil inside his estate in Albania, where his *Elioud* strength was amplified.

She glanced out of the corner of her eye at the brooding *drangùe* standing nearby on the cruise ship's sun deck.

Learning that he'd once been married had done something to her view of him.

She'd already stopped thinking of Mihàil as a rich European playboy who may have ties to the Albanian mafia. The truth was that he was a lot like her: living a life to cover for his real mission to save innocents.

But now that she'd spent more time with him, her heart told her that he didn't fully embrace that cover. Oh, he was wealthy and escorted beautiful women to photo-op-worthy events and venues. Yet he'd said that love-making wasn't a casual, physical act but rather meant to bind two souls together. If he made love to her, he'd said, he'd make her *his*.

What would it feel like to be his? To belong to him? Something told her that it would be like flying and being devoured by fire at the same time.

She laughed softly to herself. *How appropriate for a dragon man.*

The long-dead Luljeta had been his. She'd stake her life that only Luljeta had ever been his. Mihàil did not have sex. He did not *fuck*.

Sharp jealousy twisted in her gut.

Olivia shivered and looked fully at the angel man who'd captured her imagination. Images of his naked chest rose before her mind's eye to taunt her only to be replaced by memories of him fighting next to her at the Belvedere.

She closed her eyes and breathed in deeply, clutching at the railing in front of her. Now she better understood the words *terrible beauty* and *awe*. Mihàil embodied the first two and inspired the other. She'd been so focused on their cover lives and escaping Vienna that she'd ignored the reality of what he was. If she hadn't, she would never have acted the hurt and betrayed lover. Shame burned her as she remembered attacking him. They could never be lovers. They weren't *that* much alike. He'd made that starkly clear when he'd told her that he'd tried to live as a man and how much it had cost in lost lives, including the woman he'd loved.

When she opened her eyes again, she found that she was playing with the wedding band that she still wore.

"You will not have to wear it much longer." Mihàil's low baritone sent goosebumps racing down her spine.

She looked up at him. He'd moved closer while she was thinking.

"It's just strange having it on," she murmured.

He smiled. It was rueful. "I, too, find this gold band an odd sensation."

"Didn't you wear a wedding band before?" Why was her heart in her throat as she asked?

He shook his head. "It was not the custom during my marriage. My parents wore half of a gimmel ring before their ceremony, though my father kept his in a small pouch most of the time. And then my mother wore both once they were married. She gave me the set after my father's death."

"Gimmel ring?" she asked, puzzled.

"*Gimmel* is from the Latin for twin. Here." Mihàil pulled an ornate ring from his right pinky finger. She'd noticed it before but had thought it was a family heirloom. He held it out to her.

Olivia took it. It was very heavy and not at all a modern style worn by a fashionable European playboy. A diamond and a ruby were set in a raised yellow-gold bezel. Strangely, a visible seam ran between the gems. On either side, carved hands clasped red-enameled hearts. Ornate, enamel-filled scrollwork bordered the top and bottom of the setting. She saw a Latin inscription on the outside edges of the gold band.

"Let me show you."

Olivia handed the ring back to Mihàil, watching closely as he slid it back onto his finger before pinching it with his other thumb and forefinger. A moment later, he pulled half the ring off and handed it to her. Surprised, she accepted the diamond and raised it for closer study.

"For a time, the custom was for each betrothed partner to wear half of the wedding ring. Then, at the ceremony, the groom would give his half to the bride, signifying their union."

"Is that what the inscription says?" Olivia asked, fascinated. "*Homo Non Separabit...*"

"*...Quod Deus Coniunxit,*" Mihàil finished. "Whom God has joined together, let no man separate."

Olivia handed the ring back to him. "A pretty symbolism."

Mihàil slid it next to its partner. "Yes, although it meant the husband did not wear a ring." He paused, not meeting her gaze and looking uncomfortable. "You should wear the engagement ring until we reach Budapest."

Olivia swallowed and, biting her lip, nodded. Mihàil reached into his pants pocket and pulled the diamond ring out. The sun struck a dazzling glint from the flawless gem as he slipped it back onto her trembling hand. Next to the antique gimmel ring, it seemed ostentatious and impersonal. He said nothing but dropped her fingers as soon as the ring was in place.

They fell silent as the ship came into dock. After a moment, a crew member came around to inform the passengers that they were free to disembark and explore Bratislava on their own. At this, Mihàil placed his hand on Olivia's lower back and guided her toward the stairs. As they reached the pier, Olivia saw Jack and Amelia, who smiled and waved. Without conscious effort, Olivia adopted the Caterina persona as she clasped Mihàil's hand before smiling broadly and waving back at the British couple. Jack grinned and nodded but gripped

Amelia's arm above her elbow and urged her to continue along the waterfront toward the city.

"Relieved to tour Old Town without our new friends?" Mihàil asked as Amelia pulled her arm away before scolding her husband.

"What?" Olivia said, looking up at him in confusion.

"You just heaved a heartfelt sigh," he said, smiling.

"Hm?" she asked, bemused by his ever-shocking blue gaze.

"Never mind," he said and laughed.

By unspoken consent, they parted from the main stream of disembarking passengers and headed east toward the Blue Church. The sky was clear, the temperature mild, and the cobbled streets lined with pastel buildings, cafés, and restaurants. Although they left behind many of their fellow travelers, hundreds of tourists jammed the narrow streets. Despite this, Olivia drank in the Gothic and Baroque architecture, the fountains and statues, the umbrella-covered tables, and the immaculate streets. The Slovaks loved their capital, and it showed in how well they cared for it.

After a leisurely twenty-minute stroll interspersed with stops to browse a souvenir vendor and to listen to a harpist, who sat straighter and played better at the attention, they arrived at the Art Nouveau church painted a delicate, fairy blue and roofed with blue-glazed tiles. Officially the Church of St. Elizabeth, it looked as if it had been assembled from fondant for a wedding cake, complete with a tall, round bell tower and white-sugar details.

Inside, Olivia ran a hand over the blue-painted back of a pew near the altar before sliding into the seat. She watched curiously as Mihàil knelt on one knee, crossed himself, and then slid into the pew next to her.

They sat quietly for several minutes. A few other visitors had also found seats. No one sitting spoke, and those curious individuals who came only to view the inside chatted in hushed tones along the back and sides.

"My cousin Emily would have loved this church," Olivia said before she could stop herself. She toyed with a flyer that a street musician had shoved into her hand as they'd walked. Without really thinking about it, she folded the top down a third and then tore along the fold line until she had a square.

Mihàil said nothing, but she felt his attention on her.

She began folding the square as she continued. "She was like my sister. I don't have any siblings, but we grew up in nearby towns, so we spent a lot of time together. We were going to go to the same college, live in the same dorm and everything."

Something hard lodged in her chest, but she'd learned a lot about self-control from her *sensei* and her time as an intelligence officer for the Company, so she kept folding the paper. Mihàil placed his hand on her upper back. It was oddly soothing even though he did no more than rest it there.

"Emily was such a romantic. And outgoing. Not me. I was too shy and nerdy. She got me a date to her prom, took me shopping for a dress. Did my hair and makeup. Made me practice dancing." Olivia had started talking in a fast monotone, chopping her sentences up to get them out. She hadn't talked about her cousin since she'd testified at Emily's ex-boyfriend's trial. But she folded the paper with sure fingers.

"She was a very popular girl, always had lots of friends. Boys liked her. She dated a few. Then she met Jin in AP Biology. He was her lab partner. Emily felt sorry for him at first. She was very compassionate, always noticing when someone needed help. Animals too. So Jin was someone she wanted to help. She said he was nerdy. Like me."

Here Olivia gave a shudder and the folded paper slipped from her fingers. Mihàil picked it up and handed it to her. The hand on her back began to rub gentle circles.

"Emily and Jin dated for two years. The whole time he'd been suspicious of all her friends. Jealous. Controlling. Angry. He punched a locker at school once. Another time, he picked up a chair and flung it. It caught her foot. I think she broke a toe, but she wouldn't tell her mom. The summer between our junior and senior year Jin found Emily in a hammock with another boy. He dumped them out, and she hit her head hard. I tried to tell her that she had to get away from him, that he wasn't a good guy. She thought he was just immature. I tried to tell my aunt and uncle that something was broken in Jin, but he was always well behaved around them."

Olivia stopped talking. She was shaking and breathing shallowly. She closed her eyes and calmed her breathing. It was a long time ago. Why did it feel as if it had just happened?

"Emily finally broke up with Jin her senior year. She was happy, making plans to go to college out of state. But he kept texting her. He'd leave her pleading messages in her voicemail. He told her that he couldn't live without her. That they belonged together. He stopped hanging out with all his friends. His mom took him to a psychiatrist, but he refused help. She came to see Emily and asked her to talk to Jin. A month after graduation, Emily met him for a talk after work at his house.

"They found her body the next morning half submerged in a marsh. It was July Fourth, which is Independence Day in the U.S. Jin had strangled her with a bungee cord in his garage, then slit her throat. He then methodically dumped her body and cleaned up the evidence. I testified at his trial a year and a half later. He's serving a life sentence with no parole."

By the time that Olivia finished her story, she'd quit shaking and spoke in a flat voice. In her hand, she held an origami eagle.

Mihàil pulled her into his side before stroking her hair. "Is that why you became the harlequin?" His voice was gentle. It eased into her numbness like water down a parched throat.

"Yes," she whispered.

Mihàil turned her face up towards him, and the look in his eyes nearly broke her. He swiped his thumbs across her cheeks, and Olivia realized that tears sheeted down them. He kissed her softly and then pulled her closer. Even though it was warm in the church, she burrowed against him.

"Why the paper?" he asked after she'd stopped crying.

Olivia sat up. She felt drained but different somehow. Lighter. She held the origami eagle out on her flat palm.

"My therapist suggested that I focus on folding origami during our sessions," she said, not looking at him. "Keeping my hands busy helped me to talk to her." She handed the origami to him. "It's an eagle."

Mihàil cocked his head. "So it is." His gaze moved towards hers. "Albania is said to be the land of eagles."

"I know." She nodded. "I always preferred eagles to cranes. They're fearless and rule the skies."

She watched in surprise as he stood and walked to the altar where he set the folded paper down.

As they left the Blue Church, Olivia noticed the two Germans from their cruise wandering around the walking paths, but the two men seemed unware of their presence. She frowned.

Mihàil's protective urges had surged as Olivia shared her heartbreaking tale, so that was perhaps why his battle senses were exquisitely responsive as they left the Church of St. Elizabeth. The two men who had had dinner with them the night before were taking photos as he and Olivia headed away from the church, but he knew immediately that they were following him and Olivia.

He took her hand in his, smiling down at her when she looked up at him. Her watercolor eyes were red-rimmed and bright from crying. He hummed and shifted his harmonics again as he had done in the Blue Church, satisfied when Olivia's harmonics shifted with his. Though she might not trust him enough to tell him all her secrets, she trusted him on this elemental level in a way that he had never experienced with any *Elioud* before. As they synced, he felt her harmonics mesh with his in an intensely satisfying thrum. Olivia subtly straightened next to him, and when he said something to her, the gaze she turned on him had sharpened and lost its grief.

"Where are you taking me?" she asked. "Does it have something to do with our dinner companions from last night?"

Mihàil grinned, pleased at her quickness. "I thought that we would walk through St. Michael's Gate before touring the rest of Old Town. Do you mind?"

"Not at all," she assured him. "You can take me shopping for a Swarovski piece to commemorate our visit. There is also a quaint café close by that has very filling gnocchi. I'm rather hungry after our sparring."

Mihàil enjoyed their short walk to the last medieval gate of Old Town Bratislava, especially because it gave him the opportunity to observe how well

Olivia kept track of their tail. By now, he suspected that the two men targeted wealthy travelers to rob. Olivia's three-carat diamond had certainly caught a gleam in their eyes the night before. The stroll that they had taken afterwards on Handelskai would have been ideal for lifting valuables from the various cruise ship passengers, who tended to be retired and wealthy.

"You know, my dear," he said, smiling down at her. "I think that we should make sure to get a *very* special Swarovski piece, one that will dazzle any who lays eyes on it."

"I agree." She lowered her eyelids coyly. "I expect nothing less. You've set a very high standard, my love."

Mihàil knew that Olivia only played a part, in this case, a willing accomplice in an impromptu mission, but the words "my love" made his heart squeeze and his temperature rise. Ignoring both, he steered her into the Swarovski shop where they browsed conspicuously among the special-edition sculptures costing thousands of euros. At Olivia's excited and very audible gasp, Mihàil smiled. She had found the Swarovski recreation of the statue of St. Michael and the Dragon erected at the top of the gate's tower.

"That is perfect," he said, drawing his wallet from an inside jacket pocket. His battle senses had been tingling the whole time that they shopped among the crystal decorations. With a flourish, he pulled out a credit card, carelessly displaying the stack of bills inside, and handed it to the salesman. "Please wrap our selection very carefully. We are still shopping."

The man nodded and turned away from them. Olivia clapped her hands together before whirling and, standing on tiptoe, planting a kiss on him. Her eyes sparkled.

"What's the plan?" she asked in a low voice before settling back onto her feet.

"After lunch, we return to visit the Instítute Dior before ascending to the sixth floor of the tower to look out over Old Town," he said. "It is a tantalizing view."

She pressed her lips together and narrowed her eyes thoughtfully. "Yes, the castle beckons, but there are so many interesting stops along the way. It may take us all afternoon to make our way back to the ship carrying our precious Swarovski statue."

He nodded gravely. "Indeed. We will need to be very careful with it."

SEVENTEEN

The two Germans hunted the wealthy Italian newlyweds.

Friedrich and Johann watched the blithely happy couple stroll arm-in-arm from the Swarovski store across Michalská Street toward a set of large arched carved doors open to foot traffic. Inside the building, a wide cobbled hall led between restaurants and shops toward another arched doorway a few dozen meters away. The couple walked at an unhurried pace without looking behind them before they entered a traditional Slovak restaurant near the far entrance on the right.

Friedrich continued walking past and out the other entrance. Johann, who'd stopped and pretended to read the directory outside a set of glass doors leading to offices on the upper floors, returned to Michalská to wait. He sat at a wooden table covered with an awning at an outdoor restaurant in the middle of the street where he could see the entrance to the Slovak restaurant.

They had their quarry trapped.

But an hour later when the woman left the restaurant, she was alone. She headed back toward Michalská as Johann pondered what to do. The woman had the diamond ring and the Swarovski statue. She'd be a profitable target and easier to overwhelm alone. The man wore expensive tailored clothes that accentuated his superb physique. If he caught Friedrich lifting his wallet, he'd likely put up a fight.

Johann grinned at the thought. Working out with a trainer in a weight room was no match for a man skilled at dirty street fighting who had no qualms about blood. The well-groomed husband might land a punch, but that's all he'd manage. But an altercation, no matter how brief, might make snagging the wallet too risky if it brought undue attention. Friedrich would have to be very, very careful.

Decided, Johann sent a text to his partner. "Eyes on her. Divide and conquer."

An answering text said, "No eyes on him yet."

Johann watched the woman enter a high-end salon that had a window front on the street. She wandered through the empty retail area until she reached the perfume section where an impressive number of bottles lined open shelves.

Johann called Friedrich before slipping his cellphone into his jacket pocket where the call would remain open. They wore blue-tooth earbuds to coordinate their efforts.

"Find him," Johann said. "He's probably in the toilet. While you *charm* him, I'll just happen to run into the blushing bride in the salon. Meet outside the souvenir shop on Michalská in fifteen minutes."

"Understood."

Friedrich entered the restaurant. Johann waited five minutes and then threw down some euros to cover his bill. There was no need for a police officer to be called. He heard Friedrich ask about the Italian. A woman told Friedrich that he was in the far corner of the restaurant drinking beer.

Johann smiled as he crossed the street and entered the wide, arched doorway. His smile broadened when he entered the salon to see that only the Italian woman was present. However, female voices murmured from a back room. He caught a handful of words related to skin care and determined that a client was receiving treatment.

Perfect.

As he sidled up to the Italian woman, he heard the Italian man—Aleso—through his earbud.

"Ah. Welcome, Friedrich. I wondered when you would join me."

That made Johann's stride hitch a little. The woman, Caterina, looked over at him. Her expression showed no surprise. Instead, there was a curious little curl to the corner of her mouth. Like the Mona Lisa's mysterious, cat-that-ate-the-canary smirk. Doubt percolated in his gut.

Aleso continued although Friedrich had said nothing. "Please, sit. Yes, that beer is yours. Our lovely server Adéla brought it for you."

There was a muffled sound followed by a grunt and a heavy *thud*.

"Really, I insist that you sit while my beautiful, clever wife greets your friend Johann."

As those words entered his hearing, the Italian woman's hand flashed and clamped onto his arm at the elbow. Her thumb dug into the crevice. Surprisingly, it hurt like hell.

"*Schiesse!*" he swore and jerked his arm spasmodically. But her iron grip didn't change.

"Johann," she said with every indication of warm satisfaction as she pivoted before locking his arm under hers and pinching the soft flesh between his thumb and forefinger with her other hand.

His arm felt like it was breaking.

"So good to see you!" she continued. "Aleso and I wondered when you and Friedrich would catch up with us." She bent in closer and said companionably, "The anticipation has been almost more than I can bear, though I do adore shopping for perfume."

Sighing dramatically, she tossed her head. Her blond hair slid on her shoulders. At that moment, a woman came from the treatment room. When she saw them, she stopped and asked if they needed help with anything.

"Oh, yes!" Caterina responded, her voice sounding frantic. "My husband has seizures. Do you have an extra room that we can use? He needs to lie down before he falls on the floor. Quickly! I can't control him when he convulses."

Alarm transformed the woman's face. "Yes, yes, of course! This way."

Caterina tugged Johann forward as he began to disagree. He stumbled at her side. His arm was on fire. Fine pinpricks of sweat broke out above his lip and on his forehead. If only he could reach the blade he had in his boot....

The salon employee stood in the hall gesturing toward an open door. "There is a bed. What should I do?"

Caterina smiled at her while jabbing an elbow into Johann's ribs when he tried to speak. His hand had grown numb. His eyes watered.

"Please, give us some quiet. Light and noise bring his seizures on. Perhaps if we get him inside, he won't begin thrashing."

Her eyes wide, the woman nodded and backed toward the front of the salon. Out of the corner of his eye, Johann saw her turn away. In his ear, he heard Friedrich whimpering.

Then Aleso spoke. "Never worry, dear Friedrich. Caterina has Johann safely in hand. Do finish your beer. It will be the last one you enjoy for a while."

Caterina hurried him toward the treatment room. As they neared the doorway, she released him. Painful prickling pulsed through his arm and fingers. Instinctively, Johann hunched forward to rub his hand. A moment later, she was on him. She wrapped an arm around his neck and pulled his torso toward her chest, drawing him down with a knee in his lower back as she braced herself against the doorframe. He clawed at her forearm under his chin. But it was too late. She'd locked her hold around his neck while simultaneously shoving the back of his head forward. Dark splotches flashed over his vision.

His final thought before passing out was, "Who are these people?"

As Johann sagged against her, Olivia swung away from the doorframe and eased him onto the padded cot in the treatment room. Working quickly, she tugged his hands behind his back and tied them with the cord of a nearby small appliance. She grabbed a second appliance and looped its cord around his ankles. Finally, she gagged him with a hot, wet towel and left him face down.

"Don't worry about the knife," she said as she stood up to study her handiwork. "I left it for the authorities to find. Of course, if it's one used in a crime, Johann, it won't go so well with you."

He squirmed vigorously in response, nearly falling from the cot. Sighing, Olivia punched him in the head, knocking him out. The blow would leave him unconscious for a few minutes, long enough for the authorities to find him before he could wriggle out of the bindings and escape.

From the doorway she took a photo of Johann with her cellphone.

"*Ciao!*" She blew the unresponsive criminal a kiss before snapping the light off and shutting the door. As she walked into the salon, the employee approached her, concern shining on her face.

"He's resting now. Thank you so much." She opened her purse and pulled out a stack of euros. "This should cover any damage he may have done."

The woman accepted the euros with a bemused expression on her face. Olivia had nearly made it to the shop door before she called out, "Wait! What about your husband?"

In the distance, sirens sounded. Olivia laughed and waved a nonchalant hand. "He won't be there long, I promise."

Outside in the cobbled passageway, she pulled her cell out and sent a quick text to Stasia with the photo attached. "Gift-wrapped and waiting."

Stasia's response was quick. "*Sono molto contento.*" *I am very content.*

A gentle tremor caressed her skin. *Mihàil.* Olivia had begun to discern harmonics in his movements. She realized that she'd been familiar with harmonics her whole life but hadn't perceived it before. It was a continuous pressurized hum that only now seemed quite obvious when she felt the subtle alterations that the *Elioud* made. Mihàil had told her that directing personal harmonics was a very powerful tool that he'd teach her how to use once they were safe at his estate outside Shkodër in Albania.

Slipping her phone into her bag, Olivia looked up in time to see Mihàil leading a docile Friedrich by the arm toward her. Sunlight from the far doorway haloed his figure and threw his face into shadows. His electric blue eyes fixated on her, sending a current up her spine. Heat pooled in her belly even though goosebumps rose on the backs of her arms. She stood straighter and waited.

Mihàil stopped by the picturesque bench near the entrance. Friedrich dropped onto the bench, closing his eyes and appearing to go to sleep as they watched. Mihàil looked up at her and grinned. It was a mischievous, lighthearted grin that dropped years from his countenance. Olivia's heart caught and a strange emotion swelled inside her chest. Before she could examine it, he spoke.

"We are a good team. If we were not being hunted by the Austrians, I would say that we should offer our services to Interpol."

"We could probably make a deal with Interpol to get the Austrians off our backs," Olivia offered without thinking. She added hastily, "Maybe. I don't really know how Interpol's jurisdiction works."

Mihàil gave her a quizzical look and offered her his arm. She slid her own inside and laid her hand on his forearm before asking, "Shall we go up into the tower now?"

They watched from the top of the tower as a team of armed Slovakian police arrived five minutes later. As Mihàil had suspected, the men were wanted in various countries, including their native Germany for murder. The itinerant, petty nature of most of their crimes had allowed them to elude detection for some time. At least until new software at Interpol had identified an international pattern and linked the two men to it. Now they topped the most wanted list in four countries. Once Stasia's contact at Interpol identified them, it was a simple matter for her to alert her counterpart in Central Europe, who then alerted Slovakian law enforcement.

As far as Interpol was concerned, an anonymous tip had led to Johann and Friedrich. Yet as Mihàil watched, one police officer disappeared through the wide arched doorway while the two men were being secured with zip ties and led to a waiting van. Though Mihàil couldn't be sure, his long years of appraising infrared signatures and nimbuses as well as posture and profile usually gave him a pretty accurate read on someone. This police officer was conscientious and thorough, he would bet on it. A moment later, Mihàil saw the officer inside the Instítute Dior speaking with the employee who'd unwittingly aided Olivia. After several minutes, he motioned to another officer, who stepped in with a pen and pad of paper, before leaving. When the diligent officer didn't appear outside immediately, Mihàil guessed that he'd gone to interview Adéla.

"It looks like one of the Slovakian officers wants to know more about the Italian couple who left Johann and Friedrich," Olivia murmured next to him. She had her cellphone pressed to her ear, relaying updates from Stasia. "As impromptu bait, this escapade should work nicely."

Mihàil inhaled deeply. Her warm, rose-filled scent had become a constant lure *and* warning. After all, roses had thorns. Finally he responded. "Yes, it will do."

He kept his gaze forward. Olivia's ability to read him made it imperative that he did not give away his thoughts in his expression. They had agreed that it was necessary to leave hints of their escape like breadcrumbs for Asmodeus. Their good deed, though unplanned, should serve. Timed well, and Asmodeus would not catch up with them until they were safe in Albania. What he had not made clear to Olivia was that the Dark *Irim* already had an acolyte among the intelligence agencies that they had encountered. And that acolyte was not in a coma. He was monitoring reports closely, perhaps directing field officers to find them.

Mihàil knew that Olivia would figure this out on her own eventually—she was too smart not to do so—yet he waited to tell her. He needed to know more. Besides, at this point, their evasive tactics were the same whether an angel or a human tracked them. And the end game favored them: Asmodeus would never deliberately follow them into Albania without another Dark *Irim* ally. But he would be forced to come if his foolish human acolyte did.

And the acolyte would.

It was a given that the acolyte was as arrogant and greedy as his master—but dangerously ignorant. Asmodeus would never tell his human servant about the power that servant wielded over him. He would kill his acolyte before it could be used. He had learned that lesson, very hard and very thoroughly, almost five hundred years ago. Mihàil had taught it to him.

Without knowing more about the acolyte or Olivia, though, Mihàil could not risk the only advantage that he had over his ancient foe.

He had called Olivia an enigma. It was time to change that.

Below them the last of the police got into their cars and drove through St. Michael's Gate. The din of activity dissipated along with the clumps of curious shopkeepers and tourists.

"I believe that is our cue to leave, Cat," he said.

They descended to Michalská and headed west, away from the departing police vehicles and toward the castle.

"Stasia has proven to be rather indispensable," he said as they strolled, arm in arm while window shopping. "Though Miró has quite a network of his own, it is always better to have fresh sources on which to call."

"True," Olivia said, gazing across the street. Then she smiled at him. He caught no uneasiness in her features, yet he still sensed her shift into wary alertness.

Mihàil allowed her to steer them to the other side of the street where there were more storefronts with large windows. As they approached a bridal shop, Olivia's thumb toyed with the set of rings on her third finger. She never looked aside. He said nothing but took in the gown with its elaborate chapel-length train that appeared to be detachable from a cocktail-length dress. Olivia would be stunning in it. He could see her striding down an aisle, her serene gaze fixed on his, holding a white bouquet of calla lilies, roses, and freesia.

A toxic mix of jealousy, fear, and guilt stabbed him.

He had no right to imagine her walking down an aisle towards him. The sooner they got to his Albanian estate, the sooner he could focus on determining exactly what *Elioud* gifts she had and then training her to use them. He would be able to distance himself from her then, to subdue his almost insanely powerful attraction to her. He turned his gaze forward and picked up his pace. Silently she adapted to his stride.

"How did you meet Miró?" she asked, looking up at him. Her eyes had opened a little wider. All innocence.

Mihàil knew that she was deflecting the conversation away from Stasia. He almost wished that they were sparring again. Then he would be able to extract details from her more easily. Defending against an attack to the head made it impossible to dissimulate during questioning.

He sighed. Olivia had trusted him with the heartbreaking reason that she became the harlequin. He owed it to her to be honest whether it got her to open up about her connection to Stasia or not.

Even so, Mihàil could not look at her as he said, "I killed three of my cavalry officers who were vying for him at a festival held to celebrate the birth of Prince Ömer in 1621."

Olivia drew up short. "'Vying for him'?" she repeated.

"They wanted to buy his sexual favors."

"What?" she asked. "Was he a prostitute?"

"He was a *köçek*. A boy made to cross dress, dance, and have sex with men," he said, his voice rough. He walked faster, his movements swift and jerky. "The Ottoman Turks stole young boys for two hundred years from their homes in the Balkans and Asia Minor. They were seven or eight years old and very comely. The Turks trained them for six years in dancing and drumming. Miró was wrenched from his home in Split, his father and brother killed when they tried to stop the janissaries. When I met him, he was fourteen and beginning to grow a beard."

Mihàil assumed that Olivia had known that the janissaries were elite soldiers during the Ottoman Empire who'd been conscripted into the sultan's personal guard from conquered Christians in the Balkans. His own father had been a janissary. But she'd clearly not known that they'd also stolen children from families like their own for the Ottomans to use as performers and sex slaves. He could see her empathy and compassion for his oldest lieutenant, who must remind her of the victims for whom she donned her harlequin hood.

"What was going to happen to him?" she asked when Mihàil fell silent.

"When? That night? Or when he began to look like the man he is?" Mihàil laughed without humor. "*Köçek* became musicians in their troupe after they were no longer pretty and hairless. Miró was not going to last that long."

"How do you know?" Her low voice held a trace of understanding despite her question.

"His eyes." Mihàil remembered the dead expression in Miró's gaze as he gyrated and thrust, miming the sexual act. "Our gazes met while my officers fought over him. If not that night, one night soon he was going to kill the man who tried to use him. And then he would have been executed."

She didn't speak for a moment. Finally, she said, "You were still Asmodeus's acolyte."

"Yes. I was also the *Silahdar Agha*. I commanded the sultan's Yellow Banners, his bodyguards."

"Saving a victim doesn't sound like something the partner of a Dark *Irim* would do."

Ah. There. She'd assumed that he was the hero, not the villain. He didn't want to correct that assumption. He did it anyway.

"No." He swallowed hard. His throat had gone dry. "But killing rivals does."

Her gaze flashed to his. It held a mix of shock and horror.

Mihàil had not felt such terror since Luljeta had died, but now that he had gone down this path, he forced himself to finish. Miró had forgiven him a long time ago for the sick impulse that had forced Mihàil to act. He had made his peace with the Archangel Michael and the Lord Most High. But none of that seemed to matter in the face of Olivia's potential rejection.

She searched his gaze. His heartbeat sped up.

"You wanted to be the one Miró killed, didn't you?" she murmured.

He dipped his chin in mute reply.

"But he didn't."

He kept his face forward as he went on. "I bought Miró from the troupe. Every night for a year, I went to his chamber and sat on a cushion while he danced. Every night I intended to do this–this unforgiveable thing that would push him into stabbing me in my sleep. And every time I came to his room, life returned a little more to his gaze. He grew into a young man, full of intelligence, strength, and grace.

"Finally, at the end of the year, Miró asked me why I hated life so much when I had so much power, money, and high position in the sultan's palace. I could not tell him. When I said nothing, he asked the question that saved my life."

"What was that?"

"He asked me why I loved him so much that I would continue to suffer rather than use him to take my own life. I realized that he was right. I did indeed love him. I would rather go on living knowing what a miserable bastard I was than to steal his dignity because I was a coward. We have been like brothers ever since."

Her warm hand took his icy one. "Asmodeus never had a complete hold on you, Mihàil."

Mihàil looked at her. He saw acceptance shining in her eyes. "Shortly after, Zophie appeared. I recognized her as one of the singers with Miró's *köçek* troupe that I had brought into my household so that he would have a friend. Little did I know that she was our guardian angel. She told me that rescuing Miró, no matter why I had thought I was doing it, had redeemed me in the Archangel Michael's sight. He broke Asmodeus's hold over me, and I was free to leave Istanbul with Miró."

He left it unsaid that the Archangel's intercession had left Asmodeus in a coma for a hundred years and meant long penance for him.

He blinked and looked around them.

While confiding in Olivia, he had unconsciously shifted his harmonics and sped up. Now they stood in the brilliant sunshine before Bratislava Castle. Mihàil didn't know what it meant that she'd kept up with him, but it didn't matter. Her hand was still holding his.

For the first time in more than 500 years he thought that he just might be able to fly.

EIGHTEEN

After Bratislava, Olivia sensed a significant shift in her relationship with Mihàil. The look of relief on his face after he'd told her about Miró meant that he'd expected her to pull away from him afterwards. Perhaps he hadn't intended to reveal so much. Or perhaps he'd risked it anyway given her own deeply personal disclosure. Whatever the reason, they'd opened up to each other, creating an unexpected bond, and it scared her. Coming on the heels of his rejection of anything physical, she'd rather not feel so drawn to him.

Their easy partnership in taking the two German criminals down both surprised and alarmed her. She'd been a covert operative long enough to know that that kind of chemistry didn't happen often. It was one of the reasons that she'd recruited Stasia in the first place. Even though they'd never worked together before, she and Stasia had played off of each other exceedingly well during their first and only joint mission infiltrating a Serbian arms dealer's circle. When they'd discovered a few young women being held as sex slaves at the Serb's rented Venetian palazzo, they'd shared a single, intense look. While the Serbs were being cuffed, hauled away, and processed for a long stay in an Italian prison, she and Stasia had taken out the guards at the palazzo and led the women to a hospital.

However, most of the time field operatives kept a wary distance even from operatives from their own side. If her experience with Fagan was any indication, this unwritten code was the wisest course.

No doubt it was also the wisest course with a 570-year-old angel hybrid being stalked by a powerful demon. Yet her wariness towards Mihàil was evaporating by degrees the longer that she spent with him. If she didn't go her own way soon, she might not be able to leave at all.

Olivia glanced sideways at the tall, sexy *drangùe* walking next to her. They'd docked at Budapest and disembarked this morning before checking into a Hilton overlooking the Danube. In keeping with their cover identities, they'd requested a honeymoon package and made a great show of fawning over each other in the lobby. But Olivia's senses had started tingling while they stood at the concierge desk, and her instincts told her that they were being watched by someone who didn't buy their cover story.

Someone who tailed them now as they walked to the Széchenyi Bath.

The problem was that her itchy instincts didn't tell her whether it was an operative, a former hostile contact, or an agent of the Dark *Irim*. The *bogomili* that she'd encountered couldn't pull off anything as subtle as surveillance, but she didn't know enough about angelic abilities to rule out Asmodeus controlling the observer directly or indirectly.

Olivia watched Mihàil from the corner of her eye. The *drangùe* showed no hint that he knew that they were being followed. That probably meant that their tail was an ordinary human with an unremarkable infrared signature. Someone who wouldn't set off the battle senses of a seasoned warrior like Mihàil. A covert operative then, Austrian or CIA. She couldn't be sure which, but she'd bet her *bō* that it was CIA.

Fagan knew where they were.

Leaving breadcrumbs for Asmodeus hadn't been the wisest course if she hoped to remain under Fagan's radar. But she couldn't risk telling Mihàil about her status as a spy who was out in the cold. As far as she knew, Fagan hadn't burned her yet, so she needed to keep her covert identity intact. Despite knowing that it was the only play she had, Olivia found herself uncomfortable about not coming clean with Mihàil.

She could evade a CIA substation chief, but she'd never evade a demon who could track her harmonics with pinpoint precision. Not unless and until Mihàil trained her how to mask her harmonic signature. If she was unwise enough to leave him before she'd been trained, Asmodeus would find her. Trained or untrained, if Asmodeus found her, he would use her as leverage against the *drangùe*.

An image of Mihàil lying pale, his fingernails and lips purple tinged, filled her mind's eye. It shocked her how intensely she hated the thought of him being wounded again or worse, killed—especially if it happened because he had tried to protect or save *her*.

She darted a glance at Mihàil, who, sensing her gaze, smiled and took her hand in his. It felt unbelievably good to have his large, warm fingers intertwined with hers.

Olivia closed her eyes briefly and swallowed.

No, she couldn't allow herself to fall under Asmodeus's control. She'd rather find a way to make Mihàil hate her, to think that she'd gone Dark, than to allow Asmodeus to use her to hurt him. It would also make it easier for her to return to her day job at the Company when she finally found a way to come in out of the cold.

And that's what she wanted, right? She was a CIA operative stationed in Vienna who moonlighted as a vigilante against sexual predators. She might have a few drops of angel blood in her, but she really didn't want to get caught up in some epic, eternal battle between the forces of darkness and the angelic host. She just needed a little *Elioud* training, and then she'd bolt.

That's the way it had to be.

So she kept quiet about their tail. If Stasia were here, they could work together to identify whoever it was and plan how to handle the surveillance. But the Italian spy was waiting for Olivia to contact her before leaving Vienna. Olivia would have to stay sharp or she and Mihàil would be the target of a snatch-and-grab in the meantime.

The City Park came into view ahead. Covering about 300 acres, it was a little more than a third the size of Central Park in New York City. As with its American counterpart, there were numerous attractions, including a zoo, an ice-skating rink that became a pond with rowboats in the summer, an art museum, and the Széchenyi Bath, one of the world's largest thermal baths.

As Olivia and Mihàil drew near to the impressive Neo-Baroque building that housed the extensive complex of indoor and outdoor pools, steam rooms, and saunas, Olivia recognized the familiar gray-haired profiles of Amelia and Jack.

Snuggling against Mihàil's side, she said, "There are our two British friends. Should we invite them to join us for lunch?"

Mihàil's forehead wrinkled as he studied her. "I thought we were spending the time here alone," he said, a question in his voice.

"We could." *We shouldn't for my sanity, however,* she thought to herself. She cleared her throat. "But being social will help sell our cover." *And keep anyone from getting too close and making a play for us.* She squeezed his hand. "Not too social, just a little social."

Something flitted through his gaze that looked like disappointment, but he nodded. Olivia ignored the small surge of triumph that filled her at seeing his reaction. Even though a part of her—too large a part, if truth be told—wanted him to want her all to himself, she couldn't risk it. Maybe he could do it. Hell, he escorted beautiful women all the time with no apparent attachment. She operated better with a barrier.

Smiling to take the sting from her action, she tugged her hand free of Mihàil's grip and waved. "Amelia!" she called. "Jack!" Then she hurried up the steps toward the middle-aged couple.

Amelia turned, and catching sight of Olivia, beamed. "Caterina!" She held out her arms and drew Olivia in for a quick peck on the cheeks and a brief squeeze of her shoulders. "So lovely to see you! I guess our schedules aligned." She elbowed Jack, who beamed at Olivia before turning to his wife to whisper loudly that she should leave the newlyweds alone.

Olivia laughed. "That is quite all right, Jack. We would love to keep you company. You agree, do you not, my love?" She smiled back at Mihàil, who stood erect on the step below her with his face on the same level as hers. Electricity leaped and sparked between them. She swallowed hard and shifted her stance.

Mihàil dipped his chin. "As you wish, Cat." He stepped up and slipped an arm around her waist, sending a thrill through her. "My only desire is to make you happy."

Olivia's smile lifted the corner of her mouth, but she barely glanced at him. She wondered if he knew that she wanted to put some distance between them. Heart beating faster, she focused again on Amelia and Jack.

"I am positively dying for a soak in one of the mineral baths inside."

"Me, too," Amelia said, smiling. "We bought tickets with a cabin for dressing and storing our things."

Olivia looked up at Mihàil, whose warm bulk and spicy scent had started to play havoc with her senses. "We have a cabin, too, do we not?"

"Yes. In fact, we can enter the spa without waiting in line." He gestured toward a separate priority entrance in the grand main lobby, which was dominated by a centaur statue and fountain. "I suggest that we find our cabins on the far side of the outdoor pools rather than stopping in the first block near the main entrance."

"Right, mate," Jack said, nodding as he headed toward a desk for guests with tickets. "I don't care what we do just so long as I get to try that thermal beer spa."

"Thermal beer spa?" Olivia asked, frowning. She looked up at Mihàil as they followed along behind Amelia and Jack.

Mihàil shook his head and shrugged in answer.

"A thermal bath with beer added to the water," Amelia said. "They say the hops, malt, and yeast are good for your skin. It's supposed to have a very pleasant herbal aroma. Like aromatherapy."

"I don't care what it smells like," Jack called over his shoulder as he navigated through an arched entryway towards the interior of the spa. "I care about the taps on the side of the wooden tubs. We get to drink as many pints of Czech Ale as we can manage in forty-five minutes, mate."

Amelia clucked and hurried to catch up with her suddenly speedy husband, who studied a map of the complex on his smartphone as he hustled down a long hallway tiled in dramatic black and white squares. Olivia chose to gape at the surroundings. The outside of the sprawling Széchenyi Bath had awed her with its ornate stone façade featuring imperial colonnades, copper domes, bronze horsemen, and formal gardens. But the inside of the hundred-year-old spa nearly overwhelmed her. A water motif dominated the interior of the main hall. Mythological water gods and goddesses, monsters, and mermaids mixed with dolphins, swans, fish, shells, and clams in fantastic, detailed mosaics, reliefs, and statues that abounded in niches and cupolas. Various scenes, from drinking and bathing to irrigation, told wordless allegories about the history of humanity and water. Even the radiators had decorative metalwork. Through it all, the scent of sulfur chloride from fifteen different pools heated with water from a thermal well almost a mile underground infused the humid air.

Mihàil, as if sensing her confused wonder, slowed his pace. "Perhaps we should start with a visit to the outdoor pools after we change?"

Olivia nodded, wordless.

At the end of the corridor, they passed a steam room, the aroma sauna, another sauna, and a small octagonal pool before they reached a doorway to the outdoor pool area. Ahead of them, Amelia and Jack wove among chaise lounges and people on their way to the far side of the pool deck where a wing added to the original spa building enclosed lockers and individual changing cabins. As she walked, Olivia took in the pools and the guests enjoying them with the trained senses of a covert operative. She heard at least half a dozen languages being spoken and guessed that most of the visitors were tourists, though along one side of the thermal pool she saw middle-aged men up to their armpits playing chess on large, waterproof boards and gossiping in Hungarian.

They crossed between the outdoor thermal pool with its phosphorescent green mineral water and the large rectangular lap pool with its familiar cerulean blue. On the far side of the pool area, Olivia knew that another pool with jets and a large, authentic whirlpool beckoned. Pavers filled in the deck area. Everywhere there were stone balustrades, old-fashioned lampposts, arched windows, black-and-white tile, statues, and stone urns filled with bright-red geraniums. The golden-yellow stone of the spa building complemented the sparkling pools and the July sky filled with fluffy clouds.

In short, this public facility offered bathers Old World charm and graciousness for about fifteen American dollars.

It was also a defensive nightmare.

There were very few means of egress and little-to-no cover. A sniper could own the top of the grandstand next to the entrance to the zoo and pick off dozens while panicked swimmers careened about trying to escape or take cover.

As they neared the steps that led up to the patio bordering the fitness center beneath the grandstand, Olivia's upper back itched. She gazed back toward the pool area as casually as she could, but no threat stood out to her. It was unlikely that Fagan would send in a strike team, anyway. That kind of thing only happened in blockbuster movies featuring bulked-up A-list movie stars who would dazzle the audience with their extraordinary tactics while the professionals wearing Kevlar vests and combat gear displayed all the skills of the proverbial Keystone Kops. No, her itching meant the surveillance had followed them into the Széchenyi Bath.

"Is something wrong?" Mihàil asked quietly as they headed toward the fitness center on their way to the changing cabins.

"I'm not sure," she murmured, prevaricating. "My gut tells me that we should stay alert."

Mihàil placed his hand on her lower back as he guided her through the French doors after Jack and Amelia.

"I am always alert. Where you are concerned, that alertness is akin to vigilance."

A thrill of pleasure zinged through her from her chest to her groin at the intensity in his velvety baritone. She squelched it coldheartedly. Instead, she focused on her plan to make her own way once Stasia arrived in Budapest to back her up.

"You won't have to worry so much if you show me how to mask my harmonic signature. Surely you can teach me that before we get to your estate?"

He looked down at her, his expression unreadable. "Perhaps."

Olivia let the subject drop. It would never do to signal her plans to him. He'd clearly decided that she was travelling to Shkodër with him.

They walked through the fitness center past the infrared sauna before exiting into the lobby for the entrance near the zoo. Jack took a left, so they followed him past the beauty salon and Thai massage room. On the far side, lockers filled a window-lined corridor with a row of small dressing cabins behind them.

Jack slowed to a halt and turned to them. He studied his phone and gestured. "Up ahead is a spot for gettin' a massage from some private masseurs, if that's your thing."

"Ooh, smashing!" Amelia said, already starting to move past her husband. "These old bones would love a massage."

Jack shook his head and continued. "Beyond the massage spot is a block of cabins. To my way of thinkin' it's a bit out of the way and not likely to be overrun with a bunch of Joe Bloggs displayin' their nethers." He turned to follow his wife, who had already made it halfway down the row of lockers away from them.

When Mihàil and Olivia caught up to Jack, he stood outside a cabin door with his hands crossed. He eyed them. "The missus is already inside gettin' into her suit."

Mihàil stopped and gestured at a cabin door. "Would you like to change first?" he asked Olivia.

Olivia glanced at Jack and back at the door. The cabin could be more accurately described as a stall. Before she could answer, Jack spoke.

"No need to play the old codger, mate, just 'cause you're hangin' out with one. Go inside with your bride. There's more than enough room for the two of you."

Mihàil flashed the other man a grin and pulled the door open with a flourish. "Indeed. After you, my love."

Olivia swallowed and entered the tiny room. Fortunately, there were no mirrors. Those were on the walls outside between the doors. Besides, it wasn't as if she hadn't seen most of his body—more than once—in the past few days. Turning to face a corner, she set her tote bag between her feet.

A moment later the door latched shut and Mihàil's heat enveloped her. Smoky hints of musk, clove, and cedar swirled around them. Olivia's heart rate sped up. She tried to breathe through her nose to mask the shallowness of her breathing but found herself panting anyway. Mihàil's chest pressed against her back.

"Let me help," he whispered, his lips brushing her ear. His own breathing sounded shaky.

His hot, large hands grasped the hem of her blouse and tugged upwards. She raised her arms as he drew it up over her head. Gooseflesh covered her bare skin even though the confined space was stifling. Mihàil slid partway down and, reaching around her leg, stuffed the blouse into her bag. Then he stood up, the hard muscles of his arms and chest pressing the soft cotton of his polo shirt into her suddenly sensitive flesh, and proceeded to undress her wordlessly.

Olivia couldn't have spoken if she'd wanted to.

Her thoughts swam. Every movement, every touch was tortuous pleasure. Mihàil's fingers moved to the clasp on her bra, and their heated gentleness lit a conflagration in her. The band fell open and the cups sagged. He brushed the strap from one shoulder, then the other. Olivia shivered as he pushed the straps down each arm. Then he bent in the tight space to slip a strap over her slack hand, kissing her shoulder softly as he did so.

Olivia quivered.

He reached around her other side and tugged the bra free. His fingertips caressed the smooth plane of her abdomen, sending a jolt all the way to her core. She felt her bra drop and wedge itself between her thigh and the wall. The next moment, it was completely forgotten as Mihàil's hands rose to cup her breasts.

She let out a tiny moan and leaned into him. He shifted his hips, and his thick erection pulsed through his chinos against her buttocks. She moaned softly again.

His lips moved to the base of her neck, and she let her head fall to the side, giving him access to the exquisitely needy area. Her breasts had grown heavy and full. They ached for him to knead and stroke them. Her hardened nipples burned for his fingers to tug and play with them. She craved his hot mouth on the pebbled flesh, his tongue circling until he sucked one in, hard, while the other hand teased and tweaked the other nipple. She grew wet, dampening her panties. The sudden sharp ache in her core made her suck her breath in and push against his groin.

All at once, Mihàil's hands fell from her breasts. Before Olivia, still swimming in desire, could process the change, the cabin door popped open and the cooler air from the hallway shocked her over-heated skin. Then Mihàil stepped out and shut the door behind him, leaving her trembling and blinking and wondering what in the hell had just happened.

Running his hand through his hair, Mihàil swore, low and vicious, as he lurched drunkenly away from the cabin and the overwhelming temptation to return and finish stripping Olivia before sinking to his knees and giving her exactly what she deserved.

He swore again, and closing his eyes, shook his head. He had to tamp down on thoughts like that or he would never make it to his estate without doing the one thing that he absolutely must not. He could not understand it. Ever since Luljeta's death, he had been impervious to the charms and attractions of scantily clad, beautiful women—and he had spent time with some of the most beautiful in the world in the past seventy-five years. What was it about Olivia that got him so steamed up?

Mihàil opened his eyes and looked around the deserted corridor running between dressing cabins. Jack had disappeared. He had probably gone to find the thermal beer spa, which sounded pretty enticing to Mihàil right now. Would Olivia be offended if he paused in playing the doting husband and sought some space between them? She had seemed perfectly content to spend the afternoon with Amelia and Jack, suggesting that she was a great deal wiser than he was being at the moment.

Taking one last look at the cabin door, Mihàil adjusted his harmonics (along with his pants) and set off at a pace more natural to an *Elioud* as he went in search of beer or anything cold, wet, and guaranteed to quell his suddenly blazing libido.

NINETEEN

Olivia stood for several moments, trembling, with her hands clenched in loose fists at her side. Despite being bare from the waist up, she felt flushed, dizzy, and overheated. Dropping her head down, she closed her eyes and breathed through her nose as her *sensei* had taught her to do so long ago when she'd first started training and pushed herself too hard—hard enough to vomit on more than one occasion.

"You cannot master the form until you master yourself," she heard him say now in memory. "You're wasting your energy trying to dominate it. Make it your ally instead."

She let herself inhale, tightening the back of her throat so that her breathing sounded loud in the small, enclosed space. Long ago, she'd learned to loosen her mental grip on her awareness, letting it slide away from her as she exhaled. The ability to control her awareness had enhanced her ability to observe and evaluate her surroundings. Once she'd discovered this technique for herself, her martial arts training had progressed rapidly. It served her well in other areas too. As a sniper, in surveillance, even in maintaining her cover during an op, she would unconsciously control her breathing and thereby control her focus.

What was it about Mihàil that so knocked her off balance despite her best intentions?

She let the thought go on an exhale, instead listening to the sound of her breathing rise and fall like the tide. She imagined the sun on her skin and warm sand between her toes. Then she noticed something that she hadn't noticed before: the hum of her own harmonics threading through and supporting her breath. Her harmonics seemed to quaver with her jittery, unfocused thoughts, but as she regained control, they smoothed into a quiet, even hum.

Did she already possess the key to controlling—and thereby masking—her harmonics?

Curious, she tried to control the hum, but the more she focused directly on it, the more it tightened and slipped from her control.

You're wasting your energy trying to dominate it. Make it your ally instead.

So she let herself relax and follow the hum, her awareness and breath aligning with her soul's harmonics as a child watches for just the right moment to jump in time with a rope swinging between two other children.

Her consciousness of her surroundings blurred. Everything disappeared except her chest rising and falling and her harmonics vibrating. At the edge of her vision, she caught sight of a nimbus limning her skin. It seemed to shimmer in time with her harmonics and her breath. She accepted its presence without wonder. Lifting her hand, she ran a fingertip through the nimbus, imagining that it blurred and elongated as she breathed. Cloudy wisps clung to her finger and frayed the nimbus's edge.

Then she began focusing on retracting the nimbus into herself. It resisted, but she found herself silently encouraging the nimbus to snuggle against her skin, to dim its glow. As she focused on the nimbus, she slowed her breathing and quieted the hum of her harmonics.

The measured pendulum of her chest eased to a stop. So too did her hum. The nimbus winked out. For a long moment, Olivia didn't breathe. Her vision clarified to discern microscopic details in the cabin. Grains of dust and particles of grime, fine hairs, brushstrokes in dried paint, and chips in woodwork all assailed her view. Her sense of smell sharpened. The scent of sulfur chloride suffused the air and nearly drowned the lingering trace of cedar and musk from Mihàil's presence.

A text alert on her smartphone sounded. Olivia didn't startle. Instead, she allowed her lungs to expand gradually. When her breathing returned, it was unhurried. Her harmonics and the nimbus also returned, both even and sure.

Olivia straightened and blinked. She wasn't sure what exactly she'd discovered, but she had every intention of revisiting this link between her breath, her harmonics, and the mysterious glow emanating from her skin.

Letting out a heavy sigh, she rolled her shoulders and bent to rummage in her tote bag for her phone. The text was from Mihàil.

"Grabbed a locker. Will change elsewhere. Meet later? Silicone band locks cabin."

She bit her lip to control the smile that threatened. He apparently had been as affected by their brief interlude as she had. She'd just finished sending him a reply and grabbing the silicone wristband with its coded security chip when a knock came at the door.

"Caterina?" It was Amelia's voice.

"A moment, *per favore*," she called and tugged her cover-up from her bag before pulling it over her head.

She opened the door to see Amelia standing there wearing a terrycloth cover-up and flip flops with a tote bag over one shoulder and a large-brimmed hat in her hands. She turned the hat around and around.

"What's the matter?" Olivia asked.

"Have you seen Jack?"

"He was waiting outside when we got to our cabin."

Amelia's gaze went beyond Olivia to the small room behind her. "Aleso is gone too? I thought you were taking so long because you were both changing."

Although there wasn't anything suggestive or even a hint of reproof in Amelia's tone, Olivia blushed. She felt strangely guilty for putting the other woman through this charade, especially because they *had* behaved like newlyweds. "The cabin is too small. Aleso has gone to find a locker." She hurried past this embarrassing revelation. "Do you want me to help you find Jack?"

Amelia closed her eyes briefly. When she opened them, she appeared to shake off her worry. "No, I'm just being barmy, that's all. He's likely gone to find that thermal beer spa and will send a text once he's had a pint."

"Come with me to the whirlpool until then," Olivia said, laying a consoling hand on the older woman's forearm. "Only allow me to finish dressing first."

Amelia frowned and then nodded. "I'll pop over and make an appointment for a massage while I'm waiting. You can find me there when you're ready."

Olivia smiled and nodded in return. Pursing her lips, she watched Amelia head back toward the room that Jack had pointed out a little while before. Was Jack's disappearance odd or nothing out of the ordinary?

Tucking the thought away, she returned to the cabin and donned her swimsuit in quick, efficient movements. Amelia had just finalized a time as Olivia joined her, so they traced their steps back to the outside pool area. Listening to Amelia describe her upcoming massage with only half her attention, Olivia scanned the outside area for signs of surveillance. Nothing alarming caught her attention.

Clouds drifted across the sun, darkening the day for a moment. Olivia shivered. Where had their tail gone?

The whirlpool was in the center of a large pool twenty meters in front of them. As she and Amelia approached the wide, shallow steps entering the crystalline water, a couple got up from a nearby bench. Olivia steered her companion to it so that they could deposit their towels, flips flops, and Amelia's tote bag before entering the water. Amelia chattered away. Olivia sensed that the longer it took Jack to respond to Amelia's repeated text inquiries, the more the older woman's nerves frayed.

Instinctively, she took Amelia's hand, which was colder than it should be on this hot July afternoon, and began rubbing her thumb over its veined back. She wished that she knew how to raise her internal temperature to warm her companion. Yet another thing that Mihàil could teach her. Even so, Amelia's babble subsided as she let Olivia lead her across the pool among clusters of bathers gossiping in the chest-high water.

Olivia let the swirling current pull them between the two tiled walls forming concentric circles in the middle of the pool. The walls were lined with benches that were filled with laughing and talking bathers. When they reached a space on the bench lining the inside of the inner circle, Olivia and Amelia squeezed in together.

"That color looks marvelous on you," said a familiar voice with an aristocratic British accent.

Startled, Olivia glanced at the blond woman in the red swimsuit next to her. Even with the dark sunglasses, she recognized Zophie.

"What are you doing here?" she asked without thinking.

"Mmm, enjoying the sun. And this pool is divine. So relaxing." Zophie turned her head and slipped her sunglasses up. Her serious gaze contradicted her frivolous words. "Amelia's husband Jack is not finding his visit to Széchenyi Bath so relaxing, I am afraid."

Olivia's heart jolted. "What's happening? Where is he?"

"Someday soon, Olivia, you will trust Mihàil enough to tell him what your instincts and experience tell you is happening," the guardian angel said.

Olivia squirmed and looked back at Amelia, who didn't seem to notice them talking. She returned her gaze to Zophie.

"Even if I wanted to tell him that I'm worried about Jack, he's off somewhere."

"Oh, he is repeatedly plunging himself into cold water." Zophie grinned and slid her sunglasses back onto her face. The smile evaporated. She gestured with her chin. "Do you know that fellow? He seems quite intent on you in a way that is not exactly flattering."

Olivia looked in the direction that Zophie indicated. A dark-haired, fully clothed man wearing sunglasses stood next to the balustrade lining the terrace beneath the grandstand, his hands crossed before him. She recognized him. His name was Miles Baxter, and he was one of the Company's best operatives, a specialist in extracting hostile targets. Many of his operations were covert and off book, and he often operated naked and illegal—meaning he had no diplomatic immunity. To pull off this high-wire act, Baxter excelled at shadowing his targets, and no one was better at escape and evasion. He'd once survived for three weeks in the Carpathian Mountains after a black-ops mission went sideways in the Ukraine. That meant eluding capture for 400 miles and fending off bears and wolves once he reached the mountains.

And there he stood, staring at her.

"Oh, crap," she whispered as her insides liquefied into an icy gel. "He's got Jack." It wasn't a question.

"Yes." Zophie's voice thrummed with strong emotion, which Olivia wouldn't have been able to identify even if she wasn't momentarily stunned out of rational thought.

Baxter nodded once, turned, and disappeared inside the baths.

She had no doubt that he'd left his contact information at the service desk inside the main entrance. In taking a civilian, he'd done what he needed to do to get Olivia to come to him of her own free will. The only way Jack walked free from this was if Olivia outmaneuvered Baxter, who had no reason to leave Jack alive and every reason to cover his trail. However, Baxter would not have been sent to capture her. Fagan wanted Mihàil; she was just a means to that end. Where Jack was her bait, she was Mihàil's. And she was as expendable, maybe more so, than Jack. The question was: could she rescue the British man without drawing Mihàil into danger?

How vulnerable *was* Mihàil?

He might still be weak from his *bogomili* injury, but she suspected that he could handle one, perhaps two or three, ordinary humans if it came to that. However, Baxter worked with handpicked extraction teams that he assembled depending on the job. For Mihàil and Olivia, he would include a sniper. So even though Mihàil could defend himself in a small face-to-face confrontation, he'd be as vulnerable to a hidden shooter as any normal human—unless he had some sort of long-range angelic sniper radar that he hadn't told her about.

On the other hand, she and Mihàil *did* work well together as a team, some-thing that Fagan and Baxter might not have accounted for. If Stasia or Beta were here to back her up, she wouldn't even consider risking Mihàil to save Jack. But there wasn't time to call on either of them. The trick would be involving Mihàil without revealing her covert identity. She'd managed to avoid revealing the truth before, so there was a chance that she could pull it off again. Either way, she had no choice. She had to act now. Jack's life depended on it.

Having considered the situation, Olivia turned to speak to Zophie. The angel had disappeared. Amelia, however, sat staring at the doors to the terrace through which they'd come twenty minutes earlier. Her pale face and wide eyes filled Olivia with guilt. It was her fault that Jack had been snatched by one of the most ruthless field operatives the CIA had. She should have anticipated that Fagan would bring in someone like Baxter, should have known that anyone she had more than casual contact with would be potential leverage. Yet another reason Fagan had to be stopped. There was no room for someone like him in the Company. Boundaries between civilians and those who played the game had to be enforced or they'd already lost what they were fighting to protect.

Unfortunately, Olivia was going to have to lie to Amelia to protect her and buy herself some time while she recovered Baxter's message.

Amelia caught Olivia's gaze on her. Shaking her head, the older woman forced a laugh and leaned over to pat Olivia's hand. "What a pea brain I am! All moony over a man who has never missed an opportunity to have a pint while you've been abandoned on your honeymoon. I can't think what has gotten into your husband to leave you here with me."

At the other woman's observation, Olivia had her answer. It was always best to keep things simple and take care of two things with one lie, albeit one liberally seasoned with the truth.

"I will share a secret with you." She leaned in and lowered her voice. "Aleso and I had to take a break from each other. He is off somewhere cooling down." She sat upright and smiled brightly. "I will send him a text and tell him to look for Jack while you are being massaged. It is too big a place, however. I will leave a message for Jack at the service desk telling him where you are in case something is wrong with his phone. Perhaps his battery is dead."

Amelia's eyes glistened and she smiled. "Thank you, my dear. You've eased a foolish old woman's heart."

"Do not worry, *cara*. I am sure that Jack is enjoying the thermal beer spa and has no idea that you miss him." She squeezed Amelia's hand before standing up. "Trust me and go enjoy your massage."

Mihàil forced himself to remain calm and cool. The fact that Olivia wasn't answering his texts or her phone didn't mean anything in this sprawling pool complex. She'd sent him that text about looking for Jack almost thirty minutes ago while he was still in the plunge pool. There was every chance that he'd missed her during his complete circuit of all the interior rooms, and she was likely too busy keeping watch on Jack to ensure that he returned to his overly anxious wife. Even so, Mihàil wished that Olivia had given him a time and place to meet up. Given that they weren't exactly a team yet, it probably hadn't occurred to her that they might spend most of the afternoon chasing each other. That was going to change once they got to Albania, however. Their spontaneous work yesterday in Bratislava had convinced him that he and Olivia worked well together.

He headed toward the massage room where Olivia had said that Amelia would be. It was a short walk from the dressing cabin that he'd rented earlier. Some instinct made him bypass the massage room and continue toward the cabin. As he approached, he scanned it for Olivia's infrared signature. There was nothing. In fact, the ambient temperature of the cabin matched that of the hallway. Warm, but no trace of elevated heat from a living being. Frowning, he stepped forward and tried the handle. The door hadn't been pulled fully shut and the latch slipped free.

Mihàil shoved the door open. Olivia's tote bag was gone. On the small wooden bench in the corner lay the bright blue silicone wrist band that he'd given her to lock the door. His mind went blank even as his temperature soared. Grabbing the silicone band, he whirled and traced his path back to the massage room. Without knocking, he opened the door. Inside a white-coated massage therapist bent over Amelia's plump calves. Both women looked at him, their wide eyes gleaming in the dim room.

Amelia found her voice first. "Aleso?" It came out raspy. "What's wrong?"

Mihàil tamped his rising emotions down. Clearing his throat, he asked, "May I speak with you?"

Amelia looked at the massage therapist. "Will you leave us for a moment?" The woman nodded and, wiping her hands on a towel, left them.

"I apologize for interrupting." His voice sounded like gravel, and he tasted smoke. He cleared his throat. "Did Cat tell you that she was going to look for Jack?"

If possible, Amelia's eyes got wider. After a moment, she shook her head. "You don't know where either of them are, do you?" Her voice wobbled on the question.

"No." When she flinched, he went on using his *drangùe* charm. "Please, there is no reason to worry, Amelia. The Széchenyi Bath is a wet, echoing warren. Cellphones do not like water, and batteries die." Even as he said this, his own doubts twisted his gut. He didn't believe in coincidence, and the evidence was that Olivia was gone without any attempt to notify him. But there was no reason to alarm the older woman more than she was already. If nothing else, he didn't need the added attention. "Finish your massage and meet me in the main lobby. In the meantime, I will check at the service desk. We will find them."

Despite his charm, Amelia rolled to her side and heaved herself to a sitting position, clutching the sheet to her freckled bosom. "None of this makes any sense. First Jack disappears and now your bride. I'm not staying here one more minute." She swung her feet to the floor. "I'm going with you."

Mihàil sighed to himself. Having to escort Amelia was going to slow him down, but he had little choice at the moment.

TWENTY

S tasia preferred to do her intelligence gathering alone and during the day-light. She'd learned a long time ago that most people thought that oper-atives skulked around in the shadows, dressed in black gear more suited to cat burglars or acrobats than a professional or working-class woman. It was true that she sometimes needed stealth, speed, and flexibility, especially when she helped Olivia on her missions, but there was a time and place for everything. This was the time for intelligence gathering, not kicking ass. Not that she'd dressed in her ass-kicking suit since that *Elioud* had destroyed her *surujin*. Of course, that didn't mean that she was unarmed.

Her hand strayed to the BC-41 knife tucked into the side pocket of the bag slung over her shoulder. The BC-41 was for close work, however, which she wanted to avoid. Inside her right boot, she'd clipped a Kel-Tec P32 for an arms' length defense. At six and a half ounces, the American handgun was exceptionally light, making it ideal as a concealed weapon for a small woman walking in a neighborhood known for its crime rate. And, if her instincts were right, a hotbed for *bogomili* indoctrination and training.

The back of her neck tingled briefly before the sensation winked out. She didn't turn around. If she hadn't become hyperaware of the reserved *Elioud,* she knew that she'd never have caught even that slight inkling of his presence. He was that good. She let a frown drift between her brows. In fact, he was so good that she wondered if he wanted her to know that he was following her into Brigittenau, Vienna's Twentieth District.

Sighing in annoyance, she shrugged and lifted her head high. Good luck to him. He was welcome to try keeping up with her. As long as he didn't get in the way or otherwise interfere with her efforts, she would tolerate his presence. But she didn't extend trust easily. She would never have survived in this business if she did. And something about the silent, handsome angel hybrid rubbed her the wrong way. Maybe it was the fact that she felt as though he saw through everything she did. Those cool blue eyes had stayed trained on her the whole time that she was trying to interrogate the surviving *bogomili* at St. Elizabeth's. She got the feeling that he knew before she did that it was a wasted effort. The shell of a man had no brain activity beyond that which allowed him to watch children's TV programming, to which he kept his gaze glued no matter what she did to attract it.

Stasia squinted, remembering. Had that been a glint of humor in Miró's eyes when the wretched *bogomili* failed to react to her leaning over him to straighten his blanket? Or leaned away from her bosom to see the TV screen as she plumped his pillow?

It didn't help that the nursing staff uniformly seemed to find Miró swoon-worthy. There had been several female nurses who appeared to have palpitations at the sight of him. Stasia gave the *Elioud* credit, though, for appearing oblivious to his effect on these glassy-eyed women. She didn't think that she could have tolerated a smug acceptance from him along with everything else.

But there was more than one way to extract information from a target, and Stasia was exceptionally good at reading people and situations to learn more than what was explicitly conveyed. It was one of the skills that had kept her alive all these years: not only did it allow her to anticipate violence, but it also gave her the ability to manipulate targets out of acting violently. She'd been a literature major at university. Along with her own innate empathy and her family's long history in law enforcement and the military, that training had given her a unique insight into a range of motives, goals, and plans for all kinds of illicit activities. She also secretly loved the fictional British detective Sherlock Holmes, whose devotion to evidence-based deductive reasoning helped shore up her reliance on her gut.

That's why Stasia found herself walking along the canals of Brigittenau this morning dressed in non-descript, modest brown clothing. Though she'd gotten no cooperation from the surviving *bogomili* at St. Elizabeth's or help from Miró, she had gleaned a couple of details. First, the surviving *bogomili* had a Serbian accent. Second, she knew where he'd come from prior to the attack. The *Bundespolizei,* Austria's federal criminal police, had tracked his address to this industrial Viennese neighborhood where a third of the residents came from Turkey and the Balkans—the same region where other *bogomili* had ravaged refugee camps. The *Bundespolizei* had no other leads on the Serbian *bogomili,* so for now their investigation had moved to identifying motive for both *bogomili* attacks and making sure that they had no connection to the terrorists who'd stormed the music festival. Stasia, however, thought a visit to Brigittenau might turn up something that they'd missed.

She slowed as she neared a corner market plastered with advertisements for packaged foods and prepaid cards. Perhaps this small store offered her a way to shake her tail? She stepped inside and approached the bank machine. It always paid to have an errand to cover her true intentions.

She punched in her account code, her gaze watching the reflection on the ATM screen. There! A flare of white light dazzled her for a moment. It could have been sunlight striking a car window, but she knew better. It was a devious *Elioud* warrior. He'd passed the store without entering. Quickly she finished her transaction before stepping into an empty aisle where she stepped out of her loose trousers to reveal white leggings. Next, she slipped out of the lightweight oversized jacket that covered her tunic dress. Then she pulled the band out of her hair before donning a large, floppy-brimmed sun hat that she'd collapsed flat and stuffed into the bag. Finally, she slipped on large sunglasses, the kind that highlighted the eyes rather than hid them, and headed out to her final destination, an older residential building.

Perhaps she should have shared what she was doing with Miró instead of trying to lose him. *As if his presence would be helpful.*

Given her previous interrogation of the Macedonian *bogomili,* she'd found the Serbian specimen puzzling. The other *bogomili* could at least tell her about their beliefs and mentioned a leader. In fact, they spoke in coherent sentences. They knew what they were, what they were supposed to do, and why. The

Serbian *bogomili* knew nothing about what he was or why he was in the hospital. And Miró had done nothing with his *Elioud* magic to extract any information locked in the zombie's brain.

That thought drew Stasia up short. She covered by backtracking and turning into a café to buy a coffee.

There was something odd about this *bogomili,* she reflected while she waited. He'd smelled healthy. As a rule, *bogomili* stank. Their rotting insides exuded from every pore, crevice, and breath. The *bogomili* who'd died at the Stadtpark had been in such an advanced state of decay when the coroner examined them that the authorities were bewildered. How had anyone dumped so many bodies in the open without being seen? The subsequent attack at the Belvedere seemed to have clarified the situation for the *Bundespolizei,* whose current working theory was that a group of refugees infected with an unknown necrotizing virus were attacking tourists. It was during this attack that the *Bundespolizei* officer was killed. And, in an odd twist, the eyewitness to the killing had retracted her story.

The good? Olivia and Mihàil were now officially wanted as witnesses, not murder suspects.

The bad? The *Bundespolizei* had no clue about what was really going on.

Stasia reached the building with the Serb's flat. The entry fronted the corner, but the streets were bare. She pushed the call button for the manager's office.

Five minutes later, the door was opened by an aging Viennese man. He peered at her through rheumy eyes, his glasses propped on a nest of white hair.

"*Guten tag,*" she said, greeting him with a wide, warm smile and extended hand. "I have come about the flat, *si?*"

He squinted at her before taking her hand and shaking it. "Come in, please. Why you should wish to rent a flat in Brigittenau is a mystery, but you are welcome to fill out the papers and tour it nonetheless." He turned to lead her through the cramped entryway and down a hall toward his office.

Stasia waited until she was inside to slip off the sunglasses. She refrained from looking back over her shoulder as she stepped over the threshold.

The *Bundespolizei* had requested a warrant for the rental information on the Serbian *bogomili's* flat, but she'd been unable to discover what, if anything, they had learned. It was doubtful that they would have noticed anything that might connect him to Asmodeus. She needed to access the paper files this man kept to determine if there was more there.

"Please, Frau Fiore, take a seat. If you will be so good as to fill out the rental application, I will go to the flat to make sure that the cleaning company has finished. It has only just become available."

"That is unnecessary, Herr Bauer. A little dirt will not affect my opinion."

Herr Bauer straightened and blinked. "That does not matter. It is not my practice to show flats unless they are clean and ready for occupation. Now, if you will excuse me."

Stasia nodded, and Herr Bauer left her alone. As soon as she heard the doors to the elevator slide shut, she sprang from her seat and went behind the desk to the old-fashioned filing cabinets lining the wall. Quickly she found the one containing the Serbian *bogomili's* folder and scanned the contents. Then she used her smartphone to take photos of all the documents. When Herr Bauer returned, she was seated again, staring at the application and tapping a pen on the desk.

"Is something wrong, Frau Fiore?" the manager asked, frowning.

Stasia smiled at him, making sure it was even wider and warmer than before. "Oh, no, Herr Bauer. It is just that I am not fond of writing so many little things, this and that about where I have lived and for how long...it is very trying, you see. Might I see the flat before I finish? It would inspire me to fill in all these empty spaces."

His frown deepened. "I do not—"

A young woman knocked on his open office door, interrupting him. She was wearing a uniform and should have seemed nondescript except that her short spiky hair was white blond and almost as arresting as her blue eyes.

"Excuse me, Herr Bauer, but we have discovered a problem with the plumbing in one of the flats," she said when he turned toward her. "Please, we need you to come right away."

Herr Bauer let out a heavy sigh. "Please wait, Frau Fiore." He turned away without looking at her.

The cleaning employee did, however. Stasia was shocked when those blue eyes focused on her. "You might want to move quickly," the woman said and then winked before pivoting to follow Herr Bauer.

Stasia blinked, trying to process what had just happened. A moment later, she accepted it and jumped up, grabbed her bag, and left the office for the stairs, which she took two at a time. On the third floor, she found the *bogomili's* flat and pulled out her lock-picking toolkit. A minute later she'd opened the door and slid inside, using the hem of her tunic on the door handle.

A mess greeted her. Clothes and food cartons covered every surface of the small living space. The tiny kitchen had food molding in dishes stacked in the sink and along the counter. The entire flat stank of old socks, cigarettes, and overflowing waste bins. Herr Bauer should send his cleaning company in here—after she'd finished, of course. Wrinkling her nose, Stasia directed her gaze around until it landed on the best place to start her search: a small console littered with mail and newspapers next to an empty bottle of *slivovitz*.

She tugged on a pair of leather gloves and stepped to the console to flip through the papers. A flyer for work training at Caritas Vienna for the Compulsory Integration Year caught her attention. The local office for the UN High Commissioner on Refugees referred many refugees to Caritas for a variety of programs. Scanning the flyer, she saw a phone number written in the upper right corner. Stasia folded it and tucked it inside her bag. She'd visit the Caritas office later for more information and track down the source of the phone number.

"Somehow I doubt that you have found an advertisement for the best strudel in Vienna," said Miró behind her.

Stasia whirled, the P32 in her hand. The damn *Elioud* leaned against the wall next to the door, his arms crossed. His eyelids drooped over his icy-blue irises, lending him a sleepy air. But the piercing gaze was predatory. Stasia's heart pattered against her ribcage. The walls of the flat pressed in against her.

The angel hybrid blocked her egress.

Lifting her chin, she said, "I expected you sooner." She was proud at the confidence that rang in her voice.

Miró's gaze dropped. Stasia couldn't tell if he studied her mouth or her chest but the temperature rose until she felt damp between her breasts and under her arms. Before the smoldering intensified further, he brought his gaze up to her face again. Gooseflesh sprang out on the back of her arms. She gritted her teeth and smiled. It didn't reach her eyes.

"Hm? Yes, well, I admit that I lost you at the market, but it was only a temporary setback." His melodious voice caressed her. *Porca miseria!* It lured her! She almost took a step toward him but stopped herself. He tilted his head. "Have you gathered any useful intelligence on the hospitalized *bogomili*?"

"I am not inclined to answer whether I have or have not." She took a step toward him, her hand steady on the P32. His gaze tracked her and the tension increased, increasing her annoyance in equal measure. "You have been less than forthcoming, *Elioud*. You already took whatever information that *bogomili* had and then gave him amnesia. Why should I share anything with you?"

Miró acknowledged her assessment with a slight nod. "We can protect humans better if they have less conscious knowledge of angelic activities."

A complex scent of bergamot, leather, sage, and ash wafted toward Stasia as she stepped closer.

That awareness prompted a thought. "Is that why the *bogomili* did not smell like an abattoir?" she asked. "Did you heal him?"

"Not exactly," he said, his voice lowering to velvet. Stasia shivered. Miró's gaze sharpened and his scent deepened. "I simply delayed the inevitable by clearing his memory of the evil that he let into his being. Now he has returned to a state more closely resembling an average human, though it cannot return his higher-order thinking ability, I am afraid."

Stasia halted an arm's distance from him. The dangerous proximity had accelerated her heart rate to a painful staccato. He hadn't straightened from his casual slouch, but his dark silk suit and white shirt did little to obscure his broad shoulders and muscled chest. He radiated heat and restrained power.

She eased closer to bell the tiger, bringing the P32 to his chest. "You know more about the *Bundespolizei* officer who attacked Olivia than you told me, *si?*"

Miró ignored the muzzle kissing his breast. "He was a vessel. Asmodeus possessed him. To do that, Asmodeus would have had to interact with him in person."

"Is it the same with the *bogomili?*"

"Yes."

"We both know that the *Bundespolizei* officer had been investigating terrorist cells among the Balkan refugees in Austria."

He nodded, never taking his gaze from hers.

"A few weeks ago, I traveled to Macedonia. *Bogomili* are quite active in the refugee camps there. Asmodeus must have traveled with them, perhaps lives within the Balkan refugee community here."

"Not necessarily." For the first time since she'd met him, Miró looked uncomfortable.

"What have you not told me?" Stasia whispered, moving still closer and lifting the tip of the P32 to caress his jaw. "Do you think to play me for a fool?"

For a moment, the air thickened and heated around them. Miró's lids dropped to veil his gaze, and he leaned ever so slightly closer to her. She wouldn't have known except that the weapon barrel slid a hair's breadth. She was so close that she couldn't avoid taking in the dusting of gray at his temples, the fine lines at the corners of his eyes, and the fullness of his mouth. His unique scent enveloped her until her own lids drifted down, and she started to lean toward him.

"Never," he said, startling her out of her reverie to see him standing on the other side of the entry, his arms folded as he leaned against the wall. Although it was a mirror pose to the one he'd held a moment before, all signs of casualness had evaporated, along with the smoky heat. In fact, his eyes had grown icier if possible.

Stasia shook her head to clear it. *What had just happened?* Glaring, she asked, "Why are you here?"

Instead of answering, Miró said, "Asmodeus has a partner."

"Ah." She nodded. After a moment, she slipped the P32 into her bag. She wasn't going to shoot him—yet—so she might as well put it away and try to have a civilized conversation. "Not a brainless minion and not a vessel."

"An acolyte." When Stasia's gaze sharpened, Miró clarified, "We call humans who work for Dark *Irim* without losing their agency *acolytes*. They fit a certain profile."

"Terrorist?" Stasia asked the obvious.

"Possibly." His face was grave. "Terrorism is a hallmark of Asmodeus's influence on humans. It is probably no coincidence that the terrorists attacked while Mihàil was at the festival."

"The *Bundespolizei* has not found a connection between this *bogomili*"—Stasia gestured around the flat—"and the terrorists or they would have told other agencies."

"Terrorists are not the only humans who fit the profile. Given that the acolyte is the nexus between the *bogomili*, the *Bundespolizei*, and the terrorists, we are most likely looking for an intelligence operative, someone who would have had contact with the dead officer."

It didn't escape Stasia's notice that Miró had used the pronoun *we*. "*We* are back to my question. What makes you think that I will share anything more with you? I do not need you to find this accomplice." She tossed her head and stepped closer to him again, ignoring the way her heartbeat kicked into high gear as if she were a meek little rabbit and he was the big bad wolf about to devour her. "*I* could be the acolyte, *amico mio*."

At her announcement, Miró's hand shot out and gripped her wrist with hot fingers. When he leaned down to look in her eyes, his own burned with a blue-white intensity that shook her to the core. "Never say that, Ms. Fiore. Both the *bogomili* and the acolyte are bound to Asmodeus. If you get too close, he will sense your true nature and come for you. *That* is too dangerous for you to handle alone."

He leaned back and his gaze grew distant and impersonal. "Besides, Ms. Fiore, it is more likely that the acolyte is your boss." As her eyes widened at his suggestion, he let go of her wrist and continued, "As I see it, it is in your best interest to work with me, not only for your sake but for your friend's sake. Ms. Markham and Mihàil may not have to worry about murder charges, but the acolyte will stop at nothing until he finds them for his master. *We* must find him first."

Stasia refrained from rubbing her wrist though she felt branded by Miró's touch. She thought about her friend, who'd threatened him with such bravado even though she was the one in dire straits. "For Olivia's sake then, I will work with you, but I do not trust you."

"That is too bad," he murmured and tossed something toward her. Stasia caught it by reflex, though she nearly dropped the heavy, flexible object. Before she realized what she'd caught, she heard someone in the hallway and a few seconds later a jingling at the door. "Perhaps this will help mitigate my faults. I trust that you can handle yourself? We will meet again later."

The door opened, and Miró disappeared in a blur of light. Stasia glanced down and saw that she held a gleaming *surujin*, its smooth links held together with a simple leather thong. As Herr Bauer stepped into the flat, surprise lifting his sagging features, Stasia smiled.

"Herr Bauer, I am *so* happy to see you," she said, already planning to teach an infuriating *Elioud* a lesson the next time that they met.

TWENTY-ONE

Joseph Fagan, director of the CIA substation in Vienna, was used to getting results for ops under his authority, and this time it was no different regardless of the fact that the Austrian authorities had cleared Olivia Markham and Mihàil Kastrioti. Markham had defied his order to bring the Dragon of Albania in, and in fact had facilitated his escape. He'd known as soon as he'd met her that she was going to be more trouble than she was worth, sterling career notwithstanding. He'd decided almost as quickly that he would burn her any chance he got. He'd run a few dozen field officers in his career with the Company, but she was the most dangerously insubordinate that he'd encountered. Given that operatives were cultivated for their ability to think quickly and handle situations on their own, that was saying something. The great majority didn't question their orders or their superiors. He suspected that she was running something on the side, though exactly what it was he had yet to discover. No matter. She couldn't be allowed to continue her maverick ways.

Stenson knocked on his open door. "Sir, Baxter has made contact."

Fagan looked up, excitement making his pulse kick up a notch. "Where?"

"Budapest, at the Széchenyi Bath. You were right that they'd left Vienna on a river cruise."

A grin split Fagan's face. By Stenson's sudden alarmed look and step back, he figured it wasn't the most pleasant-looking expression, but no matter. He felt triumphant, *damn it,* and the familiar rush of adrenaline from the chase fueled the blood in his veins. Though he missed the raw edge that pursuing a target in the field gave, there was something almost sweet about his command of the mission from here at the substation. His ability to synthesize disparate pieces of field intel into a coherent tactical solution made him feel downright omnipotent. Godlike in fact.

He stood up and waved at Stenson to follow him to the tactical operations center, which was really just a large conference room with multiple workstations, a white board, and a screen for projecting real-time video. There would come a day when he would have control of a much more important, much larger TOC in a more challenging environment. Of course, given the way things had started heating up these days in Western Europe with the increasing terrorist attacks and bands of roaming refugees assaulting citizens in public swimming pools, shopping districts, and Christmas festivals, that could mean staying put right here in Vienna, albeit with a larger command.

If he helped the situation along, then all the better. What was the saying? He who helps himself...the grin returned as he recalled that it was God who supposedly helps 'he who helps himself.'

Fagan entered the operations center with Stenson on his heels. "Sitrep?"

All seven heads turned towards him. It hadn't taken long for the staff at the substation to comprehend Fagan's command style and to conform itself.

"Sir, Baxter made contact with Markham via a British national."

"What do we know about this Brit?" Fagan asked, his voice sharp, his gaze on the screen where a still image of a middle-aged man had appeared. "Is he MI6? How did Markham make contact with him?"

"Negative, sir, he's a civilian," said an analyst in the far left corner of the room. "Jack Davies, retired aircraft mechanic from Bristol, and his wife Amelia, a retired schoolteacher, are traveling on the river cruise from Munich to Budapest that Markham and Kastrioti boarded two days ago. As far as we can tell, their contact with Markham and Kastrioti was purely circumstantial. It appears that the Davies shared seating at dinner with our targets."

Fagan squinted, thinking. He directed his inquiry to his second-in-command. "Stenson, what's Baxter's play here?"

Stenson cleared his throat. "Sir, Baxter took Davies from Széchenyi Bath to an undisclosed location. He left meet information for Markham. He intends to lure Kastrioti once he's gotten control of her."

Of course. Markham would never let some harmless old geezer suffer at the hands of one of the Company's best snatch-and-grab experts. She'd try to free the old man, and then Baxter would have her.

"Does he have any reason to believe that play will work with Kastrioti? The man's a notorious playboy. Surely he'll abandon his pretty companion if she's caught. I know I would. He'll be less encumbered."

Stenson looked uncomfortable. "Baxter sent an operative to fill in for one of the crew in Bratislava. Kastrioti and Markham traveled as newlyweds. Their behavior has been convincingly passionate."

Fagan wasn't sold. "Markham is a trained operative. Selling a romance is definitely in her wheelhouse."

Stenson nodded. "True, but Baxter's asset learned that Markham and Kastrioti were seen in a steamy embrace when they had no idea that they were being observed. The next morning, they apparently had a lovers' quarrel that ended with sparring on the sun deck. Baxter believes that the playacting crossed a line."

"When Baxter reports in, tell him I want mission details, location, team-member capabilities. I know he likes to run his missions autonomously, but I want to know everything. If what happened at the Belvedere and again in Bratislava is anything to go by, Kastrioti and Markham work exceptionally well together, whether they're boning each other or not. If Markham brings Kastrioti to free the Brit, they will be more than a match for Baxter. Or if Kastrioti does the stupid thing and goes after Markham, he will still be formidable. I want to step in sooner rather than later if the mission goes sideways."

"Yes, sir," Stenson said.

Fagan remained in the tactical operations center, the familiar current running through his veins. He studied the map of Budapest that one of the analysts had left on the main screen with a red circle highlighting Széchenyi Bath. He played a game with himself trying to predict where Baxter had taken the retired Brit. Maybe he took him to the Ròmai-part, a section of the Danube riverbank near the old Roman baths. Or perhaps Feneketlen Lake located near the Buda Arboretum?

And then Fagan let his gaze travel farther west toward the Buda Hills and the Normafa Park, and he got that sharp tingle when he knew that he'd identified a target.

The Children's Railway. Baxter would take Davies to the Children's Railway and station a sniper at the nearby Elizabeth Lookout. The wedding-cake-shaped stone tower sat on top of János-hegy, the tallest hill overlooking Budapest, with views for three hundred and sixty degrees. A team member would be stationed at the Zugligeti chairlift at the base of the hill. Depending on whether there were four or five members on the team, another person would surveil the Normafa train station to observe access to the lookout by train or car. One would tail Markham of course.

Fagan felt something akin to joy, or at least what he imagined joy felt like: a kind of weightless excitement. Even if Markham chose to take the longer route around the hill to the suburb of Budakeszi and approached János-hegy from the west unobserved, she wouldn't have a fixed location to target. Baxter would have set a meet time that gave Markham only enough time to get to the Buda Hills from the Széchenyi Bath. She'd have no time to scout or get close before Baxter and the Brit got onto the Children's Railway. An artifact of the communist era, it was run almost entirely by older children. He suppressed his grin again. No need to look like a goofy idiot at the idea of miniature human shields.

"What's the visibility to Elizabeth Lookout, Cramer?" Fagan asked.

The named analyst glanced back, confusion in his gaze. "Sir?"

Fagan held his temper in check. "Elizabeth Lookout to the west. How much groundcover is there?"

Cramer scrambled to find the answer to his boss's question. "The tower is surrounded by dense tree cover except for a paved terrace around the perimeter and a driveway at the entrance that leads to a road on the south. Anyone approaching will be largely invisible for three quarters of its perimeter until the last few meters, sir."

Fagan didn't acknowledge the information. Cramer waited a moment and returned his focus to his workstation. The new substation chief wasn't known for thanks or compliments, and Cramer knew enough to get back to the task at hand.

"Sir?" Stenson stood at Fagan's right shoulder, a phone receiver in his hand. "It's Baxter."

Fagan took the phone. He jumped right to the point. "You're at the Children's Railway."

"With a team of four."

"Overwatch on the tower?"

"Affirmative. One at the chairlift, one following Markham. I have the package."

Triumph flooded Fagan. He'd been right. "Has Markham contacted you?"

"Affirmative. I expect her within the perimeter of Normafa Park in 10."

Now down to brass tacks. "What's the play?"

"Markham will board the train at the Normafa station. Her tail will board at the same time. The package and I will board at Virágvölgy."

"The children are a nice touch."

Baxter didn't acknowledge Fagan's interruption. "All four of us will disembark at the János-hegy station and walk to the lookout where I will put the package on the chairlift. The operative at the lift has orders to take the package out before he reaches the ground. Markham's tail has confirmed that she left Széchenyi Bath alone and dumped her cellphone as instructed."

"As far as we can tell, she hasn't been in touch with any of her old contacts. Officers in the field have been alerted to her presence and instructed to inform us if she contacts them." Fagan paused before delivering the salient information. "She's on her own. How do you plan to alert Kastrioti?"

"We left him instructions to wait at his hotel. An informant on the staff will notify us if Kastrioti deviates. Once we have Markham under control, we'll send him proof of life and instruct him to meet us at the lookout."

Baxter went silent, but Fagan sensed that he had more to say. "You worried that you won't be able to get an experienced field operative under control?" he asked.

"She knows how we operate. And I've read her file. She's not about to let a civilian die. What play is she going to make?"

"You said it. She knows how we operate. So you know how *she* operates."

Baxter grunted. "In the next 10 minutes she'll make a move, likely on the tail."

"Leave your radio on VOX. I want to hear what's happening as it plays out."

"Copy that."

Fagan nodded to an analyst sitting next to Cramer. "Murphy, put Baxter's radio on loudspeaker."

"Yes, sir."

A moment later the room was filled with the live audio feed from Baxter's radio. The visuals on the main screen had also changed to show live video from the sniper's network-connected scope. It turned out to be a slow-moving kaleidoscope of trees punctuated by a swath of pavement filled with a few dozen people entering and exiting the stone building. A few more people milled around the nearby chairlift. If the tail lost Markham, the whole mission dynamic changed in her favor.

"Misfit 1, this is Misfit. Report."

"This is Misfit 1. Target approaching Normafa station. The train arrives in three."

"Copy that. Leave your radio on VOX, Misfit 1."

The video from the sniper's scope swung in the direction of the lower station hidden in tree cover. It would have been an almost impossible shot even if it had been visible. Tense moments passed until audio filled the room again.

The voice returned labored and panting as if the tail had broken into a dash. "Misfit, this is Misfit 1. I lost visual on target. Repeat. Target disappeared as train approached station. Target may have jumped onto the train."

Fagan pursed his lips but said nothing. This wasn't a surprising move and the tail should have anticipated it.

Suddenly Misfit 1 vocalized "oof!" Then there came a solid *thud* and all sound from Misfit 1's mic stopped. The analysts around Fagan swiveled their heads toward him. He scowled back at them, and they hastily turned away.

"Misfit 1, sitrep." Baxter remained calm. "Misfit 1?"

There was no answer.

"Murphy, pinpoint the GPS for Misfit 1's radio."

"It's at Normafa Station. Wait. Now it's gone, sir."

"Misfit, you've lost a team member. We get no GPS for his radio. Target likely on the train. Proceed with extreme caution." Fagan's blood pumped. He felt like he was flying.

"Copy that." Baxter paused. "Misfit 2, this is Misfit. Give me a sitrep."

"This is Misfit 2. Nothing unusual to report. Still got dozens of civilians entering and exiting the lookout tower."

"Misfit 3, this is Misfit. Status report."

"This is Misfit 3. No unusual activity at the lift."

The tension in the tactical operations room thickened enough to cut with a chainsaw. Fagan wished that he'd had enough time and enough clout to call in a satellite overwatch and drones. Someday he would. For now, all they could do was wait in the strained silence as the minutes ticked by.

Murphy, intent on his monitor, called out, "Sir! The GPS from Misfit 1's radio is back! She's at the entrance to the chairlift on top of János-hegy. "

At almost the same instant, Misfit 3 said, "Wait. Holy shit! It's Markham!" She'd broken protocol by speaking the target's name. "How the fuck did she get here so fast?"

Baxter's voice came next. "Confirm, Misfit 3. Target hasn't had enough time to run almost two kilometers uphill through the woods from Normafa station."

"Positive, sir! She wasn't there one moment, and then she was! It's like she materialized out of thin air. Should I engage?"

"Bring her to the János-hegy Station and wait for me, Misfit 3. Leave your radio on VOX."

"Copy that, Misfit."

The sniper's scope swung between the invisible János-hegy Station and the nearby chairlift, but only tourists appeared to be on the road leading from Elizabeth Lookout to the train. Misfit 3's bone-conduction mic wouldn't transmit any sound until she spoke, so silence filled the room except for the occasional squeak of someone's chair and the low-grade hum of laptop fans.

"Where the fuck is she?" Misfit 3 whispered as she came into sight on the video feed, scanning the road as she walked toward the János-hegy Station.

"Right here," Markham said over Misfit 1's radio. "Can't you see me?"

On the heels of Markham's question, the sniper spoke. "This is Misfit 2. I've got eyes on target but no shot."

From the scope's video feed, they saw Markham emerge from the trees lining the road and launch herself at Misfit 3. The two women disappeared into the trees on the south side of the hill. What followed was a thunderous and disjointed rain of profanity and grunts, mostly emanating from Misfit 3's bone mic.

Fagan found himself leaning toward the screen, focused intently on the lushly green leaf cover as if he could discern the progress of the hand-to-hand combat below. Both operatives were skilled and the fight seemed to last forever, though in reality it took three minutes. At that time, the radios went silent, but only Misfit 3's GPS remained operative—and stationary. She'd lost the battle.

"Misfit, you've lost another team member," Fagan said. Despite Markham's successes, he couldn't help the exhilaration he felt. Maybe it was because of them. Taking Markham down was going to be all the sweeter when it happened. He dialed Baxter on his cellphone. "Target is monitoring your radios. Board the damn train with the package."

"Where is she?" Coldness threaded Baxter's voice.

"Unable to ascertain. Markham has found some way to disable the GPS on Misfit 1's radio to mask her movements. Signal your status using your radio once you've secured the package on the train. Let her come to you."

Baxter had to keep Davies alive and stay on the train in order to control Markham, who would never forget the civilians around her. Several strained minutes passed as the tactical operations room waited for Baxter to radio in that he'd gotten onto the relative safety of the train.

"This is Misfit. I got the package on the train. We should reach János-hegy in 20 minutes."

Ten more minutes elapsed before Baxter spoke again. "Markham, we know you're monitoring our radios. Stop wasting time. If you want Davies safe and sound, you'll meet us at János-hegy Station."

"I wasted just as much time as was necessary," Markham said.

"Sir," Murphy called.

"You've only got one member left on your team, Misfit. Isn't that right, Control? Baxter keeps his teams lean, but he'd definitely have a sniper."

Fagan rose to her bait, anger and excitement warring within him. "Markham, this ends now. The only option you have is whether Mr. Davies walks away unharmed."

"Sir," Murphy called again, sounding more urgent. Fagan ignored him.

"Really?" she asked. "Aren't you curious about where I am right now?"

"Sir." Murphy had stood up and turned so that he could grab Fagan's attention. "The GPS from Misfit 1's radio shows that target is on the Children's Railway seven meters from Misfit."

Fagan stood immobile, listening. The remaining analysts sat in stunned silence, looking at him.

"How the hell is she getting around so fast?" Baxter asked over the radio.

No one answered.

Markham mused, "Where could the sniper's best line of sight possibly be?" She answered her own question with a laugh. "Not on Baxter, that's for sure."

A moment later, Baxter said, "Markham, have a care. As you can see, I have line of sight on Mr. Davies as well as on this lovely young train employee named Márta."

Olivia turned to face the open train car behind her own. Baxter stood at the far end, one hand gripping the arm of a terrified-looking girl and a Glock pointed at her head. Jack sat hunched over, his hands clutching his own head, whose hair was matted and bloody. She suspected that the older man had tried to defend Márta and gotten the butt end of the Glock as reward. The remainder of the car was empty despite the other train cars being full on this beautiful July day. Baxter would have directed the girl to refuse entry to anyone once he and Jack had gotten the car to themselves. Behind her sounds of panic and distress punctured the riders' low murmuring as they realized that there was an armed man within range of their seats.

Olivia's heartrate picked up. She felt as though she'd swallowed an ice cube, now lodged at the base of her esophagus. She fingered her St. Michael medal and sent a swift prayer that she hadn't played the wrong tactics. Children were supposed to be off limits, and as far as she knew Baxter hadn't crossed that line before. But Márta's obscenely large eyes warned her to be careful about testing Baxter if it meant mission failure.

She decided to go with bravado.

"Fagan, why am I not surprised that you're an amoral slime ball who would stoop to using a child as leverage? Is Stenson onboard with Misfit holding a Glock to a twelve-year-old's head? How about the rest of the team in the op center? You okay with this? Márta's so white I think she's going to pass out any moment."

Baxter scowled but didn't release Márta.

Fagan laughed. It sounded especially harsh through the stolen earwig. "Who gives a damn what Stenson or Murphy or the rest of the crew here at the substation think, Markham? The only thing that matters is what *I* think. And I don't have a problem with using anybody or anything to motivate an AWOL operative to cooperate."

There was no point denying her status. In fact, perhaps she should play to her strengths now that she had an audience. Fagan may claim that no one else's opinion mattered, but she thought it was worth buying time to bring her colleagues into the situation. If Fagan overstepped his authority too far, she was pretty sure that Murphy and Stenson would both report him to Langley, the first because he was a decent person and the second because, well, he was ambitious. And they all had history together. Fagan was the outsider.

"That's just it, Fagan. I'm willing to cooperate. I have been all along. You just don't seem too willing to listen to the judgment of your experienced field officers, something I'm sure that Misfit already understands." She was careful to use his call sign in front of Jack and Márta. "Am I right, Misfit?" She smiled and waved at the deadly serious man across from her. He didn't react, a reaction in itself. In fact, his face had gone blank.

"The question is, Markham, who's to be in charge. That's all. I gave you a direct order to bring Kastrioti in."

"You gave me a job but didn't wait for me to do it. I've found no evidence that Kastrioti"—her tongue tied at the impersonal reference—"has ties to the Albanian mafia. If he does, he would have already contacted someone about an extraction or safe house. He wouldn't be traveling alone with me."

Olivia eased toward the barrier between the cars on the slow-moving train. It would be next to impossible to get into the car with Baxter, Jack, and Márta before both hostages were shot. At that moment, Jack raised his head and his gaze locked onto her. He looked neither shocked nor forgiving. Guilt spiked in her breast.

"Come now, Markham. You're helping him. You're not exactly a credible source. For all we know, he has a security team at a discreet distance while you two play at being lovers."

"So the answer is to kidnap two civilians and hold them at gunpoint? On a supposition? Where's your evidence?" On an instinct, Olivia began climbing over the barrier. Baxter bared his teeth but did nothing as she swung her legs over, wobbling a little as the train jerked around a bend.

"I've built a career on supposition." Anger sharpened Fagan's tone. "I'm never wrong."

Olivia stopped on the inside of the train car with Baxter and the two hostages. "I'm sure that will console Amelia Davies after Misfit kills him. Those are your orders, right, Misfit? Best do it yourself since I disabled your team member at the lift."

She stepped forward. She needed to keep Fagan engaged just a little longer....

Baxter stiffened. Márta yelped as he gripped her arm tighter. The tension in the train car had reached a high voltage.

"Misfit, sixty seconds to János-hegy Station," Fagan said. "If Markham cares for the welfare of innocent civilians so much, she'll let you secure her without a struggle. Misfit 2 remains on overwatch, and he's unfortunately not been a party to Markham's impassioned pleas."

Olivia looked at Baxter and nodded. He tilted his chin in response, dropping his hand from Márta's arm. The young railway employee staggered away from the sudden loss of support and went down on one knee, crying out in pain. The Glock swiveled to cover Jack, who'd half risen from his seat. The retired Brit sank back wordlessly.

"Don't worry, Jack," Olivia said, addressing him for the first time. "It's almost over. You and Márta and everyone else will leave the train at the station. I will stay with my friend Misfit."

Jack's eyes narrowed. "A Yank spy."

She nodded, unable for the second time to deny the truth about herself.

"And your boss wants 'Aleso,' but you don't want to give him up."

She nodded again.

"So you got caught up in the game." Something flitted across his expression and he nodded again, the tightness around his eyes gone. "Makes sense. Plain t'see there's somethin' goin' on between you two."

Before Olivia, shocked, could take in Jack's words, the Children's Railway eased into János-hegy Station. Márta dashed past Olivia and down the steps onto the platform, but Jack paused as he passed her, laying a hand on her shoulder.

"Take my advice, love," he said concern showing in his gaze, "and don't play the game. There ain't any winners."

Olivia nodded, unable to speak as Jack left the train. Baxter took his spot, the Glock held at the small of her back this time.

"Misfit, local law enforcement arrives in five. You need to get the package off the train. Head due west through the park toward Budakeszi, which doesn't have jurisdiction and hasn't sent any units. You can regroup there. Misfit 2, cover Misfit's exit."

Baxter prodded Olivia, who shoved Jack's admonition to the back of her thoughts and got off the train. A few dozen people waited at the station and more strolled down from the lookout tower, unaware of the drama unfolding around them. Those who'd been on the train scattered like magnetized metal filings away from its idling cars, some pushing against the flow from the tower while even more scurried south on János-hegyi Way. Those fleeing that direction were met by Budapest police cars, sirens flashing and wailing as they attempted to maneuver among the panicked passengers and tourists.

She and Baxter had barely stepped beneath the covering canopy of trees when a brilliant white light flared from the top of the lookout tower. Olivia smiled. Baxter, caught off guard, turned to look behind them. As he did, Olivia slammed a foot against his instep while grasping the wrist holding the Glock with both hands and yanking him closer. Off balance, he stumbled. Olivia released him as soon as he moved, grabbing a handful of his shirt and propelling him hard toward the ground. He instantly rolled, bringing the Glock up and firing into empty air.

"What the hell?" He wavered, blinking in confusion.

"Here I am," Olivia said, kneeling at his side before delivering an open-handed chop to the vagus nerve on the side of his neck. Baxter fell back, limp. Olivia removed the Glock and stuck it into the back of her shorts. Into her bone mic she whispered, "Misfit down. Repeat. Misfit down."

Then she dropped the comm set on the ground.

TWENTY-TWO

Mihàil reached the base of the Elizabeth Lookout blazing white-hot and vibrating too fast for human eyes to detect. If Zophiel had seen him, she would have remarked that he practically flew toward Olivia even though his wings were more suggestion than actual angelic energy.

He'd known where Olivia was even before he'd gotten to the service desk at the Széchenyi Bath and found her note for him, though something had eased in his chest when he read her message. They'd grown closer after Bratislava, yet he'd sensed her wariness and the unspoken wall between them. Given the way that he'd manhandled her in the dressing cabin, he'd half expected her to try to disappear, leaving the diamond engagement ring and gold wedding band behind without any explanation.

He would have found her, of course. He might not have András's tracking abilities, but he could find Olivia Markham anywhere on the face of the Earth. Even if she learned to mask her harmonic signature, he would still find traces of its essence if he searched. That's because he knew her on a harmonic level now. Their nimbuses had merged more than once, his imprinting on hers. Hers imprinting on his.

She'd gone after Jack, who'd been taken by the CIA. She hadn't wasted time explaining, but she'd asked him to come. That's all that mattered.

He was furious anyway.

Furious at the unbelievable danger that Olivia had been in until he'd gotten to the lookout tower. And even more furious when he'd found a sniper at the top, harmonic disturbance echoing in the park below from the combat in which she'd engaged. Alone. She'd put herself in incredible danger. He was fast and deadly, but those attributes didn't matter if he wasn't there to fight at her side.

Mihàil reached Olivia as she stepped away from the prone man at her feet. Behind them turmoil reigned among panicked tourists, overwhelmed railway personnel, and grim-faced police officers trying to assess and control the situation. Ignoring them, Mihàil grabbed Olivia's upper arms.

"Are you all right?" At her wide-eyed nod, he savagely tamped down his desire to shake her and pulled her into his arms instead. "What the hell were you thinking going after Jack without me?" he asked, radiating blistering heat and smoke fumes. From long experience, he knew that humans and *Elioud* alike found his battle rage terrifying, but he didn't care.

Olivia didn't pull away. Instead, she sank against him, shivering. Mihàil wanted to bathe in her coolness, to ease his own fiery temperature before he combusted with rage, desire, and need. Somewhere inside, he felt the last icy current dissolve in molten conviction. He had to take a step back or be consumed.

Gripping his response with an iron will that had been honed over centuries, Mihàil stepped away from Olivia. His hands wouldn't release her, however. He drank in the sight of her, his vision taking in details only apparent to the *Elioud* along with more mundane ones such as the swollen bruise on her left cheek, the long tendrils of fine blond hair sprouting haphazardly from her hairband, the torn and dirty white shirt, and the filthy walking shorts on her lean, shapely legs. He forced himself to breathe slowly, to cool his skin and fingertips, to adjust his harmonics to a more human level. With satisfaction, he watched as Olivia's own harmonics evened, her breath slowed, and her temperature steadied to match his.

She raised her hands to his arms, her slender fingers sending shockwaves through him, and fixed her serious gaze on his. Her blue-gray eyes had deepened to slate. Where their arms met, hand to arm and arm to hand, their nimbuses flared and danced before settling into a stable new hue.

"I'm sorry." Her voice sounded scratchy.

Mihàil's eyes widened as he scented a trace of smoke on her breath. Nodding, he brought his fingertips to her bruised cheek, tenderly tracing healing heat over it. Olivia, closing her eyes, dropped her injured cheek into his palm. They stood there as long as they dared, but when the man on the ground groaned, they both snapped alert.

"I'll explain later, but right now we've got to get back to the hotel and grab our gear," she said. "We need to find a place to lay low and figure out our next steps."

Mihàil nodded. She pulled a weapon from the back of her shorts and tucked it inside the front, pulling her blouse over it. Then she set off down János-hegyi Way through the milling crowd, Mihàil following with his hand on her lower back. He adjusted his harmonics as they moved so that he disappeared from human sight. Olivia's harmonics adjusted at the same time, he noted with a private smile.

At the base of the hill, they got on the bus at Normafa just moments before police cars came wailing into the station to shut down service. Mihàil said nothing to Olivia about avoiding public transportation. She looked to be at the end of her energy and a short bus trip would do her more good than the risk of being spotted.

Olivia leaned back in the seat and propped her head against the window, closing her eyes on a sigh. Mihàil waited a moment before sliding his arm behind her and shifting closer until she turned and pressed her face against his chest. He moved the hair from her forehead with a delicate finger. Already the bruise on her cheek had faded to an ugly yellow-green and the swelling had gone down.

What was she hiding?

Once before he'd asked her why the CIA was after her, and he'd allowed her to shut the inquiry down because he'd been so startled when she'd responded by battling wills with him. He'd also been too aroused to think clearly and wanted to put some physical and emotional distance between them. Now he realized another, far more troubling, response to Olivia's display of *Elioud* will: subconscious pleasure. Despite all of his stated reasons for avoiding any entanglements, he'd been evaluating her from the beginning as a potential mate.

That made him angry.

He'd let his guard down. Mihàil should have recognized the danger sooner. After this latest incident, he'd bet that the acolyte was a member of the CIA, not the *Bundespolizei*.

If so, being with Olivia increased his danger.

Because the CIA had targeted her. If the CIA could find her, the acolyte could find him. It was only a matter of time. The question was whether he'd be at full strength and ready for the assault by then.

She opened her eyes and tilted her head back to study him.

"You're angry with me."

"Absolutely. You could have been hurt or killed." The savagery of his tone shocked him.

Olivia blinked several times before answering. When she did, her face and voice were inscrutable. "I wasn't."

Mihàil wanted to press her for answers, but she turned and looked out the bus window. Though she didn't move away from him, he noticed that her nimbus had retreated so far against her skin that it was nearly invisible. Her harmonic signature, so unstable from grief just a few days ago, had settled into an even, almost imperceptible, hum. They finished the fifteen-minute bus ride in silence. All around them, talk of the incident at Elizabeth Lookout occupied the other riders. Most speculated that it had been a terrorist group. He heard a couple in the back of the bus talking about an unknown woman, a tourist by her accent and clothing, who'd fought several of the terrorists. Mihàil pulled Olivia tighter against him in response, blurring the edge of his harmonics, which in turn blurred Olivia's. They would be vague and unidentifiable if anyone looked their way.

When they returned to the Hilton, Olivia allowed him to lead her to their suite. Once there, she stripped and pulled on a pair of dark chinos, a black-silk t-shirt, and walking shoes. Though her movements were swift and efficient, Mihàil saw the ugly reddish-purple bruises blossoming on her body. A red haze descended over his vision. He wanted to incinerate something.

Tamping his jaw shut, he turned and changed into black chinos and a dark button-down shirt before pulling on a pair of loafer-style walking shoes. He wished he had his combat boots with him. He donned sunglasses.

Olivia brushed her hair into a neat ponytail before pushing it under an American-style cap and slipping on a pair of sunglasses. Then she grabbed a backpack from the back of her closet and jammed the weapon she'd picked up into it. Mihàil refrained from questioning her. Instead, he went to the safe and removed his wallet and their passports.

"Leave the Italian passports," Olivia said, moving toward the door. "Those covers have been burned. Leave your cellphone too. It's likely been compromised."

Mihàil's eyes narrowed, but he said nothing and returned Aleso and Caterina's passports. He'd be without a passport until Miró and Pjetër arrived tomorrow. He added his cellphone to the safe. It had been a burner anyway.

Olivia didn't look around as she left the suite, setting off toward the elevators before he could reach her side. Once they exited the lobby onto the street, she headed south through the Castle District until they reached Szent György Square where she hailed a taxi.

"Soroksár. Solid Apartmans," said Olivia, sliding into the backseat. Mihàil's eyebrows rose at her sure command. She'd used a German accent.

The driver pulled into traffic, whistling. "It is good that you are going south," he said. "There was an incident at Normafa Park and the police are shutting down this district."

Olivia gave a non-committal grunt and kept her face turned toward the street.

Mihàil relaxed into the corner of the seat. Perhaps a little *Elioud* charm would go a long way here? Friendly tourists would be less memorable than silent ones.

"What has happened?" he asked, also using a German accent. He ignored Olivia's glare. "We were shopping at the West End Center."

The man shrugged. "Who knows? The news reports say that there was fighting and a man grabbed one of the little girls who work on the Children's Railway and pointed a weapon at her head. I think it is likely the refugees. There is more and more unrest around them."

Mihàil shook his head. "It is the same in Germany. The refugees are leaving here to go there. Merkel will have to address this soon for everyone's benefit."

The driver nodded. "Some say there was a woman who saved the little train conductor. The BBC has found a witness who saw her disarm the man with the gun. She is a hero. We need more like her when trouble happens."

At this remark, Olivia spoke. "I don't believe it. It sounds like a fairytale. Women are vulnerable to men, especially men with guns." Mihàil heard the subtle sarcasm under her words. More than that, he heard truth.

The driver nodded again. "That is so. But where children are concerned, they are like lions." He looked over his shoulder as he changed lanes. They took a right over the Danube. "But she was not alone, our hero. She had an angel fighting at her back. Witnesses saw him fly from the rooftop of the tower. When the police got there, they found that the door was blocked, but on the other side was an unconscious gunman whose rifle had been tied like a pretzel."

Olivia glanced at Mihàil. He couldn't read the expression behind her dark lenses, but she didn't have to send him a mental message for him to know what she was thinking. She knew that they'd just sent up a large flare for the acolyte, whether she suspected that the acolyte was CIA or not. After that she said no more, leaving Mihàil to make misleading small talk until they arrived at a tall yellow house. Though unfamiliar with the particular neighborhood, Mihàil knew that the airport was a twenty-minute-drive west. He paid the driver and then followed Olivia to the front door. There, an unsmiling middle-aged man met them and handed Olivia a key without speaking. She led Mihàil down a dark hallway toward a set of steep stairs. At the top was a small attic flat.

Once inside, Olivia dropped her backpack on the dining table. She took her sunglasses off and tossed them on the table along with her hat. Then she turned to face him. Resignation and something else—wariness?—shadowed her features.

"I'm CIA," she said before Mihàil could speak.

Her announcement hit him like a punch to the gut.

"What?" he asked, trying to process her words.

Suddenly everything about her, her proficiency with weapons, her cool-headed fighting during a terrorist attack, all of it made sense. She'd been trained in more than martial arts.

She gripped the back of a chair, her knuckles white. "My job at ABA-Invest in Austria is a cover. Was a cover." She closed her eyes for a moment, swallowing hard. "I was assigned to get close to you."

The answer had been staring him in the face. On some level, he'd already known it. Another thought hit him. Could the acolyte have used her from the beginning? Was Olivia actually a Grey *Elioud* all along? He hadn't believed it. He didn't want to believe it. "Why?"

Tension crackled between them. The air heated and the aroma of smoke blossomed.

Olivia's eyes widened. Their blue deepened. "I'm breaking protocol and burning my cover with you."

Mihàil clenched his jaw. His temperature rose further. "You could be working for the acolyte."

She held his gaze a moment longer and then sighed and sat down. She pinched the bridge of her nose, a gesture that perversely made Mihàil want to smooth the lines from her forehead. "Not knowingly." She paused and dropped her hands to her lap. "The CIA believes that the Dragon of Albania runs the Krasniqi clan. They suspect that you are the Dragon. Interpol has been watching you for some time as well, but no evidence ties you to the Krasniqis. My job was to find it."

Mihàil laughed. *Unbelievable.* "I *am* the Dragon of Albania, but I do not run the Krasniqis. I hunt them."

"I know." Her certainty warmed something inside his chest. "I was supposed to bring you in after the Belvedere, but I refused."

Mihàil remembered her cellphone conversation as they ran through the park to escape. "The asshole." He also recalled that it was the second time that Olivia had clashed wills with him—and won. After all, she hadn't told him whom she'd been talking to.

Olivia nodded. "Regardless, I'm a rogue operative and expendable."

"Apparently so was Jack." Mihàil ran his hand over his face and lowered his body temperature. It took a great deal of willpower to rein it in, but he managed. He sat down next to Olivia and took her hand. "It is my turn to be completely honest. Asmodeus prefers to target secret organizations, which are defined by deceit and manipulation. After the Belvedere, I thought that his acolyte would be among the *Bundespolizei*. Now I am certain that the acolyte is CIA. There are too many coincidences, including you."

Olivia looked solemn. She nodded. "Of course. That makes sense."

She stood and went to the small galley kitchen to retrieve a bottle of apricot *pálinka* and two glasses. She returned, sat, and poured them each a dram. She saluted him with hers and then tossed the brandy back before pouring a second glass.

"So where does that leave us?" she asked, her gaze on her hands as she rolled the glass between her palms.

He tasted the *pálinka*. Its sweet heat made him want to ignore everything but the beautiful, desirable woman sitting less than an arm's length from him. He wanted to taste her sweet heat, to dribble apricot brandy on her bruises and lick them dry with a delicate, healing touch. But he was a *drangùe*. He couldn't give in to his own selfish desires for fleeting physical pleasure. Or its aftermath.

Because then Olivia would be his.

He shot a penetrating look at her. The thought had been too swift, too forceful. Had she heard it?

But Olivia sat brooding over her *pálinka*. Feeling his gaze on her, she looked up. Her blue-gray eyes conveyed nothing, but her hands continued to roll her glass back and forth.

"Are we safe here until Miró and Pjetër arrive tomorrow?"

She nodded. "This isn't an official CIA safe house. It's part of my other, unsanctioned, activities."

"As the harlequin."

"Yes."

Mihàil frowned, thinking. "What about the team that we just battled at the Lookout? Will they continue on their mission?"

"Yes." Olivia sipped her brandy. "Baxter, the team leader—the man at my feet when you showed up—he will have eluded the Hungarian police. The other members on the ground will also have gotten away. The sniper on the rooftop will be out of play, however."

"Can I conclude that Pjetër will be watched in Vienna?"

She nodded.

"Good," he said and swallowed the rest of his *pálinka*.

Olivia looked startled.

Ignoring her, Mihàil poured a second, more generous dram. "We can use you to lure the acolyte here." Then he tilted his head back to drain the second glass. He slammed it down on the table. "And imprison Asmodeus once and for all."

"Imprison Asmodeus?" She sounded confused. "Has he awakened from his angelic coma?"

"I think not. He would have come after me directly knowing that I am still vulnerable and without my lieutenants. He would not have sent a human team at all." Mihàil shook his head. "No, Asmodeus is not directing his acolyte, of that I am sure. And that makes *him* vulnerable. The bond Asmodeus has with his acolyte is much greater than the hold he had over his vessel at the Belvedere. We can use that against him."

Mihàil stopped while Olivia considered his words. He knew that she would understand what that meant. And she didn't disappoint him.

"So controlling the acolyte means controlling Asmodeus."

It was his turn to salute her.

András may have extended enough trust to the enigmatic Wild *Elioud* named Beta for her to leave Vienna on her own, but he'd never promised not to follow her. He couldn't help it. He was an *Elioud* tracker, first and foremost, and her prickly determination to remain aloof and alone begged for him to shadow her to her destination. He didn't doubt that she thought she could handle any opponents, but he suspected that she'd mostly faced *tutyimutyi* men and *bogomili*.

Tutyimutyi men by definition were weak, lazy cowards. *Bogomili* couldn't think about tactics beyond those of wild dogs. A little tougher to overcome, but not impossible for a trained fighter, unless they came in numbers.

So he had waited until Miró had confirmed that Mihàil and Olivia had safely sailed out of Vienna, and then he'd followed Beta's faint harmonic trail. It might have been impossible even for him to track her after so many hours, but his brief physical contact at their last encounter had provided him with enough harmonic energy to distinguish her unique signature among the cacophony clouding Vienna.

At the memory of his hand wrapped around her bicep, András inhaled sharply. What an *agyilag zokni!* Mental sock indeed! What was she thinking? Any *büdös* villain with a modicum of training would break such a delicate creature should he get his hands on her. True, she could keep most men at arm's length with that wicked chain whip of hers...but once any of them got inside its protective guard, she wouldn't be able to withstand a direct assault. As fast as she moved (he grinned, recalling his ass hitting the floor at their last encounter), she couldn't evade all opponents. Eventually one of them would catch her.

András knew that he shouldn't care what happened to the slender, dark-haired woman and that he should have stayed in Vienna until it was time to fly with Mirò and Pjetër to Budapest. There was even good reason to think that she and the other two women were Grey *Elioud,* despite the fact that that minx Zophiel had played a role in their meeting Mihàil. Zophie had a generous heart and always held hope that someone could be redeemed. A necessary quality in a guardian angel to be sure, but András had no desire to risk Mihàil or their fighting triad for the slim chance that the three women could be brought onto the battlefield against the forces of dark angelic beings, of whom Asmodeus was only one among many.

Even so, he was intrigued by Beta. She reminded him of a standoffish black cat that he'd had as a child, a suspicious creature that would allow him only a stroke or two before darting away to safety. And yet when this black cat had been hurt, she'd found him even though she could scarcely walk from the gash in her side. She'd allowed no one else, not even the veterinarian, to come near or touch her.

It was he who'd snuck a sedative into a morsel of food that she nibbled from his hand, allowing her to be treated. András had nursed the little black cat back to health, cleaned her stitches, changed her bandages, and made sure she had food she liked to eat and a soft bed to sleep on in the corner of his room. That cat had become his shadow, and more than once she had alerted him to danger. He had called her a *gomba,* mushroom, though she had never become the kind of pet one would describe with an endearment.

When András found a group of teenage boys—many of them older and rougher than he was at the time—tormenting the terrified Gomba, promising to repeat their previous injury to her, he had flown into a fury. Though he hadn't yet reached his full height, András was as tall and sturdy as several of the other boys and managed to land more than one punch and a few kicks. Nevertheless, he had been beaten severely by the time Mihàil, Gomba in his arms, came upon them. She had run at the *drangùe* fearlessly, nipping at his feet and meowing insistently until he followed her back to the empty lot where her beloved human lay on the ground, curled in a ball and covering his face with his arms. Mihàil had administered the discipline the thugs deserved and brought home a neophyte to train.

"Admit it. You like her," said Zophiel, now sitting next to him. The guardian angel passed him a *makový koláček,* a fruit-filled Czech pastry. "Why else would you follow Ms. Černá all the way to Ostrava?"

András grunted and ate the pastry in two bites. He refused to look directly at his interrogator. They sat on the parapet of the Science and Technology Center overlooking the heart of the converted Dolní Vitkovice industrial complex. Tonight, workers swarmed over the grounds installing signs and structures to handle the upcoming Colours of Ostrava Music Festival. For four days, more than forty thousand people would listen to concerts of all types of music at almost two dozen stages.

"She is at the Bolt Café," Zophie said, pointing beyond the Small World of Technology building. Angled walkways outlined by bright white lights twisted around the tower where the modern café was sited. "You should go visit her."

András shook his head, wiping his hand on his jeans. "No. I can keep track of her from a safe distance. Wouldn't want that nasty chain whip used against me, would I?" He grinned at her.

"No, indeed not," Zophie agreed, nodding. "But how do you feel about her using it against the two Cămătaru brothers who have cornered her?"

András whipped his gaze toward her, heat seeping from his pores. Then he turned, staring at the Bolt Tower as he studied the infrared signatures nearest to Beta. Their sickly colors matched the identification of the Romanian mafia family. Unaware that his own harmonic signature had grown agitated and ominous sounding, András stood to jump from the parapet to the ground.

Zophie dropped a cool, weighted hand onto his shoulder. András looked up at the guardian angel, who was no longer as diminutive and cute as she had been. "Perhaps you would care to go slowly?"

András held her gaze for a moment before dropping his. "Of course." Then he raised his eyes again and his gaze blazed. "Slow or fast—it makes no difference. The strike of her chain whip will be as a kiss compared to what I will do to them if they should move against her."

The towering *Elioud* turned and stepped over the parapet as if descending stairs.

"Good man," Zophie said before clapping her hands over her head. Thunder rumbled in the distance in response. She smiled before rising into the air, her voluminous and diaphanous wings bright against the night sky. Only one person on the ground below glimpsed her disappearance in a vivid bolt of lightning, and he attributed the sight to the aftereffects of staring too long at the lights on the tower.

TWENTY-THREE

After her talk with Mihàil, Olivia retreated to the flat's bathroom and the large tub with jets there. Her body ached. She'd pushed it to the limit over the past week, and she needed the soothing hot water as much as the time to think. Mihàil had left her alone to go to the nearby Lidl grocery to pick up food and to buy a burner cellphone. He wanted to call Miró to update him about the CIA situation and to ask his lieutenant to transport the surviving *bogomili* at St. Elizabeth's to Budapest. Apparently Asmodeus didn't know that his minion had survived, and Mihàil had some plan to use the creature against its master.

As the tub filled with water, Olivia picked up her latest cellphone, the one that Stasia had put into her go-bag. She studied the phone's directory and saw that Stasia had saved a contact number for her and for Beta. Good. She needed them. But first, she called Amelia to make sure that she and Jack were all right. When Amelia answered, Olivia claimed to be from a news service looking for more information about Jack's role in the afternoon's events. The other woman readily confirmed that she and Jack had been at the Szechenyi Bath when he had been taken against his will to Normafa Park. However, she said nothing about Aleso and Cat and confided that her husband's story was more than a little suspicious.

"The old fool claims that American spies took him hostage in some scheme to capture a member of the Albanian mafia. I think he had too many pints and wandered off," Amelia said. "If you ask me, he made up the whole story so that I wouldn't be angry with him. You'd do best, dear, to find someone who was actually at the Lookout."

Olivia thanked her and hung up.

It was hard to tell what it meant, but Amelia's omission of the young Italian newlyweds struck Olivia as odd. Could Mihàil have altered the older woman's memory somehow? If so, that was a useful skill for a covert operative. Perhaps he would teach it to her.

At that thought, Olivia suddenly wanted to see Stasia and Beta, to know that her life hadn't been upended permanently. She was a covert operative, a damn good one. And she had a personal mission to stop sexual predators when she could. She didn't want anything more. She'd just forgotten herself in this legend, this cover story of a newlywed bride with a handsome, sexy husband who made her weak with longing and need.

She called Stasia, who answered on the second ring.

"*Ciao.*"

"Are you alone?"

"*Un momento, per favore,*" said Stasia. Her voice was muffled as if she spoke to someone nearby. When she spoke again, she sounded as if she were walking. "Budapest?"

"A team sent to take Kastrioti. Needless to say, the team failed."

"Ah. Where are you?"

"Soroksár. Have you learned anything?"

"I have found something. The *zombi* still at St. Elizabeth's. He is a Serbian refugee. It seems that he knew the *Bundespolizei* officer."

The tub was full. Olivia closed the tap and ran her fingertips over the water. Her bruises throbbed in response.

"What do you know about this *Bundespolizei* officer?"

"He investigated possible terrorist cells among the refugees. After the attack at the music festival, he was assigned to liaise with other intelligence services."

"Was the Serb a terrorist then?" Olivia nudged her shoes to the floor before tugging her socks, pants, and underwear off. She sat on the tub's edge and swung her feet into the hot water. Her t-shirt and bra would have to wait. Out of nowhere she remembered Mihàil's hands on her breasts. She shoved the memory from her thoughts.

"The *Bundespolizei* does not think so, but then they do not admit that their officer could be the link between the attackers at the Stadtpark and the terrorists at the festival."

A voice in Stasia's background interrupted. The sound over the cellphone grew muffled. Olivia took advantage of the break to stand and yank her t-shirt over her head. Hastily she pressed the cellphone back against her ear and reached up with her free hand to pinch her bra hooks open. The band loosened.

Stasia spoke to her again as she slipped the bra off and dropped it to the floor. "Our Croatian friend told me that the Dark *Irim* has an ally, someone called an acolyte. All the signs point to an intelligence officer, one who had contact with the dead *Bundespolizei* officer. I am gathering intelligence on the operatives that he debriefed after the music festival."

Something was buzzing in Olivia's exhausted brain, trying to come into focus. She stepped into the bath and sank into the hot water with an inaudible sigh.

"I wonder which CIA analyst it was. The new substation chief's a perfect candidate. He's a prick of the first order," she said, sliding under the water's surface until only her neck and head remained dry. Even as the words left her, she knew that they were true. In fact, she'd known it as soon as Mihàil said that someone from the Company was in league with the Dark *Irim*.

Fagan had transferred to Vienna two weeks ago after spending two years in the Balkans.

"Liv, there is something that you should know," Stasia said, interrupting her thoughts. She sounded grave. "The dead *Bundespolizei* officer met with Fagan an hour before he showed up at the Belvedere."

Ok, so maybe she wasn't such a damn-good covert operative after all. She really should have put this together before now. "Kastrioti wants me to lure the acolyte here. It sounds like the script for doing that is writing itself."

"Is that such a good idea?"

Olivia knew what Stasia alluded to. "I burned my cover, Staz."

"I see." Her friend's tone remained neutral.

"He would have figured it out. He already had suspicions after the music festival. At the time, he thought the CIA was after me for something the harlequin had done. After today's attack, he determined that the acolyte is CIA. It was only a short mental leap from there to *me* being CIA."

"The acolyte is your boss, *cara*."

Olivia stared at her thighs. Their skin had grown deep pink in the hot water, but the bruises from the Misfits had deepened to a dark purple. She'd been without her weapons, so all of her combat had been up close and extremely hands on.

"Two birds, one stone, *cara*."

"*Che significa?*"

"I need to get back in, Staz. Taking Fagan out of play not only makes that more likely, but Kastrioti says that it can be used to neutralize Asmodeus. Then we can return to our regularly scheduled lives as intelligence officers by day, super heroes by night."

"I do not think that the *drangùe* will be so amenable to that plan," said Stasia. "He seems smitten with you."

Olivia scoffed. "I think what you meant to say, Staz, is that he lusts after me. But he has already told me that he doesn't engage in casual intimacy and that he doesn't want anything more. It makes him more vulnerable or something." Her bitter tone stunned her.

"Ah, I see." Stasia sounded sympathetic. "What about *Elioud* training?"

"I see no need for that if we're not joining Kastrioti's little band. Besides, I've already figured out some fascinating *Elioud* tactics that I can share with you and Beta. How soon can you get to Budapest?"

"I leave tonight. Officially I am investigating the events that happened today. I have to make some arrangements, but I should be there before first light."

"Good. I will call Beta. Is she back in Ostrava?"

"*Sì.*"

"Then text me when you get inside the city limits. We can arrange to rendezvous somewhere."

Olivia dialed Beta after Stasia ended their call. Beta answered immediately.

"I am going to take his head off," her friend bit out without preamble.

"Whose?" Olivia asked, lifting her right toes out of the water. How long had it been since she'd had a pedicure? Really, how long had it been since she'd taken care of any of the routine grooming that a healthy young woman typically did? She wouldn't want to look too closely at her shins for the stubble sprouting there. Then again, the livid bruises obscured it pretty well.

"That *velká kráva* who has been following me for three days," Beta growled. "He is as subtle as a noxious fart."

Olivia recalled the giant *Elioud* whom Beta had nearly throttled at Mihàil's Vienna dining table and laughed. He was as far from being a big cow as an athletic, muscular male could be. For one his size, he was exceptionally graceful, quick, and quiet. She wondered why he'd been tailing Beta and whether Mihàil had anything to do with it. If so, they had another reason to shake these *Elioud* warriors. She didn't like being watched or second guessed. Neither did Stasia or Beta. Especially not Beta.

"Want to get rid of him permanently?"

"I just said so."

Olivia sighed, shaking her head. "Get to Budapest. Stasia will be here in a few hours. A lot has happened since I saw you in Vienna, but the short story is that I plan to get back in with the Company and get these *Elioud* oafs out of our lives, and I need your help."

Beta muttered something in Czech that Olivia didn't catch before saying, "Of course I will help you. But I cannot promise not to turn that stinking *velká kráva* into roast beef first."

Olivia laughed at her friend's dark tone. "I don't know. András seems more like a prime piece of sirloin to me. Just make sure you lose him and head to Budapest. I'll text you a place to meet without prying *Elioud* eyes and ears."

After ending the call, Olivia listened for Mihàil but heard nothing. Grateful for the solitude, she closed her eyes. As she'd raced to save Jack this afternoon, she'd slipped into her training and kept her breathing calm and even. And she'd noticed that the harmonic hum had responded. Almost on instinct she found that she could change the rate and pitch of her harmonics until she moved at a different speed from those around her, whose harmonics seemed fixed at a steady rate. This unlikely discovery was what had allowed her to surprise the Misfit team members.

She wondered what else she could control without being explicitly taught. What about her infrared signature? She'd managed to heat her fingertips enough to turn the eyes of Asmodeus's vessel into bubbling jelly. She frowned, looking down at herself. Nothing stood out except the pink of her skin and the faintly glowing nimbus that she'd glimpsed earlier. She shrugged mentally. Perhaps it was something that she would never master.

That would be too bad. She'd love to be able to defend herself with something that couldn't be stripped from her. If nothing else, she could escape zip ties and black hoods by melting or burning them.

Closing her eyes again, Olivia focused on the hot water, imagining that her breath flowed out into the water on an exhale and pulled heat from the water on an inhale. Sweat beaded on her forehead and she slowed her breathing even more, drawing the heat deeper into her torso and holding it there. Her breathing slowed until she held it. For a moment she felt weightless, unable to ascertain where her body ended and the water began.

The door to the bathroom burst open.

Mihàil stood in the doorway, a thunderous look on his face. His gaze locked onto hers, and she was shocked to see fear there. Relief quickly washed it away.

She clapped her hands over her breasts and squeezed her thighs together. Even so, she felt exposed as never before. "Well?" she asked, hearing the strain in her voice.

He said nothing, but his gaze devoured her.

In fact, his eyes burned so blue that she had the uncomfortable feeling that he could read her very soul. That's when she realized that he'd sheltered her from his full attention until now.

Something had changed.

Olivia swallowed the sudden lump in her throat. She forced herself to speak again. "What is it?"

Still Mihàil said nothing. Instead, she saw a soft white light limn his form, emphasizing the planes and hollows of his face and the dark stubble along his jaw. The soft hum that she'd come to associate with him vibrated the air between them, bringing a heated caress to her neck and shoulders. Her eyes widened as she felt that heat slide over her skin, skimming her collarbone and hands where they splayed over her chest. The warmth soaked between her fingers and cupped her breasts, now heavy and full.

Olivia's eyes fluttered closed as she tilted her head back, unable to resist the slow descent of heat along her belly and flank that wrapped around to her shoulders and lower back. The pressure massaged the aching muscles there. She sighed and relaxed into the warmth as it soothed over her hips and kneaded the tight flesh of her buttocks, slowly and deliberately pouring like heated honey over her thighs and calves. Invisible fingers tugged on her toes and stroked the soles of her sore feet.

She sighed again, so relaxed after Mihàil's ministrations that her hands slid down to the hot water. Her thighs eased open.

Across the bathroom, Mihàil groaned. His hum deepened as heat shot up her thighs like lightning, pooling at their apex.

Eyes half closed, Olivia lifted her head and looked at Mihàil. In his gaze she saw a dragon. It should have terrified her. Instead, she'd never felt so safe or so desirable than she did right at this moment.

She held his stare, wordlessly urging him to continue. Finally she managed to whisper, "Please."

At that, Mihàil's eyes flared with hunger. His smoldering look traveled down her body, setting it on fire wherever it touched. Olivia's nipples tightened in response, shooting a taut arrow of desire straight to her groin. Her own liquid heat rushed to meet Mihàil's where it had soaked into her hidden folds and licked along their contours.

His scrutiny returned to Olivia's face, pinning her in place with its intensity while warm, invisible fingers massaged her breasts, another circled around and around her engorged bud, and yet another slid inside her.

Olivia gasped and then moaned as the silky heat rose and retreated inside her like the slow surge of waves on a shore. *Oh, sweet lord.* It felt so incredible. Warm and wet and intense.

She wanted Mihàil inside of her. Now. She wanted his big, hot body over hers, his arms encircling her as her legs tightened around his waist. She wanted to feel him filling her, possessing her, taking her, while she ran her hands over the corded muscle in his arms and shoulders, urging him between passionate kisses to *go harder, go faster, go deeper.*

She tried to speak, to call him to her, but the air vibrated around them and there wasn't enough to breathe into her lungs. Mihàil's lips parted. His eyes became two brilliant slits, and his jaw tightened. The pressure on her swollen bud increased while heated waves rocked her core with tidal force. She couldn't think anymore, could only focus on the mounting urgency between her legs. They shook so hard that water streamed from her thighs.

Everything around them disappeared from Olivia's awareness except for the twin blue beacons of Mihàil's eyes. As her world shattered, sending her flying into a million pieces on a harmonic boom, she heard him give a hoarse shout of triumph.

Olivia slumped, boneless, against the side of the tub and rested her cheek against its cool rim. Her chest rose and fell. She felt overheated and slightly dizzy. Mihàil leaned against the door frame, his own chest expanding with deep breaths. On his skin, a sheen of sweat glistened and dark spots dampened his white linen shirt. After a moment, he ran a hand over his face, shook his head as if clearing it, and stepped to her side. Bending, he lifted her in his arms before sitting on the side of the tub with her on his lap. While she snuggled against his chest, he toweled her dry. Then he carried her from the bathroom into the bedroom where he pulled down the covers and laid her against the cool cotton sheets. He left her there, drowsy and spent, only to return a few moments later with a cold, wet washcloth, which he used to wipe her face, chest, and the back of her neck. As she luxuriated in the soft sheets, he moved away to unpack a t-shirt from his bag before lifting her and pulling it over her head.

Olivia allowed him to draw her arms through the sleeves, his familiar spicy scent filling her nose. She wanted nothing better than to sleep, to bask in the afterglow of *whatever* it was that had just happened between them, but she couldn't. Sighing, she sat back and watched Mihàil as he unbuttoned his damp shirt and took it off. His beautiful body gleamed in the warm glow of the bedside lamp. The incision over his right pectoral muscle had tightened into a thin shiny line, visible only when the light caught it. Though he looked fully recovered, she read fatigue in the line of his neck and shoulders.

Sitting on the edge of the bed, he turned to look at her, tenderness muting the lingering ferocity in his eyes. Ferocity and something else. Hope? Fear?

Olivia searched his gaze. "That wasn't casual, was it?" she asked.

He shook his head, watching her. "No, it was not." His voice was gruff. He took her hand and held it in his. "But neither was it true lovemaking. That I will not do until you are sure that you can accept the consequences."

"The consequences?" she asked. If they were going to have this talk, then she needed for him to be blunt. "Are you afraid that if you make me yours it will lead to a lot of suffering and evil?" She tried to sound light, but she heard the mixed fear and anxiety in her voice.

"No." His gaze never wavered. "I am speaking of the consequences for you, Olivia."

She would show him what the consequences were for her.

Leaning forward, she cupped his cheek before caressing his jaw. His breath hitched when her gaze dropped to his mouth. Slowly she touched her lips to his. Full and firm, they parted beneath the gentle probing of her tongue. With a groan, he gripped the back of her head and, angling his own for more control, plunged his tongue against hers. Time slipped away and Olivia forgot everything but the intoxicating mastery of his mouth taking hers.

At last, she pulled back. Mihàil looked as dazed as she felt. Triumph arced through her.

"You, Dragon Man," she said, smiling, "will be mine."

Light flared in his eyes at her words, but he restrained himself. Instead, he studied her face as he responded. "Yes, but that is not all."

She sighed. It was time to lay her cards on the table. "I know who the acolyte is, Mihàil. Or at least, I think I do."

His hand holding hers tightened and grew warm. His gaze sharpened as he leaned closer. "Who?"

"My new boss, Joseph Fagan. He came from the Balkans two weeks ago. He knew about the attack at the music festival and tried to use it to grab you in the chaos."

He grew thoughtful. "You did not know about the CIA officers on the square."

She shook her head. "Fagan's arrogant and clearly doesn't think much of me as a field officer. He gave me no notice or chance to object."

"And he tried to have you killed."

At Mihàil's reminder, Olivia's anger—and temperature—flared. "At the time, I thought Fagan had failed to make sure that his team knew who I was and that Miró saved me from being killed in the fog of battle."

Mihàil's fingers cooled, bringing her temperature down. "Was he responsible for the armed team that tried to 'escort' us after the music festival?"

She nodded. "He was the suit that András knocked out. Too bad he didn't incinerate him."

"Yet you left my Vienna residence, presumably to return to the CIA?" There was an edge in Mihàil's voice that Olivia didn't like. "You chose to reject my protection for him?"

"I left the home of a *suspected Albanian mafia lord* that I was assigned to gather intelligence on," she said, pulling her hand from his. "And my boss ordered me to report in. I wanted to confront him about disregarding my judgment and putting me in danger for his own glory. Besides, I don't like feeling imprisoned. Your *Elioud* defenses just begged to be defeated."

Mihàil ignored her bait. Instead, he took her hand again and held her gaze. "Your boss in all likelihood *orchestrated* the terrorist attack knowing that I planned to attend the music festival," he said grimly. "I have been concerned that Asmodeus would find a way to use you to attack me when he has been doing exactly that all along."

"If I help you lure Fagan here, then you can do whatever it is you plan to do to Asmodeus." Olivia's fingers strayed to her St. Michael medal. "You won't have to keep me close." Despite herself, her voice broke a little as she spoke, but she kept her gaze steady.

"And you can go back to your job at the CIA and take on predators as the harlequin," Mihàil said. "Is that it? You think that I am only interested in protecting myself?"

Olivia heard incredulity in his voice. She lifted her chin. "Until a little while ago, yes. After what we just shared, I want to believe that you want more."

Mihàil's eyes blazed and the room grew warm. When he spoke, his words resounded. "I want you by my side and in my bed, now and forever. Today's events made that abundantly clear."

Olivia shivered and liquid heat shot to her core. Just like that, she was ready for him. She tamped her reaction down. While her traitorous body exulted at the thought of being in Mihàil's bed, her heart wanted more. "I don't want to be in your bed just so you can protect me."

"I will protect you whether you are in my bed or not." He began rubbing the back of her hand with his thumb. "This is not about physical union, Olivia. We are already connected, you and I."

At Mihàil's words, vibrations began to hum along Olivia's arm, moving through her entire body. Her harmonics responded, syncing with his. A nimbus flared to life around him. A matching glow emanated from Olivia, merging with his until she couldn't see where her nimbus ended and his began.

"You also have power over me." He looked at her, his eyes dark and intense. "Show me, Olivia."

Olivia searched his gaze and knew that what he said was true. After a moment, she took a deep breath before focusing on her harmonics. Mihàil's shifted in sync, sending a thrilling vibration through her. In wonder, she watched as their nimbuses flared and danced.

She brought her gaze back to Mihàil's face. Pride and admiration radiated from him only to be replaced by a somber expression. "Making love now will bind us on a spiritual level. There will be no going back. Your fate and mine will be forever entertwined."

"So I have no choice then?"

At her question, his face lost all expression. When he answered, he spoke carefully. "You have a choice, Olivia. This connection will always be between us, but it does not have to become more. I will always be aware of you. I will always know where you are, and I will always come to your side if you need me."

He paused, his gaze searching. "I want more. I want yours to be the first face I see when I wake and the last before I go to sleep. I love you, Olivia Markham. I want to marry you. But I am a *drangùe*. By marrying me, you will become my *zonjë*, my lady, and bound to my duty as the Archangel Michael's general. You cannot return to the CIA or to being the harlequin."

TWENTY-FOUR

B eta stared through narrowed eyes at Nutu ("Little John") Cămătaru,
ignoring his younger brother Sile (short for Vasile), who stood on the
catwalk behind her. The pudgy, aging Romanian mafia boss believed that he
and Sile had blocked her egress. It was just like the *vûl* to think that *he* had *her*
where he wanted her. She stroked the heavy steel dart of her chain whip where
it lay against her thigh, hidden under her jacket hem.

Nutu pursed his lips, studying her. He cocked his head to look around at Sile.
"*This* is the one causing us so much trouble?" He straightened his head, shaking
it. "Too skinny. She'd cost us even more money if we put her on the sidewalk."
He laughed. It was guttural. "*We'd* have to pay *them* to stick their dicks in her."

Beta said nothing. Let him keep talking. It meant that he didn't consider
her a threat. She could sense Sile easing toward her, his hulking form radiating
warmth and body odor on the evening air. She shifted her weight and forced
herself to hold the handle of her chain whip with a relaxed grip. Its warm steel
kept her calm.

Nutu focused on her, his gaze holding hers. If he was surprised at her un-
flinching regard, he didn't show it. "I showed your picture around. It seems we
have a mutual friend in the VZ." The VZ was the Czech military intelligence
service. Beta tucked that insight away for later perusal—and pursuit.

"He says you are a lone wolf. Always disappearing for days and weeks. That,
he says, has made you a legend even among the legends." His gaze sharpened and
became predatory. "*I* say no one will notice you're dead until it's too late. But
first, I'll collect your debt to me." He let his gaze travel down her. "Or a fraction
of it anyway."

Beta saw the almost imperceptible nod he gave as he finished speaking. She didn't need it. Sile's heat and stink formed a miasma around her so thick it choked her. She flung the dart toward Nutu as she pivoted, driving the elbow of her whip arm into Sile's face and wrapping the chain whip around Nutu's neck at the same time. Sile grunted and dropped to his knees like a sack of cow dung. Instantly Beta swiveled back toward Nutu, yanking the chain whip across her body and tightening it around his neck. He took an involuntary step toward her, his hands going to the link pressing against his windpipe. His eyes bugged.

Beta allowed herself a small smile as she jerked Nutu closer. "Your country has a saying: 'Don't sell the skin until you have caught the bear.' Or should I say wolf?" Now Beta let her smile grow, imagining gleaming incisors and a feral light in her eyes. Perhaps Nutu caught a sense of her imaginings because his eyes grew wide and his skin paled. He stilled.

Or perhaps he'd just caught sight of the giant oaf looming behind her. Of course the *velká kráva* would show up after she'd taken down her quarry. She sniffed and tightened her grip on the handle of the chain whip. Nutu gagged and struggled. He wanted to help? Alright then. She'd let him help.

Sile lumbered to his feet. Here was another thick skull.

Beta pulled Nutu to her, leaning on his weight as she kicked Sile, who flew away from her into András. Seconds later, she'd shoved the mob boss, unwinding her chain whip from his neck. He stumbled backwards into the catwalk railing and went down hard.

She was sprinting down the catwalk before she heard Nutu's head clang as it hit the railing. Behind her came the sounds of bone hitting flesh and flesh hitting metal interspersed with curses, grunts, and groans. She palmed the railing and dropped over the side onto the catwalk below. As she stood, she chanced a glance over her shoulder. András had his back to her. She knew that he would pick up her trail at the base of the former blast furnace that housed the café, but once she reached her car, he would need more time to track her.

That he *would* track her, she had no doubt. Two days ago, she'd been astounded that he'd found her here in Ostrava. Afterwards, she'd let him shadow her, giving no sign that she knew that he was there. In those two days, she'd tried to determine how the *Elioud* followed her. It was something non-technological. She'd searched all of her belongings and found no hidden tracker. Her cell phone was a burner, but she dumped it anyway and got a new one. She abandoned her rental car with its hackable navigation system. Still András stayed on her tail. Whatever he used, it wasn't perfect. She'd lost him for half a day in the industrial park that housed Liberty Ostrava, the largest steel mill in the Czech Republic that happened to be a ten-minute drive south.

As a result, she'd gotten an idea for a trap, one that would kill two flies with one blow.

Beta raced along the angled catwalk, going over the railing until it leveled into a viewing platform. There she found the rappelling equipment that she'd stashed earlier. In moments, she was on the ground and running toward the stolen car that she'd parked next to the information center.

Thank all that was holy that these *Elioud* didn't appear to have wings. She'd have a head start at least.

"Fly number one is dead," she said as she slid behind the wheel. Leaving the headlights off, she started the car before looking out the windshield. A massive shadow plummeted from the top of the tower to the pavement, no wings necessary. Grumbling, she stepped hard on the gas pedal. The car shot forward. "Fly number two I'm going to kill with my bare hands."

Miró watched as Anastasia Fiore exited the front entrance of the nondescript office building where her agency had its Vienna substation. Unlike Mihàil and Andràs, his *Elioud* senses weren't strong enough to track her after only a handful of brief physical contacts. He'd been forced to touch her at their last meeting in order to attach a tracker to her, though it wasn't the touch that she'd focused on, that is, his grip on her wrist. In the space between a heartbeat and a breath, he'd sped his harmonics enough to slip it into her bag and onto the sheath of her BC-41. She might dump the other contents of that bag, but she'd keep her fighting knife with her.

Low muttering and a few choice words came from the backseat of the car. Miró turned and fixed his gaze on the man sitting in the backseat across from him.

"You promised to play with that quietly."

The man's wide dark eyes looked up at him, a disturbing mix of sly innocence shining in them. "I turned the volume down."

Miró let his nimbus flare and an edge of *Elioud* authority enter his voice. The interior of the car heated twenty degrees. The man's eyes widened farther. Sweat beaded on his forehead and upper lip. "No more muttering and absolutely no naughty words or I will have to take the phone away from you for the rest of the trip. Do I make myself understood?"

The man blinked a few times, his gaze suspiciously bright. He looked out the side window. "Yes," he said, his lower lip pushed out.

"Good." Miró turned back toward the front. Ms. Fiore had gotten behind the wheel of a Fiat and now pulled away from the curb into the empty street. He waited to tail her. He could afford to hang back out of sight with the tracker, which was a good thing. She was too good an operative to overlook a car following her. Despite her earlier agreement to work with him, he knew that she would do everything she could to keep him unaware of her movements and her discoveries.

That was fine by him. He'd had his own investigation into the *Bundespolizei* officer to occupy him as well as his errand to pick up his passenger. In between, he'd helped Pjetër pack and close up Mihàil's Vienna headquarters, though that efficient and hardworking man could have done it without any meddling from a less-than competent *Elioud* warrior. But now it was time for him to bring Stasia up to date and to learn what she'd found.

Miró studied the map currently displayed by the Cayenne's built-in navigation system, which he'd tied to the tracker. She appeared to be headed toward the sixth district. *Olivia's flat.* Of course. Olivia would have called Ms. Fiore to join her following the attempted extraction in Budapest. A stop first at her flat made sense. That meant that his and Ms. Fiore's paths were destined to converge whether she wanted them to or not. He shot a glance at the man in the backseat.

He couldn't ask for a better chaperon or reminder about the consequences of Asmodeus's evil presence in the world.

Annoyed at the direction his thoughts had taken, Miró dialed Ms. Fiore's cellphone as he maneuvered the Cayenne into the street.

A moment later her husky voice answered, calling to mind her large, hazel eyes and sweet scent. "*Ciao.*" She sounded wary.

"Ms. Fiore."

She sighed. "There is no avoiding you, is there?"

"I suggest you do not try," he said, letting a pleasant tone vibrate in his voice.

"No need to use your *Elioud* charm on me. I despise insincerity." Startled, Miró almost didn't hear her next words. "Next time, drive a less obvious car. A white Porsche makes a poor tail."

Tightening his lips, Miró said, "I suppose that I should be grateful that you spare me *your* charm, sincere as it is." He heard a slight hiss at the fair hit. "As for the appropriateness of my vehicle, there is no need to tail you as I am driving directly to Ms. Markham's flat. By the way, the Cayenne has plenty of room. Feel free to pack whatever you need."

There was a long moment of silence.

When Ms. Fiore spoke, her voice was flat. "What makes you think that I am riding with you?"

It was Miró's turn to sigh. "As you said, there is no avoiding me, Ms. Fiore, at least not for the near term."

"Fine. Wait outside Olivia's flat. I will not be long."

"As you wish."

He'd barely finished speaking before she disconnected.

Twenty minutes later, he sat parked a block down from the building. Ms. Fiore's Fiat was nowhere to be seen, but he assumed that she'd left it parked in the garage. It was almost two a.m. and the street was deserted, which set his battle senses on edge. Behind him, his passenger hummed softly as he saved wingless animated birds from their enemies, animated green pigs. There was a trace of disturbance in the harmonics of the neighborhood, like the last fading ripple after a small pebble has been tossed into a pond. Miró scanned the street for a hundred meters in either direction of the front entrance but sensed nothing out of the ordinary, either on a human or angelic level. Yet he didn't believe in coincidences.

All at once his passenger erupted into howls and began rocking back and forth, his hands over his ears.

Miró sent a powerful burst of harmonics at the man, who slumped over against the rear window, unconscious. No need for him to be alert now that he'd served as an alarm system for approaching *bogomili*.

Slipping his door open, he slid out of the Cayenne, speeding his harmonics as he shut it carefully. In the moonlit darkness, human eyes—therefore *bogomili* eyes—wouldn't be able to detect him except as a flitting shadow.

Crouching, he ran down the block toward the trio, which had begun to move toward the entrance.

As he got within twenty meters, he sent a harmonic shock wave at them. It should have knocked them off their feet, stunned. But it didn't. They kept walking. One turned, looked over his shoulder, and grinned.

What in St. Michael's name was going on?

Miró stopped short. That's when he realized that the *bogomili* wore full facemasks and gloves. He'd seen that clothing before, but he didn't have time to figure it out. The grinning *bogomili* had halted and now waited for him.

Slowing his harmonics to syncopate strongly with those of the *bogomili*, Miró moved in close, less surprised this time when the *bogomili* resisted the disrupting vibration. The man's movements slowed, however, as though the air had become water.

Miró, who had developed his own fighting style using syncopation, jabbed at the *bogomili*'s face, timing his strike with his heavy harmonic offbeat. The brain-dead minion's head snapped back, its grin wavering. This time, he wobbled as he returned upright. Miró didn't wait for the other to recover his balance. Dancing around the *bogomili*, he hammered him with lightning blows to the torso and head.

The *bogomili* tottered as if buffeted by strong winds. Miró's dancing around him had created a minor harmonic vortex in counterpoint to his steadier harmonics and it was only a matter of a leg sweep to topple him. Miró knelt and delivered a swift fatal blow to the *bogomili.*

He didn't look back as he jumped and swiveled toward the two *bogomili* who had managed to bypass the security system for Olivia's building. One had entered the building. One waited on the steps guarding the door.

Even before he got within five meters of the guard, Miró knew that he would be unable to repeat his maneuver. Although humans had no ability to control their harmonics, which were set at a steady rate, the harmonics of the *bogomili* in front of him now varied. Strangely, the harmonic vibration emanated a short distance from the man's body, leaving a still space like the eye of a hurricane.

Miró switched to steady, slower harmonics and noted that the other's shifted to match after several beats.

"Try this," he said and raised his core temperature. Though the night was warm, his fingers steamed.

The *bogomili*'s eyes widened. These men may have lost a lot of their higher-level thinking, but they recognized danger in their limbic systems.

A beat later the *bogomili*'s infrared signature disappeared as if covered with a shade. Before Miró could interpret that bit of information, the *bogomili* launched from the top step toward him, knocking him to the ground. Miró embraced the *bogomili* with arms and legs. Heat radiated from him, yet the man's clothing absorbed it.

They scrabbled and grappled. Miró couldn't get a solid purchase on the man's heaving form. It was like wrestling a lumpy, slippery fire-retardant blanket—not exactly something Miró had trained as an *Elioud* warrior to overcome. Only a few moments had passed, but Miró thought of the third *bogomili,* unhindered in his approach to Olivia's flat. He sped his harmonics, rolled the other man onto his back with his thighs pinning the man's arms, and jabbed stiffened fingers into the blurry white oval that the man's face had become.

This time, his heated fingertips struck exposed skin. An inhuman shriek pierced his harmonic veil along with the taint of burning flesh and the stink of decay. No matter how many times he fought one of these minions of Dark *Irim,* he would never grow immune to that smell. Gagging, Miró leaned on his fingers, pressing into the *bogomili*'s skull as he again shifted his harmonics into a short, directed burst aimed at the man's unprotected face. A sharp crack cut the shriek off and the man's body went limp.

Miró sprang from the dead *bogomili* and jumped to the stair landing. By the time he reached the vestibule, the door to Olivia's flat stood open.

He stopped in the doorway. Nothing moved inside the darkened main room. In fact, he detected no heat or harmonic signatures anywhere in the flat.

But that didn't mean anything with this group of *bogomili*.

Miró slowed his harmonics and sent out pulses of low-frequency sound. Angelic sonar, Mihàil called it. Usually, he could ping any living creature with it. The resulting echo would be distorted predictably by the typical harmonics. But these *bogomili* wore something that actively adapted their harmonics to his. The response would be both late *and* wrong.

Yet it was the whisper of fabric on fabric that alerted him to the attack from behind.

Whirling, he raised his arm to block and caught a blow that sent him staggering. The *bogomili* kept coming, however, his momentum unbroken by Miró's lower mass and off-balance stance. They tumbled together to the floor, Miró hitting his head against the doorjamb on the way down where they lay half inside and half outside the flat. Stunned, Miró did nothing while the *bogomili* wrapped meaty fingers around his neck and squeezed. His vision darkened.

Abruptly, his attacker wrenched his hands away and began writhing. Miró sucked in several large breaths while his vision cleared but couldn't immediately make sense of the struggle above him.

No matter. He'd end it.

He flashed angelic white light.

The *bogomili* stopped thrashing and began moaning. The moaning became a choking sound and then the man toppled back into the hallway. Somebody dragged him off of Miró.

He shoved upright to see Ms. Fiore bent over the *bogomili*, one hand on her upper thigh as her chest heaved and the other gripping one end of her *surujin*, which was twisted around the *bogomili*'s throat. She turned and retched.

"I am sorry," he said, aware that the aftereffects of the flash would leave her dizzy and disoriented. Already a sharp headache had started behind his eyes. Ignoring it, he stood. "Thank you for coming to my aid."

Nodding, she wiped her mouth with the back of her hand and wrinkled her nose. "Gah! Do they have to smell so bad?"

The *bogomili* whimpered in response.

She jerked the *surujin* tighter until he passed out. Raising her face, she looked at Miró. Her large, almond-shaped eyes gave away nothing. She nudged the man with her toe. "What should I do with him?"

Miró sighed. "Let me take care of him."

He knelt to place his hand on the *bogomili*'s face, applying intense heat and adjusting his harmonics to a high-pitched vibration. After several moments, he sat back, running a palm down his own face. By St. Michael, he was tired.

"Is he dead?" Ms. Fiore asked, watching him.

"Yes." He looked up. "Let us hope that Asmodeus is still in his angelic coma, and these minions were set to watch Olivia's flat." He began stripping the *bogomili*'s jacket. The body would decay in minutes now, leaving nothing behind but clothing.

"Why are you doing that?"

"These *bogomili* are dressed oddly. I suspect that their clothes have something to do with their ability to withstand some of my *Elioud* weapons."

Ms. Fiore picked up the strange facemask that had fallen from the *bogomili*'s head when she'd wrenched him off of Miró. "There are sensors of some kind embedded in the lining."

"Bring it." Miró stood. "Have you packed what you need?"

She nodded, swaying.

Miró steadied her, withdrawing his hand almost as soon as he'd touched her. Turning away, he said, "I have some chocolate in the Cayenne that will help."

Outside the building, Miró stopped and knelt by each of the dead *bogomili*, sending a concentrated burst of heat into them until nothing remained but ash. As he got to his feet, the ash rose in a column of harmonic wind that scattered when he joined Ms. Fiore. She said nothing, her gaze trained on the dispersing ash for a moment, and then they walked in silence back to the SUV. It was all Miró could do to stay upright on the way.

Ms. Fiore's eyes narrowed as she took in the slumped figure in the back seat, but again she said nothing. He stored the *bogomili* gear and her bag in the trunk before rummaging for the chocolate and a couple of water bottles in a large kit. His head ached sharply and fatigue melted his bones. Acid churned in his empty stomach.

He tossed a bottle at Ms. Fiore as he slid into the driver's seat. She got in beside him.

"Who is our guest?" she asked after they'd been driving ten minutes.

Miró glanced in the rearview mirror. Then he looked briefly at Ms. Fiore. "You do not recognize the Serbian *bogomili* from the hospital?"

Ms. Fiore twisted in her seat to stare at the man. After a minute, she swiveled to face forward again. "Why do you have him?"

"He can be used against Asmodeus. More to the point, he can tell us whenever there are other *bogomili* around."

She nodded and sipped on her water. Her wide eyes had a glazed sheen and fatigue pinched the corners of her generous mouth.

"Eat the chocolate, *signorina*."

Defiance sparked in her gaze, but she dutifully tore the wrapper and nipped a corner of the bar. The scent of chocolate made his stomach twist.

"Here," she said.

When he took a chance to look at her, she held a square of chocolate toward his face.

"Eat." She pressed the chocolate against his lips.

He kept his face forward.

"I can hear your stomach grumbling."

Miró allowed her to slide the chocolate into his mouth. He left it on his tongue where it began to melt. After a few moments, his headache eased. He opened his water bottle and took a mouthful. He was parched, but he knew from long experience that he needed to go slowly or he'd be sick.

"There is a portfolio on the floorboard," he said to distract himself.

Ms. Fiore brought the leather case to her lap and opened it. She studied the photos inside, flipping each one over into a neat stack.

"Recognize the *Bundespolizei* officer from The Belvedere?" he asked. "The man he's meeting is CIA."

"This photo was taken an hour before the attack." She'd seen the time-stamp. "How did you get these?"

He lifted a shoulder and let himself reach for his chocolate bar. "These were in a cache of documents from a contact I have at the Russian embassy. After Mihàil told me about the CIA team, I sorted through them. His name is Joseph Fagan, and he arrived in Vienna two weeks ago from the Balkans."

"So he could have come into contact with the refugees and the *bogomili* in the camps."

Miró nodded. "What is more, I have identified the eyewitness who initially named Mihàil and Ms. Markham as the *Bundespolizei* officer's killers. She is an American attached to the embassy named Susan Larsen. Video surveillance puts her with the *Bundespolizei* officer at The Belvedere twenty minutes before Olivia arrived. Her photo and stills of that meeting are also in the portfolio. Ms. Larsen has a fondness for haute couture and carries high student-loan debt. Recently, she received a large payment from a company known to be a CIA front."

Ms. Fiore looked at him. "This Joseph Fagan, he is the acolyte, no?"

"That would seem so." Miró's mouth tightened as he said this, which made his temples throb. He rolled his head and stretched his neck. He began to work at the wrapper of his chocolate with one hand while he drove with the other.

"Let me help you." Her fingers brushed his as she removed the bar from his grasp, setting off a tingle. He snatched his hand back and drummed his fingers on the steering wheel to hide his reaction. A moment later, she held out a square between them. Her movements stirred her subtle scent, which had permeated the interior of the Cayenne without him noticing. Anise, vanilla, and something slightly smoky combined with the sweet fragility of iris. It was feminine and sensual and deeply heady. And it eased his headache from the angelic white light much better than anything he'd ever tried.

Clearing his throat, he accepted the chocolate and popped it in his mouth. Silence descended between them. Miró wished—not for the first time in his long life—that he was either as impervious to emotional currents as Mihàil or as insensitive to them as András. Instead, it was his lot to be the *Elioud* spy, the master of deception, intrigue, and innuendo. For that reason alone, he suspected, he imagined currents swirling between him and Ms. Fiore. He didn't know which was worse: the possibility that the currents were real or that his fevered brain wanted them to be.

They drove for about forty minutes before Ms. Fiore sighed and said, "Can we please stop at that rest station up ahead? I need to use the toilet and buy a coffee."

"As you wish." Miró's headache was gone, but he had the dehydrated feeling that accompanied drinking too much wine. A brief stop to stretch his legs and clear his head wouldn't hurt.

He pulled into the rest station at Nickelsdorf on the Austrian side of the border. Ms. Fiore disappeared into the well-lit main building to take care of her needs. He parked and got out of the Cayenne, reaching for his cell phone as he stretched his back. András hadn't responded to his earlier texts. That was worrisome. The giant *Elioud* might be goofy and lack finesse when it came to interpersonal affairs, but he was indomitable in battle. If they were going to be facing Asmodeus's acolyte or even a human black-ops team, he wanted the Hungarian at his back.

At the border, he typed *Will rendezvous with Mihàil in two hours. Where are you?*

His friend didn't respond so Miró did what he had to do. He checked the tracking app that he'd put on András's phone and only accessed in dire emergency. Frowning, he realized that the *Elioud* tracker was almost 350 kilometers northeast of the rest station. Miró quickly swiped the coordinates into mapping software. Ostrava, Czechoslavakia? What was in Ostrava?

The coordinates matched an address for Liberty Ostrava, a steel mill. What in St. Michael's name was András doing at a steel mill?

"Here."

Miró looked up to see Ms. Fiore holding out a paper cup with a lid, the kind that held coffee.

"It's hot chocolate. I figured that would help you the most."

Surprised at her thoughtfulness, Miró accepted the cup.

"Want me to drive?"

Miró, in the act of taking a sip, paused to study his companion, but she had her cellphone out and was peering at the screen. She seemed sincere enough. And they had more than an hour until they reached Budapest. Glancing at the back seat at the still unconscious *bogomili*, he shrugged and headed to the passenger side of the Cayenne.

"Why were you frowning?" she asked as they crossed into Hungary and the A4 turned into the M1.

"Hm?" He blinked. Funny, the hot chocolate was making him sleepy.

She glanced at him. He noticed that her eyeliner had wings at the corners, accentuating the almond shape of her eyes. She looked mysterious and exotic, like a modern-day Cleopatra. Smart. Devious. Not to be trusted.

"When we were at the rest station. You were frowning at your phone."

Miró found it hard to concentrate on what she was saying. He knew that he'd been about to have an important thought. What was it?

He lifted the hot chocolate to his mouth and sipped as his thoughts came slow and ill-formed. It was almost as if he'd been drugged....

"What did you do?" he asked, his tongue a swollen mass that stuck to his palate.

She shrugged a graceful shoulder. "What I had to."

Miró winced and reached for the switch to lower his window, intending to throw the spiked drink out, but his fingers wouldn't obey him. The paper cup dropped into his lap, sloshing the contents onto his pants. His last thought before he lost consciousness was that he was glad that it had grown tepid first.

TWENTY-FIVE

For the first time in nearly three hundred years, Mihàil knew despair. The look on Olivia's face after he'd told her what she'd have to give up to be with him had sent him from the safe house. He hadn't waited for her to answer what was essentially a marriage proposal. At that thought, he shook his head and scoffed. First a fake marriage and honeymoon, now an ultimatum. How romantic!

"How authentic," murmured Zophie at his side.

"Authentic?" He didn't look at the guardian angel though he was glad that she'd appeared. She didn't always show up when he wanted her and often appeared when he didn't, but right now her company eased him.

"Being your mate—your *zonjë*—means doing whatever it takes to combat the Dark *Irim* that walk among humanity. If Olivia is the one for you, then she has to know and accept it all. That's what love is, *djali im*."

Mihàil heard the endearment and his despair lightened, bringing a sense of shame. He should never despair, not when he had a guardian angel and the blood of an *Irim* flowing through his veins. Yes, he loved Olivia and didn't want to live without her. But he would do what he must, what he was called to do. He was a *drangùe*.

He looked over at Zophie, who for the first time in memory stood shoulder to shoulder with him. She wore her hair long and straight in a demure style and was dressed in nondescript dark clothing. He realized that she was here to keep him focused and remind him that there was more at stake than his feelings.

"Thank you. I will not forget again."

"Yes, you will," she said and punched him in the shoulder.

And to remind him of his personal failings, of course.

"Besides," she said, sliding her arm through his and strolling faster, "Olivia just needs a few moments to recognize how exciting and unpredictable being married to a *drangùe* is. It is much better than being a staid CIA officer."

Just as Mihàil started to say that he doubted that Olivia would describe her career as "staid," his cellphone rang. Slipping his phone to his ear, he looked down. Zophie had disappeared.

"Are you here already?"

"No." Even over the cell line, Miró's voice sounded strained. "I am awaiting a ride just inside the Hungarian border."

"Tell me." Mihàil's brain and demeanor switched into command mode, all thoughts of Olivia's possible rejection gone.

Miró sighed. That was indicative in and of itself. The man was so restrained and self-contained that he would lose consciousness before anyone knew that he'd been injured or overwhelmed. Mihàil and András made it a point to keep an eye on their friend for telltale hints that he was in trouble.

"First and foremost, I am a victim of my own stupidity." Miró might be self-contained, but he was always brutally honest. "I let my guard down with Ms. Fiore, and she drugged and abandoned me on the side of the M1."

"Ah." Mihàil found that tidbit fascinating. Miró *never* let his guard down with anyone but Mihàil and András—his experience as a *köçek* had only enhanced his natural reticence as a truthseeker. Mihàil tucked Miró's confession away for future reference. "You were escorting Ms. Fiore to Budapest?" He hadn't expected that of his lieutenant.

"After I followed her to Olivia's flat, I realized that she planned to meet Olivia." His lieutenant paused. "I will ensure her safety once we engage Fagan's team."

Mihàil smiled to himself. *Very fascinating.* "Pjetër?"

"As ordered, he has packed the necessaries and shut down the mansion. A crew comes tomorrow to move out anything left and the property manager resets the security system afterwards. By the end of the day, it will be as if we had never been there. Pjetër arrives at Budapest airport at 7 a.m."

"András?" Mihàil hadn't been surprised when Miró told him that the *Elioud* tracker had disappeared shortly after he and Olivia sailed from Vienna. The Hungarian had gone after Olivia's Czech friend. Though he was affable and optimistic, András had learned at a young age to trust but verify. Nevertheless, Mihàil needed his largest fighter in Budapest to handle Fagan's team. "He has not responded to my texts or calls."

"Before I lost consciousness, I tracked him to Ostrava. Ms. Černá works for the VZ, which has been tracking an influx of arms in that region. András, or at least his cellphone, is still there. Should I head to Ostrava to investigate?"

Mihàil ran his hand through his hair, thinking. "No, I need you here to start planning how to handle Fagan's team. Send me the coordinates for his phone. I will send Daněk to make sure that András has not forgotten that he has other responsibilities in case he has found some demons or minions with which to amuse himself."

"If she is anything like Ms. Markham and Ms. Fiore, I suspect that Ms. Černá has provided him with more than enough distraction." Miró's tone was wry. When he spoke next, the humor had gone. "*Gospodaru moj*, there is something else."

Miró's use of the Croatian honorific "my lord" signaled the seriousness of what he was about to say. Mihàil's battle intuition flared. "What is it?"

"Ms. Fiore and I encountered *bogomili* outside Ms. Markham's flat who wore the same gear that the team that intercepted us in Vienna wore."

Mihàil swore under his breath. *Bogomili* were a pain to tackle when they swarmed but largely easy to disable or kill. Because Asmodeus didn't care how many *bogomili* died in his battles against the *Elioud*, he'd never bothered making them less vulnerable. They were pawns and replaced as quickly as he could find more spiritually weak humans—that is, in no time at all. In fact, Asmodeus could and had created vast armies of minions. The last time was during World War II. The scale of his efforts had spawned literally thousands of copycats among the Dark *Irim* and lesser demons around the world. But Asmodeus much preferred smaller *bogomili* teams now to play cat-and-mouse games with Mihàil and his lieutenants.

It must be the acolyte's handiwork.

"I trust that you obtained pieces to examine?"

"Yes, and in that at least, Ms. Fiore did not make things harder for me. I have a facemask and a jacket. Both have microelectronics embedded in their fabrics. The facemask has a camera. I will know more once I can study them."

"Do you also have the surviving *bogomili* from St. Elizabeth's?"

"Yes."

"Good. Contact me when you are ten minutes out." Mihàil paused before adding, "Oh, and Miró, do not disable Ms. Fiore's engine while she is driving."

"That never occurred to me." Even though Mihàil had been teasing, Miró sounded vaguely offended. "Besides, I have no way to determine if she is still driving. She has turned off the GPS in the navigation system and removed the tracker that I put on the SUV."

"But not the tracker that you put on her."

"Indeed. I may be gullible, but I am not *that* gullible."

Miles Baxter had been a field operative long enough to know never to be surprised. Flexibility in everything was the key to adapting to changing situations on the ground. So he wasn't surprised when Olivia Markham contacted Stenson or that Stenson contacted him—without reading Fagan in. What surprised him was his own response. Olivia Markham intrigued him. He didn't know Markham beyond her young reputation with the Agency, which was that of competent junior intelligence officer. But he'd known dozens like her. Experience told him that Markham likely wouldn't be around for him to collect when he needed it. No reason to flirt with trouble on the chance that he was earning a favor for the long term. Yet his gut told him something different, and that's what intrigued him. Why did he think that Markham had something to offer that would justify going around Fagan, a narcissistic megalomaniac if he'd ever met one?

The experienced operator that he was, he'd hired a trusted local to watch the Hilton after he'd grabbed the Brit. It was never wise to underestimate a target, and he'd stayed alive and effective this long because he always had a contingency plan. As a result, he knew that Markham and Kastrioti had returned to the hotel and left some minutes later laden only with backpacks. The asset had managed to tail them to Szent György Square and capture the license plate number of the taxi that they took. After a few calls, Baxter knew the pair's exact location.

But he hesitated. Sure enough, he got the call that Markham wanted to meet—without Kastrioti. He agreed and then sent the rest of the team to watch their safe house. Either Markham would cut a deal to turn over the Albanian, saving him and his team a lot of effort, or they'd grab Kastrioti anyway.

Contingency meant flexibility. Flexibility had allowed Baxter to adapt to the new situation on the ground. It would lead to ultimate mission success. And Fagan had nothing to do with it. A nice bonus.

Markham had insisted on picking the meeting site, which hadn't fazed Baxter in the least. She was unlikely to attempt to do him any harm, and despite her obvious skill at hand-to-hand combat, he had no qualms about taking her on if it came to that. On the other hand, he had no intention of detaining her; whatever Fagan's issue with Markham, she was still a CIA officer. Until it was shown definitively that she was a rogue operator working to harm American interests, Baxter had no interest in bagging her for Fagan's petty ambition.

Markham had picked the Budapest Park concert venue fifteen minutes' drive north of her safe house. A smart move, especially on a clear Saturday night when a popular band played. It also meant that she didn't suspect that he already had a fix on Kastrioti's location.

As Baxter neared the entrance to Budapest Park, he eased into the crowd still thronging the sidewalk even though it was past two a.m. Markham would have called him from the park after she'd arrived and found a spot to watch him enter. His job was to saunter along the food stalls lining the broad walk in front of the open-air stage until she approached. He did so, ambling for twenty minutes before making it all the way to the concert pavilion without any contact, not even a tingle on the back of his neck from being watched. Baxter had turned and headed back toward the entrance when Markham slipped her arm inside his as if they were on a date. She held a 9mm muzzle against his side with the other hand.

Nicely done, he thought. Aloud he said, "Let's go somewhere else."

Markham said nothing. Instead, she leaned closer and walked faster. Baxter allowed her to lead him past the park entrance and north. On their left, the dark water of the Danube River reflected the lights of Budapest's buildings in liquid gold. Budapest was a uniquely lovely city at night. Some might prefer Paris or Rome, but this Eastern European capital rivalled those famous cities of love. Unbidden, the thought that he could be strolling arm-in-arm with a beautiful woman on a romantic outing instead of a tense intelligence operation seized him. In response, he shoved it where he sent all of his sentimental musings and focused on the task at hand.

They walked in silence for ten minutes. Up ahead, the lights of the Liberty Bridge, formerly called the Franz Josef Bridge after the Austro-Hungarian emperor, outlined the ornate structure. It was a favorite lovers' rendezvous. It was also ideal for covert meetings. His senses began to tingle. Was Kastrioti waiting on the bridge?

"I wouldn't have harmed the girl," he said suddenly.

Markham squeezed his arm. "I know."

A dark figure separated from one of the trusses and stood in the center of the empty bridge as they approached. It wasn't Kastrioti but a petite woman wearing a mask that reminded him of Spiderman except that this one was creepily featureless. She also held a short chain, its ends weighted. If he had to guess, it was a throwing weapon. Markham nudged him forward with the 9mm. Baxter silently and instinctively evaluated his options.

A soft sound, more a movement in the night air, caused him to look over his shoulder as they stepped onto the bridge. Another dark figure, tall and slender and also masked, stood behind them. Despite the dark clothing and obscured face, it was clearly another woman. Something thin and metallic dangled at her side. Markham had backup, and Baxter had no idea who they were. He also had no land exit from the bridge.

He stopped. Markham stopped too.

"You've got a team." He let appreciation color his voice. "I had a feeling that there was more to you than your file suggests."

"Is that why you agreed to meet?" She'd taken a step back and now aimed her 9mm at his face in a two-handed grip.

"Partly." He looked again at both women stationed on either side. "Does Fagan know about them? Is that why he has such a hard-on for you?"

Markham shook her head. Her gaze was as unwavering as her grip. "They're friends who are doing me a favor."

"I'm not your friend," Baxter said.

"So don't do me any favors."

Baxter laughed and widened his stance, shifting to the balls of his feet. Tension clogged the air around them. "Interesting piece of advice. Tell me, why did you have Stenson contact me if not for a favor?"

"What I want to talk about is a mutually beneficial deal. I have something you need, and you have something I want."

"To come in from the cold," he supplied, "around Fagan. How do I know you aren't as dangerous as he says you are?"

"You know or you wouldn't be here. Stenson wouldn't vouch for me if I was a rogue operative."

Baxter acknowledged this with a chin dip.

"But it's more than that. You know that Fagan is the one who is a threat."

Normally Baxter didn't let anyone make bald statements about his judgment, but he let this slide. After all, Markham was right. He nodded again and waited to hear her terms.

"I know your team is watching Kastrioti," she said.

Baxter didn't let his surprise show. There really was more to Markham than her file documented.

"They'll never take him, not without my help."

Baxter studied her. His gut told him that she wasn't bluffing.

"What do you want in exchange?"

"That's easy. Fagan."

Baxter threw his head back and laughed. The sound carried across the Danube. The woman in front of him shifted her feet and began twirling a weight at her side.

"You've got ovaries, I'll give you that," Baxter said, wiping at the corner of his eyes with his thumb. He couldn't remember the last time he'd laughed. He didn't laugh on missions. Well, there was that one time with that mousy Latvian hacker who'd run around a warehouse like a madly spinning pinball. Baxter had laughed so hard that he'd had to sit down and get a grip on himself. Later, he'd downed a whole bottle of vodka. Still. He couldn't recall laughing until he cried since he'd been a goofy teenager in New Jersey messing around with friends and fireworks.

Markham appeared to wait until he regained composure. He saw speculation in her eyes.

"I may not be your friend," she said quietly, "but here's a piece of friendly advice: take some time off, Baxter. You need a little R and R."

Baxter coughed and swallowed and felt his hilarity die. "And how do you propose that I deliver him to you? He's in Vienna."

Markham smiled. Baxter noticed for the first time how beautiful her blue-gray eyes were, how luminescent her skin. At the moment, she looked angelic, haloed in the gold light from the municipal buildings behind them. He almost started laughing again at the thought of an angel holding a 9mm with a practiced grip.

"Get him here to direct the op against Kastrioti and me."

When he spoke, the cold edge had returned. "Fagan knows that I don't cede control on the ground. Period. He won't buy it."

"I think he will if he's got Stenson whispering in his ear, especially if he overhears you complaining to your team that you don't want him to come. You and I both know that he's monitoring your comms. It's a short step from there to running your team in person."

"Carrot and stick." Baxter eyed her through narrowed eyes. "I think Fagan is right to see you as a threat."

"Only to those who threaten the innocent."

Baxter would have laughed if anyone else had uttered those ridiculous words, but he believed Markham. "Okay, let's say Fagan decides to ride roughshod over me and come to Budapest. How do I know that Kastrioti won't have skipped out beforehand? He has to have figured out that the CIA is after him. He'd be better off heading to Albania where he's treated like a local lord."

"You've had someone watching us since Bratislava. You know that Kastrioti is in love with me."

"Yes." He couldn't blame the Albanian. Right now, Baxter himself was half in love with her.

"He asked me to marry him."

Baxter shook his head. *Poor bastard*. Aloud, he said, "I'll contact you when Fagan takes the bait."

Markham nodded once, lowered the 9mm, and signaled to the petite woman with her chin before backing toward her taller friend. As she joined the other woman, Baxter called, "A piece of friendly advice? Don't underestimate Fagan. I've known some hard operators. He's in a class all his own."

Fagan stood in the nearly empty TOC, watching footage from the earlier botched attempt to take Kastrioti in Budapest. He asked the technician to slow the footage down repeatedly. Something bugged him about the sequence of events.

"Again, at half speed," he ordered. The young woman twitched at his command and her fingers flew over the keyboard. Fagan scarcely registered her nervous speed, though normally it gave him no small thrill to yank on his subordinates' strings like a master puppeteer.

The timestamp in the lower right of the recording flashed its counting. All at once, Fagan knew what bothered him.

"Stop right there. Note Markham's position and the time, then move forward frame-by-frame until her next position appears. Note her position and time again, and then calculate distance between those two points and what speed target had to maintain to move between them."

"Yes, sir." The analyst bent to her work, her nerves settling into the defined task. "Sir?" She turned to face him, her features noticeably pale. "I ran the numbers more than once. They don't make sense. There must be a glitch in the recording."

Fagan gave her credit for facing him when she feared his ire. But then, he knew what she didn't: the numbers didn't make sense. "There's no glitch, Wilson. Markham moved between point A and point B faster than humanly possible."

Wilson blinked. "Sir? I don't understand."

Fagan brushed her off. "There's nothing for you to understand. Now dump the footage onto a USB drive and erase the recording from the main system." No sense in keeping evidence of Markham's abilities. It would raise flags.

Wilson blinked again, clearly shocked. Then she focused on his face, saw what was there, and straightened her shoulders. "Yes, sir."

Fagan gave her credit for that response too. Wilson was a smart woman. He took the USB drive that she handed him and returned to his office, shutting the door. He checked his voicemail on the phone that his demonic partner had given him, but there was nothing. He had heard nothing from the Dark *Irim* since Asmodeus had sent his minions against Kastrioti and Markham at the Belvedere more than four days ago. Fagan wasn't sure what that meant, but he was certain that their quarry was in danger of getting away.

Tapping his fingers on his desktop, Fagan decided to check on the *bogomili* that he'd set to watch Markham's flat. Asmodeus had humored him when he'd asked for his own *bogomili* hit squad, saying that he grew bored of the brainless creatures and would enjoy watching Fagan torment them. Or use them to torment people. Either way, it was amusing to the Dark *Irim*, who promptly ignored the group, except to ask Fagan why he needed so many playthings.

Fagan, for his part, had quizzed Asmodeus about how the *Elioud* tracked the *bogomili*. As an intelligence operative, he'd wanted to employ counter-measures to make the *bogomili* more effective as a tool.

Waving a dismissive hand, Asmodeus had said, "They have angelic senses, though they're inferior to mine. They can read the spiritual vibrations each human makes. You can think of it as angelic sonar. And they have infrared vision, too." He'd said all of this while watching with sneering avarice as a group of immigrants accosted a young Viennese woman. In his hands, he'd held his profane *subulam*, the one that he'd consecrated to his use.

From this brief description, it was simple enough for Fagan to work with a weapons supplier to develop an anti-thermal-imaging fabric for his braindead grunts. Not that that was any great design breakthrough. The intelligence community already used the technology for black-ops missions in hostile territories. Camouflaging the *bogomili* harmonics proved to be the trickier part of his anti-*Elioud* uniform, but Fagan's supplier integrated extremely sensitive sensors to cancel or redirect vibrations within a three-meter radius. Then Fagan had gone to a black-hat programmer to create a set of machine-learning algorithms that trained the sensors to adapt to an angel's harmonics. Of course, that had meant that he'd needed to wear a training module in his own clothes that used Asmodeus himself as a model.

Fagan grinned. He'd created the world's first smart textile for fighting angelic beings.

His good humor died, however, when the app that he used to control the sensors on his smartphone detected no vitals or movement among his crew. His anger grew, in fact, when he realized that all but two sensors had no readings at all. Someone had destroyed his clever armor. The two missing sensors belonged to a facemask and jacket. His anger died as quickly as it came, bringing his good humor back like the sun burning off dark clouds. Swiftly he tracked the GPS sewn into each item. They were together and were moving along the A4 south toward the border with Hungary. Putting two and two together, Fagan surmised that his surveillance squad had been dispatched and that either a *bogomili* had been captured or someone had been smart enough to realize that the uniform had secrets worth studying.

He laughed outright.

One of Kastrioti's associates had gone to Markham's flat and encountered his *bogomili*. And now he or she was taking a tracker to his quarry. He'd created an unintentional Trojan Horse.

He wouldn't wait on Baxter to locate Markham and Kastrioti. Baxter had been allowed to run his operations for too long. He wouldn't cede command on the ground to Fagan. True, he was a highly effective operator with a loyal and skilled team, but there was a chain of command, and Fagan was at the top of it. Fagan had every right to take the reins if he deemed it critical to mission success. And one of Fagan's prerogatives was sending in a new team. A team that he so happened to have ready and waiting, one that was incapable of being anything but loyal to him, with a pilot as a member. Again, he'd had the foresight to target a critical asset. After this, Asmodeus wouldn't question his need to have so many "playthings" any more.

Where *was* Asmodeus?

The Dark *Irim* had been irate the last time that Fagan had taken the lead on trapping Kastrioti at the Vienna music festival. And he'd almost had him, too, making it at least as good as the other attempts that Asmodeus had directed. Fagan almost wondered if the Dark *Irim* was envious. If so, how would he take Fagan going after Kastrioti without consulting him? Was his silence a test?

Fagan stared at the app as it updated the GPS positioning of his smart armor. He really didn't have time to ponder the question, not if he wanted to get to Budapest and scout the location. Baxter may not have Fagan's good luck in having tracking details hand-delivered to him, but he was very likely hours away from sniffing out Kastrioti and Markham's location if he hadn't found them already. Though Baxter's team was good—the best, actually—at finding and acquiring a target, they didn't stand a chance unless Fagan outflanked the *Elioud* with his smart-armor-wearing goon squad.

He called Asmodeus one last time just in case. Never let the Dark *Irim* say that Fagan hadn't done his best to reach him. But he was delighted when the call went to voicemail. Asmodeus always knew where he was and had an uncanny ability to discover what he was doing. He also moved with the speed of an angel.

Let him come stop Fagan if he had a problem with what Fagan was about to do.

TWENTY-SIX

M ihàil waited in pitch-black shadows a block down and across from the Solid Apartmans building. There were two infrared signatures outside, one on top of a nearby roof and the other a block up on the same side of the street as he was. They were being surveilled, likely by the CIA team from this afternoon.

He swore, low and soundlessly. He'd been too preoccupied with his dramatic declaration to Olivia and beating a hasty retreat afterwards to be fully alert to their perimeter. It was a bad sign that he'd allowed his battle senses to be quiescent. How in the world would he explain this to St. Michael? Did the Archangel even know what Zophiel was up to, encouraging his *drangùe* to fall in love and lose focus? Was it a test? If so, he was in danger of failing it.

Scowling, he scanned the neighborhood for the infrared signatures of the other two team members. There were no obvious lurkers outside any of the houses. It took a couple of minutes, but then he found a third infrared signature on another street a block west. Given the relative location, he guessed that someone waited in a surveillance van.

His cellphone vibrated. It was Miró, who must be ten minutes away. He tapped his earwig and said, "We have company. Three individuals."

"Who is unaccounted for?" Miró sounded fully alert and aware now.

"Indeterminate. Given that Olivia left the safe house two hours ago, I would hazard a guess that it is the team leader Baxter meeting with her."

"You sent her?" Miró's voice held a hint of skepticism.

"We discussed the options." Mihàil still didn't like the fact that he'd allowed Olivia to meet with Baxter alone. "She argued rather persuasively that it would be better for her to approach Baxter without me."

"She is no longer a Wild *Elioud*."

"I am well aware of that fact." Mihàil pinched the bridge of his nose at his sharp tone. He shouldn't snap at Miró. "But she is not under my command."

"Will she be at your side then?" Miró had guessed at his commander's feelings. He and András both deserved to know that Mihàil had asked Olivia to be his *zonjë*.

"That remains to be seen." He paused to wrest his emotions into order. "For now, we are working together to bring Fagan here. Have you heard from Danek?"

"I have done better. András himself called. Daněk is flying him here."

"Good. We are going to need him." Mihàil sensed Olivia behind him and turned to watch her approach. Though it was faint, her nimbus shone softly in the dark. His heart clenched. She was so astonishingly lovely.

Miró interrupted his thoughts. "Do you think that Baxter's team is going to move against us ahead of Fagan's arrival?"

"Not if Olivia has any sway with him." He studied her face, which was inscrutable. "I am confident that she was successful."

Miró cleared his throat. "It has only been a few days since you were injured. Perhaps we should fall back to another location."

That observation caught Mihàil by surprise. He scanned himself. For such a grave injury and such a short recovery period, he felt remarkably well, especially given his burst of angelic white light yesterday afternoon. True, he wasn't at full strength, but he felt close. Puzzled, he watched his nimbus flare as Olivia came to stand next to him, its edge merging with hers in a gentle overlap. Their energies wove together, boosting and fortifying his strength. Understanding dawned. Olivia made him stronger, whole. Did she feel it too?

He turned his attention back to Miró. "Negative. Olivia has returned. Find a location to await further orders."

"Copy that." Miró ended the call.

Mihàil wanted to touch Olivia, but he restrained himself with drinking in her presence instead. Even here, an invisible filigree of rose, freesia, and ginger wafted around her—warm, familiar, and enticing. She looked at him, her large blue-gray eyes luminous in the low light provided by her nimbus. Astonishingly, *deceptively* lovely. Olivia's captivating exterior hid a tough, resourceful interior.

"Were you successful at meeting with Baxter?"

"Yes. It's as I thought. He'll let us know when Fagan arrives in Budapest." She gestured with her head toward the safe house. "I gather that you've discovered his team watching the safe house. Was that Miró?"

He nodded. "András will be here soon." He studied her demeanor. Something was off, but he couldn't tell what. "Ms. Fiore?"

"Stasia is checking in with her agency. She's awaiting my instructions."

Olivia stuck her hands into her jacket pockets and kept her face forward. She seemed to be trying to gather her thoughts. Or her courage. He wasn't sure which. Finally, she looked at him, and one hand strayed to the St. Michael medal around her neck.

"Mihàil, I can't do it. I can't marry you." The words tumbled from her mouth.

Something cold stabbed his heart. He'd never felt anything so devastatingly chilling, not even the *subulam* that Asmodeus's vessel had broken off in his chest.

Turning away, he said, "I see." So Zophiel, ever the optimist, had been wrong. Being the *zonjë* of a *drangùe* was too much to ask. Of course it was. Even if she'd loved him, he should never have asked it of her. A vast sense of isolation and loneliness flooded him. There would never be another woman for him. He would never love another. An eternity stretched before him without her.

He felt Olivia's gentle fingers on his arm. "Mihàil, I'm sorry. I care about you—a lot."

Shoving his disappointment and grief into the cavern where his heart had been, Mihàil looked at her. "We need to plan the meeting. Are you sure that you are fine with me taking Fagan at your safe house?"

Olivia's gaze searched his face. Concern radiated from her, but Mihàil consciously pulled his nimbus back into himself and dropped his temperature. He needed to put some distance between them so that he could focus on the mission at hand.

She looked as though she wanted to say something and then thought better of it. Her hand dropped to her side. Shrugging, she said, "It's compromised already. I'll need a new location. Besides, once you take him, it won't matter what he knows, will it?"

He shook his head. "We will transport him to a secure location. He cannot be allowed free access to people, let alone intelligence resources for the most powerful government in the world."

Olivia looked uneasy. "That government will want him back if they learn where he's being held. Then you really will be a criminal no matter what Stenson does with your CIA file."

Mihàil refrained from saying that he could teach her how to use her *Elioud* charm to modify Stenson's memory of this operation, limited as it was about the details. He would have to settle for wiping Baxter and his team's memories instead, leaving only Olivia and Ms. Fiore with knowledge of who had grabbed Fagan. Olivia would be forced by self-interest to protect that information, though it would be a test of her ethics how she chose to do so.

It was the start of her future as a fully aware *Elioud*. Would she become Grey or stay White?

Mihàil shook himself. He had to focus. "I will worry about that if and when it comes to pass. Where is Baxter now?"

"At our hotel scrubbing our presence but pretending to follow a lead on our location. Fagan has to believe that Baxter's team has just gotten into position and is planning the best way to take you."

"A sniper would be useful to them."

She nodded. "Baxter expects that Fagan will use that excuse to justify arriving with a shooter."

"How soon can Fagan get here?"

"That depends on where the nearest asset is. My guess? As soon as dawn."

Mihàil's cellphone vibrated. He tapped the earwig to answer. "Yes?"

"Daněk's helo touches down in five in a clearing half a klick east of your location."

"Good. The surveillance vehicle is due west of my location approximately forty meters. Be ready to move on my order."

Mihàil turned away to scan the perimeter of the safe house and the neighborhood again. Nothing had changed since his last scan. If they moved quickly, they could disable the three team members already on site. Without looking at Olivia, he said, "Leave."

"What?" She sounded startled. "Did you just order me to leave?"

Still not looking at her, he gestured and spoke again, more roughly than before. "There is no need for you to remain any longer. Return to Vienna. You may even reach there in time to have an alibi once Fagan goes missing."

Despite his efforts to dampen his awareness of her, Mihàil was still too acutely aware of Olivia's scent, her heat, her breath, and her harmonics. He heard the hitch in her breath at his words, felt the disruption in her harmonics. He needed to have her gone before taking Asmodeus's acolyte. After a moment, he looked at her.

In the darkness, Olivia felt Mihàil's stare. He'd gone dim and cold as soon as she'd rejected his proposal. Inside she was still reeling from the sharp sense of desolation that had flooded her when she'd touched his arm. It had come from Mihàil, but it had been met with a fierce response from within her. Her brain told her that she couldn't marry him, but her heart grieved. She didn't know how to leave him. His harsh command left her panicky and breathless. It was too soon. In other words, it was way past time. Best to get it over with.

It also sparked her ire. How could he be so callous?

"What about Baxter and his team? How are you going to handle them?" She narrowed her eyes. "You plan to take them out now, don't you?"

"It *is* the best tactic. Baxter will lead Fagan here, and we will already be in position in place of his team, who by then will be chasing leads that we suggest to them." He sounded impatient now.

"Using your *Elioud* charm?" Suddenly Olivia's ire died. Of course, Mihàil was the consummate commander. He had that to sustain him and make him forget her. He didn't need her after all. Tears pricked her eyes, and she was glad for the darkness.

"Olivia." Mihàil's voice broke on her name. "Please leave. I am finding it exceedingly difficult not to pull you into my arms and never let you go. If you cannot be my *zonjë*, then you need to return to your life as a CIA officer and let me and my *Elioud* warriors take care of Asmodeus's acolyte."

It hurt to hear the raw emotion in his voice, but Olivia knew what Mihàil was doing. He was reminding her exactly what he was asking her and what was at stake. She also knew that if she couldn't be certain that she would fight at his side in this ancient battle against evil, she shouldn't be here. She shouldn't stand in his way.

Turning, she hunched her shoulders. At least she wouldn't have to carry an image of him watching her walk away. As she walked away, she touched her St. Michael medal. *Please let him find a true mate. Someone worthy of him.*

Behind her, she sensed Mihàil turning back toward his surveillance of her safe house. She heard him say, "Miró, get ready to take the surveillance van, a block west of my position. Wait for my signal."

To the east came the sounds of a helicopter flying low. She glanced over her shoulder as she made her way south toward the next street. Mihàil, looking in the helicopter's direction, showed no signs of alarm. It sounded closer than the airport. András must be flying to the nearest open field. She'd wondered how he could arrive so quickly after Beta had led him into Liberty Ostrava, where her infrared signature had been masked by the heat from the blast furnace. Apparently angel hybrids had to borrow wings when they needed to get somewhere quickly.

Olivia was approaching the next intersection when a *bogomili* jumped her.

He came barreling out from behind a tree and was on her in seconds. She reacted, twisting to the side to deflect some of his forward momentum. But her feet hadn't been planted, and his clutching hands carried her along with him to the ground where they ended in a tangle of arms and legs. Fear shot adrenaline through her. He was huge and heavy and wearing clothing made of slick fabric. If he pinned her, she would be nearly powerless against him. Scrabbling against the pavement and the awkward grappling of the feral minion, Olivia managed to free her torso. She needed to get to the 9mm in her jacket pocket. As he struggled with her, the *bogomili* panted, releasing a miasma of foul breath that made her woozy. He grabbed for her throat, but Olivia bucked and turned, blocking his hands with a forearm while punching his head.

He laughed.

Olivia's fear turned to outright panic. She jabbed her fingers at the *bogomili*, aiming for his eyes but missing. He howled as her fingertips connected with his cheekbone. She heard a *sizzle-pop* and realized that her fingertips radiated a faint red in the early morning light. In fact, she felt feverish. Heated air rose between them, trapping the *bogomili*'s stench in a cloying haze. Bile rose in her throat, choking her.

Olivia frantically jabbed her fingers at the *bogomili*, who howled and thrashed. One of his paw-like hands knocked her hand aside with such force that it slammed into the pavement and pain shot up her forearm. In the next instant, he was lifted from her and flung across the street, hitting a fence. Mihàil stalked after him, nimbus flaring and fists ready. Olivia rolled, coughing and gagging, until she lay on her side on the grass. Her whole body, already bruised from her earlier combat at Elizabeth Lookout, throbbed. Her forearm shrieked at her. Clutching it to her chest, she sat up to watch Mihàil, who had seized the moaning *bogomili* with hands that glowed red and smoked.

Something sharp poked the back of her neck.

"Ms. Markham. I'm afraid you've lost your chance to come in from the cold." Fagan's low voice caused gooseflesh to erupt on Olivia, who shivered. "Curious weapons, these *subulae*. Primitive, harkening to an ancient era. But they get the job done. More than done, in fact. Do you know that when inserted into the base of the skull, just here"—he demonstrated by sliding the tip up to rest at her hairline—"this wicked tool releases the soul to wing toward its eternal destination?"

Olivia's heart squeezed. Had she misread Baxter? Was it her fault that Fagan had taken them unaware?

Mihàil spun around to face them. His eyes blazed within his phosphorescent nimbus. He had never looked more angelic than he did now.

The big Albanian stood about ten meters from Fagan on the other side of the street, Fagan's possessed pawn twitching on the ground behind him. It had been an inspired gambit, if Fagan did say so himself. He'd been right to think that Kastrioti and Markham would have a falling out. Markham loved the game too much to leave it. She also chafed at authority, something that Kastrioti exuded in spades. So while Baxter was still sucking his thumb at the Hilton, Fagan had tracked the angelic armor to a nearby street. Not knowing what they were walking into, he'd been canvassing the area using his *bogomili* as scouts when he'd stumbled on Kastrioti and Markham and seen her walk off alone.

Fagan heard the helicopter as it descended about a kilometer away. Another of Kastrioti's associates had arrived. It was no matter. Whoever it was had arrived too late to halt what was about to happen. Though he greatly enjoyed having an audience.

"Stand up, Ms. Markham. Your erstwhile lover and I have some things to discuss." To motivate her further, Fagan jabbed her in the side with his Glock. She trembled in response, sending a thrill deep into his groin. There was something about having a beautiful, aloof woman on her knees before him, powerless to ignore his commands.

Markham stood with the poise of a ballet dancer. He could tell by the set of her shoulders that she intended to engage him as soon as she thought he was distracted. The problem was, he wouldn't get distracted. And he wouldn't drop either of his weapons. That would be beyond foolish against an active field agent who was younger and more agile and had extensive hand-to-hand combat training. No, give him a 9mm and a silencer any day. They were the great equalizers.

Fagan looked at Kastrioti, who looked furious enough to spit bullets. Now time to test the rest of his theory about these two. Markham might have walked away from Kastrioti, but *he'd* come running to save her.

"I have no use for her," he said, ignoring Markham's stiffening at his bald statement. "But I think you have a vested interest in her wellbeing, don't you, Kastrioti? Or should I call you the Dragon of Albania?"

Kastrioti said nothing, but his fists clenched. He inhaled, his chin rising and his eyes narrowing.

Fagan grinned and jabbed the tip of his *subulam* against Markham's skull, causing her to stumble. Kastrioti took a step, but Fagan kept his Glock trained on her. He grabbed her upper arm and pulled her back.

A moment passed. Fagan waited. He wondered if Kastrioti considered stalling until his associates arrived. Such a tactic would only seal Markham's fate, however. He saw when Kastrioti realized that.

"A dragon whose wings have been clipped, it seems."

In response, Kastrioti linked his hands behind his head and dropped his knees to the pavement.

"No, Mihàil!" Markham shouted. "Don't do this! Don't do this for me!" She drove her elbow into his gut, and he let go of her arm.

He had, however, anticipated her escape attempt. Before Markham got more than a step forward, he slammed the Glock into the side of her face. She crumpled.

Kastrioti, to his credit, made not a sound. On the other hand, if a gaze could scorch concrete and steel, his would have set the world on fire.

Fagan dragged Markham upright and fastened her to his side before approaching Kastrioti. She staggered along, her head lolling. When they got within three meters, he shoved her toward her lover. As he'd anticipated, Kastrioti caught her instead of letting her hit the ground. Fagan hurried behind the Albanian. He shoved the Glock into the back of his waistband. He didn't need it. Kastrioti could put Markham down to engage him, but he wouldn't risk it at such close quarters.

No matter. Fagan would help Kastrioti let her go.

Smirking, Fagan pulled a modified black hood from his pocket and slipped it over Kastrioti's head before the big man realized what he was doing. A flexible collar, locked with his thumbprint, closed the hood around Kastrioti's neck.

Kastrioti remained passive as Fagan worked, clearly unworried about his situation.

He should have been.

Fagan slid his smartphone out and pressed the play function on the harmonics app that he'd had written for controlling the sensors in his smart textiles. In response, Kastrioti jerked and twitched, his hands falling powerless to his sides. Markham tumbled to the pavement.

Fagan hit pause on the harmonics app, and Kastrioti fell face forward. Then he bent over the prone Albanian and tightened high-security handcuffs around his wrists. Standing, he depressed the comm button for his earwig. "Now."

Sixty seconds later, a black sedan screeched to a halt next to them. Two of his *bogomili* jumped out and lifted Kastrioti into the back. Fagan slid into the front passenger seat and the car made a U-turn and sped away.

In the rearview mirror, Fagan watched Markham roll onto her side and struggle to her feet. The *bogomili* that he'd left behind circled her, grins splitting their stupid faces. She pulled a weapon from her pocket and got off a shot before the second one was on top of her.

Kastrioti groaned.

Fagan looked down at his captive. "As I said, I have no use for Ms. Markham." And then he let the app disrupt Kastrioti's harmonics until the Albanian lost consciousness.

Twenty-Seven

Olivia heard the car carrying the man she loved speed away. That's all she had time for before the second *bogomili* crashed into her. She stumbled backwards, barely keeping her feet on the ground. A noxious cloud of breath washed over her, stinging her eyes and making her throat burn. She jammed the 9mm into the creature's gut and fired again and again until the clip was empty. His heavy weight pressed down on her, his hands going for her throat. Dropping the useless 9mm and flinging her arms up to block his hold, she stepped back to give herself space to knee him twice in the groin before sliding her foot down to smash his instep.

It wasn't enough.

Laughing, the *bogomili* grappled her, his hand catching her uninjured arm and wrenching it behind her back. Despite the shriek of pain from her other arm, Olivia grabbed the wrist of her captured arm so that he couldn't break it. Then she stomped down on his foot and threw an elbow at his head, following it around until she had his head in a lock of her own. As he sagged, she grabbed a wrist. It was her turn to yank his arm up. She didn't stop until a loud crack and a grunt signaled that she'd broken it.

Panting, she pushed the creature away from her and staggered back, throwing the useless 9mm to the pavement. Her head ached, she was dizzy and nauseous, and her vision was blurry. Her right forearm was probably fractured. Even if she had her *bō*, she would have trouble defending herself. The *bogomili* swayed across from her, blood soaking the fabric over his midsection. His right arm dangled uselessly. He grinned, his eyes glinting in the streetlight. Out of the corner of her eye, she caught a moving shadow and flinched.

A moment later, the other *bogomili*, the one that she'd shot first, wrapped his arms around her thighs and pulled her down hard. She managed to twist and land on her shoulder instead of hitting her head. The *bogomili* trapped her legs underneath him. Frantically Olivia punched at him, but he only smirked at her glancing blows.

Darkness blocked the streetlight.

Olivia stopped struggling and looked up. The first *bogomili* stood above them, a *subulam* in his good hand. Now his smile sent a chill deep into her chest.

"Time to liberate your soul, *Elioud*."

Awareness filled Mihàil slowly. He was slouched against something hard, his hands bound so tightly behind his back that he couldn't feel them anymore. They were going to hurt like a demon doused with holy water when he got them free. After several moments, he realized that the hood that Fagan had put over his head remained in place. He wasn't in the car, however. Whatever he rested on, it was as hard and unyielding as concrete. His buttocks ached. Gradually he became aware of the penetrating cold. That and the pervasive scent of blood and offal. Taken together, those two sensory inputs suggested a specific site, one designed to hamper his *Elioud* gifts.

He was in a refrigerated room at a slaughterhouse.

A shudder ran through him. He instinctively raised his core temperature, but he knew that he couldn't sustain it indefinitely. Thermogenesis burned a lot of metabolic fuel, which is why *Elioud* used it sparingly. Healing required thermogenesis. The graver the illness or injury, the more thermogenesis depleted the body's resources. His recent penetrating chest wound meant that his body couldn't generate enough heat to incinerate the hood or soften the carbon steel of the cuffs so that he could slip out of them.

It wasn't all bad. True, he couldn't see through the hood. But he still had the ability to read infrared signatures. If anything living moved in this environment, he'd know it. He could hear and smell. His legs were unbound—though he needed to get the blood flowing again in them or his muscles would cramp and betray him. And whatever Fagan had done earlier to disrupt his harmonics no longer affected them.

Clenching his jaw, Mihàil eased upright. Painful pins stabbed his thighs and upper back. The fresh scar on his chest throbbed and burned, reminding him yet again that he wasn't at full strength. Inhaling slowly, he shrugged his shoulders as high as they could go. Some of the tension in his arms released, but he knew that it was only a matter of time before his arms would be useless. Rolling his head, he tried to relax the muscles in his neck.

There were several meat-processing plants within driving distance from Budapest. Mihàil listened. He had no idea what time it was, but he could detect no sound or movement within the facility. Perhaps there were no Sunday shifts. There might not even be any security, let alone a guard who checked more than the locks on outside doors. That was just as well. Normal humans were unlikely to be able to help him against the acolyte and his *bogomili* henchmen. And he couldn't protect them from being wounded or killed. Or turned into more *bogomili*. Better that he faced the enemy alone, thank St. Michael.

Mihàil would make sure that enemy would wish that he'd never laid hands on Olivia. At that thought, the memory of Fagan smashing his Glock into Olivia's face seized him. Anger and anguish wrestled in his gut. He hadn't protected her.

Sensing nothing living, Mihàil began humming, matching his harmonics to the carbon steel of the handcuffs. As he manipulated his pitch, the bonds between the carbon molecules began to elongate. Just as he was about to switch the wave pattern of his own harmonics to allow him to move outside the cuffs, massive white noise swamped him.

And then he lost consciousness.

When Mihàil came around, he had no idea how much time had passed. Though he read no infrared signatures or heard any sound, his battle senses told him that someone stood within a meter of him. He kept his breathing even, hoping to discern more about this presence, but he couldn't. Even so, his intuition told him that it was Fagan. After several trying minutes, Fagan shifted. When he spoke, his voice came from a few centimeters away.

"As you must know by now, your extraordinary *gifts* are useless."

Mihàil responded by headbutting Fagan. Thirty seconds later, the white noise overwhelmed him. But not before Mihàil had anticipated it by shifting his harmonics into an inverse of the lower sound frequencies in the white noise, effectively canceling them. Although the remaining sound frequencies nearly swamped his thoughts, he stayed conscious. He could also hear more of the sounds in his environment, which were lower pitched.

Someone joined Fagan, who now stood farther away. "Leave it! I'm okay."

"But you need medical attention, sir! It looks broken." Rustling and scraping filled the air. "Let me just clean the blood off."

"I said leave it. If you must do something, give me some of this." More sounds came.

"Are we going to kill him, sir?" The sycophant's eagerness turned Mihàil's stomach.

"Not yet. Asmodeus has plans for him."

"But you haven't heard from him, sir. Surely he will approve."

"I've got twenty-four hours here before I have to move him or kill him. Too bad Markham's dead. I would have especially loved playing with her."

Mihàil ground his teeth to keep from growling and alerting his captors. For an instant, his harmonics vibrated at such a pitch that they swamped the white noise entirely.

"Sir, do you see that?"

"What?"

"Smoke. Doesn't it look like his hood is smoking?"

Footsteps approached. Something tugged on the hood.

"Hm. Perhaps he's short circuiting." Fagan laughed. "Did you hear that somewhere in your lizard brain, Kastrioti? Markham is dead. Sorry now that you sacrificed yourself for her?"

Mihàil, now fully aware, said nothing.

After a moment, Fagan asked, "Did Russo's team find the helo pilot and passengers?"

"Negative, sir. They secured the abandoned helo, however, and are flying it here so that it can't be used by Kastrioti's people. They're fifteen minutes out."

"Very good. How long before Gerson's team arrives with the missing armor?"

"They're having trouble locating it, sir."

"What?" Sharpness lent an edge to Fagan's voice. A moment passed. "The tracker shows that it hasn't moved in the last two hours. What's the problem, and why wasn't I told before now?"

"The tracker was found in an empty SUV at that location, sir." Nerves made the underling's voice thready. "But the pieces of armor weren't there. The team is conducting a grid search now."

"So my armor is missing along with whoever drove it from Vienna."

Mihàil exulted silently. Miró, András, and Daněk remained free. And Miró had found Fagan's tracker. He'd left it to lure Fagan's team.

A moment later, Fagan confirmed Mihàil's hunch. "I'm showing Gerson's team in the same vicinity as the tracker. Raise them on the comms now."

"Yes, sir." Several moments passed. "Sir, Gerson isn't answering. None of the team members are." The underling sounded scared.

"Damn it!" Mihàil almost flinched at the explosive profanity. He sensed Fagan's pacing. "We should assume Gerson's team has been ambushed and the tracker cloned. Someone will be coming for Kastrioti. When was the last time you spoke to Gerson?"

"Twenty minutes ago, sir."

"So we could have almost two hours or ten minutes then."

"Sir?"

"What's so hard to understand, Price? Gerson's comm can be cloned, too. He could have been compelled to call us from the road. Get it?" Fagan's anger was palpable. "I'm betting Kastrioti has a rescue mission underway. We need to get ready. Help me with him."

Mihàil felt hands under his armpits and then hands on his ankles.

"On three," Fagan ordered. "One, two, three!"

Mihàil was lifted and carried across the room accompanied by much grunting. Twice he was dropped to the floor, once banging his head so hard that bright lights flashed behind his eyes. Then they stopped and struggled with him. A security cuff was removed from one wrist, but before he could react, his arms had been shifted to the front and his wrist bound again.

"Damn bastard weighs a ton," Fagan panted. "Here. Lift him. I'll put the cuffs over the hook."

Five minutes later, Mihàil hung from his hands with his feet dragging the floor. Staccato footsteps announced his captors walking and stopping a few meters away.

"Not quite," Fagan said. "Bring your cuffs. We'll use both, one each on a hook."

They returned. Someone removed one cuff and replaced it with another before lifting that arm and anchoring its cuff. Then his hand was pushed out to its limit, awakening his formerly sleeping shoulders and arms in terrifying agony. A groan escaped him.

"A familiar pose. Their side does like to play martyr." Fagan sounded satisfied. "If we leave him there long enough, he just may become one."

"He'd look better naked," the sycophant observed.

"Indeed. See to it."

Rough hands fumbled with Mihàil's clothes. After some tugging and tearing, his skin was bared to the freezing temperature.

"It looks like he's been recently wounded, sir. Hanging there has got to be excruciating for him."

"You surprise me, Price. At best, I didn't expect you to be more than an extra set of hands. But I like to give credit when credit is due. This is truly inspired."

"Thank you, sir."

"Come. He's not going anywhere. You and Jameson need to take your positions. I have a kill box to see to."

Olivia's head, shoulder, and forearm were killing her despite the painkiller that Miró had given her earlier. He'd taken one look at her bruised cheek, and muttering something about a concussion, had forced her to sit on the sidewalk while he'd sent someone named Daněk after ice. And *force* was a mild way of putting it: he'd somehow reprogrammed a *bogomili*, the one he'd snatched from the Vienna hospital, into guarding her. The delusional killer had held her immobile on his lap with an arm around her. When the ice arrived, the *bogomili* had dutifully held some wrapped in a towel against her cheek, alternating in twenty-minute intervals with her shoulder and forearm for the past two hours. Olivia was certain that everything ached because of the cold.

In fact, she couldn't get warm.

It was July and she sat shuddering and covered in gooseflesh. Perhaps it was just delayed shock on top of the concussion. She'd been a heartbeat from dying when Miró had grabbed the *bogomili* above her and snapped his neck while Stasia slit the other *bogomili*'s throat. Then they'd left her and joined András, Beta, and Daněk in hunting the *bogomili* teams that Fagan had left behind. Across from her, the two bodies of the *bogomili* that Miró and Stasia had killed lay decomposing in the early morning sun.

While they were gone, she'd sat with her devoted guard, a human being who had allied himself with a fallen angel and killed people with a wicked weapon to 'liberate' their souls. This, after watching as Mihàil had been hauled away in a black hood, hands bound behind his back. A man with the blood of angels in his veins, a *drangùe*, whose sacred duty it was to protect humans from demonic creatures. He'd sacrificed himself for her.

Was it any wonder that ice ran in her veins and her teeth chattered?

After the *bogomili* teams had been dispatched, Stasia had berated Miró in rapid, abusive Italian for not transporting Olivia to a hospital until Olivia had told her that she refused to go. Miró had remained silent during the whole exchange, his icy-blue eyes revealing nothing of his thoughts, though Olivia was sure that she saw strain in the corners of his mouth. András had paced in a wide berth around them, clearly eager for more action. Beta had stood alone across the street, her gaze scanning for new threats. And Daněk had waited at the EC130 Eurocopter, prepping to fly as soon as Miró back traced the location where Fagan held Mihàil.

Olivia hadn't spoken again until the moment when she saw that Miró's trace had finished. Then she'd shoved the *bogomili* away, and, standing, announced that she was going with him and András. Miró had simply nodded and led the way to the helicopter. Beta and Stasia had followed, Stasia wearing a heavy frown. Andràs brought up the rear, his intent focus on their surroundings belying the jocularity that she'd witnessed from him in Vienna.

That was forty-five minutes ago, and still she shook from cold. If anything, it had grown more intense instead of peaking. Was it fear for Mihàil? Or worse, grief....

Miró had been watching her. Now he leaned forward and caught her gaze. *You are suffering because Mihàil is suffering.*

Taken aback and blinking, Olivia realized that she'd forgotten that the *Elioud* could communicate telepathically. *What?*

You are cold because Mihàil is cold. The acolyte has him in a place that prevents him from raising his core temperature.

He's in a walk-in refrigerator for butchered animals, Andràs interjected. Apparently, he could hear their conversation. *The bastard's keeping him alive for Asmodeus.*

Miró never took his gaze from Olivia, who couldn't marshal her thoughts into coherency. *The key point is that he is alive, Olivia. He needs you now. You can help him in a way that we cannot.*

How?

Raise your core temperature. It will keep Mihail from freezing. Miró sounded so matter of fact that Olivia almost believed that it was as simple as him telling her to do it.

She nodded, the movement causing her head to ache. Out of habit, she touched the St. Michael medal on her chest, sending a silent prayer that she would be able to banish the ice building up inside her. To her shock, the medal was hot. She couldn't move her fingertips now even if she'd tried. For a terrible, long moment, her shaking became so violent that she could see and hear nothing. Heat coursed through her, radiating through her torso and into her limbs.

Gradually, she became aware of her breathing and then her thoughts coalesced and her shaking subsided.

If Mihàil was freezing, then she'd damn well need to be broiling to compensate.

The *bogomili* next to her shrieked in pain and dropped the now-smoking towel into her lap. Stasia was staring wide-eyed at her while Beta had twisted in her front seat, a pistol aimed at the demented creature's head. Steam filled the cabin, growing denser every second. Miró still watched her, but András and the pilot seemed unmoved.

Pace yourself or you will deplete your strength long before we land. Mihàil does not need to be warm. Just not freezing.

Olivia nodded again and took a deep breath. The cabin temperature dropped while the ventilation cleared the steam. She signaled that she was okay. Beta lowered her weapon and returned to facing front, but Stasia kept her gaze on her. The normally fierce Italian spy looked spooked. At her side, the *bogomili* had collapsed back into his seat, his burnt fingers forgotten. He muttered under his breath and leaned as far from her as he could.

Mihàil had said that he would always be aware of her and come to her aid no matter where she was. Well, if she was going to be his *zonjë, damn it,* then she'd better be able to do the same for him.

Closing her eyes, she concentrated on Mihàil. As she focused, a ghostly grid mapped itself onto the back of her eyelids. It was so like a high-resolution sonar scan that Olivia understood what it was right away. Her internal viewfinder snagged on a bright image just as her lungs began to labor.

Moments later, she felt a hand on her shoulder. Olivia's eyes snapped open to see Stasia bending over her, clearly worried. Beta had turned again, but this time she looked uncertain, her weapon out of sight. The *bogomili* had started to rock in his seat, his hands over his ears.

What is it? Miró asked.

She shook her head, unable to catch her breath. Almost as soon as the attack occurred, it let up. Sucking air into her lungs was such a relief that it was several moments before she realized that her shoulders and chest screamed in agony. Her temperature had plummeted. Gooseflesh covered her.

I don't know! Suddenly I couldn't breathe. Now my whole upper body hurts.

Panting gripped her again, disrupting her attention. The pain in her shoulders and chest eased. A wave of panic washed over her. What was wrong with her? Was she having an anxiety attack?

Her shallow breathing ended. But there was no respite this time. Her arms felt as if they were being pulled from their sockets. She sucked in deep breaths, feeling lightheaded and nauseous from the pain. All at once, she knew what was happening to her.

Something's happening to Mihàil.

Andràs looked over his shoulder. He and Miró looked grimly unsurprised, but Miró worked to reassure her.

Focus on remaining calm, Olivia. We land soon. Mihàil is very strong, but he will feel your anxiety, especially as we draw closer to him.

The labored breathing began again. She squirmed against the seat, her feet pushing her higher on the backrest. She felt as though she was slowly, inexorably, and literally, suffocating. Miró's lips tightened, but he said nothing. Instead, he deployed the oxygen mask above her seat. Glaring at him, Stasia slipped it over her face, pulling the straps snug. Pure oxygen entered her lungs, easing her lightheadedness. The bright image resolved into clarity.

Olivia clutched an armrest. *You don't understand. I've seen what Fagan is doing to him.*

The helicopter began its descent.

Miró ignored everything but Olivia. *Concentrate. What do you see?*

Panting, she held his gaze, trying to convey her utter horror. *Mihàil is being crucified, and it's my fault.*

Though she hadn't spoken aloud, both Beta and Stasia jerked as if they'd been slapped. Miró's eyes narrowed. The irises grew so frosty she thought they'd ice over. He looked toward Andràs, whose own gaze was so glacial Olivia couldn't believe that she'd ever thought he was a lovable goofball. Something passed between them.

Miró looked back at her. *No, it is not, my lady. Do you understand?*

It took Olivia a moment to realize that Miró had addressed her as 'my lady.' She gave an almost imperceptible nod. She was either going to help rescue Mihàil or die trying.

Five minutes later, the EC130 touched down in a parking lot outside an industrial complex of buildings. Olivia stared at them, her heart sinking.

How would they ever find Mihàil in that windowless monolith?

TWENTY-EIGHT

"How much longer do you plan to hang there feeling sorry for yourself?" Zophie asked Mihàil.

He opened his eyes. White dots fizzed across his vision in the thick darkness. He was breathing mostly carbon monoxide in small gulps. His head hurt. His thoughts swam.

What had his guardian angel just asked him?

Pulling himself up a few centimeters with weakening arms, he sipped a tiny stream of fresh air from an opening in the fold at the hood's neck.

Right. How much longer. He didn't have much longer.

"Or have you not yet noticed in that oxygen-starved brain that you are warm?"

With a shock, Mihàil realized that Zophie was right.

"I'm always right, *djali im,*" she said. Affection leavened the note of impatience in her voice. "Your *zonjë* shares your burden. Don't let her down now."

A thrill jolted Mihàil. *Olivia lived*. And she buttressed his core energy with her own.

Would...not...dream...of...it, he assured Zophie.

"Well, then."

Mihàil locked his attention onto the guardian angel's pure white signature. Shunting as much heat as he could to his wrists, he began to raise the temperature of the pin in the hinge of the security cuffs. For long moments, the metal remained cold. He began to quake as the rest of his body lost warmth and his arms shook from holding him up. He let his body slip back down.

"What perfect timing! She's arrived with your warriors as well as her own."

Mihàil didn't have the breath to speak. He certainly didn't have it to laugh at Zophie's ridiculous cheerfulness. It would have been irritating except for the fact that it distracted him from how arduous it was to soften a tiny amount of steel when he could melt a delivery truck in seconds at full strength. Still, he pulled himself up enough to breathe easier.

"Dear man, please hurry. Olivia is strong, but she isn't as strong or as seasoned as you. She's getting lightheaded waiting for you to free yourself."

That got Mihàil's attention. Of course. Sharing his burdens was a two-way bond. He needed to get to Olivia. Closing his eyes, he drove everything from his thoughts except breathing and melting the hinge pins in the cuffs. The increased heat emanating from his wrists roasted his eyelids. Ten seconds later, liquid steel sizzled on the frigid tile just before he dropped like a side of frozen beef. He tried to roll as he hit the floor, but he'd been hanging too long and instead landed on his right shoulder. Immediate, intense pain sent him thrashing upright onto his knees. He'd been injured in enough battles to recognize a dislocated shoulder.

"Here, let me help you." Gentle fingers tugged the hood from his head. Mihàil tried to breathe the frigid air slowly, but his lungs insisted on sucking it in as fast as they could. That sent him into a coughing fit.

As he struggled to regain his breath, Zophie draped a blanket around his shoulders. Nothing had ever felt as good as its soft warmth.

The guardian angel knelt next to him. She wore all white, her long coat, hat, and boots trimmed in fur. The purity of her presence here filled him with a familiar sense of wonder, terrified awe, and humility. That she chose, again and again, to come to his aid was no small gift. That she came into such a mundane, ugly environment reminded him of his own humanity. And his duty.

She tilted her head, appearing to listen to something beyond the storage room. "The acolyte and his *sidekick*"—the corners of her mouth curled in a slight smile as she used his word for Fagan's *bogomili* assistant—"have just realized that the helo's occupants aren't their colleagues."

Zophie's gaze came back to him. "Imagine how they'll feel when they realize that you're no longer hanging in cold storage?"

"No doubt...unconcerned," he managed to say through chattering teeth. He pulled the blanket tighter around him with his good arm. The velvety material was warmer than it should have been in the storage room, but he felt as though he'd never be warm again.

"Oh, they'll be concerned all right when you show up for their welcoming party." She lifted a bag that he hadn't noticed before and tossed it at him. "Although you might want to get dressed first."

Mihàil stuck fingers stiff with cold into the bag. Clothes and boots were there along with an insulated carafe, a protein bar, a 9mm, and a comm. He didn't bother asking where an angel procured them.

"There's painkiller in the outside pocket," Zophie said as he pulled on the clothing.

He grunted. It hurt like hell using his bad arm to dress, but it wasn't anything he hadn't experienced before. In fact, the pain helped him to focus. That and the ability to fill his lungs with fresh air, searing as it was. He'd stood and was trying to tug on the thick socks when Zophie took over.

While she pulled the socks up and then shoved boots onto his feet, Mihàil ripped open the protein bar and ate it in three bites. He found hot, sweet coffee in the carafe. Tossing the pain pills into his mouth, he swallowed them with a mouthful of coffee.

"Where?" he asked as she sat back on her heels.

She didn't have to ask what he meant. "The helo landed next to the unloading docks on the northside. You're in the south section of the building."

Mihàil stood. It was time to finish this.

Zophie stood also. "You'll need this." She cupped the origami eagle that he'd placed on the altar in the Blue Church in her palms. The folded bird of prey looked strangely quiescent, as though it were waiting for its handler to send it after quarry.

He plucked it from the angel's hands. That's exactly what he intended to do.

Fagan watched with glee as the *Elioud* team descended from the EC130 and fanned out. His earlier irritation with Price had dissipated once he'd had a moment to recall his options. It had always been possible that the *bogomili* teams that he'd left in Budapest would fail, one of the reasons why he'd imprisoned Kastrioti in the immense Hungarian abattoir.

It was a new facility south of Budapest that hadn't yet ramped up to its full production cycle of slaughtering thirty-six hundred pigs each shift. Still, the complex had been designed to move several thousand animals efficiently from stables to packaging and storage. A wide corridor separated the slaughterhouse from the meat-processing area, where the chilling room, freezer, and cold storage were. There were two internal entry points to the meat-processing area from the corridor and only a single exit from the building.

It was a natural kill box. And it was where he'd left Kastrioti hanging.

He chuckled.

By morning's end, he intended to have more *Elioud* either dead or under his control. He was warming to the idea of the latter. Barring Asmodeus's imminent return, which he'd begun to doubt, he saw no reason why he shouldn't be able to experiment on these human-angel hybrids. Asmodeus hadn't been very helpful in Fagan's efforts to develop countermeasures, and Fagan surmised that the Dark *Irim* would rather not give his human acolyte more power than was absolutely necessary. In fact, Fagan wondered as he watched a female *Elioud* climb out of the EC130 with the help of a male whether Asmodeus feared that his acolyte might develop weapons that could be used to defend against *him*. And if he could be defended against, might he not be defeated? Who knew what treasure-trove of angelic secrets might be pried from Kastrioti and his colleagues? Could he, Joseph Fagan, aspire to being like the angels?

Suddenly he recognized the female. It was Markham.

How in the hell had she survived?

Fagan frowned, his musings cut short. Had any of Price's intelligence been good?

Leaning forward, he peered more closely at the monitor. Markham wore a sling on her right arm. The right side of her face was swollen and purplish. She stumbled. The male—one of Kastrioti's *Elioud* warriors, no doubt—steadied her.

Nice. She'd be easy to deal with once he separated her from her escort. Time to scatter the herd.

"Price," Fagan said into his comm. "Showtime."

Thirty seconds later, a black Mercedes sedan screeched, fishtailing, around the west side of the stables and shot toward the *Elioud*, who fled like popcorn kernels in a hot skillet. The male next to Markham pulled her with him. Price, who'd trained with the Agency as a field agent and had superb tactical driving skills, negotiated a tight turn at the end of the lot and proceeded to drive in figure eights around the helicopter, forcing the *Elioud* to keep moving or risk being run over.

"Jameson, your turn," Fagan said at the same time a diminutive female pivoted and shot the rear window out of the Mercedes.

A box truck barreled from the depot on the main road into the parking lot. Jameson and Price had trained and worked in the field together. Within moments, they'd trapped the shooter between them, the unloading dock, and the helicopter. A second female dashed toward the first and grabbed her out of the way just in time. The giant didn't bother. Jumping, he landed on the truck's cab and slammed a glowing fist into the windshield. The truck swerved. The driver's door flung open and Jameson hit the pavement and rolled.

"Impressive," Fagan murmured, "but not good enough."

Time to bring out the big gun.

With practiced ease, he engaged the controls for the attack drone that he'd held in reserve on the rooftop of the stockyard. Swooping, he engaged the drone's machine gun, spitting bullets and flying toward Markham and her escort, who'd already started to run south. The helicopter pilot started shooting at the drone, but Fagan only laughed and took evasive maneuvers.

"Price, Jameson. Keep those *Elioud* occupied. I've got the other two."

After giving that order, Fagan ignored the fight behind and beneath the drone. Jameson and Price could handle themselves. Besides, they'd already successfully split the group in two. He dropped the drone two meters above the ground and raced toward Markham and her escort, expecting them to keep running until they could take cover under or inside the semi-trucks parked ahead.

Instead, the male *Elioud* whirled to face the drone as Markham dove for the grass and rolled. Fagan chortled and let loose a barrage. To his stunned disbelief, however, the bullets seemed to hit an invisible wall and dropped harmlessly to the ground. Anger gripped him until he remembered that he'd wanted to separate them. Now they were.

Markham sprang to her feet.

Before she could act, Fagan raced the drone toward her. At the last moment, he sent it in a sharp roll toward the *Elioud*, buzzing him. The male threw up his arms, the drone passing within centimeters of his head.

Fagan whooped and turned the drone around to buzz him again. The drone flew a few meters before bobbling as if overcome by flood waters.

Harmonic vibrations again. Damn *Elioud*.

But his tactic had worked. As he'd hoped, Markham chose this opportunity to let her escort handle the drone while she dashed toward the staff annex fifty meters away. Kastrioti was everything to her, just as she was to the Albanian. He should have realized it sooner. No matter, he'd rectify his misstep. Her love would be her undoing. He'd end up with two for the price of one.

Fagan struggled to keep the drone aloft. He had to slow the male *Elioud* down, keep him from joining Markham until it was too late. The drone lurched toward the ground, spraying bullets.

The *Elioud* staggered and fell to his knees.

Ten seconds later, Fagan lost control of the drone and the ground rose up to swallow it. Its camera went black.

Olivia's heart pounded in her ears and her breath came in huge gasps. She glanced over her shoulder to see the drone slam the ground in a fountain of dirt.

Miró, looking grim, shook his head when her stride slowed. He stood with effort and then started back the way that they'd just come, his pace increasing as he got closer to the parking lot. The Mercedes continued to accelerate and squeal to a halt along with the staccato sounds of gunfire. As she listened, the helicopter's rotors spun up.

Turning back, Olivia pulled out the smartphone that Miró had handed her as they fled the skirmish.

Here, Miró's mental voice echoed in her memory. *The plans for the meat-processing plant are in the Images folder.*

She fumbled with the touchscreen as she jogged away. As they'd landed, Miró and András had scanned the grounds with their battle senses. There were no other *bogomili* outside. The only infrared signatures that they read inside belonged to the livestock in the stables. Obviously, Mihàil was in the refrigerated area where the butchered meat was kept. But how many *bogomili* were there? And what surprises did her boss have for them?

Olivia swiped through the layout image until she saw the chilling room, cold storage, and freezer labeled. It took only a moment to identify Fagan's "surprise."

Oh. A kill box. How predictable.

Fagan thought that they'd enter his maze like dazed, cheese-obsessed mice, blind to the danger until he had them trapped with Mihàil.

Well, she had a surprise for him.

She had no intention of dashing, unthinking, straight for her *drangùe.* That was not a good tactical plan. They needed to cut the head from the snake. And the snake wouldn't be waiting in the box, no. The snake would be waiting somewhere safe, outside the kill zone. Somewhere close by where he could monitor their approach. Maybe even pilot an attack drone.

Olivia glanced up at the roofline above her. There was no way to know if Fagan hid up there, but she doubted it. He would protect an escape route at all costs. Unless he'd planned to use his helicopter....

She pressed her earwig. "Helo, check out the roof. The ringmaster may be presiding there."

"Affirmative," the pilot, Daněk, said as the helicopter rose from the ground.

"Carny team, time to pack the show up. Carny 1 and 2, grab a clown to squeeze for info."

"You got it, Boss," András said.

"Copy that," Miró echoed.

"Carny 3, cover the loading docks on this end."

Beta answered. "Copy, Carny Leader."

Olivia took a clarifying breath. Her breathing and temperature had normalized once they'd landed. Closing her eyes, she called up the ghostly image of Mihàil that she'd tapped into earlier. As she'd known, he no longer hung by his arms. He appeared to be sitting. Where was he? Maybe if she got closer, she could sense him inside....

"Carny 4, with me. There's an entrance to the staff annex thirty meters ahead."

"Copy that, Carny Leader. ETA two minutes," Stasia said.

"Carny Leader, this is Daněk. No sign of anyone on the roof. Repeat: no one on the roof."

"Acknowledged. Recon the site and grounds. Let me know if you see anything suspicious." Olivia looked down again at the smartphone screen. Where was Fagan? Had he tapped into the plant's security cameras? She scanned the perimeter of the building until she saw a camera wedged into a corner between the roof and wall. A quick glance caught three more units. There would be more.

Stasia sprinted up to her, her 9mm in a two-handed grip at her side. Her prized BC-41 rode her thigh in a sheath. She nodded. Olivia led the way to the staff entrance but halted outside.

"We're walking in blind, Staz. I don't like it. Fagan and his goons have the ability to mask their infrared signatures. For all I know, he's standing next to Mihàil with a gun to his head."

Stasia's hard gaze held hers. "Does it make a difference, *cara*?" She gestured with her chin toward the door. "We are going in anyway."

Olivia nodded once. Stasia always put her options into perspective. Turning, she made room for her friend, who tried the door handle. Locked. Stasia holstered her 9mm and brought out lock-picking tools. Fifteen seconds later, she opened the door, her 9mm back in her hand, and gestured for Olivia to wait for her to enter first. She peered inside. When she looked back, there was an odd, Mona-Lisa smile on her face. Instead of stepping over the threshold, she held the door and motioned for Olivia to enter.

Puzzled, Olivia stepped into what her intel told her was a passageway leading to the mens and womens locker rooms. As soon as she entered, she understood Stasia's mysterious smirk.

Mihàil, shadows under his eyes and stubble on his jaw, pulled her hard against his chest. Then his mouth took hers in a fierce, possessive—deeply yearning—kiss. Olivia, head swimming, relaxed against him. For the first time in her life, she felt as if she'd come home where she belonged. Nothing else mattered. They would face whatever came next together.

Mihàil ended the kiss and pulled back to look at her. His hand came up to brush a lock from her cheek before cupping it. His gaze, intense and yet tender at the same time, searched hers. "*Dashuria ime, zonja ime.*" *My love, my lady. My love. My lord.*

Mihàil's smile in response lit them both in a brief flare of angelic light.

And then he stepped away from her. As he did, the hard battle commander's visage descended over the warm lover's. He brought his hand, palm up, to waist level. On it sat the origami eagle that she'd folded in the Blue Church as she'd told him about Emily and Jin. In wonder and a little trepidation, Olivia took it from him.

"Come." The flint in his voice struck sparks in his gaze. He placed his hand on her upper arm. "We take the acolyte together."

TWENTY-NINE

A gan jabbed at the keyboard of the laptop that he'd used to tap into the meat-processing plant's security cameras. He'd known that the drone wouldn't act as more than a deterrent, but losing it before Markham had reached the building made him furious. The videofeeds streamed into a matrix onto his screen. He scanned them quickly to find those on the west side of the building where he'd last seen Markham and her *Elioud* escort. He expected to see a body on the ground. Instead, Markham stood swiping a smartphone screen.

"Come on, Markham," Fagan growled. Why wasn't she running toward the *drangùe*?

She looked up at the roofline, studying it. Then she pressed her ear and spoke. Sixty seconds later the helicopter—*his* helicopter—rose up and flew toward the building's roof.

So she thought that he might be hiding on the roof?

Fagan searched for the videofeed from the parking lot where Price and Jameson were keeping the remaining *Elioud* occupied. He recognized Markham's escort peering toward the action from behind a box truck. Fagan swore. He'd strafed that *Elioud*, he was sure of it. He should be out of commission. Across from Markham's escort, the other *Elioud* male ran in a low crouch toward Jameson, who had taken cover inside the depot and focused on firing at the giant. Unfortunately, he seemed unaware that a tall, slender female eased along the depot wall headed for him.

"On your left flank, Jameson," he said into his comm.

Suddenly a short, dark-haired beauty ran from the lot toward Markham. Even distracted by the conflict, Fagan found the way that she held her weapon and the knife strapped to her thigh extremely sexy. Who would have guessed that taking on these *Elioud* would be like playing Tomb Raider?

The dark-haired *Elioud* caught up to Markham and then they jogged toward the outside door of the staff annex. Fagan watched as the short female bent over the handle, her weapon holstered. Picking the lock no doubt. Good. Let them come inside. He grew hard thinking about what he would do to the short one when he captured her. Perhaps he'd hang her next to Kastrioti in the chilling room, her clothes stripped from her with her own knife.

A moment later she swung the door open and, weapon again in hand, leaned inside. Then she stepped back, holding the door open. She motioned Markham to enter.

Markham disappeared into the building. Fagan hesitated. He really wanted her companion to enter before acting. She stood outside, however.

He frowned. What was Markham doing?

Bright light flared inside the dim hallway. What the—?

Something fluttered through the doorway. Fagan leaned forward, studying the screen. It looked like a piece of paper. Whatever it was, it was too small and the security camera's fixed focal length made it impossible to zoom in on it. He watched in fascination as the paper floated up toward the camera's lens. It almost seemed as if it were flying on its own power.

Markham appeared in the doorway followed by Kastrioti, who was fully dressed. Like Markham, his right arm was in a sling.

Scalding rage blinded Fagan. Literally. For an excruciating heartbeat, a white haze covered his vision. How the hell had the Albanian freed himself from his security cuffs let alone dressed himself? Why hadn't he thought to put a guard on the chilling room? A *bogomili* team waited inside, but he'd deliberately left the corridor from the staff annex open until after the *Elioud* team penetrated as far as the packaging rooms around Kastrioti.

"Adams, Malloy. Target has left the building via the staff annex. Adams, exit via the loading docks and come up behind them from the south. Malloy, come up on their rear via the corridor leading outside from the annex. Wait for my signal."

"Affirmative, Control," Adams said, echoed by Malloy.

"Price, Jameson. Fall back toward the staff annex. We'll trap the target in between. Kill anyone who gets in your way."

Fagan waited for confirmation from Price and Jameson. Nothing.

"Price, Jameson! Sitrep now!"

When neither man responded, he found the videofeed closet to the lot where they'd engaged the *Elioud*. It looked like Mogadishu on an ordinary day. Glass shards from the windshield of the box truck that Jameson had abandoned glittered among shells and several automatic weapons. The Mercedes, pock-marked from large-caliber bullets, had accordioned on the corner of the stables, its driver's door open and casings heaped on the pavement. Near the depot, a compliant Jameson lay on his stomach. The tall female *Elioud* had a knee in his lower back and appeared to be cuffing his wrists. The giant male *Elioud* stood next to her, his posture relaxed, but he scanned the parking lot. In the lot next to the stables, Price stood, his weapon aimed at Markham's calm escort, who appeared to be talking.

"Shoot him, Price!" Fagan shouted just as Price dropped the weapon's barrel. Fifteen seconds later, his loyal *bogomili* soldier flung the weapon away, put his hands behind his head, and eased to his knees. The male *Elioud* looked at the nearest security camera. As if knowing how much it infuriated Fagan, he smiled and tossed the kneeling *bogomili* something. The man reached down, picked it up, and then cuffed himself.

Fagan swore. He remembered that the *Elioud* had sensitive hearing as Price's captor came closer to take custody of him.

"You're a dead man," he promised via comm.

The *Elioud* looked up again and pointed in the direction of the remaining *Elioud* trio.

"Sir, target in sight now," Adams said in his ear. "Two individuals, one injured male and one injured female, appear to be waiting for me."

Only two? Waiting? Fagan focused on the videofeed from the two cameras closest to the staff annex. Kastrioti and Markham had moved away from the building and stood facing the south side-by-side, his good arm around her shoulder. The dark-haired beauty waited out of Adams's line of sight along the north wall.

"Armed female on perimeter twenty meters from you, Adams."

Adams, pinned by the unseen shooter, remained crouching. Time to unleash Malloy from where he waited at the annex door. But now Fagan had no intention of taking any of them alive. If Asmodeus wanted his arch nemesis alive to torture or screw or whatever Dark *Irim* did to their arch enemies, too bad. Fagan was in charge here and now. And he wanted them dead.

"Two targets twenty-five meters northwest from you, Malloy. On my mark you and Adams take all three targets out."

"Affirmative," both *bogomili* said.

"Go."

Malloy opened the door at the same time that Adams leaped up, both firing. Malloy's bullets missed Kastrioti and Markham, who now stood fifteen meters *closer* to the building than they had when Fagan called out their position. The unfortunate Adams took a dagger to the chest before the armed female turned and shot Malloy, who never had the chance to realign his sights. It was over in seconds.

Now Markham and Kastrioti looked up together at the nearest security camera.

Fagan pounded the dash and screamed. Then he grabbed the 9mm on the seat next to him and turned to open the door. From the corner of his eye, something fluttered. Distracted, he looked out the driver's window. A meter up some paper hung suspended. As he watched in horrified fascination, the paper floated closer as if it were a feather in a cartoon strip. When it had reached eye level, he saw that it was folded into the likeness of an eagle. The eagle's wings flapped as it settled onto the driver's seat.

He couldn't stop himself. He reached out and took the paper eagle between forefinger and thumb. He unfolded it. It was just what it appeared to be: paper and nothing more. Puzzled, he saw that words had been typed onto one side. He couldn't read them, but the small illustration of a violin suggested that it was a flyer for a musical event. How had it gotten to him? Was it coated with nanosensors that converted sunlight into energy?

Suddenly spooked, he reached for the door handle again.

He jumped down from the cab of the box truck behind the plant's office that he'd made his temporary command post. There were a few cars in the employee lot. He'd use one of them to escape now and regroup with more *bogomili*.

He'd just set off in a jog toward the lot when Markham stepped out from the end of the truck and clocked him. As he lay stunned on the ground, Kastrioti crushed his weapon hand under a boot.

"Why am I not surprised to find you running?" Markham said, amusement clear in her voice. "Discretion the better part of valor, eh, Fagan?"

"Stupid bitch." Fagan saw the cold fire in Kastrioti's eyes at his words. He hoped the Albanian would lash out, make a mistake. He still had options.

Kastrioti leaned over instead and lifted him into the air with his good hand. He shook Fagan so hard his teeth rattled. "Enough. Time for you to pay the consequence for being Asmodeus's acolyte."

Olivia and Mihàil waited for the rest of their companions to join them on the southeast side of the meat-processing plant. Olivia's arm and head ached so fiercely that she feared she'd let her forced casualness slip. She didn't want to give Fagan the satisfaction of knowing how close she was to collapsing. She'd used the last of her strength to strike him. If Mihàil hadn't been there to restrain Fagan, she couldn't have prevented him from recovering his wits and struggling free, killing her even.

Sensing her unsteadiness, Mihàil eased closer to her side. He looked down at her, protective concern clear in his gaze. She allowed herself to lean into him. Though it was full morning now and growing hot, Mihàil's body heat soothed her. After a moment, she thought perhaps that he was modulating their temperatures together. It was going to take some getting used to, this idea that not only could she control her own body temperature, but that she could affect

Mihàil's as well and vice versa. It dawned on her that it had only been a week since she'd met Mihàil in the Stadtpark in Vienna. It might as well have been a lifetime ago.

Or a different life. She was certainly not the same person who confidently—maybe even naively for all her training and experience—donned a harlequin hood to defend a young woman from a predator with a demon's name.

Stasia reached them first, followed by Miró and Beta. András brought up the rear, leading the two docile *bogomili*, whose hands were cuffed. As the trio drew near, Daněk set the helicopter down in the field east of the facility.

"Price! Jameson! What the hell are you doing? How did they take you alive?" Fagan was so furious that his nostrils flared and spit flew with his words. "These are *Elioud*! Your whole mission is to liberate their souls or die trying."

The two *bogomili* never even looked at him.

"With these?" András asked, holding two *subula* aloft. Whatever metal they were forged with absorbed sunlight instead of reflecting it.

Olivia shivered at the clear evil emanating from the weapons of a Dark *Irim*. How had she ever handled one so blithely before? Her gaze darted to Mihàil. How had he endured having one broken off in his chest?

Daněk and the Serbian *bogomili* joined them. The Serb wore a backpack that Olivia knew contained *subula*, including the broken pieces from the Belvedere attack. The Serb hissed when he saw the other *bogomili* and lurched away from them. *Interesting*.

Fagan, looking surly, said, "This is ridiculous. You might be able to control these idiots, but I'm not about to cooperate with you. Asmodeus will come for me, and you won't be able to withstand *him*."

Mihàil, who'd ignored Fagan's complaints until this moment, stared through narrow eyes at the acolyte. Olivia didn't know how he did it, but he appeared to grow taller and more imposing despite his haggard countenance and the sling on his arm. A white nimbus flared around him.

"Indeed?" he asked. His voice was low, yet it reverberated around them. "Could it be that it is you who have something to fear from your dark master for not waiting for his command?"

Fagan blanched. Then he rallied. "Not waiting for his command? I don't have to wait to know what to do. Asmodeus wants you. He wants you badly."

Mihàil smiled. It didn't reach his eyes. "Have you heard from your dark master since he and his minions attacked Ms. Markham at the Belvedere?"

He paused but didn't wait for Fagan to answer. "You have not, yet you are too ignorant to know why or what it means."

Now Fagan bristled. "What makes you think that Asmodeus won't be here any moment?"

Mihàil didn't answer. Instead, he looked at Miró and András. "Time to bait the trap. Any suggestions?"

András gestured with his chin at Fagan. "Does he need to be alive?"

"Wait—" Fagan demanded, but suddenly his voice disappeared as if his personal mute button had been depressed. His eyes grew large as his mouth formed words but nothing emanated.

Mihàil shook his head. "No, but it would be poetic justice if he is when his master finds him, do you agree?"

"We could always leave him and his *bogomili* in the stable with the pigs," András said. "That has a kind of poetic ring to it."

Mihàil smiled again. The coldness in his gaze chilled Olivia. He looked down at her, his gaze softening for a moment, before taking her free hand in his. Its warmth and steady harmonics reassured her. And then he turned his attention back to the matter at hand.

"If I had any assurance that Asmodeus will awaken from his angelic coma before this one"—Mihàil lifted his chin at Fagan—"expires, I would consider it. However, I think that we should find an alternative solution, one that does not draw suspicion or help from any authorities. We could take them to my industrial complex in Budapest."

"No." Olivia shook her head. "That site will be watched. Zagreb as well."

"Perhaps Ms. Markham would allow us to use her flat in Soroksár," Miró said. Olivia looked at the Croatian, whose icy-blue eyes revealed nothing. She got the feeling that he wasn't a fan of hers, but after today, she couldn't exactly blame him. "Her colleague Baxter and his team are likely still there watching it. It would be rather simple to charm them to continue, at least for the short term."

"Perhaps you can charm his boss here," Stasia said to Miró, drawing everyone's gaze to her. Her own drooping eyelids made her look as though she'd just been awakened from sleep. Olivia knew that her friend played upon that impression when it suited her. "If you can give *bogomili* amnesia, why not the acolyte?" Stasia's tone was mild, but Olivia felt more than heard the sharp undercurrent in it. There was something more to her friend's comment than its surface meaning.

That's probably why she focused on Miró's reaction. For a moment the ice in his eyes melted. Olivia glimpsed volcanic heat, and then it was gone under a glacier. She peeked at Mihàil, but nothing had changed in his expression. Maybe he hadn't noticed what she'd noticed.

Mihàil spoke before Miró could answer. "That will not work. Unlike the *bogomili* who allowed Asmodeus to subsume them, the acolyte retains his own will, and his memories will be too difficult to wipe. However, it does bring up an intriguing idea, Ms. Fiore. The acolyte's memory cannot be erased, but it can be manipulated to an extent."

"Manipulated?" Olivia asked.

"Think of it as an intelligence operation, my lady," Miró said. Hearing the honorific from this taciturn *Elioud* was going to take some getting used to. "We will use his ambition and plans against him. As long as we stay close to the truth, we can convince the acolyte to remain at your flat. The longer that he looks for you two, the more secure his belief in the veracity of his situation. Eventually only Asmodeus will be able to free him."

"Which he will be compelled to do in order to free himself, and then we will have him." Mihàil turned to his lieutenants. "Miró, András. Take the acolyte and the *bogomili* to Olivia's flat and prep them along with the CIA team. Daněk, can you fly them?"

The Czech pilot nodded.

"Excellent. Let the acolyte continue on his mission then." Mihàil turned back to Olivia. He raised her hand to his mouth and kissed it. In front of their assembled friends and enemies, he said, "*Dashuria ime, zonja ime.*" This time, however, there was a note of question in his voice.

Darting a glance at the others silently watching them, Olivia knew a brief flare of panic. But then she saw the faint glow limning their conjoined hands. It was impossible to see where her fingers ended and Mihàil's began. Lifting her chin, she said, "My love, my lord" and caused their nimbuses to blaze so brightly and so wide that the entire group was bathed in blinding light.

THIRTY

A week passed and nothing happened. Fagan had set up shop in Olivia's flat directing Baxter's team to look for Mihàil and her. In the end Mihàil had thought it best to keep Baxter in the dark about what had happened at the meat processing plant.

"The fewer people charmed, the fewer potential cracks in their adherance, especially as our strength will be spred thin," he said. "Besides, Baxter is less manipulable. As an intelligence operative, he walks a line, perhaps too closely. But he has never crossed over into unforgiveable action, which is why he chose to aid you over Fagan. We could push him, but I would rather encourage him than help him along the wrong path."

Instead, Olivia contacted Baxter to say that Fagan had managed to get ahead of their plans, and that she had accepted Mihàil's proposal after all. She would not be coming in from the cold. Baxter surprised her by apologizing for letting Fagan outflank him. He surprised her even more by wishing her future happiness.

"Maybe I'll look you up one day. Your Albanian might have use for more security. That's if I don't catch up to him first."

At the end of the week, however, Baxter was becoming suspicious about Fagan's fixation and curious about why he hadn't returned to Vienna. So Miró and Stasia, now back in Italy, began fabricating sightings of Mihàil and Olivia in Romania. András volunteered to embody them. Like a will o'the wisp, he flitted from Bucharest to smaller cities and hamlets. That's all it took for the pliable Fagan to update the mission and allay Baxter's concerns. He and his team departed to chase down these ghost leads, while Fagan fixated on catching the Dragon of Albania and his rogue operative.

Beta stayed as long as Baxter's team remained, surveilling the surveillance. But the day after they'd left Budapest, she found Olivia at the coffee shop where she had gone to try to write her parents a letter. Olivia was staring at the white screen of her laptop and playing with the engagement ring that she still wore when Beta slipped into the chair across from her. The enigmatic Czech set something on the table.

It was Olivia's extensible *bō*.

"You will need this even if you are the lady of a *drangùe*."

Olivia picked it up. The smooth black metal was scuffed and scratched. Its warmth and weight felt familiar against her palm.

"And perhaps this, too." Beta slid a folded white cloth on the table toward her. It was Olivia's *zentai* hood.

Olivia set the *bō* down and touched a fingertip to the hood. Shaking her head, she said, "No, Mihàil said that I can't be the harlequin anymore. Or work for the Agency. I'm not even sure that I can return to the United States to see my family." Despite herself, a slight quaver threaded her voice.

"Wearing the *zentai* and wielding the *bō* will be helpful for a modern *zonjë* who fights alongside her lord. Of course, I have never been married, but I think that some things are negotiable." Beta signaled for the waiter, who hurried over for her coffee order. "As for your family, why are you unable to return to the United States to see them? If Mihàil can fly them over for the wedding, surely he will fly you both to visit them there."

Olivia's heart pinged at Beta's comment. She sat up. "What did you say?"

Beta, who had just accepted her coffee from the waiter, turned toward Olivia with the cup to her mouth. "Hm?"

"My family? What are you talking about?"

A glint appeared in her friend's eyes. "Oh, did you not know?" she asked. She sounded amused. "Mihàil has instructed all of us to be at his estate near Shkodër in three days for the ceremony. He sent his man Pjetër there already to arrange everything."

Olivia, trained to think and respond in volatile situations, found that her brain had shut off. "Shkodër?"

"Yes, of course," Zophie said, pulling up a chair and sitting. She wore a sundress with a white cardigan and strappy sandals. She set a large straw tote on the ground and smiled at the waiter, who had frozen while clearing a table to stare at her. "A piece of *dobos torta*, please. And a *kávé*. Thank you."

She turned to Olivia and put a delicate hand on her forearm. "You will have the most beautiful bouquet of his mother's roses. Mihàil has also ordered freesia to be flown in fresh for the table arrangements."

"Wait." Olivia closed her eyes and took a deep breath. When she opened them, Beta and Zophie both looked at her, Beta with a slight smirk and Zophie with a serene patience. "Mihàil and I haven't set a date. We have to deal with Fagan. And Asmodeus. The CIA thinks that I'm a rogue operative. My parents have no idea what I'm really doing in Europe or that I've fallen in love, let alone that I'm marrying a man who is three-quarters angel."

"And one hundred percent dreamy," Zophie said, sighing. She looked toward the entrance to the coffee shop. "And here now." She turned to the waiter, who had just walked up with her slice of cake and coffee. "I am afraid that I will need that boxed to take with me." She slipped a hand under his elbow and led him away, talking the whole time. The poor man looked besotted.

Beta stood. "I must go. Stasia and I will call you about our gowns. Please, Liv, for the sake of our friendship, do not make me wear a sheath dress. I will look like a pencil. More importantly, there is no place to hide a weapon."

"A dagger. You could hide a dagger," Olivia said, still struggling to comprehend what was happening.

Beta shrugged, clasped Olivia's upper arm in a silent goodbye, and turned to leave. She nodded at Mihàil as she passed him, her expression suddenly respectful. The look she gave Olivia over her shoulder revealed a deep awe before she shuttered her gaze and walked away.

Bemused, Olivia looked up at Mihàil, whose blue eyes caught her in their gravity. She still didn't understand what was going on, but now that he was there, nothing else mattered. He waited a moment as she took him in, her gaze caressing the hard line of his jaw and the broad expanse of his shoulders and chest in the fine silk t-shirt that he wore. When her regard reached his hands, he took her own in both of his and leaned in to kiss her. He smelled of cedar and musk and a hint of spicy clove. Olivia closed her eyes and breathed him in.

When she opened them again, he was sitting across from her, a slight smile playing around the corners of his mouth as he watched her.

"*Ciao*, beautiful," he said, his baritone sending vibrations down her spine. She felt warm, invisible caresses undulating over her skin as he merged his harmonics with his thermogenics to touch her unseen by human eyes. It was shockingly intimate in this public space. Olivia shifted in her seat and crossed her legs to tamp down the sudden bolt of desire that went straight to her core. "I gather that you have heard the good news about our upcoming nuptials."

"I thought we were putting those off until after we capture Asmodeus," she said, surprised to hear how uncertain she sounded.

He shook his head, watching her closely. "There is no way to know when Asmodeus will wake from his angelic coma. The last time it took many years, though I do not expect it to be nearly as long. Those were very different circumstances. Regardless, whenever Asmodeus returns to his senses, he will be weak and not immediately a threat."

Taking her hands, he leaned forward and said, "Our happy union should not wait on evil, my love. We will determine our fate, not Asmodeus. If what I suspect is true, we will be stronger once we are married. Asmodeus will want to prevent that if he can. I do not intend to give him the opportunity."

The warm angelic fingers stroking her moved toward her breasts and the place between her legs, touching her through the thin cloth of her summer clothes. A naughty gleam sharpened the blue of his eyes.

"None of that is the real reason I want to get married as soon as it can be arranged," he said, his low voice for her ears only.

His stroking became warmer, firmer. Olivia felt her breath catch. She was exquisitely aware that they sat in the middle of a dozen tables peopled with oblivious businessmen, shoppers, and tourists. All of that would change if she started moaning and writhing in her seat. The social pressure to remain calm and alert heightened her responses to an almost painful pitch. She squeezed her eyes shut briefly, bit her lower lip, and swallowed. When she opened her eyes again, Mihàil's own breathing had deepened, his pupils had enlarged, and there was a hint of smoke in the air. Olivia focused on her breathing, regaining control of it before this got any farther out of hand than it had.

She also brought her temperature down. Way down. Gooseflesh appeared on her arms, but she maintained her temperature in the I'm-not-going-to-embarass-myself range.

Mihàil, whose temperature had followed suit, smiled, acknowledging that she'd brought them back from the brink. He sat back but kept her hands in his, satisfying himself with rubbing them with his thumbs.

"But three days?" Olivia asked as if nothing had interrupted the flow of their conversation. "That's not enough time for me to prepare. I'm a good field operative, but even I can't make this happen. It's too tight a timeline to get a dress let alone all of the other items that I need to find."

Mihàil pulled out his smartphone. "It is your choice, of course, but I thought that you would look enchanting in this dress." He showed her an image of the dress that she'd seen on their trip to Bratislava, the one that had sent a sharp pang knifing through her chest when she realized that she couldn't even window shop because their romance was a sham.

She touched a tip of her finger to the screen, tears pricking her eyes. Looking up, she saw his beloved face and the hope waiting there. "How did you know?" Before he could answer, she went on, "Yes, yes. I would love to wear this." She leaned up and kissed him then. His warm, firm lips met hers hungrily, but she pulled back before they could get lost in the kiss.

"So dress, flowers...how about a church?"

"My family's chapel on my estate."

"That sounds positively medieval."

"It is. My parents were married there."

Olivia suddenly felt unsure again. She looked down as she played with the *zentai* hood. "Were you and Luljeta married there?"

"No. My parents did not support the marriage. We were married by the village priest."

"Oh."

"Olivia," Mihàil said, tipping her face up so that she looked at him. "I loved Luljeta, yes, but never worry that you are second in my heart. She was my wife, the love of my youth. You are my heart, my life. Only you will be my *zonjë* and fight at my side against the Dark *Irim*. What you are to me is more than I can express."

A lump choked Olivia as she heard the conviction in his words. When she could speak, she said, "Well, then, what about wedding bands?"

Now he looked puzzled. "Why not the engagement ring and wedding bands that we already have?"

She shook her head. "The ring is quite eye catching. I'm sure that you spent a small fortune on it—"

"Indeed, it cost almost 200,000 American dollars."

"Two hundred thousand—" Olivia dropped her voice when the neighboring patrons turned toward her. She covered the engagement ring with her other hand. Geesh. No wonder wearing it felt all wrong. And to think, she'd thrown it at him on the river cruise. What if it had been lost? Worse, what if she'd had the impulse to throw it into the Danube?

She held his gaze. "It's a beautiful ring, but it represents something false. It's also not me. Caterina maybe, but not Olivia Markham from Marlborough, Massachusetts. I want something less ostentatious but with more meaning, like the gimmel ring." She touched the ring on his little finger.

Mihàil twisted the antique ring, his lips pursed. "I could have a gimmel ring made with a smaller diamond."

"That would take time." She continued tracing the hearts with the tip of her finger. Surely he would have offered it to her if he wanted her to have it? "What about *this* gimmel ring?" she finally asked.

"My mother's gimmel ring?" Mihàil said, sounding surprised but thankfully not offended. "You would wear it? It is old and not very stylish. In fact, it is rather battered from being on my finger for almost 500 years."

"That doesn't matter at all to me. Besides, it seems more appropriate for fighting *bogomili*, don't you think?"

Mihàil said nothing for a moment, simply sat rubbing the gimmel ring. When he looked at her, his gaze was full of complex emotion. "My mother wanted my *zonjë* to wear this gimmel ring. At the time that she gave it to me, Luljeta was already dead, as was my father. I had no intention of ever marrying again. I slipped it on and forgot about it until a few days ago in Bratislava."

Olivia took his hand in hers. "If it pains you so much, forget I asked about it. In fact, we don't have to have an engagement ring at all, just two gold wedding bands."

"No, no—you misunderstand me. It never occurred to me that you would want to wear this gimmel ring. But it will please my mother that you wear it."

"Please her?"

"Yes." At Olivia's puzzled expression, he said, "Have you forgotten that she is an angel? She rejoined the *Angeli Fidelis* after my father's death, but Zophie says that the Archangel Michael will let her attend our nuptials. She is looking forward to meeting you."

Three days later, Olivia Anne Markham walked at her father's side up the short aisle of the Kastrioti family chapel. She carried a bouquet of fragrant white roses that the gardener had told her were called The Harlequin, a miraculous cultivar that had begun growing and blooming only two weeks before. Her grandparents, mother, and her aunt and uncle, Emily's parents, sat in simple wooden chairs on the bride's side. On the groom's side sat a dozen estate employees, including Pjetër, Mihàil's trusted steward who oversaw the mundane details of his life. In the back row, Zophie sat wearing a demure tailored dress and an elegant hat. Mihàil, looking impossibly handsome and rather intimidating in black formalwear, stood at the front flanked by András and Miró. Stasia and Beta preceded her and her father, a violinist at the back of the chapel playing

Bach's *Jesu, Joy of Man's Desiring*. And on the steps in front of the altar a priest waited to lead her and Mihàil in the sacrament.

As Olivia reached Mihàil, he took her hand, love radiating from him so that he seemed to glow with it. When it came time for them to speak their vows, they faced one another. At that moment, golden-white light lit the interior of the stone chapel as if they stood outside in the sun. After they turned toward their family and friends, the priest declared them husband and wife before Heaven and earth. Then ineffable music as of a thousand voices and ten thousand harps swelled in the space. Stunned, Olivia realized that both the light and the music emanated from her and Mihàil. Many of those gathered wept in obvious joy.

Olivia smiled at everyone, scarcely taking in their faces. Even so, she realized that an unknown woman sat next to Zophie. The woman had an ethereal beauty that eclipsed even that of Zophie, her long hair so white and fine that it could have been made from starlight and silk. She seemed to look at Mihàil for a long moment, her smile so tender and approving that Olivia knew all at once who she was. Then she turned her gaze on Olivia. Looking at the angel's deep blue eyes, Olivia felt as though she stared into the infinite. Awestruck, she dipped her chin and closed her eyes in respect. A deep silence fell on her.

Daughter. Music and warm vibrations coursed through Olivia as the angel spoke to her. *I give you my blessing. May you and my son live happily and long.*

When Olivia looked up, the angel was gone. She smiled at Mihàil, who squeezed her hand and bent to kiss her.

He awoke into unremitting darkness that echoed from a shout of great joy. For a long moment, he knew not who or where he was. He only felt ancient loss and anguish made inexplicably fresh. And then he remembered.

He remembered too who had put him here. Fury ignited in him as he realized what the joy meant. She had joined in holy matrimony with his former acolyte.

Weak as he was, he could do nothing.

For now.

But he would return to his former strength sooner or later. And when he did, they would find their united strength little consolation as he destroyed everyone they held dear...wait, what was this?

The uncaring darkness swallowed Asmodeus's outrage as he discovered the trap the *drangùe* had set for him.

With a massive effort of will, he wrestled his emotions under control. It was no matter what the *Elioud* general had done. He was only delaying the inevitable. Their long war had entered the final stage.

It was time for the Dragon of Albania to meet the Dark *Irim*'s master—a real dragon.

ABOUT THE AUTHOR

Liane Zane is the cover identity of a novelist who is an expert at hiding in plain sight. She has spent time interrogating a former Army intelligence officer and engaging in Open Source Intelligence (OSINT) activities related to Italian slang words for naughty body parts and the proclivities of Eastern European criminals. She spends her days drinking New England chocolate-raspberry coffee and gazing at the magical brook in her back yard as she plots her romantic thrillers or walking her monstrous dog along mountain trails near her estate-like home.

THE HARLEQUIN & THE DRANGÙE is the first book in her series, *THE ELIOUD LEGACY.*

Visit Liane's Website at www.lianezane.com for updates.

ALSO BY

The Elioud Legacy series
The Harlequin & The Drangùe
The Flower & The Blackbird
The Draka & The Giant

The Unsanctioned Guardians series (a prequel series to The *Elioud* Legacy)
The Covert Guardian (forthcoming)

Available in paperback, ebook, and audiobook online at all major retailers or through your local library by request. Special editions and signed copies are available from Liane Zane: www. shop.lianezane.com.